Unspoken

By Helena Harte

2026

Butterworth Books is a different breed of publishing house. It's a home for Indies, for independent authors who take great pride in their work and produce top quality books for readers who deserve the best. Professional editing, professional cover design, professional proof reading, professional book production—you get the idea. As individual as the Indie authors we're proud to work with, we're Butterworths and we're *different*.

Authors currently publishing with us:

E.V. Bancroft
Valden Bush
Addison M Conley
Jo Fletcher (JL Fletcher)
Helena Harte
Lee Haven
Karen Klyne (KJ Kenny)
Sydney Lear
AJ Mason
Ally McGuire
James Merrick
JP Preston
Robyn Nyx (RJ Nyx)
Anne Shade
JJ Taylor
Brey Willows

For more information visit www.butterworthbooks.co.uk

CATALOGING INFORMATION
ISBN: 978-1-918072-08-2
CREDITS
Editor: Victoria Villaseñor
Cover Design: Nicci Robinson
Production Design: Global Wordsmiths

Introduction

When I first planned to write *Unspoken*, I expected to have it complete within three months.

This book was always meant to be quieter than the others in the series. More inward. More emotionally precise. But life has a way of shaping the stories we tell, sometimes in ways we don't choose.

During the time I was writing it, my family was moving through an ongoing crisis. My dad experienced a serious mental health breakdown, one that required immediate attention, constant advocacy, and an emotional vigilance that left very little room for anything else. In tandem with that, my mum's dementia continued to progress, bringing with it a steady erosion of familiarity, certainty, and the roles we'd all known for so long.

There were long stretches where writing simply wasn't possible, because the headspace just wasn't there. Creativity requires a kind of quiet focus, and that quiet was being thirstily swallowed by worry, exhaustion, and the practical realities of caring, supporting, and simply getting through each day.

Progress came in fragments. A scene here. A paragraph there. In the beginning, five weeks of nothing at all.

And yet, the book kept waiting.

This story about silence inside a marriage, about loving someone while feeling lost, and about mental health struggles that are invisible to the outside world ended up being shaped by the season it was written in. Not directly, not autobiographically, but emotionally. The themes of endurance, vulnerability, and choosing to stay present even when everything feels overwhelming became sharper, more honest, because I was living them as much as I was writing them.

The delay in publication wasn't a lack of commitment or passion. It was the reality of balancing creativity with care, art with responsibility, and storytelling with the very real work of showing up for the people I love.

I'm sharing this not as an explanation that's owed, but as context, because stories don't exist in isolation. They're written by people living full, complicated lives, often carrying far more than what appears on the page.

Unspoken took longer because life demanded more. And while that was difficult, I believe the book is stronger for it. Quieter, truer, and written with the patience that only hard situations teach you.

And now to the thank yous:

To my ever-loving wife, editor, and my light: thank you for not divorcing me when I bitch about edits.

Thank you to Margaret Burris for your diligent work and friendship.

Thanks to the wonderful folk people in my ARC team: your early reviews make the pain of writing much more bearable, and of course, a grateful and eternal thanks to all you lovely readers.

And before you begin...

Postpartum depression affects far more mothers than we ever hear about, because for too long it has been suffered in silence. If you recognise yourself in any part of this book, I want you to know that what you're feeling is real, it *is* valid, and it does *not* make you a bad mother. You are not alone, and you don't have to stay in this place. Please reach out to your GP, midwife, or health visitor. Recovery is possible, and asking for help is one of the bravest things you can do.

Be gentle with yourself,
Helena

Dedication

To my wife,
Let there never be a single word
or emotion unspoken between us.
We're in this together, and I wouldn't
want anyone else by my side.

(Imagine TV announcer voice!)

"Previously in the Windy City, Shay and Rosie's friend with benefits situationship turned into far more than either of them could ever have imagined, while Gabe and Lori continued to explore the first flushes of a new relationship.

"Meanwhile, Solo's been suffering not so silently, and she feels like she's grasping at rapidly disappearing straws as she tries to hold onto her wife, Janie, who's become disillusioned with the lack of attention and love she's been getting from Solo. But there's something else troubling Janie, a secret that she can't share with anyone..."

Chapter One

How had it come to this? Solo slid down the wall onto the solid wooden floor of the kitchen. A weirdly protective numbness enveloped her whole body, and she could've been landing on a bed of feathers for all she knew…or cared.

The shield didn't extend to her heart. That *did* hurt like hell. She looked through the double doors, and her gaze rested on the dining room's liquor cabinet, daring and taunting her. Colorful bottles in appealing shapes held colorless liquids calling for her to fall into their oblivion.

Her wife, Janie, the woman who painted the brightness into her life, stopped at the kitchen counter and looked down at her.

"Please don't," Janie said quietly before she stepped around Solo and exited the kitchen.

The delicate scent of Janie's perfume reached Solo, and as she inhaled deeply, she choked on the sob she'd been trying so hard to repress. She had only ever associated Fenty with Janie since their first brief but memorable meeting four years ago, when Janie had been wearing it. Up to this moment, the scent evoked strong, positive memories and always made her horny, but today, it was a right hook to the jaw. If she hadn't already been on her ass, it would've floored her.

Solo's phone vibrated in the pocket of her sweatpants. She dug it out on auto pilot and read the message reminder: *Tell Janie one thing you appreciate about her.* She dropped the cell to the floor and skimmed it across the shiny oak, far away from her. The therapeutic tidbits she'd been religious about completing had done fuck all, had changed nothing. Gabe's voice echoed in her head: *If you want your family to stay together, buddy, you have to fight for it.*

She placed her palms flat on the floor to *ground* herself, another therapy tip that had been hit and miss so far, and closed her eyes for a little while before she got to her feet. *Fight for it.* Gabe's advice was always solid; she was dependable, and Solo could count on her for anything and everything. Whatever Gabe said was better than anything therapist Rae Trent had ever uttered, and it cost Solo nothing too. She bit the inside of her cheek—the therapy didn't cost her anything either since Janie insisted on paying. But which of them was the big breadwinner in their household wasn't one of their problems and never had been. Solo prided herself on being a modern masc that way.

She made her way upstairs, every footstep leaden and labored, and she hovered in the doorway of the guest room that Janie had been occupying for the last month. Janie glanced across at her from where she stood at the closet. The small, sad smile she offered Solo did nothing to comfort her; she'd seen that same smile on Janie's lips when she consoled a colleague who'd just lost their case and their client was about to start a ten-year stretch at Joliet Correctional Center. Solo would take that sentence over this hell right now.

No, she wouldn't. That would take her away from Janie and from their babies. She couldn't survive that any more than she thought she could survive what was happening in front of her. She chewed on her bottom lip, searching her useless mind for the right words, for any words, that could put a stop to this shitshow before it got to the final act. Gabe would know the right thing to say, especially now that she was head over heels in love with Lori. Gabe had been Solo's rock for the thirteen years they'd been in the Army together. But when Solo met Janie, it was the one thing she thought she might be alone in, the one thing Gabe wouldn't be able to advise her on.

She dug her hand in her pocket then remembered she'd abandoned her phone in the kitchen. Gabe giving her the right words might be the only way she could say something meaningful, something that didn't come out like a weak-assed murmur or just be...disappointing.

If they could get through this rough patch, Solo would give anything, *do* anything. Like writing lessons to help her put what was in her heart into actual words. Wasn't it supposed to be easier for lesbians to share their emotions with their partners? Wasn't that supposed to be one of the primary benefits over straight relationships?

Janie crossed the room and stood in front of Solo. Everything about her, from the way she looked to the way she smelled to the way she walked, all of it took Solo's breath away. It had from the moment she'd seen Janie in Club Infinite. Was any of that enough to stop this giant wrecking ball of silence from destroying their lives?

"Talk to me," Janie whispered.

Solo clamped her teeth hard on her tongue. The iron maiden squeezing her heart to pulp made the pain in her mouth minimal. *Don't go. Please don't go.* But instead of those words emerging, she shook her head. "What are the girls going to do without their mom?" she asked, her temper flaring. "Shouldn't you be thinking about them?" She'd never had trouble expressing her anger, and she instantly regretted it.

Janie's eyes flashed open, and Solo couldn't even begin to name the emotions swimming in her eyes. Therapy was supposed to have made communicating easier, but Janie had become increasingly distant and cold, often like her soul wasn't in her body, and she'd floated off somewhere else, anywhere else apparently, because she clearly couldn't bear being at home with her family. Spikes shot into Solo's heart. Her family was disintegrating right in front of her, and she couldn't do a damn thing about it.

"I *am* thinking about them," Janie said. "And they'll be better off without me." She put her hand square in the center of Solo's chest and pushed her out of the room before she closed the door.

It was only wood.

Solo could've kicked it down with little effort. But it may as well have been steel, six feet thick like the door of a bank vault. That sounded about right. Janie had locked her heart and mind in a safe, and Solo didn't have the skills or tools to crack it open.

The soft giggles of their girls filtered down the hallway. They wouldn't be "better off" without Janie, no more than Solo would. The seventeen-month-old triplets were a handful when they were both there to parent them, but alone? She couldn't–didn't want to–imagine that. She placed her head against the door. No imagination would be necessary; it was about to become a reality. She could only hope Janie didn't really mean any of what she'd been saying over the past few days, and that she'd come to her senses and realize they all belonged here, together.

The door opened, and Solo just managed to keep herself from falling into the guest room.

Janie squeezed past, rolling a medium suitcase behind her. "I'll send Amanda to pick up the rest of my clothes from our room."

"You want me to let your assistant in our bedroom?" Solo clenched her jaw. "Why can't you do it?" Goddamn, why couldn't she wrangle the mic from her anger and give another emotion voice?

Janie paused at the top of the stairs. "It has to be this way, Hannah. I don't know who I am anymore, and I can't be anything to anyone, especially you and the girls, until I resolve that... If I can."

Solo walked toward Janie and grasped the handle of her luggage. "You can do that here. I'll give you all the space you need."

Janie shook her head and pulled the case from Solo's grasp. "If I thought that would work, I'd stay." She caressed Solo's cheek with her other hand, and tears spilled down her cheeks. "But the past month hasn't changed anything. *I* haven't changed. I'm suffocating. I have to do this alone."

Janie took the stairs carefully, but Solo couldn't bring herself to offer assistance, to literally help her wife out of their home. Janie picked up her purse and paused after she'd opened the door. She took the key off her keyring and placed it on the nearby side table.

"This is still your house. You'll need that key to come visit the girls... You *will* visit, won't you?" Solo heard the cry catch in Janie's throat, and she launched herself down the stairs, three at a time, the sudden glimpse of hope almost levitating her. "You don't want to do this, JJ. Please." She sank to her knees at Janie's feet; she wasn't beneath begging if it'd keep her family together. *Fight for it*, Gabe yelled inside her head.

Janie stepped outside, her body shaking with her sobs. "I can't... I just can't."

She pulled the door shut behind her, leaving Solo staring at the slab of wood, another impenetrable barrier between them. She fell to her side and let the tears come, body-wracking cries that shredded parts of her soul. Through the watery membrane in front of her eyes, the liquor cabinet beckoned her.

Upstairs, the giggles subsided, and Chloe shouted out in distress.

Solo took a deep breath and pulled herself up from the floor. She flipped the bird at the cabinet, making a mental note to donate the contents to RB and Woody the next day, and climbed the stairs to her girls. They had to be her priority now. She couldn't afford to fall into old patterns to cope with new conflicts. Hey, maybe she'd learned something from the therapy sessions after all.

Chapter Two

JANIE HUNG ONTO THE door handle longer than she should. Was she holding it so Hannah couldn't follow? Or because she couldn't really bring herself to leave her beautiful little family? She rested her head against the doorjamb. The answer was beyond her, and *that* was a huge part of the problem. She didn't know who she was anymore, what she wanted, what she was capable of. She caught sight of herself in one of the dining room windows and barely recognized herself. But even that wasn't the biggest issue... She couldn't bring herself to even *think* about the core problem, the thing that was really wrong with her. And if she couldn't do that, then telling Hannah about it was all but impossible.

She let go of the handle and backed away, dragging her bag with her and not bothering to lift it down the stone steps. If it broke, so be it. She didn't deserve anything perfect, not a piece of luggage and definitely not the three beautiful children she'd just closed the door on. Or her doting wife. They'd all be happier and *safer* without her.

Janie threw the case into the trunk of her car, got in, and pulled out without paying much attention to any of it. She drove down the block and took a right onto Warner Avenue before swerving into the first available space curbside. And then the tears came, hot and free-flowing down her cheeks, and she wailed. The sound startled her at first, one so loud and uninhibited, so unfamiliar in expression that it had to be coming from someone else. She hugged herself tightly and dropped her head against the steering wheel. Here seemed as good a place as any to finally dissolve into the mess she'd been trying to disguise for over a year and a half.

She didn't know how long she'd been like that when she heard a gentle tapping on the passenger window. She stared into the kind-looking eyes of a gray-haired woman, her forehead marked with decades of life. When she smiled, her skin creased like folds of silk to give her an even more gentle appearance, making Janie hit the button to retract her window almost instantly.

But the old woman opened the door and sat in the passenger seat without saying anything, and Janie simply sighed. If she was about to get carjacked, it would be the most polite and least violent theft in history. Janie should just step out onto the road and leave the elderly matriarch to it. There was nothing in Janie's luggage she couldn't replace, and her Lexus being stolen would be light relief right about now.

"One of the benefits of being old is that you get to disappear," the woman finally said. "I walk all around this neighborhood—have for thirteen years, whatever the weather—and no one ever asks what I'm up to. They're all too involved with their own lives. Everyone's zipping from meeting to meeting, dropping off their kids, picking them up from soccer, racing to that next date with the guy...or girl," she said and winked, "who's going to be *the one*."

Great. A rambling homeless woman has just gotten into my car. But she was right. Janie and Hannah had lived in that house for two years, and she'd never seen this woman before... Or had she seen her without *seeing* her? Janie pulled a tissue from the center console and dried her face. "Is that a good thing? Being able to disappear?" she asked.

"Sometimes it is, yes." She patted Janie's thigh. "I used to be someone who couldn't go anywhere without being recognized, but as soon as I got old and wrinkly..." She laughed, a joyful and deep sound, and tugged the skin of her neck to the left, where it stayed a while before slowly returning to sag below her chin. "Well, then they'd look away."

Janie gave the woman the benefit of the doubt and narrowed her eyes to study her face, but she couldn't place her as a movie star of a bygone time or some other type of celebrity. "What's your name?"

The old woman chuckled and patted Janie's thigh again. "You can call me Maria."

"Is that your name?"

Maria shrugged. "No, but I've always wanted to be Maria. I look like a Maria, don't you think?"

Janie frowned. This conversation was beyond bizarre, but it had given her something else to focus on rather than her spiraling thoughts. And it'd stopped her keening like a mythic Greek widow. Temporary though both might be, she welcomed them *and* this unusual passenger. "Would you like to go for coffee?" she asked, mainly because being with someone she had zero connection with and who had no knowledge of her would be a pleasant break from her reality.

Maria smiled widely. "I'd love to." She fastened her seatbelt and pointed ahead. "I know just the place."

Maria indicated left and then another left. When she wanted Janie to turn left back onto Greenfield, Janie froze. Her home wasn't "just the place" for coffee, and how could Maria know where she lived anyway?

Maria patted her hand lightly again. "Don't worry. It's a ways away yet."

Fighting against her desire to turn right instead, Janie took the left and drove past her home, keeping her eyes on the road ahead, hoping that Hannah wasn't looking out of the window. She turned south onto Ashland after another vague instruction from Maria and drove on.

After five or so miles, Janie glanced at Maria, but she just waved her forward.

"It's *really* good coffee," Maria said and smiled, her eyes twinkling as her silky wrinkles deepened around her cheeks.

Several miles and a couple of turns later, Janie pulled up just before a corner café in Pilsen, a neighborhood she'd never gotten around to visiting. The café was on the ground floor of a grand-looking, multi-story building that had seen better days and needed a little love, if not a whole lot of gentrification. The mainly red-brick building was still beautiful though, with the corner edge featuring a white, two-story oriel window and topped with a gray-tiled turret. If someone plucked it from its foundations and planted it near her own home, it would likely quadruple in value.

Maria got out of the car and stood to the side of a bench, which was scrawled with the words, "No human is illegal" and "Borders are imaginary." Janie was reminded of an idiot colleague who'd advised her to avoid Pilsen in case she was bundled into a deportation van by accident.

Maria didn't close her door until Janie had joined her on the sidewalk.

She hit the lock button on her remote. "Did you think I'd bolt?"

Maria held her hand aloft and wiggled it from side to side. "Wasn't sure, sweetie. Thought you might've come to your senses and be wondering why the heck you were driving an old bird like me ten miles for a simple coffee."

Maria laughed that throaty yet honeyed laugh again, and Janie couldn't help but smile.

"Good morning, Maria! Who's your friend?"

Janie turned around to face another old woman in the café's sky-blue painted doorway.

"That's a good question." Maria hooked her arm into Janie's and tugged her forward. "What *is* your name?"

"Sally?"

"Copycat." Maria chuckled and tapped Janie's hand. "Is that who you want to be?"

"Honestly, I'd rather be anyone other than me."

Maria pressed her lips together and tilted her head slightly. "Well, I'm glad you're you, whoever you are. You've saved these jittery legs the ten-mile journey for my morning coffee and pancakes."

"Jittery isn't the word I'd use to describe you." Janie had seen thirty-year-olds in worse shape than Maria, which was easily explained if she regularly walked ten miles for breakfast. "And you look like you could easily walk the B of A marathon next month."

Maria swatted Janie's shoulder. "Sassy. I could *run* that," she said and winked before pulling Janie into the café.

Janie laughed at Maria's about-turn and allowed herself to be led into a space that a realtor would likely describe as quaint. A zoomer would likely call it odd and old-fashioned. Vintage sconces with warm bulbs lit the room, and the walls were exposed brick, with occasional sections painted in deep ochre and a rich olive green. A mural of a colorful eagle clutching a dark snake in its claws, on a background of what looked like local families, stretched across the entire wall behind the counter. Each corner of the painting was decorated with a Guatemalan flag. All manner of seating and tables covered the hardwood floor, and most were draped with brightly colored serapes.

"Sally, this is Mirta. Say hi to Mirta." Maria plopped herself into one of the cozy armchairs positioned on a raised platform of cobblestone tile along the length of the window.

"Hi, Mirta, I'm Janie."

Mirta smiled in a similarly gentle way to Maria. Perhaps they were sisters.

"Pleased to make your acquaintance, Janie." Mirta motioned to Maria. "And where did you pick up this roaming spirit today?"

"I was parked on West Warner having..." Janie chewed on her bottom lip. She'd been having a meltdown, but she wasn't about to confess that. "I was having a moment to myself."

"Ah, that makes sense." Mirta ushered Janie into an empty chair beside Maria and all but pushed her into it. "Maria does love to poke her nose in where it isn't wanted."

"Bleh." Maria poked her toe at Mirta's shin. "How do you know my nose wasn't wanted? She's here, isn't she? Didn't race off in her fancy car and leave me on the sidewalk, did she?"

Mirta grumbled and looked at Janie from tip to toe. "She

looks way too classy to leave a viejita standing on the side of the road. Look at you; she probably thought you were homeless."

Maria brushed at her velvet jacket. "That's offensive to homeless people, Mirta. Just because you're old doesn't mean you have to be a vieja armagada."

Yep, they were either sisters or had been friends for longer than Janie had been alive. She bit her lip, not knowing where to look.

"Takes one to know one," Mirta shot back and turned on a dime to duck behind the counter just as someone else came in.

"Well, hey there, Maria," the old guy said. "How're you doing today? Caught any fish yet?"

"No fish, Martin." Maria tilted her head toward Janie. "Just a pretty lady."

Martin nodded his head slowly as he stared unabashedly at Janie. "Quite the catch, eh?"

"More of a rescue than a catch," Maria said and shooed him away.

Janie offered Martin a smile, despite thinking that she'd somehow slipped into an episode of *Black Mirror*, where all the characters were septuagenarians and all their names began with M. Maybe she was still on West Warner in a sobbing stupor, and this was all in her head.

She glanced outside to see her Lexus shining in the sunlight. Not a dream then.

Martin ambled the short distance to the counter, where Mirta already had a to-go cup waiting for him. "Thank you kindly." He tipped his cap to her, took the drink without paying, and wandered into the street, calling out his goodbye over his shoulder.

Maybe he had a running tab. Janie didn't have much time to give it more thought before Mirta placed a tray with two giant mugs of coffee and the fixings on their table.

"Rescue, you say?" Mirta asked.

Maria looked at Janie and wrinkled her nose, as if giving

serious thought to the question. "What would you call it, Janie?"

Janie shrugged and picked up her coffee without adding milk or sugar. She needed to taste something hot and strong to convince her she really was in this unusual situation and *not* passed out in her car around the corner from her house. "Serendipity, perhaps."

"Ooh," Maria and Mirta chorused.

"That's a lovely way to describe our meeting." Maria dropped four cubes of sugar into her coffee and stirred it vigorously.

Janie stared into the darkness of her own drink and considered her own description. "Lovely but perhaps not as accurate as rescue." How was it she could be honest with two strangers and not her own wife or their therapist? She caught the quick look between Maria and Mirta but chose not to interpret it.

"Pancakes with bacon for two, coming right up," Mirta said and left them once again.

"It can be both things, Janie. A serendipitous rescue."

Maria's quiet delivery and her compassionate expression nearly undid Janie, and she drew in a long breath before taking an overly long drink of coffee to keep herself from dissolving into a hot mess on the comfy chair. "Do you make a habit of getting into the cars of strange women?" she asked, intent on lightening the mood. She'd played along with this crazy caper to get away from the inky blackness of her thoughts and didn't care to revisit them yet.

"I very much used to when I was in my heyday, but not so much nowadays." Maria winked. "You should consider yourself a special case. Or very unlucky. Dealer's choice."

Janie took a sip of coffee and smiled. The hot bitter liquid wasn't the only thing warming her insides. "I'll consider myself very lucky." She couldn't particularly reason why she felt that way, or why meeting Maria, and then Mirta, seemed fortunate, but sometimes, on very limited occasions, letting go of all logic was the only way forward.

She sat back in the chair and observed a number of people

of all ages, colors, and presentations enter the café, enthuse a greeting to Maria and Mirta, and leave with their drinks and baked goods, all without paying.

During a lull, Mirta returned to their table with the most delicious-smelling bacon and pancakes Janie had ever come across. She drizzled maple syrup all over them; she wouldn't usually drown them, but damn if she didn't need a pick-me-up today. She tucked in as Maria did the same.

"You said that one of the benefits of being old was that you disappeared," Janie said after swallowing a mouthful that tasted every bit as good as it looked, "but every single person who's come in here knows your name, and you theirs..."

Maria picked up a piece of bacon and bit down on it, looking at Janie but not saying anything. She widened her eyes slightly and leaned in a little. "Is there a question in there somewhere?"

Janie shrugged. "I suppose I'm asking about balancing the benefits of disappearing against," she gestured around the beautifully eclectic space and the steady trickle of people coming through the double doors, "being such an important part of this community."

Maria crunched her bacon noisily and then exhaled deeply as she nodded. "I'm allowing the two sides of my coin equality," she said and took another chomp of her breakfast.

Janie chuckled. "You're going to make me work for this, aren't you?"

Maria inclined her head slightly. "I don't think you're the kind of person who wants the answers handed to them on a plate with their bacon and pancakes," she said, prodding Janie's plate.

"I don't, you're right." Janie tried not to dwell on how easily Maria seemed able to read her. In court, she was renowned for her poker face, but here, her guard had crumbled all too quickly. Or maybe she'd been ready for someone to really *see* her. God knows, Hannah barely did now that the triplets demanded so much of their time and emotional stores. "But I would like to know your story." She pointed to her car on the roadside. "I did make your ten-mile journey simple this morning, didn't I?"

"You did." Maria caught some errant maple syrup about to dribble down her chin and licked it from her finger. "Though I think you would've happily been abducted by aliens too." She held Janie's gaze. "Any port in a storm, I've heard it said."

Janie had to look away from Maria's hypnotic eyes, the dark brown of them reflecting her own darkness and pulling her in. Was her desperation to take a break from reality that obvious?

"I understand," Maria said. "You're struggling, and you're searching. But right now, a little distraction is very appealing, yes?" She waited until Janie gave a slight nod. "This is okay. I'm only mysterious half of the time. The other half...not so much."

Maria's laughter filled the large space, bringing genuine smiles to every other person in the café. What Janie would give for that kind of freedom, that kind of natural expression, all while being part of something bigger than herself.

"First," Maria waggled her finger and then got up, "more coffee."

As Maria walked to the counter, looking more spritely with every step, Janie took another mouthful of pancake and sat back in her chair. When she'd woken this morning, she could never have imagined ending up in a totally new neighborhood after being gently kidnapped by a woman more than twice her age. And yet, she'd had the inescapable sensation that she was exactly where she was supposed to be.

Strange, given that she'd been feeling like a tumbleweed in a tornado for longer than she cared to remember. She was at rock bottom; she'd left her children, her wife, and her home. Embracing strange was just about the only thing she hadn't tried in her efforts to connect with her little family...

Chapter Three

Solo swung into the alley beside the garage and hit the dumpster. Normally, that would've set off a stream of expletives and had her jumping out of the car to inspect the damage. Today though, her triplets were lined up facing the custom-made maroon leather backrest in the rear of her vehicle, and they were all asleep. Even Tia, and at this time of day, that was as rare as rocking horse shit. But maybe that was down to Janie not being in the house, and after the night Solo and the triplets had endured, the last thing she wanted to do was wake them.

She pulled into her spot and got out of the car, with only rocket-fuel coffee and sugar keeping her upright. Gabe was already in the doorway at the back entrance and began to walk toward her. *Keep it together.* One bro-hug from Gabe, and Solo feared she'd dissolve into a puddle of useless pus at her feet.

"Fuck off," she said when Gabe got close enough and opened up her arms for exactly that purpose.

Gabe pressed her lips together and dropped her arms to her side. "Got it." She peered into the backseat and blew out a loud breath. "You overdose her on Benadryl? That's the first time I've seen that kid with her eyes closed."

Solo huffed. "I'd laugh if I wasn't so fucked. None of us got much sleep last night."

"I'm sorry, bud. This stinks." Gabe stepped back from the car and shook her head. "Shay and RB have arranged a baby-friendly space in the DFAC. And Woody's set up CCTV to some of the monitors downstairs, so you keep an eye on them while you're working."

"Great," Solo said, unable to apply the illusion of conviction to her words. She popped the trunk and hauled out the triplets' stroller. "I'll start on this side." She opened the door closest to Luna.

"Good idea." Gabe joined her. "Leave the leader until last."

Solo gave a half-smile. "The great Gabe Jackson is scared of my tiny Tia. If only I could tell the rest of the squad."

Gabe shoved Solo lightly and jutted her chin. "They wouldn't believe you."

"Probably not." No one other than Janie took her seriously, and now she was gone.

"Solo?"

"What?" She looked at Gabe, who gestured toward her chest. Solo looked down to see Luna and her bucket seat in her arms. When had she unclipped the retainer and taken her out? "Uh, yeah..." She clipped the car seat directly into the stroller and leaned into the back to get Chloe.

Gabe adjusted Chloe's purple beanie after Solo had fitted her seat alongside Luna. "It's going to be eighty-degrees today, right?"

"But right now, it's only fifty." Solo pushed the stroller around to the other side and opened the door to retrieve Tia. "I know how to look after my kids, Gabe."

Gabe held up her hands. "Of course you do. I'm sorry." She tapped her watch. "It looks like you're good here; I'm going to lower the flag to half-mast."

Solo glanced at her own wrist to see it was bare. Christ, she didn't remember taking her watch off. She turned quickly as Gabe headed off. "What time is it?"

"It's zero seven twenty-eight," Gabe said. "We'll be in the DFAC waiting for you."

Solo shook her head. *You can take the sarge out of the army, but you can't take the army out of the sarge.* RB had built a nice-looking room for them all to eat and have some downtime; it was more than a *dining facility*, and they really should call it something else, something more civilian. Like a breakroom.

Conscious she didn't have much time before the official ceremony to mark the 9/11 attacks began, she moved as quickly as she dared to unbuckle Tia and fasten her into the remaining stroller space. She needed her luck to hold a while longer and keep the triplets asleep. It was tough enough having to bring them to work any day, but on a day when she and the gang wanted to be in total silence six times, she'd need a miracle to keep the triplets quiet.

Solo locked the car and headed into the garage. Woody and RB were waiting at the foot of the stairs, and without a word, they helped her carry the stroller up to the breakroom. For the first time in too long, she smiled genuinely when she saw what the gang had done.

In the corner of the room, a large walk-in tent had been erected, and the door flaps were tied back, revealing three cots lined up along the wall. Each of them had a color-coded mobile: orange for Tia, green for Luna, and purple for Chloe. In front of the tent was a giant playpen containing all sorts of age-appropriate toys in the girls' colors. Solo looked above it to see a camera trained on the area and another one just inside the tent.

There would never have been a good time for her wife to have walked out, but at least she'd waited until Solo was surrounded by her friends again, and she could rely on them to help her pick up the pieces. Her smile was quickly followed by a burning sensation at the back of her eyes, and she looked up at the ceiling, willing her imminent tears to fuck right off. God, she'd gone soft. What would Gabe and the others think if she started spurting happy tears just because they'd done something nice?

Solo looked at it again. It was a damn sight more than *something nice*. It was spectacular. Honestly, she hadn't thought it through, beyond the inflatable playpen she'd shoved into the trunk. And their food. And nappies. And wipes. And a few toys... Maybe she'd been more organized than she'd given herself credit for, but still, this looked more permanent and less of an imposition. And they'd obviously all been working on it since she'd texted Gabe yesterday afternoon to tell her Janie had left and she'd have to bring the babies into work.

"You like it?" Shay slapped Solo on the back.

Solo swallowed hard and turned to face her. "I love it. Thanks, everyone."

There was a chorus of dismissive noises and hand gestures, making her glad she'd ushered her tears away. RB and Woody would've ribbed her for life if she'd shed so much as one drop of salty liquid onto RB's custom-made flooring.

Shay nudged her shoulder and pointed to Tia. "Gabe says the orange one is the little human we should all suck up to. Is that right?"

"Tia." Solo nodded. "If you want a quiet life, yeah."

"And the one in green is like a little Buddha?"

Solo chuckled at the characterization. "I hadn't thought of Luna like that before, but I guess that's a perfect way to describe her. She's kind of oblivious to Tia's powerplays and Zens out when Chloe is having a crying fit."

"And Tia messes with Chloe, the one in purple, quite a lot?" Shay asked quietly.

"Tia messes with everyone and anyone." Solo grinned at her eldest, who looked like an angel when she was asleep. But when she was awake, she could give any fallen angel a run for their money. "And Griff is her mighty steed."

Shay frowned. "Griff is the dog?"

"Yep," Solo said. "He's with a neighbor today, but I've got to figure something else out. And soon."

"It's time," Gabe said as she turned up the NPR broadcast.

Solo turned as she registered the victims' names being read out, and she and Shay joined the rest of the gang in the center of the room, lined up side by side. They all assumed the parade rest position and clasped their hands behind their backs. A few minutes later, the bell tolled to indicate the first moment of silence. She could remember exactly where she was when she heard that Flight 11 had hit the North Tower, could still smell the hot Syrian desert air that she'd never gotten used to, even after two years. It had been the hottest part of the day due to the thermal lag, which was useful for once, because her intense sweating had disguised her tears. In the minutes following, one by one, the gang had found each other and come together, reinforcing their bond in the face of the horrendous attack on their homeland.

Now she kept her eyes front, and her gaze unfocused, though she was praying that none of the triplets woke during what was left of the minute's silence. And she fought the tears, not just for the victims but also for the state of her family. The silence gave oxygen and space to all the swirling thoughts of darkness that she'd been desperately trying to quash for the sake of the girls. Because every time she thought about how their perfect little family was now broken, the grief threatened to drown her in her own tears. And as much as part of her wanted to slide down that snake into a pit of despair, the rest of her was battling hard to stay present so she could keep the triplets safe.

Another bell sounded, and Gabe turned the radio down slightly, so that it was still loud enough to hear the reading of the names as it continued. She gestured to the monitor showing their first customers waiting outside. "Looks like our sign worked," she said as she headed downstairs to open up.

RB and Woody followed, and RB pointed to the wall clock fashioned from giant gears. "We'll be back in sixteen minutes."

Shay put her hand on Solo's shoulder. "Take some time to settle your kids in. None of us can really start any work until after ten thirty anyway."

She nodded but didn't say anything. She couldn't trust her voice to hold, so she just watched Shay jog down the stairs, her braids bouncing on her shoulders. Solo drew in a deep breath and walked back to the stroller. Mercifully, all three of her girls were still fast asleep, so she wheeled them into the darkness of the tent.

She decided she wouldn't disturb them by putting them in

their new cots. There was no point waking them before they were ready. They'd all be super grumpy if she did. And after the lack of sleep they'd all had last night, it might even be possible that they'd sleep through the rest of the moments of silence and even through to lunch. Boy, they'd be hungry then, and Chloe would probably scream the place down. Solo couldn't see the rest of the gang wanting to put up with this situation long-term, but what the hell was she supposed to do about it?

Her cell buzzed in her pocket, and she pulled it out to see her dad's smiling face on the screen. She swallowed hard. It'd taken her two years before she'd changed the picture of her parents to just him, but the absence of her mom, both literally and on screen, hit harder than usual, and she made a note to change it back when she had a second.

"Is it okay that I'm calling, Han?" her dad asked. "I waited until after 8:46 Eastern."

"Sure. Is something wrong?"

"I was calling to ask you that," he said. "I didn't get my Sunday family time last night, and you didn't answer any of my calls. I was starting to get worried."

"I'm..." She choked on her attempt at a casual response. Of course she wasn't fine. Her life was falling apart, and she'd had to bring her children to a greasy, stinky garage because her wife had left her, and their nanny had quit earlier the same week to concentrate on her artwork. Solo wished she'd never encouraged the young woman to open up about her passions.

"Han? What's wrong?"

Solo dropped onto a nearby couch. "Everything," she said, then somehow managed to get the whole sorry story out of her mouth in between long silences, where she glared at the ceiling and pinched her neck hard to prevent her tears from falling.

"I'll get on a flight today," he said. "My buddies Eric and Jeff will pack the house up and send everything after me."

Solo laughed, not because it was funny, but because it just didn't seem possible. "Don't be crazy, Pops. You can't upend your life..." *Just because mine is falling apart.*

"I've been wanting a change anyway, and this is just the motivation I needed," he said.

She shook her head, not quite believing that her dad could be the solution to her current problems. "But you love Florida."

"I loved your *mom*, so I loved anywhere *she* was." He coughed, half disguising the slight break in his voice. "This place is making me old before my time. Everyone is three decades older than me and wants to play golf all day, every day. I want to see my grandbabies."

Solo wavered. "I don't know, Pops. You haven't mentioned being unhappy before. It kind of feels like you're saying what you think I need to hear, so I won't feel guilty about dragging you halfway across the country to rescue me. Again." She'd lost count of the times he'd come to her aid when she was a kid, getting into all types of trouble.

"You'll be doing me a favor, I swear," he said. "If I stay in this place any longer, I'll be dead in a few years, and that *would* be something for you to feel guilty about."

Solo snorted. "How'd you figure?"

"Because you're blocking me from making a change right now. What if you say no to me moving closer to you and the girls, and I drop dead of boredom next week? How will that make you feel," he said, sounding like he had to muffle a chuckle.

She looked across at the triplets, still fast asleep in the makeshift tent. The gang had done her proud, and there hadn't been a whiff of irritation or judgment that they'd had to create a nursery at breakneck speed just because Solo couldn't keep her wife happy. But really, how practical was it for her to be spraying a car and have to keep breaking off to tend to the triplets? She couldn't just stop in the middle of a panel. "Are you sure?"

"I'm more than sure," he said. "I'm one-hundred percent certain. Go on, get off the phone, so you're ready for the next moment of silence. I'll book my flight and send you the details. And don't worry about picking me up from the airport; I'll rent a car. You can hook me up with something more permanent when you've got time. See you tonight," he said and hung up before she could say anything else.

Solo sank deeper onto the couch, but her dad's imminent arrival lightened the heavy feeling in her heart just a little. He'd always been there for her, no matter what scrapes and stupid situations she got herself into. She couldn't wait for him to arrive, but she had a nasty ache in her gut that told her he wouldn't be able to make everything all right this time.

Chapter Four

Janie waved to Rosie through the glass partition walls as she came around to the door of the conference room and took a deep breath before she went in. Rosie's smile didn't look anywhere near as genuine as it usually did.

"Are you sure you're still okay to do this?" Rosie asked as soon as Janie closed the door behind her.

Janie bit her tongue instead of clenching her jaw. The movement was imperceptible to anyone watching, which she'd long ago discovered was useful to disguising her emotions. "Of course. I wouldn't let you down after offering to help." She bit down even harder as the words left a trail of acid in their wake. *But you've let your family down easily enough, haven't you?* She blinked, choosing not to re-engage in the ever-present diatribe in her head, and took a seat opposite Rosie. She hit the remote, and the glass walls turned opaque. "Are you sure you still want me involved? I don't want things to be awkward."

"I'm good if you are."

Rosie adjusted her blazer, her actions belying her real feelings. No matter. Janie had to take Rosie at her word, and even if this took half a year to resolve, they wouldn't have to meet all that often. "Most of our communication over the next six months can be via email after this initial meeting," Janie said, expecting the disappointed expression Rosie failed to hide.

"Six months?" Rosie ran her hand through her hair and leaned back in her chair. "How is it my mom is still able to mess with my life even though she's dead?"

Janie gave her the patient, professional smile every lawyer had to learn, because clients almost always expected miracles. "It's a process, I'm afraid. Luckily, your case isn't all that complicated because there isn't a broader identity theft problem beyond the loan being taken in your name."

Rosie sighed and nodded slowly. "So how will this work?"

"Obviously, you've already told your bank that a fraud has occurred, but we need to report it officially, to them and to the major credit bureaus. We also have to report the crime to the FTC, which—"

"FTC?" Rosie held up her hand.

"Sorry, the Federal Trade Commission. We have to file an identity theft report with them."

"Even though the woman who stole it is dead?"

Janie inclined her head at Rosie's dispassionate delivery. The memorial for Rosie's mom had only been two days ago; was Rosie in denial? Hannah hadn't shared much in the way of details about Rosie and her mom's relationship, but Janie supposed that, if the woman was prepared to put her daughter into $50k worth of debt, it couldn't have been that pleasant. Her own familial connections were complicated, and money had been an issue with them too, but at least she'd never had to deal with something quite like this.

"That's correct," Janie said. "Then I'll need you to gather any and all evidence that shows you couldn't have been the person who opened the account."

Rosie frowned. "Like what?"

"Sworn statements from colleagues, clients, friends, or anyone you might've seen or interacted with over the time period when the account was applied for and opened. Photos with metadata showing your location. Any receipts for anything you purchased during the same time: coffee, gas, restaurant bills." Janie smiled again, recognizing Rosie's growing impatience. "Whatever you can think of that will provide tangible evidence. All of it will help."

Rosie nodded slowly again as she made notes on her phone. "And then what?"

"The bank will have to investigate, and that can take up to

three months. That's one of the reasons I said this might take six months. Their wheels can move slowly, and it depends on how many cases they're handling at the time. I'll keep the pressure on, and that usually encourages them to move quicker. Most people don't tend to have lawyers deal with these things for them."

Rosie looked up from her phone and frowned. "Are you sure this isn't an imposition? I'm happy to pay for your time."

"You say that, but you don't know what my hourly rate is." Janie smiled, but this time, she gave Rosie a real one. "You don't want to find yourself in even more debt."

Rosie shrugged. "I guess not."

"And my assistant will be doing most of the work, because it's really very simple."

Rosie raised her right eyebrow, and her jaw clenched slightly. "So I should be able to do it myself?"

Janie inclined her head. "You could absolutely do this all yourself, no problem. But this way, you can put it to the back of your mind for a few months, and we can apply pressure when necessary and push for a faster resolution. I'm just saying that you don't need to worry about it being an imposition. I'm happy to do it for," she said and swallowed, "a friend of Hannah's."

Rosie's expression softened, and she put her hand on the table between them, not quite reaching for Janie. "Are you okay?"

Janie recognized Rosie's change to therapist tone and instinctively drew back a few inches. There was something about the softness of it that pulled at the emotions she was trying to keep out of view. She couldn't give them free rein, especially at work. And she was already thinking of canceling her session later this week with her actual therapist; she didn't need another one trying to get inside her head. Janie didn't want to be there, so why was everyone else so eager to join her? "I'm fine," she said and didn't hold Rosie's gentle gaze.

Rosie pulled her hand away slowly and settled back in her chair. "When someone you trust asks that question, I hope you can give them a more honest answer."

Janie sighed. "Probably not." She couldn't trust herself anymore, so what chance did anyone else have? She realized the implication of her words when Rosie half-smiled. "Not that I don't trust you. It's just—"

"Don't worry." Rosie held up her hand. "I know what you mean, and there are levels of trust. We've met once, and we hardly know each other. I wasn't expecting you to pour it out, but please tell me that you *do* have someone to talk to. Someone who *isn't* a therapist. Hannah has her team, but who do you have?"

"I have friends," Janie said, careful to control the speed with which she answered, so she didn't sound defensive. "But thank you for asking." She *didn't* have friends, unless she counted Maria and Mirta. And her work colleague Austin? Did he qualify as a friend? She'd talked to Maria for hours yesterday, and she couldn't remember the last time she'd had that kind of flowing, in-depth conversation. She and Hannah *used* to talk like that all the time. Before the triplets. Before *everything* changed. But *established* friends, like Hannah had? She'd never had one, and her other lawyer colleagues would just as soon cross-examine her than cross the line into friendship; competition to make partner didn't foster a supportive atmosphere.

There was a knock at the door, and the expression on Rosie's face switched from pitying to poisonous. Janie frowned and turned around to see Katherine Hill standing in the opening, her expression equally scornful. She was a perfect example of the colleagues Janie was surrounded with, although only Katherine attempted to bed Janie when she'd first started work here. She hadn't even attempted to hide the fact that she was married.

"I have this room booked for a client in ten minutes, and I need to prepare," Katherine said when she finally looked at Janie.

Janie nodded. "We'll be out of here shortly."

Katherine gave an exaggerated sigh. "Two minutes."

She shot another look at Rosie before attempting to slam

the door shut. Clearly, she'd forgotten it had a soft-close mechanism. Janie suppressed a smile, knowing the failure of her aggressive exit would irritate Katherine, who took any and every opportunity to express her power, such that it was. She was a wannabe alpha who was all swagger and no substance.

"I didn't know *she* worked here," Rosie said.

"I'm afraid so." Janie turned back to her and raised her eyebrows. "How do you know her?"

Katherine was a real estate lawyer, and Janie couldn't see how she might have crossed paths with Rosie. Unless she was one of Katherine's conquests that had failed epically.

Rosie narrowed her eyes. "You really don't know?" she asked, then shrugged. "I suppose her name might not have made it down the gang's grapevine, especially since Lori's only just started to use it again."

Janie shook her head. "I really don't."

Rosie wrinkled her nose. "*That's* Lori's ex-wife."

"Lori was married?" she asked. *And divorced.* Wasn't Lori only thirty-two? Janie chastised herself for being so judgmental. Being a lesbian didn't automatically make someone better at marriage than heterosexuals.

Rosie nodded. "Lori found her—" She waved her hand, clearly stopping herself from oversharing or revealing her best friend's personal business. "She cheated on Lori. At least once, though it was probably more."

Janie schooled her expression, lest she stoke Rosie's fiery hatred. *It was definitely more.* Katherine had slept her way through the firm's whole paralegal team, as well as several other lawyers in the three years Janie had worked there. "Oh, I'm sorry. I didn't know."

"Please tell me she isn't one of your trusted friends," Rosie said and narrowed her eyes.

"No, she isn't." If Janie ever were to have friends, she'd choose better than that. She tapped her fingernails on Rosie's folder before picking it up and rising from her chair. "Anyway, you can leave this with me, and Amanda will get things moving."

Rosie stood too. "Thank you for this," she said. "I know things are awkward right now. I hope everything works out for you."

Awkward was an understatement. She'd been forced to abandon her children and her wife because... *Not now.* She rubbed at her forehead and pushed the unspeakable reason away.

"If your head's hurting, it's probably due to the proximity of that Beetlejuice bitch," Rosie said, inclining her head toward the meeting room door. She opened her purse, pulled something out, and pressed it into Janie's hand. "Take these and put some distance between you and the devil woman."

Janie looked at the single-dose pill packet and nodded. "Thank you." It was easier to accept the Advil than explain that the unbearable ache in her head came from the fact she couldn't be trusted to raise her own children. Lawyering was the one thing she was still confident she *could* do, but if she didn't concentrate fully, she'd lose that too. "Amanda will send you an email with a link for you to upload the evidence you gather to prove you didn't take out the loan, okay?"

"I'll watch for it," Rosie said and headed for the door just as it opened.

An uncomfortable moment followed as Rosie and Katherine faced off, inches from each other, in the doorway. Thankfully, Katherine's vaguely chivalrous sensibilities kicked in, and she stepped aside for Rosie to pass. Janie had a feeling that Rosie had no intention of kowtowing to Katherine and would've stood there for hours if necessary.

"Thanks for waiting," Janie said as she followed Rosie out of the meeting room, unwilling to get caught in there with Katherine and the privacy glass still activated.

Katherine adjusted her tie and gave a little bow. "I'll wait for you anytime."

Janie shuddered at the return of Katherine's usual schtick and hustled as fast as she dared in heels back to her office. She collapsed against her closed door and began to sink slowly to the floor but stopped herself. "Don't you dare." Her whole life had collapsed around her, but she had to keep working. If that stopped too...

She pushed away from the door, tossed Rosie's file onto her desk, and called for Amanda. Burying herself in her latest case was the only way she had a hope in hell of surviving this.

Chapter Five

SOLO SAT IN THE therapist's waiting room, staring at the closed door and tapping the wooden edge of the seat repeatedly in a 1-2-3 rhythm. She ignored the pointed, and regular, glances from the receptionist who looked far too cool to be working in a therapist's office.

She wore a graphic T-shirt under a sleek cardigan, dark-wash jeans, and red sneakers with a cream V on the side and brown rubber soles. The outfit screamed style, not professionalism, and was the equivalent of Solo showing up to a Fourth of July parade in her fatigues instead of dress uniform.

She looked at her phone. One minute had ticked away since the last time she'd looked, and there were still no messages. The elevator pinged down the corridor, but the footsteps were too heavy to be Janie's, and someone tall and bulky passed by a few seconds later. Maybe she'd been delayed with a client or was stuck in an Uber in downtown traffic.

Or maybe she just wasn't coming and had already given up on their marriage and their triplets.

Rae's office door opened. "Still no sign?" she asked.

Solo shook her head and tapped her phone screen. "No messages either."

Rae opened her door wider and gestured for Solo to enter. "Let's get started, and Janie can join us when she gets here."

Solo liked Rae's optimism, even though she knew Janie had left Solo and the kids over the weekend. She pushed up from the chair and marched into Rae's office with renewed purpose. If Janie had given up, maybe it was more Solo's fault than she thought. She had some work to do on herself, so she should get on with it. The faster she achieved that, the sooner she could win Janie back and reunite their perfect little family.

She dropped into the simple, high-backed chair that was closest to Rae's seat, and sat erect, ready to get down to the session.

Rae gestured to the three-seater couch Solo and Janie had sat in for the previous sessions. "No sofa for you today?" she asked.

Solo shook her head. "I don't want to get comfortable. That's one of my problems, I think."

Rae took her position and readied her pen and note pad. "What makes you say that?"

Solo rubbed at the light covering of navy paint on her forearm hair, then rolled her sleeves down, not wanting the distraction. She had to be fully present, that's what Lori had said. "We went out to the theater last month for the first time since the triplets were born," she said, "and it was Gabe who had to tell me to *look* at Janie. How messed up is that?"

"Meaning?"

"Meaning that my best friend—well, from my end anyway— shouldn't have to tell me that. Janie had been ready for nearly an hour when Gabe and Lori arrived, and she looked stunning. I should've *seen* her, but I was too busy with the babies, too comfortable in our relationship."

Rae scribbled something on her notes. "Can you expand on the best friend comment?"

"Why?" Solo frowned. "This is about me and Janie."

"Yes, but this is only our third session and our first without Janie. In order to help you achieve what you want from our time together, I need to fully understand you and all of your relationships, as well as how you view them."

Solo rocked on her butt cheeks, already regretting her choice of chair. "Gabe was my sergeant in the Army, and she's the unofficial leader of our team, even now. When we were serving, she was the person I went to whenever I had any issues.

And that hasn't changed now that she's come out and moved to Chicago, now that the gang is back together." Though she'd been happy after meeting and marrying Janie, and then having the triplets, Solo had still missed her buddies and hadn't tried to replace them with new friends.

"What's making you smile?" Rae asked.

Solo put her hand to her mouth to check, almost not believing Rae. "I don't think I'd realized how much I've enjoyed the past couple of months."

"What have you enjoyed about that specifically?"

"Being so close to everyone again," Solo said. "Gabe, Shay, Woody, RB. But especially Gabe. And working together in an enclosed space, just like in the Army."

"Were you unhappy before Gabe came to Chicago?" Rae asked after adding another note.

"I didn't think I was, no." Solo looked up at the ceiling, searching her memory of the past three years. "Janie was the best thing that had happened to me, and then the triplets gave me a new sense of purpose."

Rae nodded slowly. "Do you feel like you didn't have purpose before your children were born?"

Solo pulled at her earlobe. "Yes. No." She threw up her hands. "I don't know. Coming out of the Army was hard. I had a job to do there, and it was important... But it became less so when—" It was like a giant iron hand wrapped around her whole body and squeezed, stopping the words from emerging. Three years on, and she still couldn't bring herself to talk about it.

Rae inclined her head slightly. "When?" she asked softly.

Solo tried to open her mouth, but her breathing became quick and shallow. She tugged on her ear again, pinching it hard this time in an effort to regain control. "My..." She squeezed her eyes closed. *Don't be such a fucking baby.*

"Relax and breathe slowly," Rae said. "There's no time to rush."

Solo pulled her phone from her jacket pocket, flipped to her contacts, and pulled up her dad. After they'd talked on Monday, she'd switched the photo back to one of both her parents. She showed Rae the screen.

Rae looked over her glasses and smiled. "That's a beautiful photo," she said. "Your mom died?"

Solo nodded, assuming Rae had worked it out from the contact details. "2021. Breast cancer. Forty-nine." She swallowed, the short, sharp sentences sticking in her throat like mini cactus balls. "I had to get out and start a family—Jesus." That couldn't be, could it?

"What's wrong?" Rae paused, mid-writing.

"Did I just use Janie to start a family?" Solo got up from her chair and went to the window. She scanned the street, but there was still no sign of her wife. How long would it be before she couldn't call Janie that anymore? She turned back to face Rae. "Is that why Janie says I'm so distant? Because it was never really about her, and only ever about her having the babies?" Solo stumbled at the horrific thought and had to rest her butt on the windowsill. "No wonder she's left me."

"Slow down, Hannah," Rae said. "Tell me about when you first met Janie."

Solo smiled widely, very much aware of it this time. "I was on leave, and I'd gone to blow off some steam in Vegas. I was at a club called Infinite." She glanced at the ceiling again, instantly able to recall the layout of the club, the dark lighting, the pounding bass, and then...Janie came from behind and walked past her. She inhaled deeply, as if she could almost smell Fenty over the scent of the fruity candle in Rae's office.

"Tell me what you're seeing," Rae said.

Solo sat in her chair again before describing the experience. A tingle ran through her whole body as she retold their meeting.

Rae smiled. "What you're feeling now, does it seem real to you?"

Solo nodded and sighed deeply. "It was real. It *is* real."

"And when you used to think of starting a family," Rae said, "did you think about how you wanted to feel about the woman you'd do that with?"

Solo gave a short huff. "I wanted the real thing." Just like she'd seen in all those Hallmark movies she loved and watched in secret for years, not that she was going to admit that to anyone, even her therapist. "And I got that with Janie. I love her. I love Janie." She rubbed the heel of her hand on her forehead. "I feel like I'm being run over by a tank, doc. This therapy shit is brutal."

Rae chuckled. "Indeed it is."

"Why is my own brain fucking with me?" Solo pulled at both her ears. "If I don't know what I'm feeling, how am I supposed to fix everything?"

"There's a lot going on in your life right now, Hannah," Rae said gently. "And there's been a lot of changes happening too. You told me how the garage was your dream, and it's been a whirlwind over the past two months since your team all came back into your life. All of that while you're trying to raise not just one child but three. Then there are the problems in your relationship with Janie. And it seems like you may not have fully processed the grief over your mom's passing. That's a lot for anyone to parse out and make sense of."

Solo dropped her head against the high-backed chair. "Jesus, doc, are you trying to tell me I'm going to be in therapy for the rest of my life?"

"I'm not going to *tell* you anything, Hannah," Rae said. "You're going to work out all the answers for yourself. That's why therapy is so hard."

Solo frowned. "But you're going to help me, right?"

"I'm going to give you some tools to help yourself."

Solo rolled her eyes. Why were therapists so expensive if the client had to do all the work?

"I know that must sound strange, and you might be wondering what you're paying for," Rae smiled as if she knew exactly what Solo was thinking, "but I promise you that the changes you'll make and the realizations you'll come to will be all the more powerful because you'll be the one in control of them."

"Okay," Solo said slowly. "But you *are* telling me that it's going to take some time to work everything through?"

"I am," Rae said. "But I can't say how long that will take. I *will* say the more work you put in, the more results you'll see. Lots of people go to therapy but not all of them are actually benefiting. Mainly because they're not giving everything. They hold back because they're afraid of what they might discover... about themselves and about their relationships." She waved her finger between the two of them. "That's why this relationship is paramount. You have to trust me. You have to believe that I can hold whatever you tell me, without judgment. If you're too concerned with what I might think of something you want to share, you'll end up keeping it to yourself, and we won't be able to progress beyond it." She smiled. "Does that make sense?"

"I guess," Solo said, "but it makes me want to shit my pants too."

Rae chuckled. "Our own demons can be frightening, Hannah, but I'm sure you'll find the courage to face them."

Solo sucked in a long breath. "I want my wife back, and I want to raise our family together. I don't care how painful and scary it's going to be, I'll do whatever it takes."

"Good." Rae motioned to her office door. "It doesn't look like Janie's going to make it today. Do you want to continue without her?"

Solo swallowed hard, the dual meaning striking her heart like a fifty-caliber bullet. She didn't want to *continue* without Janie. She didn't want to be a single mom to their girls. So if she had to cut herself open and lay herself out with the doc's tools, then that was exactly what she'd do. "Let's keep going," she said.

"Excellent. Perhaps we could come back to what you said about your friendship with Gabe. You said you were her best friend, but there seemed to be some hesitancy."

Solo held in a scoff and reminded herself Rae had to know her in order to help. "I look up to her. She took me under her wing when I joined the Army, and she made me part of her team. Woody and RB went to school together, then came into the service together in 2006, so they were already pretty tight. Lightning—sorry, Shay—joined in 2004, at the same time as Gabe, and they became friends when Lightning dragged Gabe out of the path of enemy fire in an ambush."

Rae paused from her note-taking.

"I know what you're thinking," Solo said. "How could someone like Shay drag someone like Gabe anywhere?"

Rae looked up and inclined her head slightly. "Is that what you think?"

Solo grabbed her phone again and flicked to a picture of them all from Rosie's photo shoot the previous weekend. She thrust it toward Rae. "That's Gabe, between me and Shay."

Rae tipped her glasses forward and looked at the photo for a few moments. "I see the discrepancy in size and bulk between the two of them, yes. Do you have trouble believing Shay could've pulled Gabe out of harm's way?"

Solo sat back in her chair and studied the shiny image as she clenched and unclenched her jaw. "Gabe's around fifty pounds heavier than Shay," she said and put the phone back in her jacket. "I just..."

Rae waited, her pen nib resting on the paper. *Did* Solo have to trust her with *every* thought? Even the ones she hadn't voiced to anyone?

"I just don't see how she did it," Solo finally said, filling the taunting silence.

"People are capable of extraordinary feats of strength under the right, or wrong, circumstances," Rae said. "Does it bother you that Shay rescued Gabe?"

Solo wrinkled her nose. "*Rescued* is a bit dramatic. I think the rest of the squad had the situation under control, and the enemy was already retreating." As the words came out, she began to realize what Rae was trying to get her to admit. "You think I'm jealous of Shay's relationship with Gabe, don't you?"

"What *do* you think of their relationship?"

Solo gripped the arms of her chair. Therapy was going to be regular bouts of frustration then. "I wish it'd been me." She threw her hands up. "There. I said it. That's trust, right?"

"Thank you." Rae smiled softly. "But that doesn't answer my question."

Solo yanked her ear hard and glared at the door. It'd be so easy to get up and leave. Janie hadn't shown up, and this was supposed to be couples' therapy. Why was she the only one spilling her guts? She looked back at Rae, who appeared so comfortable in every way. Was her life so perfect? Was she even in a relationship? Who was she to tell Solo to do anything? She'd had enough orders when she was a soldier to last her the rest of her life; she didn't need anyone else dictating what she should and shouldn't be doing.

She pushed up from the chair but headed to the window instead of the door. Lori had warned her these sessions were going to be hard. Gabe had said she had to fight for her family if she really wanted it. And Solo had never backed down from a fight, even when the odds were massively against her.

"I'm jealous of it." Solo pressed her forehead against the glass. "I want to be Gabe's best friend. And I'm not. Shay is. And I kind of resent her for it."

"If RB and Woody are best friends, like Shay and Gabe, what are your feelings about your place in the team?" Rae asked.

Solo couldn't decide if she liked the way Rae had essentially ignored her silent tantrum or if she didn't like that Rae hadn't acknowledged her irritation. "No one other than them took me seriously in the Army, but even they thought of me as the baby of the group, always in need of extra care or having to be bailed out of some trouble or other."

"And what about now?"

Solo scanned the street, but there was still no sign of Janie. Had something happened to her, or had she just given up on them? "I honestly thought I'd outgrown all of that, but Janie leaving has brought the curtain down on that charade." She turned back around and retook her seat. "I had to take the triplets to work on Monday, and that could've been a nightmare…"

"But?"

"But the team was amazing. They created a sleeping space and a play space for the girls, and Woody set up monitors, so I could keep an eye on them all day." Solo shook her head. The triplets had adapted surprisingly easily to their makeshift environment and had been better behaved than they'd ever been. Even Tia had left Luna alone for the majority of the day. Part of Solo wanted to believe that they'd sensed her need for them not to be any trouble, but that would mean they were aware that one of their moms had left them. Solo didn't want them knowing that at all, didn't want them thinking they weren't perfect enough to keep Janie at home with them.

The thought burned her brain like acid, and she tried to shake it away.

But now that it was there, she couldn't do a damned thing to evict it. Was *she* not enough for Janie to stay? If *she* went away, would Janie come back for the triplets?

"That sounds like a good thing, your team coming together to help you and your girls when you needed them most," Rae said.

"But it's a return to form, isn't it?" Solo picked at the wooden arm of her chair. A splinter slipped into her nailbed, but the pain from her heart was taking up too much space in her brain to really register it. "Baby Solo needs rescuing again."

"Isn't that what families are there for?" Rae asked. "Chosen families perhaps even more so. You rescue each other. Like Shay rescued Gabe. Like you rescued them all with the garage financing."

Solo inclined her head, considering that for a moment, before she shook the idea away. "That was Janie's money."

"Yes, but would Janie have invested in the team if you hadn't told her how important that dream was to all of you?"

Solo shrugged. "I guess not."

Rae tapped her notebook, catching Solo's attention, and she glanced up at the wall clock. "That's all we have time for today, Hannah. You have this slot as long as you want it. Do you want to check with Janie before you decide anything?"

Solo frowned. "I'm not giving up, doc. I'll talk to Janie, and if she's willing to come to these sessions, that'd be amazing. And if she doesn't..." She tugged on her ear again, not quite believing what she was about to ask. "If she doesn't, can we have another session every week to keep, you know, working on me?"

Rae nodded. "I think that would be a great idea, Hannah," she said and smiled. "We talked earlier about how hard therapy is, and I can see that you struggled to stay in the room with me today. But you did, and that's fantastic. It bodes well for future sessions." She stood and began to walk to the door. "I think it's clear that you're prepared to do the difficult work required to help yourself *and* your family."

Solo got up and joined Rae. "Thanks, doc. I appreciate it." She left the office and jogged down the stairs to the parking lot. At her car, she stopped to take a second. She'd fought for freedom for oppressed communities across the world, fought for her country against terrorists, even fought for her life a couple of times, but this fight for her family was going to be her most challenging battle ever.

Chapter Six

"I NEVER THOUGHT YOU'D leave your family." Austin sat back on the sofa in the corner of the bar and shook his head slowly. "Are you sure that's what you really want?"

Of course she wasn't sure. She wasn't sure of anything. That was part of the problem. Navigating life and all its complex decisions had never been much of a trial before, but then...everything had gotten muddied and complicated. And dangerous. She squeezed her eyes shut and tried to block the memory.

But she failed. Just like she'd failed to banish the horror movie from her brain countless times before. She'd messed up, and her conscience was never going to let her forget it.

And why would it? If she was allowed to forget what she'd done, if she didn't learn from it, God knows what could happen. She shook her head. She deserved this punishment. The mental torture would stop her from dreaming that she could slip back into Hannah's arms, from hoping to ever hold her children again.

"Janie?"

She looked across at Austin, so comfortable in his skin, so confident in his self-identity. When he'd taken an interest in her after he'd moved to Chicago from their office in Houston, she'd been a little starstruck by his charm. And his understanding; that'd made her guard drop too. But unlike Katherine Hill, Austin's interest had been purely professional. When she talked, he listened. *Really* listened. *His* eyes didn't wander to the baby monitor or to any one of the highchairs where the babies sat. He gave her his full attention. Of course, it made sense that Hannah's attention had wandered. Hannah hadn't known why the triplets needed her complete attention, but she'd clearly sensed it. She'd clearly made the connection that Janie shouldn't be trusted with their children.

"Janie? Are you okay?"

She offered Austin a smile, and he raised his eyebrows.

"You don't have to smile at me unless you mean it," he said. "You should know that by now."

She laughed lightly. "We've been talking for a little over a month. I don't think that qualifies me to make that judgment."

"You don't?" Austin frowned. "I feel like I know you better than people who've been in my orbit for decades. When two people connect like we have, friendship isn't measured in time."

Her answering smile was far more genuine this time, albeit a little tentative. She'd been wondering if she could truly count Austin as her friend once that spark of attraction had faded, but now he'd given her permission to do exactly that. "I don't know what I want. I don't really know who I am anymore." She took a long sip of red wine and gazed beyond Austin into the crowd of other lawyers gathered at the bar, demanding service. If Janie worked here, she'd spit into the glasses of many of the people who frequented the place. The thought made her study her own glass, but she'd always been pleasant and polite to all the staff, regardless of her mood or if she'd won or lost her most recent case.

"Are you talking to someone about this?" Austin asked.

Janie motioned toward him with her half-empty glass. "I'm talking to you."

"You know what I mean, Janie," he said, raising his eyebrows. "You need to talk to someone who can help you parse out this conundrum."

She scoffed. "If only it were that easy."

"I thought you said you were seeing a couples' therapist. Couldn't she—"

"Oh, crap." Janie tilted her head back and blew out a long breath. Would the examples of how poor a human being she was never stop coming?

Austin frowned. "What's wrong?"

Janie slipped her phone from her purse and checked the calendar app. *This* was why she didn't deserve a family. "We had a session tonight." She closed her eyes briefly. "But I conveniently forgot."

"Isn't that what you have an assistant for? To keep you apprised of your commitments?"

Janie tapped her messages app and sighed inwardly at the unopened message from Amanda doing exactly that. "She did. And she tried to tell me something as I was leaving the office, but I was in too much of a hurry to get a drink with you. Seems like I was determined to miss it." There were messages and missed calls from Hannah too, but she couldn't bring herself to read or listen to them, couldn't bear to hear the disappointment in Hannah's voice. She was fighting so hard to keep their family together when really, she should just let Janie go and find someone worthy of the titles of mom and wife. She deserved someone better and so did the triplets.

"Maybe you need a therapist just for yourself before you dive back into couples' therapy," Austin said. "Maybe that's why you sub-consciously stopped yourself from going to that appointment."

Janie emptied her glass and nodded toward the bar. She'd need a top-up if they were going to continue this conversation. "Do you want another?"

"No, thanks."

She didn't miss Austin's slight frown, but she *did* choose to ignore it. She needed a boost to get her over hump day, and she wasn't going to let his judgment stop her. When she got to the bar, she considered ordering a full bottle but then quickly changed her mind, not wanting to add aspiring alcoholic to her burgeoning list of flaws.

"Same again?" Chris asked as he took her glass and deposited it below the bar.

Janie glanced back at Austin, who gave her a tight smile. Then she surveyed the rest of the room and saw several of her other colleagues with empty glasses lined up on their tables. Their job was stressful, and they needed a little kicker here and there. Right now, so did she. "Yes, please." She flashed her card to pay.

Chris poured more than the measure she'd asked for into a fresh glass. "Rough day?"

"Rough year," she said, without thinking to censor her answer. How cliché to pour out her troubles to the bartender and yet struggle to speak to a professional.

He laughed lightly. "Anything you want to talk about?"

She registered the look in his eyes that made it clear he was offering more than just his shoulder to cry on. She glanced over at Austin again, and he widened his eyes. Clearly, he'd interpreted Chris's expression as she had. Janie shook her head. "Not really." She didn't need further complications in her life, and she wasn't about to start cheating on Hannah, even though they were technically separated. Austin had been a similar temptation, but she knew now that she'd misinterpreted their instant friend connection and the ease with which they'd fallen into intimate conversation. "Thank you, though," she said and placed five dollars on the bar.

He gave a rueful smile and slipped the cash into his pocket. "I'm here until eleven," he winked, "if you change your mind."

Janie took her glass and returned to the table without a backward glance. Austin shifted slightly and glared at Chris, so she assumed he'd stared at a particular part of her anatomy as she walked away.

"If you do decide to end your marriage," Austin said, "there'll be a line of wannabe replacements."

Janie inhaled sharply, the prospect of letting go of the love of her life sharply stabbing her heart. But she didn't really have a choice. It wouldn't be fair to Hannah to keep her hoping against hope that their family could ever be whole again.

Austin reached across the table and touched Janie's hand lightly. "Hey, I'm joking. Badly, obviously. There's something going on with you that you're not telling me." He squeezed her hand gently when she opened her mouth to protest. "And that's okay; you don't have to tell me anything. But you should seriously consider getting your own therapist to work things through." He withdrew his hand and gestured to a group of their colleagues heckling each other like hyenas around the pool table. "You don't want this to affect your work, or that pack of coyotes will be all over your professional carcass."

Janie wrinkled her nose. "That's gross, Austin."

He nodded. "It would be. They'd be picking over your cases like they're pulling flesh from—"

"Stop," Janie said. "Seriously. I get it." She glanced over at them but quickly looked away when Katherine caught her gaze and gave Janie her signature seduction smile. She'd repulsed Janie before, but now that she knew Katherine was Lori's ex, and the woman Lori had referred to only as "the lawyer," the strength of that revulsion had grown exponentially. She still couldn't believe that the wicked ex-wife she'd heard Hannah and Gabe talk about was at her own firm when there were over five hundred other law offices in the city she could've worked for.

"You know I'm here for you, Janie," Austin said. "If you need to talk about *anything*, I'll hear you."

She had to look away from the intense kindness in his eyes. Kindness she didn't deserve. If he actually heard the reason for the darkness dragging her down, Janie couldn't see him sticking around. She'd lose his friendship just like she'd lost Hannah and the girls, and selfishly, she couldn't face that. There was also the extremely large issue that she couldn't even bring herself to voice the problem in her head, let alone say it out loud, to Austin or to a therapist. "Thanks. I appreciate you," Janie said. "I just think this is something I need to work through by myself for a while."

"Okay, but just remember I'm here. And don't get lost in

the darkness alone." Austin looked slightly beyond her, and an unmistakable sadness overtook his usually bright green eyes.

Janie nibbled on her lower lip, trying to decide whether or not to press for more detail. He obviously had some personal experience that had left a mark, if his expression was anything to go by. Perhaps focusing on someone else's story might allow Janie some temporary relief from her own.

"So how do you know Rosie Morgan?"

Janie looked up to see Katherine by their table, holding two glasses of wine. She glanced back at Austin, and he rolled his eyes. The mist of melancholy had dissipated, and his nose twitched as if to indicate a bad smell.

"It's something I'm doing pro bono," Janie said. "She's a new client."

Katherine half-sneered. "I'm sure you could find more worthy people to fulfill your ethical duty. Has Phillip signed off on it?"

Janie arched her eyebrow. "I have full autonomy to choose whom I provide free legal advice to. I don't need Phillip's permission."

Katherine huffed. "You do if you want to make partner before you're fifty."

"I think you might be mistaken, Katherine," Austin said.

Janie dropped her shoulders slightly, glad for his intervention.

"Whatever," Katherine said and held out one of the glasses to Janie. "You look like you need this."

Janie gestured to the table. "Thank you, but no. I only just got a refill."

Katherine put it on their table anyway and gave Janie her signature smile as she took the seat between her and Austin without asking. "It's a ninety-dollar glass of Sangiovese. It can breathe while you finish," she wrinkled her nose in the direction of Janie's wine, "whatever that is."

Janie lost her desire to drink at all and looked at the door, half-hoping for a disgruntled client to burst into the bar and end them all. No one would mourn a roomful of dead lawyers.

"How *did* you end up with Rosie Morgan as a pro bono client anyway?"

Janie sighed at Katherine's persistence and the reminder of how she knew Rosie. "She's a friend of a friend," she said, knowing that, unlike with Austin, she really didn't have the right to call Rosie or Shay a friend. But "my estranged wife's best friend's best friend's current fuck buddy" didn't exactly roll off the tongue, and it'd be far too much personal information to share with a vampire like Katherine.

"You need new friends." Katherine scoffed and leaned in, far too close. "Seriously, you should stay away from her."

Janie tried to tamp down her piqued curiosity. How had Katherine managed to twist events in her own mind that her ex-wife's best friend was the enemy, someone to warn everyone about? "Funny, Rosie said a similar thing about you. She mentioned something about you cheating on your wife."

Katherine recoiled slightly before recovering her arrogant air of composure. "My ex-wife was a dead fish in bed." She shrugged and gave that stupid smile again. "And I'd be doing gay women city-wide a disservice if I kept my talents to myself."

Janie had to look away but saw Austin mouth, "Oh my god," as he wiped his hand over his mouth, clearly to stop himself from laughing in Katherine's face. How had sweet Lori fallen for this schtick? She was so much better off with Gabe. "You've got a pretty high opinion of yourself," Janie said, deciding to engage since it was taking her mind off other things.

Katherine looked smug. "Ask around. It's not my opinion: it's everyone else's. You can always find out for yourself to be sure," she said and winked. "You're bound to get bored of looking after three little rug rats. Screaming, shitting nipple-suckers." She laughed loudly and shook her head. "You're way too sophisticated to end up being a tired old soccer mom."

The words struck Janie's heart like an electric shock. "What do you know about being a mother, you censorious cunt?"

Austin reached across the table, but Janie had already

pushed her chair back and was standing over Katherine, barely controlling her desire to smash the glass of ninety-dollar wine in Katherine's face.

"You should stick to chasing twenty-somethings looking for a sugar daddy, you sad little Peter Pan. Emphasis on the *little*," Janie said, remembering something Lori had said about the size difference between her ex-wife and Gabe and knowing it was something Katherine tried to compensate for with elevator shoes. "You're such a patriarchal cliché, clinging to your youth by fucking girls half your age. You should know they're only doing it to climb the corporate ladder. They laugh about you in the break room, about how easy it is to seduce the desperate old mini butch into getting them a promotion or a salary bump." The red mist began to clear a little, and the sad, almost frightened look in Katherine's eyes made Janie hit pause on her diatribe. She glanced at Austin, who looked like he'd just seen Dr. Jekyll turn into Hyde, and beyond him, her colleagues and lawyers from other firms wore varying expressions of surprise, amusement, and disdain.

Janie gathered her phone and purse. "I'll see you tomorrow, Austin," she said.

"Wait," he said and began to rise from his chair. "I'll come with you."

She shook her head. "There's no need. I have to go," she said and headed out of the bar with her back straight and her gaze focused on the door, ignoring the whisperings that would be winding their way across tomorrow's grapevine. *Have to go where?* her inner voice taunted. She couldn't go home. Home was where Hannah and the triplets were, and she couldn't go back there, no matter how much she wanted to.

What were they doing right now? How was Hannah coping on her own? *Just fine without you, obviously.* The truth didn't just hurt, it wounded and scarred. But better her than her children or her wife. Janie choked back the tears as she ordered a Lyft. *Where are you going?* the app asked. Her finger hovered over

Home for far too long, until she was able to draw it away and type in the name of the hotel apartment where she was staying. Home... She might never have a home again.

Chapter Seven

Solo was hoping that the scent of garlic in Janie's signature tomato pasta sauce would bring her a sliver of peace, a familiar anchor in the swirling tempest of her new reality. It didn't. Instead, it reinforced the devastating loss of her wife's presence, of their old and beautiful reality. And the fragrance was powerless against the lingering aroma of whatever scientific experiment each of the triplets had somehow conducted in unison in their diapers earlier. The persistent tang hung in Solo's nostrils like, well, like a bad smell.

Usually, this was easy. She cooked as Janie watched their babies. But preparing dinner this evening was like climbing Everest, while her three tiny human tornadoes had been unleashed on her dad in the living room. He'd had the best of intentions when he'd offered to come live with her and help look after the triplets. He'd arrived with his impeccably neat life packed into two suitcases, leaving behind sunny Florida for the relentless demands of his three granddaughters. Three days of grandparent boot camp later, and she was sure he'd rather have stayed put, waiting for the early death he'd predicted for himself.

Still, it was unusually quiet down the hall, and silence, where her girls were concerned, was rarely golden. This week in particular, it had been an ominous prelude to some disaster or another. Monday saw glitter glue all around Griff's neck and head as they'd tried to secure bright orange pom poms to give him a lion's mane. She'd known that's what they were attempting when she'd seen the *How Do Lions Say I Love You?* picture book on the floor alongside their long-suffering dog. Tuesday evening ended with wet coffee grounds distributed in an impressively even pattern all across the pristine white carpet in Janie's office. Neither she nor her dad had figured out how they'd gotten to the coffee or how they'd secured access to the office.

"They're being super quiet, Dad," Solo called down the hallway, hope and suspicion battling for supremacy. "You haven't slipped some whiskey in their milk, have you?"

"Of course not. I'm just...admiring their artwork, honey." His voice, usually a booming baritone that filled any room with ease, was an octave higher and laced with a small hint of panic.

Solo identified his strained reply as "granddad attempting to herd feral cats with a limp pool noodle" but decided to let it go. Ignorance could be bliss, at least for a little while longer. She drained the pasta into the sink, and she could almost hear Janie's voice warning her not to burn herself on the steam. It rose around her like a suffocating blanket, reminding her she was alone. The void Janie had left in the house pulsed with unanswered questions, and her gut twisted with phantom pain she couldn't find the source of.

The beautiful sound of Tia's giggle penetrated the bubble of self-pity Solo had slipped into. That laughter and the chaotic beauty of the past few evenings were both her salvation and a painful reminder of what she'd lost. But she was determined to win Janie back and convince her their little family was worth fighting for, just like Gabe kept saying it was.

"Dad, just make sure they're not eating the crayons this time," Solo called out. One panicked phone call to 911 after Chloe had snacked on a purple crayon had assured Solo they were non-toxic, and that her little girl would likely only have a mild case of diarrhea. Chloe's digestive system *had* been surprisingly creative and what she'd produced could've easily been mistaken for a missing Jackson Pollack masterpiece.

"Nope, not eating them. They're being—"

A grunt stopped his response, and she heard a series of soft thumps. No doubt that would be Tia playing Tarzan on her pop pop's chest. "Everything's fine," she told herself out loud. She put the pasta in a serving dish and poured the tomato sauce on top. Just as she lifted the pot to carry it to the table, a high-pitched, triumphant squeal soared down the corridor into the kitchen.

Tia. Always Tia, the girls' ringleader and the tiny anarchist who seemed to view Solo's rules as suggestions and parental authority as a challenge to be overcome. That'd been fine when it was directed at Janie, but now that it was Solo's turn, it wasn't quite as amusing.

She placed the pot on the trivet, took a deep breath, and headed into the living room, trying to prepare herself for whatever chaos lay in her future. But she couldn't have imagined the scene in front of her when she crossed the threshold. Her dad stood in the center of the room, with Chloe under one arm and his other hand grasping Luna's diaper, since she'd apparently shed the rest of her clothes. A quick scan of the room indicated that the triplets had had a little success trying to dress Griff in Luna's bright green tutu. Her dad's normally immaculate silver hair was disheveled, and his cheeks were smeared with red and blue crayon. But *he* wasn't the masterpiece...

The living room wall, once a calming shade of pale pistachio, was now a vibrant swirling mural of color. Tia clutched a crayon in each fist like she was warring with her canvas, and she was currently adding a bright yellow sun to her creation, though it could just as easily have been an angry lemon character from some animated movie. Her tongue was poking out in super-focused concentration, and her eyes gleamed like a mad scientist's.

She met Solo's gaze and offered a giant smile. Solo couldn't decipher whether or not Tia was conscious of the havoc she'd caused. Or maybe she was just proud of it.

"I gave them paper, Han." He nodded vaguely toward a single, crumpled sheet lying on the floor and bearing a single, forlorn purple squiggle. "I turned my back for a few seconds."

"That's all she ever needs," Solo said, looking over Tia's artwork. It was impressive, really, what she'd managed to achieve in the tiny snippet of time she'd been unsupervised. Abstract squiggles joined vaguely humanoid shapes together, all under the sun, or maybe it was an emotional lemon. Tia had been interrupted, and it was too soon to tell definitively.

A bubble of laughter started in Solo's chest, fighting against her exhaustion and the persistent thrum of sorrow, and then it jumped out of her mouth. Tears pricked her eyes, not from sadness, but from the sheer unadulterated absurdity of it all. This was what kids did. And wasn't that beautiful and something to be celebrated? "Oh, Dad, what did you let them do to our innocent walls?"

He released his grip on Chloe and gently placed Luna on their playmat. "I tried, honey. I really did." He ran his hand through his hair, but that did little to un-muss it. "But Tia's a painting ninja, and..." he gestured wildly, "there are three of them!"

Solo couldn't stop more laughter, which Tia clearly interpreted as encouragement, because she let out another triumphant squeal and slammed her orange crayon onto the wall to begin drawing another multi-limbed creature from her own little universe.

"Tia, no, baby. Stop." Solo tried for the stern tone she'd heard Janie use and failed miserably, unable to stop her own wide smile. She knelt down to gently take the crayons from Tia's vice-like grip, wishing for all the world that Janie was there to play bad cop while Solo took photos of Tia's wall art for the Trouble Town Triplets Insta.

Tia's bottom lip began to wobble. "Mine!" she said and tried to pull her crayons away.

Solo remembered from one of the many parenting books stacked on her bedside drawers that this was the age her girls would begin to experience new emotions, like possessiveness and anger. She and her dad were in for a rough ride over the coming months. "We draw on paper, Tia. Right?"

Tia stuck out her bottom lip as she relinquished the tools of her new trade, and then she dropped to her butt. "Eat?"

Solo smiled and gently touched her finger to the end of Tia's nose. "You hungry?" she asked and rubbed her stomach. Tia nodded and looked settled for now, so Solo turned to see how her dad was doing. He sat on the playmat with Chloe and Luna on either side of him. Solo picked up Luna, and she wrapped her crayon-streaked arms around Solo's neck. "Did Tia draw on you too, Luna?"

"Luna pretty," she murmured and burrowed her little face into Solo's neck.

Another laugh escaped her. This glorious, messy, ridiculous life was so beautiful. And tragic... Janie's absence stabbed at her heart, and Solo took a deep breath, trying to push down and control the desperate grief clawing at her throat to get out.

"Are you okay, honey?" Her dad looked at her the way he always had when he knew something was bothering her.

She pressed her lips together tightly, stopping herself from answering him for now. Maybe later, when the girls were in bed, and when they could watch a replay of Sunday's Bears' game and have a couple of beers... Maybe then she could allow the words to come out of her mouth.

But not now. Not in this precious moment. She had to keep it together and make everything as normal as possible for the triplets.

Luna raised her head and pointed at the wall. "Pretty."

"It is pretty." Solo kissed Luna's forehead then popped her back down beside her dad. "But maybe next time, we could make a pretty picture on some paper, so we can keep it, huh?"

Her dad gestured to Tia's abstract art. "Your mom would've had a fit."

Solo nodded. Her mom had always been a neat freak. "No doubt. And then she would've found a way to turn it into a teachable moment about what special mom trick could remove crayon from the wall without damaging the paint."

There was a giggle behind her, and Solo turned around to see Tia grab a discarded crayon and dart over to a blank piece of wall near the doorframe. Once there, she continued the swirling pattern that formed the background of her masterpiece.

"Tia!" Solo cried, but it was too late. And what did it matter, really, when the whole wall would have to be repainted anyway?

Her dad chuckled. "She's got spirit, that one," he said then jiggled Chloe in his arms. "They all do. Creative too, just like their momma. The apple hasn't fallen far from the tree."

A warmth spread through Solo's chest at the thought that at least one of her girls might be artistic like her, and it pushed against the cold ache of her loneliness. She lifted Tia into her arms, and Tia immediately tried to decorate Solo's face. She disarmed the toddler and strapped her into the orange highchair by the table, then she scooped up Luna and Chloe in turn, and deposited them alongside their sister in their color-coded seats.

"That's an ingenious idea," her dad said, "but it makes me glad that me and your mom had you and your brother a couple years apart."

Solo nodded. "Whenever you had new friends over, they could never tell who was who in the baby pictures." She motioned to herself. "People still might have trouble telling the difference."

Her dad chuckled. "I guess. Your mom never did insist you wore a dress."

Solo didn't miss the sadness that flicked across his eyes, but it quickly disappeared. She wanted to say how much she missed her mom, but now wasn't the time for that either; they'd have to fit a lot of talking around the three-hour football game. "Watch the spider monkeys while I get dinner," she said and headed to the kitchen.

She didn't dawdle and quickly reheated the pasta, sauce, and meatballs before bringing them to the table, along with sippy cups full of juice for the girls and soda for her and her dad. She used a couple of wipes to clean the triplets' hands and then served the food for them all.

He curled his lip and raised the glass of Pepsi. "I think I deserve a glass of something alcoholic."

"Sorry." Solo gestured to the empty liquor cabinet. "I donated it all to Gabe's house on Monday." She shrugged, recalling the alluring array of colorful bottles as she stared at them from the hallway floor a few nights ago. "It was a bit too much temptation for me."

Her dad tsked. "Of course. I'm an idiot. Ignore me."

Solo shook her head and grinned. "And besides, I think you kinda fell down on the job tonight." She motioned to the wall.

He grumbled. "Nah, that's nothing a trip to Home Depot can't fix. Where's your closest one?"

Solo shrugged. "We used Ace Hardware a few blocks away. They mixed some special colors because..." She blinked rapidly and tugged on her ear. *Because Janie wanted walls the same color as some of her books.* She focused on Luna, who seemed to be struggling with her spoon. She'd given up and was using her fingers to pop the tiny meatballs in her mouth, but Solo had read that was still okay because it helped with sensory stimulation.

"Whatever," her dad said. "You should make sure it's washable though."

Solo glanced again at the Great Wall of Crayon. "I'll take pictures before we cover it and print them for the playroom. I want to keep everything they create. I want... I want Janie to see it."

Her dad muttered something she didn't catch, and she didn't care to ask him to repeat it. If he'd wanted her to hear it, he would've said it louder.

"Has she answered any of your calls yet?" he asked, shaking his head slowly before he put a giant forkful of food into his mouth.

"She texted last night to apologize for not making the therapy session." But she hadn't offered an excuse or any promise of coming next week, even though Solo had pressed for that.

"Is she coming to see your girls over the weekend?"

Solo clenched her jaw. She'd pressed for that too, but Janie had been non-committal. Solo was trying to give her the space she needed, but why did that mean Janie didn't want to see their beautiful babies? "Probably," she said, hoping it'd be true if she believed it. "I've got some light beer. We could watch the Bears and Vikings game when we've gotten the girls to sleep."

Her dad looked up from his plate at her and raised his eyebrows. "Sounds good if I don't fall asleep before them," he said. "They're exhausting, and I'm rusty in the grandparenting skills department."

"You're doing great, Dad." She squeezed his shoulder, relieved that he'd accepted her sledgehammer subject change. "And I'm so grateful you're here."

"I'm investing in an industrial-sized roll of butcher paper though." He waved his fork at the wall. "And a straitjacket—for me. I've got a feeling I might need it before the week is done."

Solo chuckled. The laughter had helped. So had her daughters' crazy artistic antics. And her dad being there was helping too. She hadn't forgotten the hell she was in but tonight had let her put it down just long enough to feel its absence.

But what she would've given to share this messy, hilarious chaos with Janie. She swallowed hard, the emotion sticking in her throat. She had to pull herself together for the girls. Janie had disappeared on them physically; they didn't need Solo doing it mentally. She had to be present, and she had to be the best mom she could be until...until she got Janie back. The girls needed her.

And so did Solo.

Chapter Eight

JANIE HAD LEFT THE message unopened for four hours. When the gray checks turned blue, Hannah would expect an answer, and Janie wanted to ignore it as long as possible. But it was a constant, nagging presence in her purse, a portent of dread, and she eventually succumbed.

They miss you. When can you come home? x

Her stomach churned. They were simple words, non-confrontational, yet they hit like a direct assault because it was a cruel, impossible request. Janie's chest tightened, steel bands cinching around her ribs until each breath was a shallow, painful effort. Why couldn't she just stay silent and unresponsive? And if she did, how long would Hannah persist before she realized she was wasting her time and love on a wife who didn't deserve it?

She'd been surrounded by silence in the rented apartment. The walls were sound-proofed, so the busy lives of her many temporary neighbors didn't encroach on the absence of Tia's naughty little giggle, or Luna's cute squeal, or Chloe's precious gurgles. And that silence held its own kind of torture, a crushing and suffocating iron maiden reinforcing her loneliness. It had driven her out of the vacuum within those four walls and somehow, she found herself driving back to the small café in Pilsen. She hadn't *chosen* to head that direction, not really. It was more like an instinctual movement toward something she couldn't name, a magnetic pull toward the strange women she'd met a few short days ago.

She figured it'd probably be closed this late on a Friday anyway, and maybe she'd drive to the aquarium and sit on the spit of land surrounding it. The view of the city from there was stunning; it was somewhere Hannah had taken her early on in their relationship... Perhaps she wouldn't go there. She needed somewhere new, somewhere not dripping with memories of her family.

But there were still lights on in Maria and Mirta's little establishment, and the same space she'd occupied last Sunday was empty, so she pulled in and cut the engine. She didn't move for a while, trying to decide whether or not this had been a stupid idea. No imaginary force had drawn her here. She *had* chosen to come. *Because I'm desperate*. Desperate for what? The two old women were strangely wonderful to her, and the few hours she'd spent with them had been somehow magical. But maybe her vulnerability and weakness had caused her to grasp at the unusual offer of a break from the reality threatening to overwhelm her.

The gentle tapping on her passenger window was familiar and comforting. Janie looked into the same kind eyes and saw that same silken, gentle smile. Just as before, she rolled down the window, and Maria ignored it, getting into the passenger seat instead.

"We must stop meeting like this or people will talk," Maria said and wiggled her bushy eyebrows.

"That'd be a hell of an age-gap," Janie said without thinking.

"Sass," Maria said. "I'm not a day over thirty; I've just had a hard life. It's working for my old friend Dutch." She tapped her nose.

"I'm sure it is." Janie frowned at her conspiratorial smile, since she had no idea who Maria was talking about. Why had she come here?

"Anyway, you're too old for me." Maria's wrinkles multiplied with her deep smile. "Have you come for coffee?" she asked. "Our decaf is made with the Swiss Water process. No chemicals here."

Janie looked at the café, a beacon of light and life on the otherwise dark and quiet street. Every seat she could see was full: a group of young people were huddled over their laptops, an elderly man sat in the window seat with a newspaper spread across his small table, and a young woman with more piercings than Janie could count was engaged in animated conversation with another woman who could easily have been Maria's sister. The connection between the seemingly *un*connected people was almost tangible, like colored cosmic string joining them all together. So many people sharing a moment, sharing this special place. "It looks busy," she said quietly and moved her hand toward the start button.

Maria wrapped her cool hand around Janie's, and she squeezed gently. "You came all this way for *something*," she said.

Janie sighed deeply and dropped her hand. "I did?"

Maria nodded, and her eyes sparkled. "A special treat. Come on."

Janie didn't know what she'd come for, but it definitely wasn't that. She got out of the car anyway and once again noticed Maria didn't close her door until Janie joined her on the sidewalk. "Did you think I'd bolt?" she asked, her mood lightening as she enjoyed the easy repetition of their first meeting.

Maria wiggled her hand from side to side, then laughed in that same honeyed way that had set Janie so at ease before. She hooked her arm in Janie's and tugged her toward the café.

Last time, Janie hadn't noticed the chime above the door that welcomed them with a cheerful metal tinkling. It seemed so old-fashioned but suited the place perfectly. The warm air, scented with freshly baked pastries and strong coffee, hit her nostrils, and she relaxed a little more.

"Janie! We hoped you would come back." Mirta came from around the counter and wrapped her arms around Janie.

She stiffened a little at the uninvited contact, and Mirta's embrace grew tighter in response, like a human swaddling blanket. Janie's body uncoiled without her permission, allowing her to take comfort from the unexpected gesture. She couldn't remember the last time someone had held her this long, and despite herself, she didn't pull away. Hannah used to, but things had changed since the triplets had come along.

"Let the poor girl go, Mirta," Maria said. "She's come for something sweet, not an awkward hug with a sour *viejita*."

Mirta released Janie slowly and smiled. "*Paja!* I'm not a *total* stranger. And I'm not the one who jumped in her car like a *vieja loca*." She wrinkled her nose toward Maria before taking Janie's hand to lead her to the only empty table. "I'll be right back with just what you need."

"Thank you," Janie said, doubting it, but she smiled anyway, not wanting to reject their kindness or upset either of them. But it was more than that, wasn't it? She didn't want to burst whatever bubble of unreality she'd been absorbed into. However alien this situation was, she didn't want it to end. Surrounded by all these strangers, most of whom had looked up and smiled, every inch of difference marked her out, and yet... Being among them, especially Maria and Mirta, sent a flicker of something dangerously close to relief through her.

Maria took the seat opposite her, looking at Janie in a way that made her want to sob and shrink away. The deep knowing in her brown eyes was intimidating but comforting, like there was nothing she hadn't seen before, like nothing could shock her or spur her to hasty judgment.

"How have you been?" Maria asked, her soothing voice somehow lowering Janie's internal volume.

Janie sifted through the detritus of her week. Client meetings. Court appointments. The disastrous night out when she'd publicly destroyed a colleague. And then there was the grinding ache of missing her children, her wife, and the life she'd dismantled with her own hands. "Fine," she said, hearing it sound as flat and hollow as she felt inside.

The door chime drew her attention away from Maria's inquisitive gaze, and a group of five young men came in, loud and energetic. Janie didn't want to react the way she did, fear zipping through her like a lightning strike, and she hated herself for it on so many levels. The fact that she wasn't alone and that there were at least thirty people around her should've provided some safety, but it didn't. Thirty people were useless against the potential of five guns. And she knew of so many horror stories, so many women powerless in the face of male entitlement.

She became aware of Maria's hand on her forearm, and her heartbeat slowed slightly.

"Relax, patoja."

Heat flushed Janie's neck and face, mortified that Maria had registered her discomfort. The guys were clearly local and had far more right to be there than she did. "I'm sorry," she whispered, hating the years of learned dread. No matter how formidable she was in a courtroom, out on the street that counted for nothing.

"Don't worry."

Janie twirled her wedding ring and tried to concentrate on its solidity beneath her fingers instead of monitoring the men in her peripheral vision. Once again, she noted that no payment was made. If this had been her first time here, she would've assumed some nefarious activity, such as gang members providing protection to the café in exchange for cash and unlimited coffee. Criminals needed caffeinating as much as the next person. But she hadn't seen any money or card transactions on her last visit either. "I've never seen a café operate an ongoing credit policy," she said, unable and perhaps unwilling to suppress her interest in discovering more about the enigmatic Maria and her adorable café.

Maria chuckled. Her soft wrinkles deepened, and her eyes sparkled mischievously, belying her age. "Is that what you think is happening here?"

Janie bit her bottom lip and frowned. "Isn't it?" The possibility that the place might be a front for a drug cartel disappeared almost as quickly as it had popped into her head. *That would require money to be crossing the counter, idiot.*

"Some things should not be for sale. A great cup of coffee, a safe haven, a little community. These things should be available to all."

Perfectly on cue, Mirta returned with a tray of coffee and pastries for two. "Torrejas," she said after she'd clearly recognized Janie's furrowed brow. "Be prepared; the flavors will fire in your mouth."

"Explode," Maria said, shaking her head. "The flavors will explode."

Mirta rolled her eyes. "My word is better." She walked away before Maria could dispense another language lesson and whispered something in one of the young guy's ears. He grinned widely and dipped his head, in obvious reverence.

Janie frowned at her lack of understanding and looked again at what seemed like a gooey bread pudding. "I bet that dish has all my sugar intake for a week."

Maria waved her hand. "Paja! Dessert is good for the soul." She picked up a spoon and offered it to Janie. "Eat."

Janie took the utensil and scooped a little of the torrejas into her mouth. The hits of cinnamon, orange, and clove did fire in her mouth, and it tasted divine. "Damn, that's good." She munched another couple of bites, wanting to enjoy it while it was hot. But the sweet treat didn't deter her query. "How can you keep this place open with that concept?" she asked, staring at the steam rising from her mug instead of focusing on Maria. It all seemed so risky and open-ended, so utterly foreign to her own existence.

"I knew a girl once," Maria said in almost a whisper. "A long time ago. She was very famous, and the whole world knew her name. But no one knew her. Everyone around her wanted a piece, a story, an autograph, a picture. She was surrounded by people constantly: managers, agents, fans, but she was terribly, terribly lonely."

Maria took a bite of her torrejas and followed it with a sip of coffee. Janie waited for more, but Maria looked beyond her for a long moment, and for the first time since they'd met, Janie saw a sadness in Maria's usually bright and joyful expression. "What happened to her?" Janie asked when the silence stretched on for too long.

Maria switched her gaze back to Janie, unwavering and direct once more. "She thought the world was a transactional place. You give a performance, you get applause. You give an interview, you get a headline. You give your time, you get paid."

Her bottom lip twitched slightly, as if the retelling of this story was painful, and Janie began to wish she hadn't prompted her to continue.

Maria made a clicking sound. "But she found out the hard way that true connection, true community, cannot be a transaction." She waved her finger in front of Janie's face, her playfulness returning. "It's a gift. A risk, sometimes, yes, but a gift."

Janie sat back from the table slightly and clasped her hands in her lap. Maria's story was beginning to sound like an allegory, and she was holding up a mirror to Janie's soul. She'd navigated her world precisely this way all her life; her parents had taught her to do exactly that. You give something, you get something. *Don't give away anything for free, especially your time.* She could practically hear their words.

"I'm not... I'm not lonely." The lie tasted like ash on her tongue. "I'm just private. I'm not like Hannah, with her whole band of sisters she can rely on. My problems are just that: mine."

"Hannah is your wife?" Maria asked, looking at Janie's hands.

Janie frowned at how easily Maria continued to read her. She glanced at the wall beside them and noticed the arrangement of framed tarot cards. Maybe Maria was some kind of white witch.

"And her sisters?"

Janie ran her finger over the rim of her mug. "They're her tribe. Hannah was in the Army for thirteen years, and now they're all out. They've just opened their own garage together. I guess Hannah is the kid sister of the bunch." They were bound by shared experience, and their mutual trust had been earned under fire. She'd always stood outside that circle, assuming her contribution of stability and a good income and now a financial stake in the business would be enough. Just the kind of transaction Maria was talking about.

"But why do you think of your problems as your own, to carry alone?" Maria asked softly. "They are like rocks, Janie, pressing on and crushing your soul. A secret, perhaps a guilty one, becomes bigger the more you hide it, the more you add layers of your fear. In the end, it isolates you and keeps you from the people who could help you lift it from your soul."

If Janie had shared her own guilty secret with a therapist, she'd believe that Maria had read through her session notes. But she hadn't. Why was her guilt so obvious to someone who was two coffees away from being a complete stranger? "No one can help me lift this," she mumbled, thinking of the Greek myth of Atlas. "What did the girl do?" she asked, still eager to know if Maria's cryptic tale had something to do with the café's cashless operation. "What was she famous for?"

Maria's eyes crinkled at the corners, and she waved her hand as if she were wafting away a bothersome mosquito. "Oh, something noisy and bright and utterly exhausting. Something that required her to give a lot of herself, though she got very little of meaningful substance in return. *Her* loneliness became like a rock too. And the more she tried to hide it from everyone around her, the heavier it became. The more she pretended it wasn't really there, and that it wasn't affecting her, the more isolated she became." Her gaze flickered across the café and settled on Mirta. "Eventually, she came to realize that she could use the fame and the money it had brought her to build something real, something that was about community and bringing people together." Maria motioned around her. "Something like this place."

Janie's heart hammered against her ribs. Maria's tale wasn't an anecdote. It was her origin story. And apparently a lesson for Janie in the value of vulnerability and community that directly refuted her transactional mindset. Without thinking about her own vulnerability and the danger of opening herself up to this strangely intuitive older woman, Janie pulled out her phone and showed Maria a photo of her beautiful family. "Hannah wants me to visit the girls."

Maria smiled at the picture. "And you don't want to go," she said, as if already knowing all the facts.

Janie swallowed and shook her head slowly. "I can't. They're all better off without me."

Maria huffed. "Janie, you are a mother. And mothers are an essential part of a child's world. You are their sun and moon. Your absence is not the gift I talked about. It is a wound that can never heal. You're inflicting that wound on your daughters out of guilt, and you're calling it protection. You must talk to Hannah. Share this burden before it consumes you all."

Janie flinched. The thought of punishing her kids, even indirectly, sliced at her heart. She squeezed her eyes shut and was immediately back in the house, reliving the horrifying moment that had changed everything. Janie waking from a slumber she shouldn't have slipped into. The ensuing silence before the air exploded with the frightened cries of the triplets, and the bone-deep terror at the terrible realization of what had happened. All because she'd been so careless, so complacent.

Cold tears crept from their hiding place and coursed down her cheeks. "She wouldn't understand," Janie said, her voice cracking. "The girls are her life. If she knew I'd put them in danger, she'd hate me forever." As she said the words, they molded into a viable option. Wouldn't it be for the best if Hannah thought about her that way? Then she could move on, find the girls another mom, a *better* mom. Someone who deserved the title.

Maria sighed. "Your fear is blinding you, Janie. You think you're being selfless, but you're indulging your guilt. Hiding will not help any of you. You're punishing yourself, yes, but you are also causing deep confusion and pain for the three little people who need you and the woman who loves you."

Janie didn't respond and simply lost herself in Maria's eyes, which seemed to hold centuries of wisdom. Her kind weathered face, a portrait of empathy, held no judgment. Janie's defenses crumbled, and her chin trembled. "I don't know what to do," she said, the admission a quiet, painful surrender.

Maria rested her hand on Janie's arm, and Janie focused on it, on its warmth and on her soft skin, and how young-looking her hands were.

"This is not a thing that can be fixed in a single moment," Maria said softly. "But you do have to start somewhere. And a visit to your children could be the first step toward healing, for all of you. It will say, 'I haven't gone anywhere. I'm here. I'm still your mom.'"

More tears than she could cry welled in Janie's eyes and blurred her vision. A fierce, protective fear gripped her. The memory was too fresh, the terror too absolute. What was there to stop it, or something worse, from happening again? "I was so stupid. So careless. I haven't changed. There's no pill to take that will make me a perfect mother."

Maria squeezed Janie's hand. "There is no such thing. Every mother tries their best. You can't guarantee that you'll get everything right. No one can. But you can face it. You can share your burden with your wife."

"I want to," Janie said, her voice as raw as the pain in her heart. "God, I want to see their gorgeous little faces. To smell them. I ache for that." She shook her head as the cold hammer of reality smashed into that desire. The image Hannah had sent her from last night, the crayon masterpiece adorning their living room wall was replaced by the terrifyingly vivid memory of the thing she'd done, the danger she'd created.

"Share the burden, Janie."

She gave a single nod and looked at her phone. The warmth of Maria's words wrapped around Janie like a comforting blanket, but it didn't change anything. Maybe if she saw Hannah, *just* Hannah, it might give her the support she needed to build herself up again, to make herself the mother the triplets deserved. But did *she* deserve that chance?

"Go to them," Maria said. "They need you, and you need them."

Janie picked up her spoon and busied her mouth with another taste of the torrejas. "This is really delicious."

Maria arched her eyebrow but said nothing, seeming to let it go, for now. As they continued to eat, and Maria talked more about the café and the community it fostered, Janie's desire for absolute isolation battled quietly with the small, persistent seed of hope and connection that Maria had planted. The fear eating at Janie demanded that she refuse to see both Hannah and the triplets, but the profound love for her children insisted that she keep the door open. Maria's stubborn, forceful compassion forced Janie to consider whether her absence really was hurting her children and her wife. Her protection was also punishment, for all of them. Did protecting them outweigh the pain they were feeling?

For now, she settled into the quiet, gentle conversation with the wise woman who'd entered her life in the most bizarre way possible. Janie was a loner by habit, but she no longer had to be a loner by choice. And maybe opening up to that possibility was the first step that might eventually lead her home.

Chapter Nine

Solo took her dark denim jacket from the chair in her bedroom and pulled it on. It usually gave her comfort and confidence, but tonight, it was like donning armor for battle. She adjusted the collar of the crisp, white button-down shirt, the starched fabric stiff against her skin, and undid the top button beneath her tie. She stared at her reflection in the full-length mirror Janie had insisted on buying and almost laughed at herself. With her hair neatly cropped and wearing her best pair of perfectly tailored black dress pants and highly polished boots, this was her go-to wife uniform, her most confident, masc presentation, and the outfit Janie liked her in—and out of—the most. Could Solo hope that it might have the same effect on her tonight?

She slipped her wallet and phone into her inside pockets and headed downstairs. The living room still resembled a colorful, cushioned warzone. The triplets, fresh from their afternoon nap, were each involved in their own interesting project. Tia was testing the structural integrity of the large cardboard box that had housed her granddad's new bedframe, while he sat cross-legged on the floor, trying to corral them all and keep them in his line of sight at all times.

She smiled. He really hadn't known what he was getting himself into when he'd upended his life and moved in with them. Caring for three eighteen-month-old girls was proving to be a highly specialized field, one he hadn't been anywhere near for over three decades. But he wouldn't be doing it alone for long if the nanny agency could come up with better candidates than the one who'd left her in the lurch just before Janie had gone.

"Chloe, the crayons are for paper. Remember?" He pulled at

the edge of a roll of drawing paper until Chloe had four feet of canvas to create on.

"Pop!" Chloe shouted, cheerly smearing her purple crayon across the chest of his crisp white T-shirt.

The knock at the front door stopped Solo from responding, and she heard it open. The comforting sounds of laughter and familiar voices drifted into the house, and Solo's anxiety dialed down a notch. Gabe's mere presence had affected her that way for nearly fifteen years now.

"The cavalry has arrived." Gabe stepped over an array of discarded toys, which looked like they'd been carefully arranged into an assault course designed to fell adults, and bro-hugged Solo.

She thought she'd stayed stiff as she tried to borrow some of Gabe's strength but knew she'd failed when Gabe pulled away and looked at her like she was trying to see into her soul.

"You okay, buddy?" Gabe asked, frowning.

Solo tried for a convincing smile. "Sure thing." She avoided Gabe's continued gaze and glanced around Gabe's bulk to wave at Lori. "Hey. You brought supplies?" She gestured toward the paper bag Lori was carrying.

Lori laughed, and her eyes sparkled. "I figured we'd all have our hands full and be too busy to attempt cooking tonight."

"Thank God." Her dad sighed. "You're an angel."

Lori tiptoed around the debris of the afternoon's playtime. "I'll take this to the kitchen and serve it up. Hannah, you look great."

The compliment lifted Solo's spirits, as any compliment from a woman as gorgeous as Lori was bound to do, no matter how shitty she felt inside. She smiled genuinely.

"Hey, spider monkey." Gabe intercepted Tia, who had abandoned her destruction of the cardboard fortress she'd built and decided Gabe's leg was the next thing to conquer.

She held her aloft with one hand, and Tia made a delighted squeal while she wiggled her arms and legs as if she was pretending to fly. Gabe clapped her other hand on Solo's shoulder, heavy and reassuring.

"She's going to be there, right?" Solo whispered. "She said yes. She'll show up, right?"

Gabe inclined her head slightly. "Janie loves you, and she loves these girls. This could never be a breakup. It's just a time-out because you've been a naughty wife."

Her crooked smile and teasing tone helped Solo to breathe a little easier. "Right." She nodded. "Bad wife."

Gabe squeezed Solo's shoulder. "What's the plan?"

"The plan is to apologize over and over for letting her down. Tell her I'm in therapy, and that I'm working on being the mature, adult wife she needs. And promise her that she'll be my priority again. Like she was when we met."

"Good." Gabe released Solo and punched her shoulder hard enough to rock her back on her heels a little. "What else? Don't just focus on the bad and what's gone wrong, remember?"

Solo nodded. "Right. I'll convince her that my neglect wasn't from a lack of love," she said, hoping she'd remember all the stuff she'd been rehearsing the whole day. "I need to remind her how good we are together and what we've built, why we said 'I do' in the first place."

"Perfect." Gabe held Tia over her head one-handed, almost touching her to the ceiling, and Lori gasped as she came back into the living room.

"Are you trying to give Hannah a heart attack before she leaves?" Lori reached up to retrieve Tia, but her outstretched arms barely reached Gabe's elbow.

Gabe grasped Lori's wrist and twisted her around in one fluid movement so that she nestled into Gabe's body. God, she was smooth. If Janie was married to Gabe, she wouldn't have left. But Gabe wouldn't have neglected her either.

"It's a test," Gabe said. "Solo's got to pop the bubble wrap and let other people help take care of the girls, so she can concentrate more on keeping her wife happy." She kissed the top of Lori's head. "Like I'm learning how to keep you happy."

Solo scoffed. "Looks like you're a natural. But it was me who said you'd fall in love with a woman you rescued on the road."

"Maybe." Gabe grinned. "But I don't have that Hallmark movie subscription like you do."

Lori tipped her head back and looked up at Gabe adoringly. "That's because we're too busy—"

Solo put her finger to her lips. "My babies don't need to hear that." She glanced over her shoulder at her dad. "And neither does he."

Gabe wiggled her eyebrows. "Anyway, back to the plan. Remind Janie that you didn't see her just as the incubator to your tiny terrors. Remind her you were obsessed with her when she could barely walk and thought she looked like a whale."

Lori nodded. "And stress the support system you're putting into place. She needs to know the fort isn't going to collapse. Tell her about your dad helping and the upcoming interviews for a new nanny."

Solo swallowed. The plan was complicated. And it was a lot to remember. "I'm terrified she's going to tell me it's too late," she whispered, her chest tightening at the thought of rejection. Was that why Janie had chosen somewhere so classy and so...public? So that Solo didn't make a scene?

Gabe and Lori shook their heads.

"It's never too late, buddy," Gabe said firmly. "Not when you love each other like you two do. Now, go. Leave us with your chaos chimps and go get your wife back."

Solo nodded. "Okay, I'm going," she said and headed out, wishing it could be as easy as Gabe made it sound.

She got in her car and drove to the restaurant on autopilot. When the valet opened her door, she jumped like she'd forgotten where she was or how she'd gotten there. She gave him the key and tried to shake it off. She'd had a few near-dissociative episodes while she'd been on tour, and alcohol had been her answer. But she'd sworn a promise to the triplets less than a week ago that she'd stay off the hard stuff, and she was determined to see that through. A beer here and there, like with her dad a couple of nights ago, didn't count. At least, that's what she was hoping.

The person at the tall desk just inside the building smiled. "Welcome to the Embers."

Solo jutted her chin. "Thanks. Table for two for Rogers." It'd been a little over a month since she'd said those words, and before that? She couldn't even remember. When had she started taking Janie for granted? When had she stopped *seeing* her?

The desk person shook their head. "Sorry, there's no table in that name. Could it be booked under another?"

Gut punch. Maybe Janie had already stopped using their married name. "Try Evans," she said, hoping she'd be wrong.

They tapped at their tablet again. "Ah, there you are." They smiled and gestured beyond the curtain separating them from the main area. "Let me show you to your table."

Solo had made sure she was Army-early to the time Janie had suggested, but she was already second-guessing herself. It just gave her more time to sit there, thinking about what bottle of hard liquor she'd order if Janie didn't show.

"Amber will be your server this evening. Enjoy," the desk person said before retreating back behind the curtain.

"Can I get you a drink to start?" Amber asked.

Solo looked across at the bar and its red-orange lighting that illuminated a vast array of high-end whiskey bottles, tempting her with their aesthetic. But she wasn't really interested in how they looked. It was what was on the inside that would help her now. "Water," she said, almost croaking the word like she'd walked an hour in a desert sandstorm.

Amber frowned and leaned closer. "Sorry, what?"

Solo glanced at her. She wasn't sorry. Looking disinterested and bored to the point of tears, the server clearly didn't even want to be there. "Still water, no ice. Thanks," Solo said, louder than was necessary.

Amber's eyebrow quirked, and she clenched her jaw for a millisecond before a practiced smile appeared. "Of course... madam."

Solo didn't miss the fleeting glee in Amber's expression. She wouldn't have minded being called sir if that was the in-joke Amber was having with herself. She'd prefer it, to be fair.

"Are you dining alone?"

Solo tamped down the desire to physically react when Amber's lips twitched after she'd asked the question. It was Saturday night, and this was a special restaurant— She stopped her internal rant. "I guess we'll see," she said instead.

Amber left, and Solo placed her phone on the table, screen up so she could keep an eye on the time without constantly shoving up her sleeve to check her watch, looking like a loser. She took off her jacket reluctantly, but the open fire a few tables away made it impossible to do otherwise unless she wanted to melt onto the chair.

Amber returned with a bottle of water and a single glass, demonstrating where she was placing her bet on whether or not Janie would show. Solo thanked her without looking up from the sleek, iridescent cutlery she was shifting and straightening. The twisted rope-like metal shafts felt nice in her palm, and she didn't want that experience ruined by another judgmental look from the zoomer. She'd just completed a spray job at the garage with a similar finish on an Aston Martin; the owner of that car wouldn't be treated to Amber's particular brand of hospitality, for sure.

Solo snapped her head up at the distinct clicking of heels on the stone floor. The sound was always a positive trigger, no matter who was filling the shoes, but she'd recognize the cadence of Janie's step anywhere. Her heart hammered against her ribs and her breath caught— So predictable. She squared her shoulders and looked up just as the heels came into view.

Janie looked exhausted but still stunning in a simple emerald dress. She'd pulled her usually vibrant auburn hair back into a severe ponytail. Her green eyes, always so warm and full of life, were guarded and...flat. Could eyes be flat? But seeing her for the first time in almost a week still took Solo's breath away, and the ache in her chest intensified as Janie's presence here reinforced her absence at home.

"You came." Solo stood and moved to pull out Janie's chair, but Janie was too quick and had already done it for herself before Solo could make it around the table.

"I did," Janie said as she smoothed her dress and sat down.

The cautious neutrality in Janie's expression pierced Solo's heart. She looked distant, with a hint of fear in her eyes. Why would she be scared? Unless she was here to tell Solo they were done forever, and she wasn't sure how Solo was going to react. Sure, they'd argued, but Solo had never gotten physical. If either of them had reason to be frightened, it was Solo. She couldn't face life without Janie by her side. Janie was her life, her oxygen, the reason she was alive.

Solo clutched at her chest when her breathing became labored.

Janie inclined her head slightly. "Are you okay?"

Solo nodded weakly and poured a glass of water. She took a long drink and tried to steady her breathing. She was being stupid. She hadn't even tried to save them yet, and she was already giving up.

Amber slipped up to the table and smiled widely at Janie. Of course she would. Janie commanded respect and admiration without even being aware of it. And she was so beautiful, no matter how straight the zoomer thought she was, she'd find herself attracted to Janie.

"Can I get you something to drink, miss?" Amber asked.

And sure, Janie looked far younger than thirty-five, so of course she'd be a miss and not a madam.

"A glass of merlot, please."

Solo recognized the professional smile that followed Janie's words. She was in full-on courtroom mode, an impenetrable wall shielding her true emotions. Janie had shut her out, and this was just a business meeting. Jesus, was that what this was? Did she want to pull her stake from the garage? Gabe and the gang would go insane. Their dream had finally become a reality, and Solo was going to be responsible for it all crashing down around them. Gabe would never forgive her.

"Why is your hair up like that?" Solo tugged at her ear. *That's* the best question she could think of? Did Chicago have earthquakes? That seemed like the only thing that might rescue her from herself. She tried to dredge her memory for *the plan*, for all the purple prose she'd been practicing.

Janie's jaw tightened. "I didn't have time to wash it after work."

Solo frowned. "You worked today? You never work Saturdays. That's—" She slammed the brakes on her motormouth. What was she going to say? That's new? Saturdays are family time. She couldn't, and shouldn't, challenge anything Janie said. She was supposed to be apologizing, supposed to be making amends. But instead, she was turning the whole thing to shit.

"I had to," Janie said. "We have a new client, and Phillip wanted the whole department in for the weekend." She glanced at her watch. "I don't have long before I have to be back."

Solo scrubbed her hand across the back of her head. "You're going back to work after this?" The tiny sliver of hope she'd had that Janie might jump into her arms and ask her to drive them home, back where she belonged, receded into the depths of her mind. She laughed at herself. Like Janie would just rush back into Solo's embrace, forgiving her for everything when she'd been such a dick since the babies were born.

Janie visibly stiffened. "I have to if I want to keep my job. And especially if I ever want to make partner."

Solo rolled her neck. She'd had to work hard to suffocate her ego when it came to Janie being the one to bring in all the money, no matter how much she declared otherwise that she wasn't *that* kind of traditional butch. Or masc. Or whatever the hell she was supposed to call herself these days. Asshole, mostly.

"Are you making progress with Rosie's situation?" she asked, trying to steer back to less combative ground. This wasn't going the way she'd planned, but maybe she'd been stupid thinking she could just dive straight into the deeper waters of their failing relationship. They hadn't talked since Janie had left their home a week ago.

Amber returned with Janie's wine. "Are you ready to order?" she asked, looking mostly at Janie.

"We need five more minutes," Solo said.

Amber gave a minimal smile and went to attend another table.

Solo flipped open the menu. "Any idea what's good here?"

"Austin said that the chef is known for her fish dishes." Janie looked into her wine glass as she spoke, then she took a sip.

"Austin?" Solo clenched her jaw, knowing she'd failed to keep the edge of distaste from her tone. Janie hadn't said outright that the guy she'd been *talking* to was also the new guy at her law firm. But there was something about the way she said his name that made Solo itch. "Austin from work?" She stared at Janie, but her wife didn't meet her gaze, seemingly fascinated with the cutlery in much the same way as Solo had initially been.

"Yes," Janie whispered and finally looked up. "And yes, we're making progress with Rosie's loan. Amanda sent correspondence to—"

"Is Austin the reason you left us?" It wasn't the question Solo *wanted* to ask, but it was one she needed the answer to.

Janie frowned before she took another long drink of her wine. "Of course not."

Solo raised her eyebrows and scoffed. "Of course not," she repeated. "Why would I think that?" She sat back in her seat and tugged at her suddenly too-tight tie.

Janie narrowed her eyes. "Please don't use that tone. You know how it gets to me."

"You know what gets to *me*?" Solo tapped two fingers on their table. "When my wife starts *talking* to a guy and then moves into the guest room, and I'm supposed to believe the two things aren't related." She nodded. "Yep, that's what gets to me."

Janie looked around and offered a small smile to the people at other tables who were flicking irritated glances their way. They were probably out for date night. Or maybe they were on their first date and had the whole exciting journey of discovery to look forward to. And then...*this*. Heartbreak. And accusations. And cheating.

"I already told you: Austin is just a friend," Janie whispered. "He was nice to me when I needed someone to talk to."

Janie's words wounded Solo like they were rocks she'd thrown at Solo's heart. "You were supposed to talk to *me*," she said, her voice cracking but still too loud for the intimate space.

Janie glanced quickly at the other tables again, and Solo noticed the sympathetic looks she received in return. Sure, Solo was the bad guy here, just like always. The immature kid who couldn't handle an adult conversation about their relationship without getting defensive. The stupid soldier who should never have been blessed with Janie for even a moment, let alone had five years with her.

"This was a bad idea," Janie said quietly and pushed her wine glass away. "I need to leave."

Solo shook her head and scoffed. "Is that why you suggested meeting here? So you could leave if it got hard? Like you've left me and the girls because that's too hard?"

Janie pushed away from the table and stood as she gathered her purse. "No, it wasn't."

Her eyes were hard and distant, a look Janie always adopted when they argued. And it killed Solo this time just as it had every time in the past. She'd caused it though, like she'd caused most of their issues. What the hell was she doing? All the shit she'd just said... Where the hell had it come from?

Solo stood and grasped Janie's wrist lightly. "Please don't go. I'm sorry. I'm an asshole. I didn't mean any of that."

Janie looked at Solo's hand then touched her gently to

remove it. She smiled, and her eyes softened slightly. "Yes. You did, Hannah. You meant every word."

Solo released Janie's hand, and her shoulders sagged. The temper she'd always had trouble controlling had fucked her over again. "I'm going to therapy," she blurted out, as if that would convince Janie to retake her seat. "Hear me out. Please."

Janie blinked, and tears tracked down her cheeks, streaking them with black mascara. "You're angry, honey. We've never been able to communicate when you're like this." She took a step back and seemed to hesitate, then she turned and walked away.

Solo had always enjoyed watching Janie leave, enjoyed the soft, swinging sashay of her hips. But that wasn't the feeling ripping through her right now. This was the same desperate and devastating pain as it had been when she'd watched Janie drag her suitcase out of the house a week ago, and steel wire constricted around her heart, almost stopping it from pulsing. Its rhythm beat for Janie. Without her, what was the point? Solo swallowed hard and dropped back into her seat.

What the hell had happened to the plan?

Chapter Ten

THE LAW OFFICES OF Richards & Wall occupied the entire forty-seventh floor of a gleaming glass tower in the Loop, a monument to the kind of polished, ambitious professionalism Janie had spent her life striving for. She had an uninterrupted view of Lake Michigan, something her clients often commented on, but the cold, blue expanse of water offered little comfort today. The way it stretched into the horizon, vast and immense, only reinforced the loneliness hollowing out her soul.

She refocused on the stack of deposition transcripts, the work a welcome, numbingly complex distraction from the reality of her home life, which was collapsing around her ears. *Damn it.* Why couldn't she keep her thoughts focused on the billable tasks she needed to stack up in order to make partner? An image of Hannah's expression when Janie had mentioned that last night popped into her head. She'd seemed distressed by the idea, even though it was something they often talked about, something that would result in more financial stability. Her progression within her firm might be even more important now that she had her apartment to pay for as well as their mortgage, and she didn't want to have to dip into the triplets' trust.

Cold fear snaked around her heart. How long would she be able to keep up the payments on two properties on her current salary? Would she have to ask Hannah and the girls to move somewhere smaller or to a less desirable neighborhood? Should she even be thinking about that version of her future? Had she already made the break emotionally as well as physically?

She flipped the folder closed and stared out of her window. Too many questions, and no answers. It wasn't a state of being she was comfortable with. Her conversation with Maria had instilled hope, but maybe she had no right to think that she and Hannah could work this out. If last night was any indication, they had a long way to go. They couldn't even share a meal together anymore; how were they supposed to co-parent three toddlers? And Janie would still have to confess what she'd done, what she'd allowed to happen.

Her gaze fell to her phone, where she'd changed the screensaver to a photo of their newly decorated living room, courtesy of Tia's creativity. A stab of grief shot through her. She was missing out on precious moments like that too. Janie turned the cell on its face and reopened the folder. If she didn't get this work done, she wouldn't even be able to keep up her responsibilities for financial support.

She didn't know how much time had passed when there were two quick, sharp taps on her office door. "Come in, Amanda," she called, expecting her assistant, who'd been uncharacteristically quiet all morning. Janie suspected she and some of the other paralegals had overindulged last night and were paying for it on a Sunday they hadn't expected to be working.

Her door swung open, and Katherine stood in the opening. The expression on her face made it clear she was still sore from Janie's recent public evisceration of her at the bar most of the firm frequented. Janie wanted to say sorry, both for the outburst and the unkind things she'd said. It didn't matter that they were mostly true. What mattered was Janie's complete lack of emotional control, a distressing signal that she was unraveling professionally as well as personally. The only saving grace was that it hadn't happened at the office. Katherine was a senior associate and widely thought of as "one of the boys" by the partners, but they rarely socialized at Oscar's, so they hadn't witnessed it. The firm's grapevine was nothing if not effective though, and Janie had no doubt the partners would've heard some version of the incident by now. She could only hope that it wouldn't hurt her chances of progression.

"I thought I'd be the bigger person and come see you," Katherine said as she stepped into the office.

Janie looked beyond Katherine's shoulder as she closed the door behind her, but there was no sign of Amanda. She must've gone to lunch, or she wouldn't have allowed Katherine to waltz into her office as if Janie was a junior associate instead of an equal. "What can I do for you?"

Katherine raised her eyebrows as if she'd expected Janie to fall at her feet in groveling apology. Her sense of entitlement irked Janie more than usual, and her regret for her behavior began to recede.

"I was going to ask for an apology for the other night." Katherine swaggered across the office and took a seat without being offered one. "But you're under a lot of stress right now, so I decided to forgive you instead," she gave Janie a crooked smile, "on the condition that you let me take you out for dinner."

Janie leaned back in her chair, not quite believing the nerve of the woman. "Why would I do that?" She flashed her wedding ring, then dropped her left hand, guilt overcoming her for using Hannah only when it suited her.

Katherine inclined her head. "You have to play nice if you want to get anywhere in this firm."

Janie gave a short laugh. "With the partners, sure. But I don't think you have that position yet."

Katherine tapped her nose, her expression smug. "It's only a matter of time. With all the new business I've brought in and all the hours I'm billing, that upcoming spot is mine. This is your chance to get ahead of the curve."

"I think I'll pass," Janie said. "I'd rather apologize."

Katherine shrugged and pushed up from the chair. "The kind of passion you showed at the bar says something different, Janie. I'll get the partnership, and then I'll get you."

Janie laughed again. "You're actually serious," she said, shaking her head. "You think me destroying you at the bar was foreplay?"

The corner of Katherine's lip twitched before she walked away. She paused to turn back after she'd opened the door. "I think you're doing too much protesting for it to be anything else."

Katherine was gone before Janie could seriously consider throwing something at her smug face. Hannah would go crazy if she knew Lori's philandering ex-wife was not just working with Janie but also putting the moves on her. Not that they'd ever had trust issues, but Hannah had very definite thoughts about the sanctity of marriage and the gross indecency of cheating spouses.

Janie got up from her desk to close her door again. The voice she heard coming from farther down the corridor froze her insides. It couldn't be.

"Can I get you some coffee, Angela?"

Phillip Wall didn't get coffee for *anyone*, and his question confirmed her worst fears. The great Angela Evans was in the building. *Her* building. Her mother hadn't been there since Janie's first day, when she'd inspected the place to make sure it was good enough for her daughter. Except that wasn't about Janie; it was about the Angela Evans' legacy. Everyone at the firm *had* to be made aware of who Janie's mom was, and the firm had to understand that they weren't just getting a new lawyer, they were getting *Angela Evans's* daughter.

"No, thank you, Phillip," her mother said with the curt chill in her voice that had put the fear of God into a thousand opposition lawyers over the years. "I didn't really have time for this trip at all, so I definitely don't have time for coffee."

Her dismissal was complete, and from the doorway, Janie saw Phillip stop and almost bow.

"Maybe next time then," he said and retreated.

Janie stepped back from the doorway before her mother could see her and slipped back behind her desk, needing the physical barrier.

"We need to talk," her mother said as she strode into Janie's office.

"Talk about what? Why are you here, Mother?" Janie realized she was gripping the arms of her chair hard, and she tried to relax her hands. Her mother surveyed the office, silently judging her aesthetic choices.

"Tell me why I had to hear about you abandoning your children from someone else," her mother hissed quietly, not trying to hide her disdain. "It's profoundly disappointing behavior, Janie."

Her mother *knew?* Janie eased up from her chair, despite the child inside wanting to crawl beneath the desk. "And how do you know anything of what's going on in my life right now?"

Her mother gave a tight smile. "I *know* things, Janie. You know Ruth is a dear friend."

Janie clenched her jaw. She should've known her elderly neighbor had snitched; anything to score points with her *dear friend* and previous employer. "This is my office. Mother. If you have a desperate need to talk about my 'profoundly disappointing behavior,' we won't be doing it here."

Her mother arched her perfectly sculpted eyebrow. "At least you're owning your actions. That'll save us time I don't have."

Janie flared her nostrils. Of course. Seconds, minutes, billable hours. Janie had known time was a commodity as soon as she was old enough to do math. She hadn't asked her mother to come here. She *wouldn't* have asked. But who had? Hannah? She clutched her chest. If Hannah had thought she could enlist Janie's parents to help repair their relationship, she sorely misunderstood them. And she misunderstood Janie too. Had she forgotten how much Janie despised their judgment?

"I suggest we go downstairs and have lunch," Janie said. She had to eat, that's what Maria kept telling her, so she might as well do two things she wasn't interested in at the same time. She grabbed her blazer and purse and led the way to the elevator, ignoring the furtive glances of her colleagues. Oh, the humiliation of having her mother strut into her office. What stories would be fabricated at the water cooler at lunch, or at the bar tonight?

"This isn't a social call, Janie. We'll have to be quick."

"Understood." Janie didn't think she could recall a single social call from her mother in her life. She tapped the ground floor button repeatedly, wanting the elevator doors to close before any brave or stupid souls tried to join them and grab a few seconds with the legendary Angela Evans.

"This is a self-indulgent crisis that could have been avoided," her mother said when the elevator finally began its descent.

Janie fiddled with the buttons on her jacket then stopped herself. She shouldn't retreat into youthful coping mechanisms. She was an adult now, and she didn't have to take this from anyone, even her own mother. Still, the familiar tension of her mere presence wrapped around Janie like a suffocating shroud. "It's hardly self-indulgent, Mother."

"No? What else should we call it? A strategic withdrawal from a marriage you weren't prepared for? A panicked retreat from motherhood, which you also clearly weren't ready for?" Her mother's eyes narrowed. "The children are my main reason for being here."

Janie couldn't respond. Her throat tightened, and an icy-cold chill rippled over her skin. Her mother was more right than she could've expected to be. And of course her mother was most concerned about her grandchildren. No doubt she didn't want her vision of a do-over parenting challenge derailed. Janie had joked with Hannah that her mother was probably planning on molding her very own set of Supreme Court judges. She'd been surprised her mother hadn't been more insistent about her involvement up to now, but she was likely just waiting for the triplets to start stringing more syllables together before she pounced.

When they'd been seated in the cold, faceless restaurant, Janie swallowed hard and prepared herself. "The children are fine. They're with Hannah and her father, and they're safe."

"I think our ideas of what is and is not safe might very well differ," her mother said. "You know how I feel about Hannah's *bohemian* lifestyle."

Despite the situation, Janie smiled internally, remembering Hannah's laughter when she'd first heard her mother-in-law refer to it that way. Her butch presentation, blue-collar father, and her decade in the Army didn't scream bohemian, but anyone who wasn't obsessed with material possessions, superior social status, and multiple zeroes in the bank was exactly that, as far as Janie's mother was concerned. "Hannah's *lifestyle* is none of your business."

"It is where my grandchildren are involved." Her mother pushed away the menus placed on their table, making it clear she wouldn't be eating. "She's ex-Army with very little in the way of career prospects. She wouldn't be doing anything if it hadn't been for you funding that ridiculous garage with her band of equally talentless yahoos."

Janie scoffed at her mother's characterization and ordered a sparkling water. She would've ordered wine, but she didn't need to give her mother extra fuel for her condemnation.

Her mother glared at her and then up at their bemused server. "An espresso then, if we must."

Janie suppressed her amusement when she recalled Hannah commenting that her mother-in-law might be a vampire, since no one ever saw her eat or drink. "Do you really not understand why I chose to settle my family here, nearly a thousand miles away from you?"

"What are you saying, Janie?" Her mother glanced around the restaurant, the way she surveyed a room when she was disinterested in or no longer had use for the person she was actually with.

"Your suffocating judgment," Janie said. "The lack of humanity. My family doesn't need that. I don't need that."

Her mother returned her attention to Janie, impatience clear in her expression. "Humanity is overrated, dear," she said with a dismissive flick of her hand. "I'm not here to discuss your perceived failings in me as a human being. We need to discuss custody."

"Custody?" Janie's stomach dropped. "Why on earth would you think we need to do that?"

"Hannah isn't fit to be a single parent, Janie." Her mother wrinkled her nose slightly. "I'm not sure she should be a parent at all. And how do you think she's going to support *three* young children right now, let alone earn the funds to send them to college? Unless you've already put your inheritance in a trust for them—if there's any left. Grandmother Evans gave you that money for your security, not to fund your wife's pet projects."

Ah, there it was. If there was anything Janie could rely on when talking to her mother, it would be this. As if their relationship wasn't difficult enough, the money from Janie's grandmother was like a splinter in a festering wound and a constant bone of contention. Janie's maternal grandmother, whom Janie adored, had long been the only person in her life who seemed to value her unconditionally rather than for her achievements, academic or otherwise.

"Grandma Susan's instructions were clear: enjoy life and prioritize family, which was something you didn't do." Janie ignored the internal voice that scoffed at her statement. Not doing that herself was how she'd ended up in this predicament. "She disapproved of your cold ambition, and she knew how disconnected you were from me as a result. She wanted me to have the means to be present, and to be a better mother than I had a role model for."

Her mother's façade cracked momentarily, long enough to reveal a flash of pure, cold rage in her eyes before they returned to their usual dispassion. "That's a malicious and hurtful distortion, Janie. She was a senile old woman playing favorites."

"That wasn't something that you could prove in court though, was it?"

Her mother arched her eyebrows. "I don't understand where all this resentment is coming from, Janie. I worked as hard as I did in order to provide a perfect life for—" She took a sharp inhalation of breath through her nose and flicked her hair over her shoulder, something she only did when she was deeply uncomfortable. "I don't have to justify my choices. Especially to someone who has completely abdicated their parental responsibilities and left her young children with a woman who's barely grown up herself. I hope you emptied the liquor cabinet when you deserted your girls. We all know Hannah likes to lose herself in the bottle. What do you think she'll be doing now that she's the sole caregiver for your children?"

Janie couldn't deflect that barb. Hannah's drinking had been a source of concern for her occasionally too. But she'd seemed to have gotten a handle on it since Janie had the babies.

Her mother's eyebrow arched even higher, and she gave a smug smile. "As I said, Hannah isn't fit to be a mother, and clearly, you agree."

"No, I didn't say that."

"Your silence said more than your words ever could." Her mother's smile grew wider. "And how was buying your wife a boat showing your girls a better role model?"

"Because it makes her happy," Janie said, hearing how weak it sounded. "And the girls love going out on the water."

Her mother laughed. "They aren't even two years old. The only things they love are food and sleep."

Janie clenched her jaw. She didn't even want to be here, let alone be having an argument about child development, which her mother still clearly knew nothing about. "I'm not having this conversation with you." She looked beyond her mother as their server approached the table with their drinks, looking wary. He placed them on the table and retreated quickly. "I decide how I spend that money and how I live my life."

"And that's working so well for you, isn't it?" Her mother gestured toward Janie. "You've fled the house *you* bought with that money, and you've abandoned your children to a stunted teenager. This is exactly why we need to establish a legal framework. It doesn't look like you're willing to return to the children, so I'll file for temporary custody immediately."

Janie's backbone disintegrated into sand, and she sank further into her chair. She'd been stupid to underestimate the depths her mother would sink to. She was no longer satisfied with controlling Janie. She wanted to take the triplets away to "raise" them herself?

"You think you're a better parent than Hannah?" Janie whispered. For all her faults, Hannah loved their children more than anything, more than she loved Janie even, or so it had seemed. "Or is this about getting your hands on the rest of Grandma's estate?"

"Children *are* expensive, dear," her mother said, her voice hard and professional as if she were providing a closing statement to the court. "But no, this is about the fact that I'm stable and can provide the structure those children need. Hannah is immature. With everything that's going on, with her *father* being her first choice for childcare, it's clear to anyone that she lacks the necessary qualities to be a good parent. I have the resources and the focus to raise them right. I can't, in all good conscience, allow the girls to be raised by a parent who's abandoned them and another who is drowning in the responsibility."

"I haven't..." Janie wanted to refute her mother's assertion, shout out that she hadn't abandoned her children, and that her marriage wasn't over. But she couldn't conjure the conviction to give the statements voice, mainly because her mother might be right. "I don't need you to *handle* my life, Mother. I'm dealing with something you couldn't begin to understand because you've never risked your heart, never *loved* anything enough to feel this kind of fear." Damn it, why had she given that information? "And Hannah is looking after the children while I do that. It was unfortunate that our nanny chose to leave the same week I had to go, but Hannah's father is their grandfather, and he's ecstatic to have the chance to spend more time with them while Hannah interviews for a suitable replacement." Of course, she had no idea what Tom really thought about upending his idyllic Floridian life to care for his three grandchildren, but from what Hannah had told her in multiple texts, he was doing okay. Nor did she know how the nanny search was going because they were supposed to talk about that last night, but that evening hadn't gone according to plan. "Don't try to exploit my personal crisis in your petty war over Grandma Susan's inheritance."

Her mother stared at her. "You're being stubborn." She pushed her espresso away, untouched, and stood. "Call me when you understand the reality of your situation," she said and walked away.

Janie closed her eyes, not wanting to succumb to the tears desperate to fall. The visit had been a brutal affirmation of her own guilt, confirming every dark thought Janie had about herself. She *was* failing, incapable of protecting her children or her marriage, just like her mother said. Had she been right, that Janie wasn't ready for either of those things? Had two of the greatest days in her life been her two greatest mistakes?

That couldn't be her main focus right now. Her mother hadn't been interested in the girls, not really, so Janie hadn't considered she might try for custody of them. She couldn't allow her absence to be leveraged into an attack on Hannah. Her mother wanted to prove they were unfit parents, and she was counting on Janie being too fragile to fight her. But Hannah *was* fighting for their marriage and their children, and she was going to therapy alone. Her anger last night had been warranted, even though Janie had been too vulnerable to face it, to hear and feel it. Janie's own pain and guilt had overwhelmed her, making it impossible to allow space to let Hannah's pain in.

But now, they had a common enemy.

Janie pulled her phone from her purse, a vortex of emotions raging within, but the fear of losing her children to her mother was stronger than shame. *We need to meet. My mother came to the office.* She considered whether or not to mention the custody issue and decided against it; she didn't want Hannah to panic and call her, especially when she had to go back to the office. She saved the message, figuring she'd send it later when she had time to talk. Right now, she had to get back to the new client work piled on her desk and try to forget the clusterfuck in her personal life.

Chapter Eleven

SOLO WOKE FROM HER late-morning nap to the sound of Chloe's blood-curdling scream coming through the monitor on her bedside table. She checked the screen to see that Tia had scaled the side of her cot and was strutting around in the middle of the triplet's bedroom. Well, as much as a toddler who'd just about mastered walking *could* strut, but Tia somehow managed it. Solo couldn't see why Chloe was so upset, unless it was simple jealousy of Tia's freedom, and Luna looked like she was still asleep. Or just meditating on the evils of her older sister.

She turned over, and all the joy of seeing her children fell through a pit in the bottom of her stomach. Just for those few blissful moments, she'd forgotten that Janie wasn't sharing her bed. She swung her legs out and put her head in her hands. Janie wasn't sharing *anything* with her anymore, and why would she after last night?

Solo blew out a sharp breath and got to her feet. No time for self-pity. She had an escape-artist daughter to deal with. She opened the door to the triplets' bedroom slowly, just in case Tia was directly on the other side. How long would it be before her little terror could reach the handle? Solo would have to google that, because she was pretty certain that locking the girls in at night wasn't an option.

Tia's eyes lit up, and she grinned widely as she stuck out her arms. "Mama up."

"Looks like you don't need morning naps anymore, little one." Scooping Tia into her arms seemed to amplify Chloe's noise, so she went over to her cot and lifted Chloe onto her other hip. "How are my amazing girls?"

"Woof," Chloe said when she'd stopped sniffling.

Griff thundered down the hallway and came to rest at Solo's feet within seconds.

"That's some hearing, Griff."

He reared up on his hind legs and planted his giant front paws on Solo's stomach, then he licked Chloe's toes, making the little girl giggle and wriggle in Solo's grip.

"Down, Griff." When he'd done as he was told, Solo went over to the giant playmat in the corner of the bedroom and dropped to her knees to put the girls on it gently. Griff got down on his belly and crawled across the floor to Chloe. A sense of pure belonging and peace washed over Solo, and she relaxed into it, accepting the gift just like Rae had told her to. *This* was how she was supposed to be feeling. *This* had been her life every day from the girls being born until the day Janie had moved into the guest room. That thought threatened to chase the momentary bliss away, but she didn't let it. Again, like Rae had told her to. "Fight the darkness and celebrate the light" was the last thing she'd said to Solo in their impromptu telephone session before her disastrous meeting with Janie. No matter what was going on in their marriage, *she* was the one still at home with their babies, and the responsibility for their continued care was hers alone. Though her dad's presence had been a great comfort, as had Gabe's last night.

Gabe. Solo needed to call her. She'd purposely avoided going home and had driven around the city until her dad texted to say Gabe and Lori had left. Solo just couldn't face the inevitable barrage of optimistic questions, not after she'd fucked it all up so spectacularly. She didn't want to see the disappointment in Gabe's expression, didn't want to see how she'd let her down.

"Hey, slugger."

Solo looked up to see her dad standing in the doorway. "Hey, Pops."

"Feeling refreshed?" he asked, concern lacing his words.

She nodded. His room was the other side of the hallway from

hers, and she was sure he hadn't heard her whispered rantings at herself or the hell she'd knocked out of her pillows for most of the night, but he clearly wasn't blind to the dark circles under her eyes. And she'd met his light inquiry about how the night had gone with silence when she'd finally come home.

"Do you want something to eat? Unless you're still full from last night's dinner, of course." He frowned. "Or did it make you sick?"

Solo inclined her head. "*I* made me sick, but yeah, I could eat." She gestured to the girls. "Help me bring them down?"

He sighed loudly. "Okay, but then you tell me more about what happened. Because it doesn't seem like things went according to plan."

She grunted. "Understatement, but yeah, I'll fill you in." She picked up Tia and Chloe, and her dad took Luna, who was now awake and muttering quietly to herself. She seemed to have her own language, and Solo couldn't wait until she started talking properly. Although, remembering the Darius Rucker song her dad had sent her when the triplets had been born, she didn't want to rush any part of their growing up either.

With the girls safely in their individual baby walkers, she followed her dad into the kitchen and relayed the sad story of her night as they prepared lunch for the girls, sandwiches for themselves, and a bowl of kibble for Griff. When she put Griff's food down, Tia immediately began bumping his bowl around with the edge of her walker. He patiently tracked its trajectory all around the kitchen, grabbing mouthfuls when he got the chance.

"It's okay that you're angry, kiddo." He gestured to Luna, flipping through the giant number book hanging on her walker. "This isn't a one-person job."

"Plenty of people are single parents. That isn't the problem." Solo shook her head. "I was the one desperate to meet up, but I ended up pushing her away. We didn't even make it to appetizers, Pops. I don't know what happened." That was a lie, and from the way her dad tilted his head and raised his eyebrows, he knew it.

"You don't?"

Solo turned to the refrigerator to get juice *and* to escape his questioning glare. She'd never been able to keep the truth from him, even when it meant she'd catch hell for it. "Her *friend* from work came up." This was the only part of the whole situation that she hadn't told him about. She hadn't been able to think about it, let alone put words to it and say it out loud.

"And?"

"I accused her of cheating on me." It wasn't exactly what she'd said, but the implication had been clear. And sometimes, talking could be far more intimate than sex. *That's* what had really gotten to her.

"You did *what?*"

Solo closed the fridge door and faced him again. "She told me she was talking to some guy at work, and—"

"Talking?" he asked, clearly unimpressed. "Since when is talking synonymous with cheating?"

"It isn't...exactly. It's what people do before they start dating."

His frown deepened. "Says who?"

She waved his question away. "It doesn't matter. She said they were just friends, but I'd already messed up. Janie always walks away when I get angry."

"Can't she handle the conflict?" He chuckled lightly. "She must be a helluva lawyer."

"Don't." Solo gripped the counter and tried the box breathing Rae had shown her. "You know how hard it is to talk to me when I'm angry."

He grunted and nodded. "You're right there. Maybe she did the right thing by walking away before you said something even more stupid."

"Exactly." She poured juice for them and put the bottle away. "I guess I just had some stupid idea that we were gonna talk all night, and she was going to remember that she loved me, that she loved our life. And then she'd come home, back to me, and back to our babies." She smacked her palm against her forehead a couple of times.

"Hey, stop that." Her dad grabbed her wrist. "Knocking your brainbox around isn't going to solve a thing, slugger."

"I want things to go back to the way they were," Solo said then shrugged. "I need her to give me another chance to be the partner she deserves."

Her dad smiled and released her hand. "It isn't me who needs to hear that," he said gently.

Solo sagged against the sink. "I know. But what if she won't see me again? What if I've blown my one chance?"

"Don't think of last night like that," he said. "But don't waste time either." Sadness darkened his eyes, and he shook his head slowly. "I thought your momma and I had all the time in the world." He swallowed and turned back to making their sandwiches. "But we didn't."

Her dad's words struck like a gut punch, and she sucked in a long breath, determined to move past the grief. "Did you and Mom ever have any problems?"

"Of course we did." Her dad chuckled. "She didn't just raise you and your brother; she raised me too. It took her a few years to whip me into shape." He sliced the sandwiches in half, then leaned against the counter. "Did you know she wouldn't have children with me until she decided I was ready to be a good dad?"

Solo frowned. "She wouldn't?"

He shook his head and smiled widely. "God knows why she decided I'd be worth it in the end, but I'm sure glad she picked me."

Her dad's smile touched her own mood, and she joined him. "I always thought you were just enjoying a few years together before you got tied down with kids."

"I guess there was a little of that too." He inclined his head. "But primarily, she was training me to be a dad and not just a father."

Tia bumped into the cabinet beside Solo and looked up at her expectantly. "Mama food."

Solo laughed. "Mama, food or Mama food?"

Tia's brow furrowed deep, making her look comically angry. "Food," she said, sounding more than a little disgruntled that she'd been forced to repeat herself.

Solo raised her hands. "Okay, okay. It's coming." She pushed away from the sink and quickly prepared three plates of cottage cheese with carrot and cucumber sticks. Then she and her dad transferred the triplets from their walkers to their highchairs in the dining room. She glanced at the wall they planned to repaint that afternoon, and a mixture of pride and sadness fought for her attention. She'd sent photos of Tia's masterpiece to Janie's phone, but they didn't really give the artwork real scale. Solo would've given anything for Janie not just to have seen it but to have been there while Tia was creating it. Maybe she should just leave it another week. Janie would want to visit the girls soon, wouldn't she?

"I'm looking forward to painting that with you," her dad said as he stood in the doorway. "It'll be just like when you were a teenager, and you used to help me with all the decorating."

Solo put her hand on his shoulder and squeezed. "Remember how Mom used to insist we stopped on the hour, every hour to stay hydrated?"

Her dad nodded. "Is that what Janie does for you?"

"Nope. We painted this whole house together." Solo grinned at some memories she couldn't share with her dad about rooms that were partly painted with their bodies. God, she missed Janie. It was like those images had faded to make room for their kids, but surely it didn't have to be that way.

"Really?" he asked, his eyebrows raised.

"Really," she said and tsked. "Janie's great with a roller. I did all the cutting in, and she painted great swathes of the walls."

He moved closer to a wall and seemed to be inspecting it.

"Are you seriously checking the quality of my wife's work?"

she asked and chuckled, knowing Janie would get a kick out of proving her painting prowess to Solo's dad.

"Maybe." He pulled back and lightly punched her arm. "You can tell her how impressed I am though."

"Maybe you can tell her yourself when she comes home." Even as she said it, the joy in her heart deflated, and the words sounded hollow and empty. "*If* she comes home."

Her dad punched her a little harder. "That's not the kind of positive thinking your mom taught you."

Solo moved past him and headed back to the kitchen for the food. "I like talking about Mom, even though it's hard. We don't do it enough."

"I keep waiting for it to get easier." Her dad picked up their plates and followed her back to the dining room. "So I can think about celebrating the years I got to spend with her instead of mourning the ones that the Big C took from us." He shook his head and sighed deeply. "Over three years..."

Solo didn't fill in the gap. She didn't need to because she had that crippling ache too. It was only now that she was separated from Janie that she could truly appreciate her dad's loss and how it differed from her own grief.

Her phone buzzed in her sweatpants, and she almost ripped the pocket in her hurry to pull it out, hoping it was Janie.

Woody got the early release of 2K25. We're coming over. OK.

Gabe wasn't Janie, but it always made Solo happy to hear from her. Though she wasn't looking forward to explaining how she'd messed up their plan to get her wife back. *What about Lori?*

Busy with a new horse coming in. Be there in thirty.

"Janie or Gabe?" her dad asked. "It's got to be one of them to put that goofy grin on your face."

"Huh?"

Her dad gestured in her direction. "Your face. It's goofy, so that," he tapped her phone, "has to be one of the two most important women in your life."

Solo shrugged. She wouldn't admit that out loud, but he wasn't wrong so she couldn't protest. "It's Gabe. The gang wants to come over to play the new NBA game."

He rolled his eyes. "You have a hoop in the back yard. Why don't you get some fresh air and play for real?"

Solo laughed. "I'm not a kid anymore, Pops. I can play video games anytime I want."

"Do you hear how that sounds?" He pointed behind her. "And what about the wall?"

She glanced over her shoulder. "It'll keep," she said, glad of a delay that might mean Janie got to see it for real. "And the triplets'll enjoy the company."

Her dad grumbled. "As long as you don't get rowdy and start cussing. You don't want the girls learning *those* words *this* young."

Solo frowned and shook her head. "You know I always appreciate a good dad moment, but it'll be fine. They all know they can't swear in front of my babies. They'll be on their best behavior."

A giant glob of cottage cheese flew past her eyeline and landed on her dad's forehead. The three girls erupted into their gorgeous giggles, and Solo had to bite her tongue to keep herself from joining them.

"I can't say the same for the triplets though," she said before she clasped her hand over her mouth.

Her dad wiped the dip from his face with a napkin and tried for a stern look. He failed miserably and broke out into a chuckle. "You need to get moving on that replacement nanny, kiddo. These kids are trying to break us, and I reckon they'll succeed if we don't get some professional help soon."

"We will, but I'm not rushing it," Solo said. "I have to make sure we get the right person, someone who's going to stick around this time." She'd just refocused on her cell to respond to Gabe when a message came in from Janie. Solo's heart jumped against her chest, and her hands shook as she opened it. She'd sent countless texts, photos, and voice messages, and Janie had responded to only a few. This was the first time Janie had initiated a conversation. She closed her eyes briefly, hoping that it wouldn't be something bad after last night's fiasco.

We need to meet. My mother came to the office.

So Janie was working today too. She clearly hadn't been lying about their new gorilla client. Maybe that explained why Janie's mom was there, unless there'd been a family emergency, and that's why Janie was reaching out.

Solo flipped to her favorites tab and hovered her finger over Janie's icon. She wanted to talk, to hear Janie's voice, but she remembered something Rae had said about taking a breath and not always going with her initial reaction to the things going on around her. If Janie had wanted to talk, she would've called. Solo flicked back to messages. *Sure. When? xx* She looked at the simplicity of her response and swallowed. If Janie wanted to meet today, should she say yes and blow off the gang? That was her first thought, so was she supposed to take a breath and reconsider? Gabe and the gang would understand. This was her life she was trying to hold together. Of course it took priority over a stupid video game.

The message delivered and showed as read immediately. Solo's heart raced a little faster, just like it had when they'd messaged each other while she was still in the service. The time difference made it difficult to message in real time, but when they'd managed it, Solo had bounced on her chair and waited, holding her breath, while the three gray dots wiggled across the bottom of the screen, showing Janie was responding. The memory rush brought a mixture of emotions with it that Solo didn't have time to "process," as Rae called it.

I can come to the garage around one tomorrow.

Solo's initial excitement ratcheted down, but only a notch or two. The garage wasn't on the same level as a fancy restaurant, but it was *something*. Janie's relationship with her parents was complicated, making every interaction with them difficult and often negative, and she wanted to talk to Solo about it, not that stupid Austin guy. *That* was progress, and after last night, she'd take anything she could get. She typed out several responses before landing on *Great xx*

She clutched her phone for a little longer, praying for more gray dots. When none came, she switched to Gabe's message. *Make it an hour. We're just finishing up lunch.* She added an exploding head emoji.

"Everything okay?" her dad asked.

She put her phone face up on the table instead of back in her pocket *just* in case Janie continued their conversation. "Maybe better than okay," she said then relayed the short exchange with Janie.

"That's great news." Her dad smiled and patted her hand. "You were worrying about nothing."

"I hope so." Solo wasn't about to make the same mistake and put too much expectation on this date like she had on last night's. Though date didn't sound right, and meeting seemed way too formal. She supposed what she called it didn't really matter as long as she didn't fuck it up again. Hopefully, Gabe and the gang would have some more advice on how to keep her stupid mouth under control, since she'd failed so miserably yesterday... If they had the patience for it. Solo was asking a lot of her chosen family, but she needed them and their understanding more now than ever.

Chapter Twelve

Yesterday, Janie had tried to wait until after work to message Hannah, but in the end, she couldn't concentrate until she'd arranged to meet her. That same lack of focus had kicked in again on her way to court today and had only been exacerbated when her judge was delayed for her case management conference. Now that was finally over, she made her way to the garage. The traffic inexplicably eased up, and she ended up there thirty minutes early.

She parked around the back and was pleased to see the bank of cars and trucks waiting for work. It looked like their financial gamble was paying off, and Hannah's dream was on its way to being a viable reality. At least one thing was going right in their lives, and Janie's mother couldn't use it against them. Janie turned off the engine and scoffed silently at her naivete; her mother could weaponize any situation to her advantage.

Janie started to walk up the alley to Bonnie's Brew to wait rather than sit in the garage waiting room. She had no idea what the rest of Hannah's friends thought about her right now, and she was in no hurry to be on the receiving end of more negativity. She was still struggling to shake off her mother's visit, and her self-loathing hadn't faded much either, especially after her aborted attempt to reconnect with Hannah on Saturday. The irony of the restaurant's name, Embers, hadn't been lost on her as she'd left, wondering if her marriage was beyond rekindling.

The garage's side door creaked open, and she glanced behind her to see RB emerging, wiping her hands on a cloth that may have once been white. Their eyes met, making it impossible for Janie not to acknowledge her. She gave a hesitant wave, unsure whether or not she should stop to talk.

RB nodded in her direction. "Are you coming in?"

Janie paused mid-step and gestured up the alley. "I was going for coffee."

"That makes two of us." RB closed the door behind her and joined Janie in a couple of purposeful strides.

"Oh... Okay." Janie tried for a smile but from RB's reaction, it was clear she hadn't succeeded.

"I'm not going to give you a hard time, Janie," RB said, and her frown deepened, "if that's what you're worried about."

She fell into step with RB, paying close attention to the pitted ground, not wanting to break a heel. "Do I look worried?"

RB raised her eyebrow and nodded. "But you don't need to. About me or any of the others. We all know Solo can be tough to take." She caught Janie's arm when Janie stumbled slightly on a loose stone and chuckled. "We've lived with her for years. It's a wonder none of us buried her alive in the desert."

"Really?" Janie risked a sideways glance at RB. "She was that bad?"

"She was *that* bad."

RB offered her arm, and Janie took it, not wanting to add a twisted ankle to her list of problems.

"She's mellowed some since you took her on," RB said, "but she's still an acquired taste."

Janie bit the inside of her cheek. They might be separated, but that didn't mean she took kindly to people bad-mouthing her wife. Although, RB wasn't *people*. She was Hannah's family. "This isn't Hannah's fault."

RB opened the door to Bonnie's and gestured for Janie to enter. "That's not the way she tells it."

The blast of cool air from inside the café made her wish she'd brought her light jacket with her, but it was the ice-cold fingers wrapping around her heart that chilled her to the core. In her shame, she'd forgotten that they were having problems before... before she'd proven herself to be a terrible mom, and that meant

Hannah thought everything was *her* fault. Janie's fears that she was also a bad wife resurfaced from their shallow hiding place and taunted her further.

RB placed an order for her team and turned to Janie. "What can I get you?"

Janie waved the offer away. "That's okay. I'll get mine."

"Don't be crazy," RB said. "What's your poison?"

"Half-fat vanilla latte, please." She smiled and glanced up at the ceiling, trying to stave off the tears in response to RB's kindness, which was another thing she didn't deserve. Especially because RB was one of Hannah's closest friends. "Thank you."

RB winked. "No problem."

They moved to the end of the line to wait for their drinks, and Janie was engulfed in a silent bubble, not sure what else to say.

After a minute or so, RB cleared her throat. "You know that you're family too, right?"

Janie opened her mouth to respond, but her mental black dog snapped the words back. *That's another thing you don't deserve.* And she didn't *feel* like family either, but how could she when she'd barely spent any time with them?

"Is there anything we can do?" RB asked after the time for Janie to respond had slipped away. "Solo is a giant pain in our butt, but she's *our* giant pain. We'll do whatever it takes to help you two get through this."

The barista called RB's name, and she seemed to hesitate before going to the counter to get her coffee tray. It was only a momentary respite though. Janie couldn't remain mute on the walk back to the garage. "I wish it was that easy," she said when RB returned and motioned for Janie to join her at the table to add the fixings.

RB shrugged. "I haven't had a girlfriend for longer than a month, so I can't begin to understand what it takes to keep a marriage going. But I've never seen Solo like this. She's...broken, but she's still trying to keep moving forward for the girls."

Another brutal stab to her heart. Janie couldn't take much

more of this. If only she'd rear-ended someone and been delayed, then she wouldn't have had to face RB. Coming to see Hannah had been enough of a challenge, but she'd really hoped she wouldn't have to talk to her band of brothers too. "I'm sorry... I don't know what else to say."

"You don't have to say anything," RB said as she loaded three sugars into one of the cups. "But I hope—we all hope—that you'll give Solo another chance." She put her hand on Janie's arm gently. "She's trying, Janie. She really is."

Janie swallowed and stumbled past RB. "Sorry, I have to go to the restroom. Don't wait." She rushed into a cubicle and sat on the toilet seat before resting her head in her hands. If she couldn't talk to RB, how was she supposed to see Hannah? Especially with the news she had.

She dabbed at the corners of her eyes with tissue and sucked in a deep breath. This was her wife, not a cantankerous judge, and it was just a conversation, not a trial. When she'd managed to pull herself together, she headed out of the restroom to see her coffee still waiting for her and RB was gone. She took a long sip, hoping the caffeine might infuse some courage, and then took the short stroll back to the garage.

Hannah was waiting by the alley's side door and gave Janie an awkward-looking wave. She looked as handsome as always in her painted-up coveralls, but dark circles under her eyes were clear signals of the stress she was under, of which Janie was the architect. And now she was going to pile on more worries.

"RB told me you were at Bonnie's," Hannah said. "I didn't know if you might want to talk there instead."

Janie shook her head. There was no telling if she'd be able to maintain control of her emotions once she began relaying the story of her mother's visit, and the garage's breakroom was about as private as she could hope for without going home. *Home... Where all her guilt originated.* That wasn't a place she could even think about going right now. "I'm good here, if that's still okay with you?"

Hannah stepped to the side and gestured for Janie to enter. "Of course. Sure. Yeah."

Her obvious nervousness was reminiscent of their early dates, and it made Janie smile a little despite the current circumstances. What would she give to go back to their first week in Vegas and start all over again? Though even if that were possible, would it solve anything? They'd still marry, still have the triplets. Knowing what she knew now, would she be a better mom? Or would it just happen again, compounding her shame?

She made her way through the garage and up the stairs to the gang's chill area, managing minimum contact with the rest of Hannah's chosen family. Aside from RB, they looked just as eager to avoid her as she did them. She stutter-stepped and clutched her hand to her chest when she saw the little nursery setup in the corner of the space. Were the triplets in there? Caught between rushing forward to see and turning to flee, Janie's breathing quickened, and she trembled.

Hannah's hand on the small of her back grounded her, and the deafening rush of blood to her ears drifted away. The nursery was empty.

"Are you okay?"

Hannah came around to face her, and the concern in her expression almost made Janie's knees give way. She remembered those looks, when Hannah's sole focus was her. God, she'd missed Hannah's attention when it switched, almost exclusively, to their babies. Where was the middle ground? Hadn't that been all Janie was looking for? To be seen as her wife and not just as the triplets' mom? "No, I'm not okay."

Maria's advice echoed in her head, but this wasn't the time to confess all that.

Hannah placed her hand on Janie's upper arm gently. "Do you want to sit down, and we can talk about it?"

Janie nodded and let Hannah guide her to the array of armchairs and sofas gathered around an industrial-looking coffee table. Hannah sat opposite her rather than beside her, and Janie couldn't decide whether that was a good or bad thing.

Janie smoothed her skirt and pressed her knees together. Hannah sat upright in her chair, legs spread wide and taking up all the available space. Janie allowed herself another small smile. She'd always liked that Hannah was unapologetic about her existence in a way that was usually the privilege of cis-men. But she pushed away the pleasant thought and refocused on the *un*pleasant reason she was here. "Before I tell you what's happening, I need you to promise that you'll stay calm. If you go off all gung-ho, you'll play right into my mother's hands."

"This is about me?" Hannah frowned. "Why is it about me?"

"Please, Han." Janie clasped her hands tightly at Hannah's instant defensiveness. "Promise me."

Hannah blew out a short breath and shrugged. "I'll try." She tugged at her ear. "And I'm sorry about Saturday night..."

The way Hannah trailed off was a clear invitation for further discussion, but Janie couldn't think about where their relationship was when the custody of their children was at risk. "We don't need to talk about that now. I think you'll be more concerned about my mother's intentions."

Hannah raised her eyebrows. "I don't think there's anything that could concern me more than losing you, but okay, I'm listening."

Janie did and *didn't* wish that were true, but she was one hundred percent certain that Hannah's fear of losing the triplets would override any others she might be harboring. She took a beat to figure out how to broach the subject before deciding to rip the Band-Aid off. "My mother wants custody of the triplets."

Hannah's mouth dropped open, and her frown deepened, like she could barely comprehend the language Janie was speaking and any more words would be totally lost. Janie bit her bottom lip and waited for the explosion. She couldn't truly ask Hannah to control her reaction to the threat; she could only hope that Hannah would remain calm enough for them to formulate a plan.

Hannah rose from her seat, mute, and wandered over to the makeshift nursery. She stayed there, staring into the tent lit with fairy lights, for what seemed like minutes. Janie thought about joining her but didn't. If Hannah had wanted her close, she would've stayed on the couch. But this situation was Janie's fault too, and Hannah probably needed the distance. God, she'd hate Janie forever if her mother took the kids. "Han?" she whispered, when the unknowing silence stretched too long for her to handle.

Hannah turned around, anger flaring in her eyes, and Janie pressed herself back into the seat. Hannah had never been violent toward Janie, but that rage frightened her. It was too animalistic, so barely controlled and volatile, like Hannah could destroy everything around her without realizing what she was doing.

"Is this because you've left me?" Hannah asked, her voice strangely calm.

Janie glanced away, unable to bear Hannah's hard and questioning glare. But she deserved Hannah's wrath. She'd broken *everything* with her carelessness. "Yes."

Hannah stalked back across the room and grasped the back of a couch. Her jaw clenched and unclenched rapidly as she stared at Janie, and it took all Janie's resolve not to run. Whatever was coming her way, she had to face it.

"So come home," Hannah said, the hardness in her eyes suddenly and completely gone. "Please."

That gaze, so full of love... Love she didn't deserve any more. Janie looked down at her hands, still clasped tightly in her lap. "I can't." She shook her head slowly. "It isn't that easy. My mother's already set things in motion."

"But if you're home, if we're together, no judge would take our babies away." Hannah's eyes implored Janie to confirm. "Would they?"

"Honestly, I don't know," Janie said. "My mother plays dirty, and she can twist the facts into whatever narrative she needs to win. It would be unusual, but...it wouldn't be impossible." She hated not only the words coming out of her mouth but also the effect they were having on Hannah. Every syllable seemed to slash at her heart, and though she hid her vulnerability and wasn't visibly recoiling, Janie knew her well enough to see the pain they were inflicting.

"I didn't realize your mother hated me this much." Hannah climbed over the couch and dropped onto it. "Has she just been waiting and hoping for this to happen?"

Janie raised her eyebrows. "What do you mean?"

"I know I'm not good enough for you, but I'm trying to be better." Hannah put her hand on the table but stopped short of reaching out. "I'm committed to therapy, and I'm working on myself and my flaws. I want to be good enough to deserve you."

Rings of cold steel wrapped around Janie's heart and squeezed. Yes, Hannah had neglected their love, but their connection had never been in question. "How could you think that you aren't?"

Hannah scoffed. "You wouldn't have left me if I was worthy of your love," she said. "And I think you only left the girls because you knew I'd die without them too."

"That's not true." Janie glanced at Hannah's hand and ached to touch her, to run her fingers up her arm and trace her tattoos, just like she used to when they'd spend hours in bed together. The intensity of her desire took her by surprise. She hadn't had room for those kinds of thoughts since she'd left their family home. She reined in her selfishness to refocus on their dire situation. "We have to figure out how we're going to fight this. The girls are the most important thing, and that's where all our attention needs to be. We can't let my mother take our children."

Hannah leaned back again and sighed. "What are we going to do about it?"

Janie took a breath, able to think a little more clearly now that Hannah wasn't quite so close. "I know the best family lawyer in the city. We'll retain him and formulate our defense. I'm sure

Grandma Susan's estate is at the root of all this. If we can prove that my mother is more interested in that money than the welfare of our girls, that might be enough for the judge to dismiss their claim."

Hannah rocked her head against the back of the sofa and tugged on her ear. "This is so fucked up." She looked at Janie again, confusion and pleading clear in her expression. "How did we end up like this?" she asked then held up her hand and shook her head. "Don't answer that. I know why, and when we get your wicked witch of a mom off our backs, I'm going to fix it. I promise."

Guilt stabbed at Janie's soul, and Maria's advice to reveal her secret shame echoed in her mind. But Janie needed Hannah to trust her, and once she knew what Janie had allowed to happen, that trust would dissolve, along with her love, no doubt. "It isn't just you, Han." She got up, and Hannah did too, reaching for Janie as she stood. Janie looked at Hannah's hand and hesitated before she took it tentatively.

It buzzed through her. The electricity. Their connection. Their love, still strong. Maybe Janie being away *had* been good for Hannah. Maybe it'd given her time to miss what they were together before they had the girls. That lack of attention *was* the thing that had forced them into separate beds, but it wasn't what had made Janie flee their home. "We'll talk properly after all this, I promise." And she'd confess her sin then. But for now, she had to force it to the far recesses of her mind. She had to be there for

Chapter Thirteen

The Halsted LGBTQ Center's gymnasium buzzed with the kind of chaotic energy that only came from competitive queers with something to prove. Solo stood at the door, watching teams organize themselves on either side of the volleyball net on the "serious" court. Lea, one of the regulars, came over to Solo and asked her to join them.

Solo gestured to the middle court. "My crew is waiting for me," she said. Though even if they weren't, she found playing with Lea challenging. The way Lea's breast implants *didn't* bounce in her boob tube was fascinating, and how her butt cheeks, which more than peeked out of her hotpants, seemed to have a mind of their own was way too mesmerizing to actually concentrate on a game.

Lea pushed out her Botox-enhanced bottom lip. "You never play with me anymore."

"That's because I like winning, and all of this," Solo waved in the direction of Lea's charms, "makes that incredibly difficult."

"Fine." Lea smiled widely and pinched Solo's cheek. "Go play with your bois," she said and went back to her team.

Solo looked down the corridor and considered backtracking. After Janie's bombshell at lunch, she'd decided not to come. Gabe had texted Solo, convincing her she needed to get out of her own head. So she'd put the triplets to bed as usual at seven and got ready. Her dad had assured her he'd be fine on his own and that sitting at home obsessing over Janie's parents wasn't going to fix anything.

"Solo, get your ass over here," Woody shouted from the bleachers at the edge of court two. "We need you on the team before Gabe claims someone from the dark side to play with us."

Solo couldn't help but smile as she made her way across the shiny hardwood floor. She'd been going to the open gym volleyball night for a year before the gang had come together again, and once she'd introduced them to it a month ago, it had quickly become a weekly institution. The sessions attracted everyone from seasoned athletes to people who'd never touched a ball in their lives, and the only rules were to try your best, talk your trash, and not be an asshole.

"Dark side?" Gabe raised her eyebrow and laughed. "What is this? *Star Wars?*"

"Close. Volleyball wars." Woody jabbed her finger at Gabe's chest. "We're creating a volleyball dynasty, and I won't stand for anything less than total victory. Solo's instrumental, you know that."

"You all take this very seriously for a community thing," Lori said and gave a small smile.

Lori had been coming for a couple of weeks, but she was often so quiet that Solo sometimes forgot she was there. Gabe's constant awareness of her however, like the way Gabe's hand found the small of Lori's back, or the way her eyes tracked Lori's movements made it impossible to miss how far gone Gabe was. It'd only been a few weeks since they'd gotten together, but they already had that quality Solo recognized from her own early days with Janie, that sense of two people learning to orbit each other, still tentative but pulled in by something undeniable. Her chest tightened, and once again, she glanced at the exit, rethinking her decision to be here.

"You okay?" RB asked.

Solo hadn't noticed her approach. RB had a way of moving through spaces like she was a ghost. It'd been a useful skill in the Army, but now it was just freaky. "Yeah, just..." She motioned vaguely at the chaos around them. "I'm taking it in."

RB studied her for a moment with those serious dark eyes

that always seemed to see more than Solo wanted to show.

"You don't have to stay if you're not feeling it," RB said. "No one would blame you."

"No, I want to be here," Solo said, realizing it was probably true. She'd been drowning for a few weeks now, in the triplets' needs, in her own spiraling thoughts about Janie, in the crushing weight of running the garage while her personal life imploded. Being here, surrounded by her people, doing something completely unrelated to any of her problems was like coming up for air.

"Good," RB said, "because we need all the help we can get."

Movement near the entrance caught Solo's attention. A tall woman with close-cropped hair and hollowed-out eyes stood just inside the doorway, scanning the crowd with the kind of wariness Solo recognized. That same skill had been drilled into her by the Army, to assess exits and threats before advancing into any space.

RB followed her gaze, and her expression shifted into something softer. "I'll be right back," she said, already moving toward the woman.

Solo watched as RB approached carefully, not crowding the woman's space, speaking in a low voice Solo couldn't hear. The woman's shoulders gradually dropped from around her ears, and after a moment, she nodded. RB gestured toward the clusters of people organizing into teams, still talking quietly, and the woman's expression shifted from wary to something like cautious interest.

"That's Van," Shay said. "RB's been working with her at the center for a couple of weeks. Former Marine, discharged six months ago, and she's been couch-surfing ever since."

Rosie smiled gently. "RB's good with her."

Solo recognized the same tone as Rae used with her. Even though she wasn't currently a therapist, Rosie couldn't quite turn it off.

"Patient," Rosie said, still observing the pair. "Consistent.

Doesn't push."

Shay circled her arms around Rosie's waist and pulled her close. "*This* is why you're reconsidering your career."

Rosie turned in Shay's arms and kissed her. "Again." She rolled her eyes. "I'm not going anywhere until the first stage of the Unity Tools project is complete. I can't leave you and your gang in anyone else's hands just yet."

Woody chuckled loudly and nudged Shay's shoulder. "I'd be happy in anyone's hands."

Shay shoved Woody away. "That's because you're a desperate butthead."

"No fair." Woody crossed her arms. "I just want some of this hotness that's running through our team like a virus."

Gabe ran her knuckles over Woody's head. "I thought you were a confirmed bachelor?"

Woody grinned wickedly and looked Rosie up and down. "I am. I want the hotness *without* the happily ever after crap."

"Are we playing or talking all night?" Gabe asked.

Solo didn't miss the glare Gabe shot at Woody before she nodded toward Solo, but she chose to ignore it and continued to watch the exchange between RB and Van. A pang of something that wasn't quite envy, but adjacent to it, rippled through her. RB had found another purpose in this work at the center, helping veterans who'd fallen through the cracks, and it showed in every careful gesture, every moment of attention she gave to people like Van. Solo had thought her own purpose was raising her girls, but trying not to drown in the sea of shit that was her life right now had overtaken that.

"Earth to Solo!" Woody snapped her fingers in front of Solo's nose. "Stop brooding and get your head in the game. We're playing Yen's team first, and I will not lose to those smug bastards again."

Gabe grasped Woody's shoulder. "You know this isn't a serious competition, right?"

"I know." Woody shrugged her off. "It's trash talk. It's part of the game."

Despite everything, Solo laughed. The easy banter, the ridiculousness of Woody's competitive streak, and the normalcy of it all was what she'd needed. "All right," she said, rolling her shoulders and forcing herself into the moment. "Let's do this."

RB rejoined them, and the game started with the usual chaos as Woody tried to organize them into a 6-2 system. Yen's team served first, a respectable attempt Gabe bumped with casual precision, making it look effortless. Shay set the ball, and Woody smashed it into the open court on Yen's weak side.

Gabe collected the ball to serve, and Solo positioned herself mid-court, still fighting to shake off the heaviness that had settled in her chest since lunch with Janie. *My mother wants custody of the triplets.* The words kept replaying in her mind. Janie had looked so defeated and small in a way that made Solo want to punch something. Preferably Janie's mother's face.

"Solo, heads up," RB shouted.

The ball was coming straight at her. Solo's body reacted before her brain caught up, and she bumped it high, sending it toward Woody at the net. Woody spiked it hard, and it hit the floor on the other side with a satisfying thwack.

"Yes!" Woody pumped her fist in the air. "That's what I'm talking about."

They fell into the rhythm of the game, and some of the tension drained from Solo's shoulders. This was good. This was normal. This was—

The ball came back over toward her, and Solo moved to receive it, but her foot caught on something, and she stumbled. Shay was beside her instantly, saving the play and sending the ball back over the net with a smooth set.

"You good?" Shay pulled Solo to her feet, concern clear in her expression.

"Yeah, just clumsy." But it wasn't clumsiness: it was distraction. Her body was here, but her mind was still at the garage with Janie, watching her explain how her parents were threatening everything they'd built.

The game continued, with points traded back and forth. Lori and Rosie cheered enthusiastically from the sidelines, and Solo noticed how Shay constantly looked at her, somehow managing to keep her head in the game at the same time, and how Rosie blew kisses that made Shay grin like a teenager. They were so new, so wrapped up in each other. As were Gabe and Lori, who exchanged little glances during plays, communicating in that wordless way new couples had before life got complicated and communication required actual words and effort and—

Solo's serve went long, sailing past the back line. "Damn it," she muttered.

"It's okay," RB shouted. "Shake it off."

But Solo couldn't shake it off. She couldn't shake off the fear, the desperation, the darkness. During a break for an injury on the other team, RB pulled Solo to the sideline to grab some water from Van. She still looked uncertain but less like she might bolt at any moment.

"Solo, this is Van," RB said. "Van, this is Solo. She's our artist-in-residence."

Van's handshake was firm but brief. "Nice to meet you."

"You play?" Solo asked, grateful for the distraction from her own spiraling thoughts.

"Nah, not since high school," Van said, her gaze darting from court to court, still assessing. "RB said it's pretty casual here."

"It's *very* casual," Solo said. "Half of us have no idea what we're doing, and the other half pretends they do."

Van laughed lightly. "Which half are you?"

"Depends on the day." Solo took a swig of water. "Today I'm firmly in the 'no idea' category."

"She's being modest," RB said. "Solo's actually good. She's just," her eyes met Solo's, "distracted."

Van nodded like she got it, which maybe she did. Whatever had hollowed out her eyes, whatever had her couch-surfing and scanning for exits, Van probably understood distraction better than most.

"You should bring your gear next week," Solo said.

"Great idea," RB said. "You can rotate with Woody's girlfriend."

Solo raised her eyebrow. "Woody doesn't do girlfriends. What are you talking about?"

"Maybe I don't, but I'll happily do her," Woody said from behind them.

She motioned beyond them toward the entrance, and Solo turned to see a muscular woman making her way across the gym. She was wearing workout gear that showed off arms covered in intricate ink of florals mixed with geometric patterns. It was beautifully done and reminded her of the rose on Janie's shoulder.

"That's Tate," Woody said. "She works as a personal trainer at the gym down the street. We met last week when I was checking out their weight room."

"And you invited her to volleyball," Shay said as Rosie handed her a water bottle. "Smooth."

"Shut up. We need a regular sixth." Woody smiled and continued to watch Tate's approach with undisguised interest.

"Hey," Tate called out and waved. When she reached their group, she gave Woody a playful shoulder bump that made her grin widen. "Sorry I'm late. I had a client who wanted to squeeze in an extra session."

"No problem." Woody gestured to the gang. "This is everyone. Everyone, this is Tate."

They introduced themselves, and Solo studied the way Woody and Tate interacted. Their casual touches, easy banter, and the way they were in each other's space. There was definitely something there. *Great*. Another couple forming while her own marriage crumbled.

Solo kicked herself for the thought. She wanted Woody to be happy. She wanted all her people to be happy, even when she couldn't be farther from that state herself.

"Okay." Woody clapped her hands together. "Tate's on our team, and we're going to destroy these guys."

The game resumed, and Solo forced herself to focus.

The ball came her way. This time she was ready and executed a clean bump with a perfect arc, delivered right to Woody's waiting hands. She set it to Tate, who spiked it with impressive force.

"Yes," RB shouted and ran around the court, high-fiving them all.

Solo grinned for the first time in what could've been weeks. Maybe Gabe had been right. Maybe she did need to get out of her own head.

The game continued, growing more competitive and more chaotic in equal measure. Tate was really good, and her addition to their team shifted the dynamic. Woody was showing off, obviously, doing dramatic dives for balls that didn't require them and talking more trash than usual. She and Tate found an easy rhythm, backing each other up for every play. That pang rumbled through her again, not quite envy or longing, but something sharp and uncomfortable.

They played for another forty-five minutes, trading wins and losses, with Woody's trash talk flowing freely. Solo just tried to be present and tried *not* to think about Janie sitting alone, God knows where, worrying about her mother's threats.

When they finally called it quits, everyone was soaked with sweat and laughing as they collapsed on the bleachers for more water and some well-deserved rest.

"That was fun," Tate said, sitting close enough to Woody that their shoulders touched. "You guys do this every week?"

"Every week," Woody said. "You should come back. We need a regular sixth."

"Yeah?" Tate bit her bottom lip and glanced down. "I'd like that."

Solo looked away and stared at her water as she emptied the bottle. She wanted to be happy for them, but the sharp ache in her heart was all-consuming.

Gabe dropped down on the bleacher next to Solo, breathing hard. "You want to talk about it?"

"About what?"

"About whatever had you playing like your head was somewhere else for the first twenty minutes."

Solo sighed. Of course Gabe had noticed. Gabe always noticed. "You know how Janie came to see me today when you were on tow duty?" She waited until Gabe nodded. "Her mother is taking legal action to get custody of the girls."

Gabe went very still beside her. "What?"

"Yeah." Solo rubbed her face. "She thinks I'm an unfit parent. And she wants control of the trust fund Janie's grandmother left her. Janie was pretty shaken up about it."

"Shit." Gabe squeezed Solo's shoulder. "What do you need?"

This was why she loved Gabe. She was always ready to act, to fix, to help. It's what had made her such a good leader in the Army, and it's what made her such a good friend now. "I don't know yet. Janie said she knew a good family lawyer. We're supposed to meet up this weekend to figure out next steps."

"You and Janie? Together."

Solo nodded. "Yeah."

"That's good, right?" Gabe nudged her. "You two working on something side by side."

Solo looked at her, saw the hope and encouragement in her eyes. "I don't know. Maybe. I just... What if everything's already gone, you know? Am I holding onto someone who doesn't want to be held anymore? How am I supposed to survive if Angela wins and takes my girls?" She coughed and put her head between her knees, not wanting to break down in the middle of the gym, in front of everyone.

"You can't think like that, buddy," Gabe said, putting her hand on Solo's back. "Janie needs you now more than ever. She needs you to show up, even when it's hard, and prove you're the woman she can count on. You can't give up."

"I'm not giving up." Solo sighed deeply and straightened up. "I'm just tired. And..." She swallowed. Could she say the word out loud? Admit her vulnerability and fear? "I'm scared. I don't know if showing up will be enough."

"It's a start though." Gabe squeezed her shoulder again. "And right now, a start is all you need."

Solo wanted to believe that. She really did. But as she looked around at her people, at Woody and Tate laughing together, Shay and Rosie wrapped up in each other, and RB patiently talking with Van, Solo couldn't shake the feeling that everyone else was moving forward while she was stuck, treading water and trying not to drown.

But at least I'm still treading. I'm still here, still trying, still showing up.

Maybe Gabe was right. Maybe that was enough.

She just had to hope it wasn't too little too late.

Chapter Fourteen

THEIR FAMILY LAWYER'S OFFICE was on the thirty-second floor of a glass tower in the Loop, and its floor-to-ceiling windows offered a sweeping view of Lake Michigan. Janie had been there dozens of times for case meetings, but today, the familiar space closed in on her, like something foreign. Threatening, even. She sat across from David's massive oak desk, with Hannah beside her in one of the leather chairs. They weren't touching, and the chairs weren't particularly close, but Hannah's mere presence promised unity, and Janie was glad not to be doing this alone.

"Okay, let's see what we're dealing with." David flipped open a legal pad and uncapped his fountain pen. "Your mother has filed a petition for custody based on allegations of parental unfitness and abandonment. Is that correct?"

Janie swallowed against her tightening throat, forcing herself to detach emotionally and just be a lawyer. "She came to my office on Sunday. She didn't say that's what she was doing specifically, but she made it clear she thinks Hannah and I are... That we're not capable of properly caring for the girls."

"What were her exact words?" David hovered his pen over the paper, ready to document everything.

"I can't remember *exactly*." Janie closed her eyes briefly, trying to remember through the haze of panic and shame. If only Lori had been there with her special memory skill. Janie should've known she'd need all these details and recorded the conversation on her phone. "She said I'd abdicated my responsibilities as a parent, that I'd abandoned my babies and left them with someone who was barely an adult." She glanced at Hannah, whose jaw twitched repeatedly like she was struggling to keep her reaction inside. "She intimated Hannah has a drinking problem that affects her ability to look after the triplets and that she was an unfit parent."

David looked at Hannah. "*Is* there a drinking problem?"

Hannah tugged her ear. "There used to be. When I was in the Army," she said. "But since the girls have been born, I mostly stick to beer and wine. And I cleared the house of hard liquor so I didn't slip back into old patterns." She shrugged and glanced at Janie. "I'm trying to be better."

Janie gave her a small smile. "That's all true, David. My mother doesn't know what she's talking about."

"Okay, that's good," he said. "And what else was said between you and your mother?"

"I accused her of doing this to get to my grandmother's trust."

David raised his eyebrows and paused his scribbling. "Ah, there it is. I recall she already tried to contest that though, yes?"

Janie nodded. "And she lost. Most of the money was for the girls, to be managed by me until they're eighteen. But if my mother could somehow get custody—"

"She'd control the assets on their behalf as their legal guardian," David said. "Smart. Vindictive, but smart." He made a note and circled it several times. "Okay, let's talk about her case. What can she actually prove?"

"I left them," Janie said quietly, not really wanting to admit that out loud. "I moved out a week ago, and—"

"Ten days." Hannah tapped the arm of her chair.

Janie chewed at the inside of her lip and couldn't hold Hannah's gaze. "I moved out on September tenth. That's abandonment, isn't it?"

"Not necessarily." David tilted his head slightly. "Separation isn't the same as abandonment, especially if you've maintained contact with the children and continued to provide financial support. Have you?"

Janie could practically feel the heat of Hannah's stare. "It's been really busy with work and having to find an apartment, so no, I haven't seen the girls since I left. But I'm still covering the mortgage, and the utilities, and everything else." When she finally looked at Hannah, she was focused on the carpet, her jaw still working furiously. She'd always been okay with Janie paying for most things, but maybe she didn't like other people knowing their financial business.

"That helps," he said, making another note. "But what about communication with your wife?" He motioned toward Hannah. "Are you two in contact about the children's welfare?"

"We text," Hannah said, though her sigh made it clear that wasn't enough. "I send Janie photos and updates. We met for dinner on Saturday...and lunch yesterday after her mother's visit."

The pause after Hannah's mention of their disastrous not-date almost undid Janie. She'd bailed too soon that night, been unwilling to bear witness to Hannah's anger and accusations. She'd been a coward.

"Even better. That shows co-parenting, not abandonment. But you should make the time to visit your children, or it won't look good." David tapped his pen against the pad. "Now, what about the fitness allegations? Is there anything your mother could point to that might support her claim?"

Janie's heart stuttered. This was the moment. This was when she should tell David about the ER visit, about Chloe and the bathroom cabinet, and about the crushing guilt that had driven her from her home.

But Hannah was sitting right beside her.

"I work long hours at the office," Janie said instead, "and I went back to work sooner than most. Hannah works five days at the garage, but she only started there about six weeks ago. The triplets are eighteen months old. It's a lot, even for two people."

David looked between them, his expression searching. "But you've hired help?"

"My dad moved up from Florida early last week," Hannah said. "He's staying with me and helping with the girls. And we're interviewing for a new nanny tomorrow. The last one left just before my wife did."

Janie heard the slight resentment in Hannah's tone, but she couldn't blame her. Janie had packed her bags and hadn't looked back, but she had damn good reason to leave...didn't she?

"Excellent." He smiled widely. "That demonstrates you're taking responsible steps to ensure proper care." He made more notes, his pen nib scratching on the paper. "Anything else? Any incidents or complaints from your pediatrician? Anything at all that could be used against you?"

The silence stretched. Janie could sense Hannah looking at her. Had she begun to question Janie's abrupt abandonment? *Tell him. Tell him now while I can control the narrative.* But the words wouldn't come. "No," she said and shrugged. "Nothing like that."

David nodded, apparently satisfied. "Good. Here's what you need to understand: grandparents' rights vary significantly by state, and Illinois is actually pretty restrictive. Your mother would need to prove that *both* of you are unfit parents and that custody with her is in the children's best interest. That's a very high bar."

Hannah sighed deeply, but Janie wasn't convinced it would be so easy. David didn't know her mother like she did, and when she discovered what had happened... "But it's possible?"

"Possible? Yes. Likely? No." David set down his pen and steepled his fingers. "Look, judges don't like removing children from their parents without serious cause. Your mother would need to show neglect, abuse, or endangerment. She'd need something substantive and documented. The fact that you're separated isn't enough. Both of you working full-time isn't enough. Even being a same-sex couple isn't enough, though I'm sure your mother would love to make that an issue."

"She's never been totally at peace with my sexuality,'" Janie said. "And she doesn't like that I used Grandma Susan's money to finance the garage start-up. I don't think she believes running a garage is a suitable career choice for a parent."

David scoffed. "Which is ridiculous and borderline discriminatory. We'd shut that down immediately. The real question is: does your mother have anything concrete? Hospital visits, police calls, CPS reports, anything like that?"

Janie's lips itched with the lie hiding behind them. "I...I don't know what she might have found. Or made up. I'm sure you're aware of my mother's reputation."

David studied her for a moment, and Janie had the uncomfortable feeling he could see right through her. They hadn't known each other that long, and they hadn't worked closely together. How *could* he know she was holding something back?

"Janie," he said, "if there's something that could come up, something your mother's investigators might find, I need to know about it now and not when we're standing in front of a judge."

"There's nothing," Janie said quickly. Too quickly. "Really. Hannah is a wonderful parent." She couldn't include herself in that statement, but she never doubted Hannah's dedication to their children. "We love our daughters. There's no reason for my mother to win this."

Hannah took Janie's hand. It was only the second time they'd touched in weeks, and the contact sent an electric shock through her system.

"We'll fight this together," Hannah said. "Whatever it takes."

"Perfect. Togetherness. That's what the court needs to see." David waved his pen at them both. "Okay. Here's what we do. When it comes in, we respond to the petition with a motion to dismiss based on lack of standing. We document your co-parenting arrangement, the help you've secured, your employment, and your financial stability. We'll line up character witnesses. We need your family, friends, and colleagues to attest to your fitness as parents. And we prepare for the possibility that this goes to a hearing."

Hannah leaned forward. "How likely is that?"

"Given that Janie's mother has money and one of the

best lawyers in the state, I'd say fifty-fifty. She might push for emergency relief, claim the children are in immediate danger, and try to get temporary custody while the case is pending." David pressed his lips together. "That's the real risk here. Not that she'll win ultimately, but that she could cause enough chaos in the meantime to hurt you and the kids."

The thought of her mother getting even temporary custody, of the triplets being confused and scared turned her stomach. Could Hannah really lose access to her own children because Janie had been too ashamed to admit her mistake?

"We won't let that happen," David said, clearly reading her fears. "But I need you both to be completely honest with me about anything, and I mean *anything*, that could be used against you. Because if there's a surprise, if something comes out in court that I don't know about, it'll make us look dishonest and undermine our entire case."

Janie nodded, not trusting herself to speak.

They spent another thirty minutes going over strategy, who to contact for character witnesses, what documentation to gather, and how to present a united front. Hannah asked most of the questions, mainly because she had no understanding of the law. Her hand never left Janie's, and Janie was content to enjoy the intimacy while she had the chance. She'd missed Hannah's touch so much over the past months, and the feel of Hannah's strong fingers covering hers comforted her deeply.

When they'd finally finished, David walked them to the elevator. "You two should talk," he said as they waited for the car to arrive. "Really talk. Not about legal strategy but about what you want for your marriage and your family. Because the judge is going to ask questions about your relationship, and 'we're separated but co-parenting' isn't the strongest position."

The elevator pinged, and the doors opened. Janie stepped in first, and Hannah followed. They rode down in silence, thirty-two floors of numbers ticking backward. Hannah's hand had slipped from Janie's when she'd motioned for Janie to enter the elevator, and the loss of contact was like a chasm re-opening between them.

"Do you want to grab lunch?" Hannah asked as they reached the lobby.

Janie knew she should say yes, should take the opening and spend time with her wife. But her mother's voice echoed in her head, as did David's warning about being dishonest. And then there was the terrible knowledge that she was lying to everyone, including herself. "I can't," she said. "I have a meeting." It wasn't entirely a lie. Maria had texted earlier, asking if Janie wanted to stop by the café. But it wasn't exactly the meeting she made it sound like. Hannah nodded, and Janie couldn't read her expression. Was it disappointment or resignation?

"Okay. Text me later?"

"Of course," Janie said easily, as if everything was so normal.

Hannah looked like she was about to say something but seemed to hesitate.

"What is it?" Janie asked, though she dreaded that Hannah might suspect her secret. She wanted to tell her, but now wasn't the right time. Janie had already decided that she'd make one final plea to her mother to drop her claim on their children, and then she could control the narrative again.

"I was thinking that I could push the interviews until after work tomorrow." Hannah pulled at her ear in that adorable way Janie had always loved. "You know, so you could come. If you want. You don't have to." She waved the notion away. "Forget it. I was being stupid. You're probably way too busy."

Janie took Hannah's still-flapping hand, sighing at how natural and good it still felt. She tried to pull back her flaring optimism, which dared to see a way back to their life. If that *was* possible, Hannah could only make that decision after she had all the facts, and right now, Janie wasn't strong enough to give them to her. "David's right," she said. "We have to show a united front to battle my mother. I'll make the time."

Hannah grinned and stroked Janie's fingers. "You will?"

Janie nodded, almost losing herself in Hannah's eyes. All that hope and love focused on her was as intoxicating now as it had been when they'd first fallen for each other. Once again, she couldn't help thinking that this short separation had achieved what months of her pleading for attention hadn't. If only she could turn back time.

Hannah pulled out her phone and nearly dropped it in her hurry. "I'll call the agency right now and reschedule."

Janie gestured to her car. "I really have to go. Text me the time you want me there."

Hannah looked up from her phone and stared into Janie's eyes. "I want you there all the time."

"Han," Janie said and shook her head slightly, "let's focus on keeping the girls at home with you right now, okay?" After Hannah gave her a contrite look and nodded, Janie headed toward her car without looking back for fear that she might fall into Hannah's arms and take the comfort that was being offered. But she couldn't. Not yet, and maybe not ever, but the slightest sliver of light in the shadows of her shame had shown itself, and that was enough for now.

The café in Pilsen was blessedly quiet when Janie arrived an hour later.

Maria was behind the counter, and she took a long look at Janie before nodding toward the corner table. "Coffee?"

"Please." Janie collapsed into the chair by the window, the same spot she'd come to think of as her table over the past week. How quickly and easily this place had become a refuge, somewhere she could exist without pretending to be okay, without holding up the mask of competence and capability. This café was exactly what Maria had wanted it to be.

Maria brought over two coffees and a plate of pan dulce, then settled into the opposite chair. "Hannah or the girls?"

Janie gave a small smile at how transparent she was, if only to Maria. "How did you know?"

"You have that look." Maria waggled her finger in front of

Janie's nose. "Like you've been talking about things you wish you didn't have to talk about."

Janie wrapped her hands around the coffee mug, savoring the warmth. "My mother filed for custody of the girls."

Maria's eyebrows rose. "I see."

"Hannah and I just met with our family lawyer. He says my mother probably can't win, but she can make things hell in the meantime. And if she finds anything to use against us..." Janie took a sip of coffee and glanced out the window, unable to hold Maria's gaze.

"Like the ER visit?" Maria asked quietly.

Janie forced herself to look at Maria. "I couldn't tell him, not with Hannah sitting right there."

"Mija," Maria said, her voice gentle but firm. "You can't fight a custody battle with secrets. You're a lawyer. You know this."

"I know, I know." Janie pressed her palms against her eyes. "David said the same thing. If something comes out that he doesn't know about, it will undermine everything."

Maria arched her eyebrows. "He's right."

"But if I tell Hannah now, especially with this custody thing..." Janie dropped her hands. "She'll think I really am unfit. That my mother is right. She'll see me the way I see myself, as someone who can't be trusted with her own children."

Maria picked at the dessert and chewed on a piece, not saying anything for a while. "Is that all that's stopping you from telling Hannah?"

"Isn't that enough?"

Maria pursed her lips and narrowed her eyes, clearly knowing there was more. "Perhaps."

Janie sighed deeply. She'd been more honest with Maria over the past ten days than she'd been with anyone other than Hannah for a long time. There was no reason to stop now. "Because I'm terrified!" she said, louder than she intended. "I'm terrified that if I tell her, she'll hate me. Or she'll look at me with pity, like I'm this broken thing that can't be fixed. I can't..." She tugged at her suit jacket and squeezed her eyes shut briefly. "I can't bear either of those things. I'm supposed to be the strong, dependable one."

"Pah." Maria wrinkled her nose. "So instead you're lying to her. And to your lawyer. And to yourself."

Janie flinched, not used to Maria being quite so blunt. "I'm not lying. I'm just not telling the whole truth."

"That's the same thing, and you know it." Maria leaned forward. "Listen to me, mija: you're building a case for your own destruction. Every day you keep this secret, you're making it worse. Every conversation you have without mentioning it, every meeting where you pretend everything is fine, you're digging yourself deeper into a hole that you might not be able to climb out of."

"You don't understand—"

"No, *you* don't understand." Maria tapped her fingernail on the table repeatedly. "You think keeping this secret is protecting your children? You think fighting this battle alone makes you stronger? All you're doing is giving your mother exactly what she needs to destroy you."

Janie leaned back in her chair, trying to escape the almost physical pressure of Maria's judgment, and looked toward the door. She could get up and leave. She didn't have to listen to this. But Maria had been the only person Janie had been able to talk to honestly since she'd left Hannah and their girls.

"I'm sorry," Maria said, her voice softening slightly. "I don't mean to be harsh. But, mija, you're running out of time. Do you really think your mother won't find out about the ER visit? What happens when she finds the hospital record and the doctor's notes from that day?"

Janie's blood ran cold. She hadn't thought about the records. Of course there were records. She'd been careful to pay on her card instead of claiming on their health insurance, but there was still a paper trail. A *discoverable* paper trail.

"Oh, God," Janie whispered.

"Yes." Maria covered Janie's hand with her own. "You need to tell Hannah everything before your mother's lawyer finds out and uses it to ambush you in court."

"I can't. Not today. I need time to figure out how—"

"There is no good time." Maria threw her hands in the air. "There is no perfect way to say any of this. There's just the truth, and the longer you wait, the worse it will get. You and Hannah need to fight this together, but this secret will pull you apart if you don't share it soon."

Janie wrapped her arms around herself and rocked slightly. The café was suddenly too small, too close, like the walls were pressing in on her.

"Let me tell you a story about my friend Elena," Maria said, settling back in her chair, and adopting her usual gentle tone.

"Okay." Janie nodded and relaxed a little.

"Elena came out when her kids were six and eight. This was the mid-eighties, so you can imagine how well that went. Her husband immediately filed for divorce and full custody. Back then, being gay was enough for the courts to brand you an unfit parent." Maria paused, and her eyes seemed to focus on a distant place, as if searching for the memory. "But Elena's lawyer told her not to worry. Times were changing, he said. The judge was known to be fair, and Elena was a good mother. They'd fight it and win. But Elena was ashamed. She didn't want her private life being dragged through court. She was frightened of what people would say."

Janie's chest tightened at the obvious parallels Maria was not-so-subtly drawing.

"So she started keeping secrets." Maria raised her eyebrows and nodded slowly. "Small ones at first. Like not telling anyone she'd lost her job, not telling her lawyer about a fight at the kids' school where another parent had taunted her for being a lesbian. She thought if she could keep everything looking perfect on the surface, if she didn't share the chaos, she'd be fine."

"What happened?" Janie asked, though she really didn't

want to know.

"Everything came out. As it always has a way of doing, mija. Always. Like water, the truth will always flow. Her husband's lawyer found out about the job loss, the missed rent payments, and all the other small things Elena had kept hidden. And when it all came out in court, the judge saw Elena had been less than honest with her own lawyer, and she was painted as unstable. Dishonest. Someone who couldn't be trusted."

Janie swallowed hard and swirled the coffee in her cup. "Did she lose custody?"

"Yes." Maria nibbled on another piece of pan dulce. "Not because she was gay, in the end. Not even because of the job loss or the other issues. But because the shame and secrecy made her look like she had something terrible to hide. The judge didn't trust her, and Elena lost her children."

Tears burned at the back of Janie's eyes. This could be her story Maria might tell another virtual stranger in a few years. "Did she ever get them back?"

Maria pursed her lips and shook her head. "By the time she'd gotten herself together and was in a position to try for custody again, her kids were teenagers. Their father had told them so many bad things about her, and they were angry. They didn't want to see her." She took a sip of her coffee and sighed, like the story had drained her energy somehow. "She has a relationship with them now, and they've worked through some of it. But they're adults, and she missed their entire childhoods. All those years, poof." She flicked her fingers. "Gone. Because she was too ashamed to ask for help. Too scared to be honest."

Janie's tears spilled over, running hot down her cheeks. "I don't want that. I don't want to lose them, Maria. But I don't deserve them. I don't deserve Hannah."

"Nonsense." Maria frowned. "You made a mistake. Don't let shame isolate you. Don't let fear keep you from being honest with the one person who should be standing beside you through this."

"But what if Hannah can't forgive me? The triplets are her life. What if she looks at me and sees what I see?"

"What if she doesn't?" Maria smiled. "What if she sees what *I* see? A woman who made a mistake, who's been carrying it alone because she's too afraid to let anyone help her carry it? What if Hannah surprises you?"

Janie wiped at her face, her hands shaking. "You make it sound so simple."

"It isn't. And you're right; it is terrifying." Maria leaned forward and took Janie's hand again. "But, Janie, listen to me. Really listen. Your mother is threatening to *take your children.* She has lawyers and resources and probably investigators who are digging into every aspect of your life. They will find out about the ER visit, and they'll use it against you. Do you want to be the one who tells your wife, or do you want her to hear it from your mother's lawyer in a courtroom?"

The visceral and horrifying images played in her mind: Hannah's face as the evidence of Janie's negligence was laid out for all to see. The devastation in Hannah's eyes at Janie's betrayal, at the realization that Janie had been lying all along, and now she was losing her children because of it. "I can't do this," Janie whispered.

"Yes, you can. You have to." Maria squeezed Janie's hand tightly. "You said that Hannah was trying to find a new nanny, yes?"

Janie nodded. "She's interviewing tomorrow, and she said she'd push the interviews to the evening so I could be part of it."

Maria smiled. "So she's including you. She's asking for your input. That is your opening, mija. Go *home* tomorrow. Help interview the nannies. And then, when you have a quiet moment, tell her the truth. All of it."

Janie wanted to argue, wanted to find a reason to wait just a little longer. But Maria's words, and Elena's story, had shaken something loose inside her. The truth was already out there, documented and waiting to be discovered. Janie could only control when and how Hannah heard it if she acted soon, but Hannah *would* hear it one way or another. "Okay," she said, dredging courage from deep within and fighting off the fear that her confession would be the death knell on everything that was important to her. "I'll tell her tomorrow, I promise."

Maria tapped Janie's hand and gave an encouraging smile. "Good. That's good, mija."

They sat in silence for a while, drinking their coffee and watching the afternoon light shift across the café walls. Around them, the café got busier. People ordered pastries and coffee, had conversations and laughed with each other, came together and shared their troubles. The world kept turning even though Janie's was falling apart. She nibbled on her bottom lip. "Can I ask you something?"

"Of course."

"How do you always know the right thing to say?" Janie tilted her head and studied Maria's deeply lined face. "How do you always have these perfect stories that make me see what I need to see?"

Maria laughed loudly. "You think I always know the right thing to say? Mija, I've made a hundred mistakes just like yours. I know what it's like to carry shame that feels too heavy to share. And I know what happens when you carry it alone for too long."

"What happens?" Janie asked, thinking that Elena's story might really be Maria's.

"It crushes you. Or you finally get tired of carrying it and set it down." Maria smiled and gave a small shrug. "I'm just trying to stop that from happening to you."

Janie's phone buzzed with a text.

Everything's shifted for tomorrow. Can you do seven? And maybe you could stay for dinner after the nanny interviews. The girls would love to see you. No pressure, just thought I'd ask.

Janie stared at the message. Hannah was hoping for more time together than just the interviews. She was offering family dinner, time with the girls, and a chance to be part of their lives again.

A chance to tell the truth.

That sounds good. I'd like that. She set the phone down and looked at Maria, who seemed to be eyeing her cautiously. "I'm going to tell her. I really am."

"I believe you," Maria said.

Janie nodded and smiled. She believed herself too. Almost.

Chapter Fifteen

SOLO HAD BEEN NERVOUS before, like when she'd jumped out of a plane for the first time in the Army, when she'd presented her first custom paint job to a client, and when she'd told Janie she wanted to have kids. But standing in their living room now, looking across the lawn and waiting for Janie to arrive for the nanny interviews, made all of those things child's play. Gabe had insisted she take the day off work, so Solo had cleaned the house twice, changed her shirt three times, and made sure the triplets were dressed in actual matching outfits instead of the chaotic mix-and-match situation that had been happening more often than not since Janie had left. A couple of times this week, she and her dad had a little trouble with the triplets' color-coding. Luckily, Tia was already pretty independent about her fashion choices. She'd thrown a fit when Solo had held up both the purple and the green sneakers.

"You're going to wear a hole in the floor," her dad said from the couch, where he was reading to the girls from a picture book about trucks. Tia sat in his lap, taking the prime position like the prima donna she was, while Luna and Chloe flanked him on either side, unusually still.

She turned to face him. "I'm not pacing."

Her dad scoffed. "You've checked that window four times in the last five minutes."

Solo forced herself to move away from the window. "I just want this to go well."

"It will." Her dad looked at her over the top of his reading glasses with that knowing expression. "You're not just talking about the interviews, are you?"

Before she could answer, Janie pulled up in front of their house. Solo's heart thudded against her chest. "She's here."

Her dad waved her away with his free hand. "Then go let her in before you explode."

Solo was at the door before Janie had even made it up the path. She opened it without considering that she didn't need to. This was Janie's house, and she could let herself in. But she'd given up her key. Whatever, it was too late and it would be too weird if she closed it now that Janie had reached the threshold and was looking up at her from the bottom of the steps.

God, she looked beautiful in a pair of simple black skinny jeans and that soft blue sweater Solo had always loved on her. Had Janie chosen it because of that? Solo stepped aside before it got any more awkward. "Hi, I'm glad you made it," she said, then wished she hadn't. Maybe her tone sounded too accusatory, like she'd expected Janie not to show, to decide work was more important than choosing a person to take care of their children.

"You sound less surprised about that than I feel," Janie said. She laughed lightly and averted her gaze, suggesting she might be just as anxious about tonight as Solo was.

"You nearly didn't come?" Solo asked, wishing she'd had the courage to kiss her wife's cheek.

"We're hip-deep in a new class-action suit on behalf of hundreds of authors." Janie shrugged elegantly. "It might end up being thousands. So it's all hands on deck and a lot of late nights."

Solo closed the door and leaned against it while Janie removed her shoes. She'd forgotten how much she loved to watch the ritual, and better still, she took it as a sign that Janie still considered this to be her home. She'd missed the sound of Janie's bare feet against their wooden flooring, announcing her presence before she was anywhere near Solo. "This isn't causing any problems for you, is it?" She didn't much care for Janie's boss, but Janie's job was an important part of her identity, *and* it kept the triplets in diapers and dinosaur nuggets.

Janie placed her heels against the stairs and shook her head.

"I explained to Phillip why I needed the time, and I've been putting in more hours than anyone else. He was fine about it."

Solo raised her eyebrows. Janie had always been very strict about keeping her personal and business life separate. "You've told him what's going on? With us? With your mom?"

Janie huffed. "Of course not. I just said we needed to interview for a new nanny because our previous one left without giving us any notice." She placed her phone and handbag on the table by the door. "He's a big fan of my mother, and I don't want him running back to her, trying to score—"

Janie was cut off by three small bodies launching themselves at her legs.

"Mommy! Mommy!"

Janie seemed to hesitate for a second before she dropped to her knees and gathered all three girls into her arms, her expression transforming into something that made Solo's chest ache. This was what she remembered Janie looking like when she was happy, surrounded by their daughters, laughing as they competed for her attention.

"I missed you guys so much," Janie said, kissing their heads in turn. "Have you been good for Mama and Grandpa?"

"I paint!" Tia said, puffing her chest and smiling widely.

Janie stroked Tia's cheek. "And it was beautiful. Mama sent me pictures."

Tia tugged on Janie's skirt and tried to pull her toward the living room. "Mommy see."

Janie allowed herself to be woman-handled by the triplets but glanced back at Solo. "It's still there?"

Solo rubbed her hand across the back of her head and chewed on her top lip. "Yeah. I wanted you to see it in person." She thought Janie's eyes got a little shiny for a moment, but she was already focused on their babies as she was dragged away, and Solo couldn't be sure.

Her dad came over after greeting Janie with an awkward-looking hug. "I'm going to take the girls to the den. It'll give you two some space for the interviews, and you can bring them in to meet the girls at the end. If you want."

"Thanks, Dad."

"Slugger?" He waited until she looked at him and squeezed her shoulder. "Breathe. You're doing great."

She nodded, not trusting herself to respond in case she got all weird, then helped him take the girls out of the way. Neither she nor Janie had any hope of concentrating on what anyone else was saying if the triplets were in the room.

They'd just gotten back to the living room when the first candidate arrived. Clara was a woman in her forties with an impressive resume and impeccable references that the agency had already checked out. She sat across from Solo at the kitchen table.

Janie slid onto the chair beside Solo. She took her mug in one hand and placed the other on the table between them. Solo looked at her slender fingers and shivered at the memory of when Janie had last touched her. Too long ago. And all the blame lay at Solo's feet for that.

"So, Clara," Solo said, "will you tell us about your experience?"

Clara launched into a detailed description of her work with twins and triplets over the past fifteen years. She was thorough, professional, and warm without being overly familiar. On paper, she was perfect.

Could they be that lucky to find the right person so quickly?

"What's your approach to discipline?" Janie asked.

Solo glanced at her, grateful for the question. They needed someone whose philosophy aligned with theirs, and Janie had always been the one to keep the girls in line, while Solo was a soft touch. And boy, did Tia know it.

"I believe in natural consequences and positive reinforcement," Clara said. "Toddlers are still learning about the world, so I prefer redirection over punishment."

Solo liked the sound of that. Natural consequences were great as long as the situation wasn't dangerous, but she and

Janie would never let anything bad happen. "What about nap schedules? Our girls are pretty routine-oriented."

Clara nodded. "I'm a big believer in consistent schedules. Especially at this age. Structure helps them feel secure."

They talked about logistics, meal preparation, and emergency procedures. Clara answered everything competently and asked intelligent questions about the girls' individual personalities and preferences, and how Solo and Janie told them apart since they were identical.

When she left, they sat in silence for a moment.

"She was great, right?" Solo straightened Clara's resume and slipped it to the bottom of the paperwork on the other possible nannies.

Janie wrinkled her nose slightly. "Yeah."

"You didn't like her?" Solo asked.

"No, I did. She's just..." Janie gazed out of the kitchen window and tapped the table lightly with her nails.

She couldn't be searching for words. Janie's grasp of language was one of the things Solo loved about her, and she always knew the exact thing to say and the perfect way to say it. So she took another sip of coffee and waited.

"She's very 'by-the-book.' I think she'll follow all the nanny rules perfectly, but I doubt she'll connect with the girls." Janie turned sideways in her seat and looked at Solo. "She didn't have much personality, and Tia won't stand for that."

Something warm and squishy unfurled in Solo's chest. She loved how Janie knew exactly what the girls' emotional needs were, not just whether someone could keep them alive and fed. Usually, Janie had to focus on practical solutions because Solo was too busy with the touchy-feely stuff. "You're right," she said. "She was a little...beige."

"Yes, beige." Janie touched Solo's arm lightly and too briefly. "And sterile."

"*That's* the word." She pulled out Clara's paperwork again and tossed it in the recycling. "Should we see how the rest go?"

she asked, enjoying spending time with her wife, despite the challenging situation.

Janie's answering smile filled the kitchen like sunlight after a storm.

Candidate two was Louise, a bubbly woman in her late twenties who'd been a kindergarten teacher before switching to private childcare. She was enthusiastic and sweet, but halfway through the interview, Chloe wandered in with Solo's dad and immediately hid behind Janie's leg when she saw Louise.

"It's okay, baby," Janie whispered, scooping her up. "This is Louise. She's just visiting."

But Chloe buried her face in Janie's neck and wouldn't look at their guest. Janie arched her eyebrow in Solo's direction, and while Solo knew toddlers were unpredictable and one reaction didn't mean anything definitive, she also trusted Chloe's instincts.

"I'm sorry," Louise said, looking genuinely distressed. "I'm usually great with shy children."

"It's not you." Janie handed Chloe back to Solo's dad, who grabbed some juice and promptly left the room without a word. "She's been through some changes lately."

Solo nodded. "She's more cautious than usual." She caught Janie's eye and saw the pain there. Janie clearly blamed herself for Chloe's increased clinginess, for the way all three girls had been more anxious since Janie left. And maybe Janie's absence was part of it, but Solo's neglect had forced Janie to leave. And then she'd been so overwhelmed and stressed that the girls had obviously picked up on it. They'd become more demanding and needy, but Solo had chosen to put it down to a phase.

After Louise left, Solo's dad returned with all three girls, and the house descended into toddler chaos for a few minutes as they dealt with diapers and a minor dispute over a toy cow that required negotiation.

Solo's heart ached as Janie dove into the madness like she'd never left, settling the farmyard fuzz with the wisdom of Solomon: Chloe could have it now, Luna would get it after snack time, and Tia could take the sheep as a consolation prize. It was so natural, so easy, so *them* that Solo's throat tightened and her chest constricted. She couldn't lose this. This partnership, this rhythm, this sense of being a team.

Carmen arrived just as they were hustling the girls into bed for a special grandad story. She was a woman in her mid-fifties with kind eyes, sensible shoes, and an air of unflappable calm that reminded Solo of her own mom. Could it be third time's the charm?

"Sorry about the timing," Solo said, ushering her inside as the sounds of toddler protests echoed down the stairs. "We wanted you to meet the girls, but they're getting cranky, so my dad's putting them to bed."

"No problem. Does your dad live close by?" Carmen asked as Janie led her through to the kitchen.

"He's living here right now," Solo said. She glanced at Janie, unsure how much she should confess to a total stranger, but Janie simply smiled and nodded. Solo took that as permission to be totally honest.

Carmen settled at the kitchen table like she belonged there. "That's nice. And so lovely for the girls. You must have a very special relationship."

Warmth flooded Solo's body. That was *exactly* what they had. "I treasure it," she said, then wished she hadn't when a flicker of sadness crossed Janie's eyes. Her relationship with her father had been practically non-existent since he'd divorced Janie's mother.

After fixing a cup of English breakfast tea for Carmen, they went through the basics of her extensive experience, her glowing references, and her certifications.

"And you two," Carmen said, looking between Solo and Janie with clear, assessing eyes. "Where are you in your relationship right now? I'm not asking to be nosy. I just need to understand the household I'd be joining."

Solo froze, unsure how to answer. Separated? Working on

it? Completely fucked up but trying to co-parent?

"We're…" Janie said, then faltered.

"We're rebuilding," Solo said, taking Janie's hand. To her relief, Janie didn't pull away. "We've had a rough time recently. We're living separately right now, but we're working on our relationship. For ourselves and for our daughters."

"That must be hard." Carmen nodded slowly, but there didn't appear to be judgment in her expression. "I appreciate your honesty. And for what it's worth, I think kids do better when they see their parents working on problems rather than pretending they don't exist."

"We're not pretending," Janie said quietly. "Work, friends, family, us. It's a juggling act, and we're trying to figure it out."

"That's all any of us can do." Carmen smiled. "Now, tell me about the girls' personalities. What makes each of them tick?"

Solo grinned. Carmen was *the one*. She didn't just want to know the on-paper, sterile information about schedules and dietary restrictions, she wanted to know about Tia's stubborn independence, Chloe's sensitivity to loud noises, and Luna's Zen-like approach to life. She asked about their comfort objects, their favorite books, and whether they were nappers or fighters.

Solo glanced at Janie and was sure they were thinking the same thing. "What do you think about the girls spending time with both of us but sometimes separately. Janie will be coming over regularly." She flinched slightly under Janie's tightening grip on her hand. Shit, she'd assumed and spoken for her. *Stupid.* "As much as her current workload allows with the added travel time from her apartment." Solo clenched her jaw, hating to think of Janie sleeping anywhere else but beside her. "I think we're hoping to coordinate so she can be here during some of your hours, help with routines, that kind of thing."

"I think that's wonderful," Carmen said. "Consistency is important, but so is flexibility. If you're both committed to being present, I'm here to support that, *not* replace it."

That was music to Solo's ears. Support was exactly what

they needed, and then she could concentrate on maintaining a healthy balance between Janie and the girls. They talked logistics, about Carmen's availability, her rate, and her potential start date, which couldn't come soon enough.

When she left, after jokingly praising the artistic integrity of Tia's wall art, Solo and Janie looked at each other. "Her," they said simultaneously, then laughed.

"Jinx," Janie said.

Solo grinned, enjoying Janie's playfulness, something she'd missed long before Janie had left. Sure, parenting was a serious business, but Solo had taken it so seriously that she'd left little room for the fun they used to have together. "Should we call her now? Or wait until we've confirmed the references?"

"Wait," Janie said. "But I think she's perfect. I like the way she's interested in our whole family dynamic and not just the triplets. That feels like it's more than just a job for her somehow."

"Yeah." Solo tentatively took Janie's hand again, and her joy elevated when Janie didn't pull away. "I liked that she didn't see our relationship issues as a barrier to our ability to parent. She's thinking of you as part of this."

Janie blinked rapidly, and her eyes shone. "I wasn't sure I still was."

Solo frowned and squeezed Janie's hand. "Of course you are. You're their mother. Nothing changes that." Why would she think that? She shouldn't suffer and miss out on the girls' growing up just because Solo wasn't the wife she deserved. "And I want you here as much as possible. The girls need you. I—" She caught herself almost making it about them instead of just the girls, which was the battle they were fighting right now. "We need you."

"Thank you," Janie whispered, "for including me in this and for not shutting me out."

Solo wanted to say that she'd never shut Janie out, but that would be a lie. She'd already done exactly that. It hadn't been deliberate, but the effect was the same. "I'm trying to do better.

I'm trying to *be* better at seeing you and making space for you."

Before Janie could respond, Solo's dad burst into the living room. Solo released her gentle grip on Janie and took a step back, feeling like she'd been caught doing something she shouldn't. But that was nonsense. Janie was still her wife, at least while they wrestled with her wicked witch of a mother.

"They won't go to sleep." He took Janie's hands in his and pulled her toward the door. "They're screaming for you, Janie. You have to make it stop."

As much as Solo wanted to be part of the moment, she didn't go with them. Janie's absence had clearly begun to affect the girls, and Solo wanted them to have as much of Janie's attention tonight as possible. She didn't want to dilute that with her presence.

She busied herself filling the dishwasher, smiling to herself as the girls' happy screams echoed all over the house, and then she took Carmen's resume into the living room to re-read. By the time Janie returned, Solo was even more convinced they'd hit the jackpot.

"He's good with them," Janie said, hovering in the doorway.

"Yeah, he is. I don't know what I would have done if he hadn't moved in." Solo had a notion of what that would have looked like, but she wasn't about to voice it. Only in the darkness of the nights she'd spent alone had she given space to how things might've turned out if she'd had to go it alone. And they'd been far right of pleasant. "Do you still have the time to stay for dinner? We could order something, or I could cook. Dad mentioned something about meeting up with some guys he met at the hardware store, so it would just be us."

Janie glanced at her watch then covered it with her hand. "I'd like that," she said. "But only if you let me help cook something. I've been living on takeout and cereal, and I'd commit perjury for a home-cooked meal."

"Deal." Solo stood, energized and buzzing that they'd get more time together. "Let's go see what we have in the refrigerator."

Janie smiled and went into the kitchen first. Solo did a little happy dance before jumping up and punching the air. She was about to join Janie but ran into her dad as he came into the living room.

"I'm going to see if it's possible to make new friends at this age," he said. "Your girls make it look easy at the park, but it's been a while since I've had to do it."

"You've got this, Pops," Solo said and grasped his shoulder. "You'll be a big hit." She glanced beyond him, nervousness nipping at her own confidence.

"Go cook dinner with your wife." He pulled her into a bear hug and slapped her back. "Show her you remember how to do something besides parent."

God, she wanted that. Wanted to cook Janie a perfect dinner then take her to bed and rediscover her all over again. But that wouldn't be tonight. It might not be any night soon. Or ever again.

Her dad left, and Solo headed to the kitchen, where Janie had tied one of Solo's aprons around her waist and was examining the contents of the refrigerator with the focus of a general surveying a battlefield. Solo tried not to get too excited and read anything into Janie not wearing her own apron; it'd probably just been on top and had been the easiest to grab.

"You've got chicken breast, some vegetables that are only slightly wilted, and," Janie emerged from the fridge holding up a bottle of white wine, "ta-da!"

"I forgot we had that." Solo moved to the cabinet to grab wine glasses. The real ones, not the plastic cups she'd been using since Janie had left for fear she'd drop one and create a death trap. That would just prove Angela right: the safe parent had gone, so of course something bad would happen. The judge would practically gift-wrap the triplets and hand them to Janie's mom.

"We bought it for our anniversary," Janie said softly. "Last year."

Solo remembered. They'd meant to drink it that night, but Tia had been teething and Chloe had gotten a fever. By the time everything had settled down, they'd both been too exhausted to do more than collapse into bed. The bottle had sat forgotten in the back of the fridge for a year, like a symbol of everything they'd meant to do but hadn't, all the moments they'd missed while drowning in the chaos of new parenthood.

"Let's drink it tonight," Solo said. "We can make pasta carbonara. I'm sure we have bacon and parmesan. And there's some focaccia bread in the freezer."

"Carbonara." Janie's face lit up. "We haven't made that in forever."

"I know. I thought..." Solo paused. She probably shouldn't be laying her cards on the table when she didn't know if Janie was still in the same game. "I thought it might be nice for us to do something we used to do together all the time, something that wasn't about the girls or the custody shit. Just us." She gave a hesitant smile, desperate for Janie to throw the fridge door shut and melt into her arms.

Janie set the wine bottle on the counter and looked at Solo with an expression that was impossible to read. "Hannah—"

"I know we're not okay." Solo held up her hands. "I know we have a lot to figure out. But I miss you, Janie. And not just as the mother of our children, but as *you*. As my *wife*. As the person I used to cook dinner with on Saturday nights while we drank wine and talked crap about everything and nothing."

Janie clasped her hands together but didn't move closer. "I miss that too," she whispered.

They stood there in the kitchen, two feet and a thousand miles apart, until Janie finally moved toward Solo. She wrapped her arms around Solo's waist and buried her face against Solo's shoulder.

Solo held her tight and cradled the back of Janie's head. Her chest cracked open. This was what she'd been missing when she'd pushed Janie away, this beautifully simple intimacy, and the solid comfort of holding and being held by the person who made life *life*.

Janie pulled back, wiping at her eyes. "Okay. Let's make this the best carbonara we've ever made."

"Deal."

They fell into an easy rhythm, just as they always had. Solo handled the bacon and chicken because Janie hated touching meat, and Janie chopped the garlic because Solo didn't like the weird thin skin sticking to her fingers. They moved around the kitchen in a dance they'd perfected over years of cooking together, and Solo could've dropped to her knees in gratitude. This was so much more than she'd hoped for when she'd asked Janie to help with the interviews.

Solo opened the wine and poured two generous glasses. "To..." She raised her glass. What were they toasting to?

"To showing up." Janie touched her glass to Solo's. "To not letting my mother win."

"To us," Solo said, not wanting to think about the custody of her children, at least for this perfect moment. "However that looks right now."

They drank, and the wine was crisp, cold, and perfect. Janie connected her phone to the kitchen speaker and chose their special lazy weekend playlist. The kitchen filled with the smell of bacon, garlic, and the yeasty warmth of bread heating in the oven.

"Tell me about the garage," Janie said as she stirred the pasta. "What are you working on right now?"

"I've just finished a custom job on a '67 Mustang," Solo said, motioning in the air as if manifesting the actual car. "The owner wanted it painted in a specific shade of midnight blue with pearl flecks that caught the light." She blew a breath through closed lips and shook her head slowly. "Getting that color exactly right was a challenge, but damn, my heart sang when that final coat went on perfect and smooth." The way Janie smiled made Solo feel seen, and she was giving Solo that look that meant she was genuinely interested but also quietly amused at Solo's enthusiasm. It was a look Solo loved and yet another thing she'd been missing. When had they last talked like this? Even when she and the gang were restoring the Brewster, she hadn't shared it with Janie.

"What about you?" Solo tossed the pasta with the bacon and egg mixture. "How's work? The new class-action suit you mentioned sounds crazy."

"It's a great case, and I should be excited about it. But I'm finding it hard to concentrate." Janie leaned against the counter, her gaze fixed on the floor. "Austin's been going over some of my work and covering for me when he needs to. Which has been far too often. I know he's worried."

Solo tightened her grip on the wooden spoon as she stirred. This guy again? Janie wasn't *his* to worry— She stopped the thought and forced her fingers to relax. He was Janie's friend and colleague. He had a right to worry about her in that capacity, and Solo had to stop being a jealous ass. "Is it the separation?" she asked and stared intently into the pot, not knowing what response she wanted. She didn't *want* to be the cause of distraction, but she also *did*, because it meant Janie was still thinking about her. A lot. "Or is it your mom?"

"Both. Neither. I don't know." Janie took a long drink of wine and briefly looked at Solo over the glass. "I feel like I'm not fully present anywhere. Not at work, not with the girls, not in my own life. It's like I'm watching myself from a distance, going through the motions."

Solo wanted to wrap her arms around Janie, say she understood, and that she should come home, because home was where she could be exactly who she was supposed to be. But the truth was, Solo had been so focused on the girls, on keeping up with her work at the garage, and on not drowning in her own exhaustion that she'd barely considered how Janie was managing. "I'm sorry," she said. "I should have asked more." Instead, she'd inundated Janie with news and pictures of the girls, and that obsession was what had gotten them here in the first place.

Janie gestured to the upper floor. "You've had your hands full."

"That's not an excuse." Solo set down her spoon and turned to face Janie fully. "You're important too. Your feelings matter. Your struggles matter. And I'm sorry that I've made you feel like they didn't."

Janie's eyes went shiny again, and Solo realized how starved for this kind of attention Janie must have been. How long had it been since Solo had really asked about Janie's day, her feelings, her life beyond the logistics of childcare and household management?

Too long. Way too long.

"Thank you," Janie said softly. "For seeing me. For this." She motioned to the pasta simmering on the stove then looked at Solo and bit her lip like she was about to say more but censored herself.

"I should never have stopped seeing you." Solo waited, hoping that's what Janie wanted to hear but couldn't ask for. She wanted Janie to move closer, to accept her simple statement for everything it meant but she couldn't quite say, and to kiss her.

Janie didn't move. But she also didn't run for the door, though she looked almost frozen in place. *Fuck.* Solo had pushed too hard, too fast. Rae had warned about that in their rearranged session that morning. Solo pushed away from the stove and pointed to the dining room. "I'll get the table ready," she said and rushed out of the kitchen before Janie could say anything, like she had to leave or that she'd made a mistake by agreeing to stay for dinner.

Things had been going so well, and they'd slipped back into motion as if they'd never been apart. And now Solo had fucked it up. Again. Maybe she didn't deserve Janie, or the triplets, or any kind of happiness. This was all too hard. She glanced at the empty, glass-fronted cabinet. Maybe after Janie left and Solo's dad came home, she'd walk to the liquor store and take refuge in some much-needed obliteration.

Chapter Sixteen

Janie stood in the kitchen doorway, watching Hannah move around the dining room, setting the table with a care that made her chest ache. Hannah pulled out the good dishes, the ones they'd gotten as a wedding gift and barely used since the triplets were born. She lit candles and put out cloth napkins instead of the paper towels they usually grabbed in a hurry to clean up the kids' mess.

I should've never stopped seeing you.

The words echoed in Janie's head, mixing with Maria's advice from yesterday: *When you have a quiet moment, tell her the truth. All of it.*

Janie had promised. But the evening had gotten away from her as she eased into being together again. The joy of choosing Carmen, the interactions with Hannah's father, and the simple domesticity of cooking dinner side by side had enveloped her in their family blanket as if she'd never left. When Janie had finally opened her mouth to confess, the words had stuck in her throat like glass, and in the gap, Solo had said the words Janie had longed to hear for months.

And now here they were, about to sit down to the beautiful dinner they'd created together, and Janie was about to destroy it all. Or lay the foundations for a new beginning. She smiled, acknowledging Maria's optimism was beginning to infiltrate her mindset.

Hannah came back into the kitchen. "You okay?"

"Yeah. Just..." Janie forced a smile. "I'm admiring your handiwork. It looks beautiful."

Hannah's answering smile was tentative and hopeful. "I

wanted it to be special."

The guilt fell in on Janie like the ceiling collapsing on her head. "Let me help you bring the food in," she said, turning back to the stove before Hannah could see her smile crack.

Hannah carried the food and wine to the dining room. Janie grabbed the focaccia bread, and the rosemary and garlicky scent floated upward, reminding her of all the nights they'd shared this exact meal, talking about their dreams and hopes, as close as two people could be.

Hannah poured them both more wine and seemed to have to stop herself from drinking it down in one swallow. Over the rim of the glass, Janie recognized the flash of panic in her expression. Where had that come from? Was she pulling back after exposing her vulnerability? That wouldn't surprise Janie, since she'd said nothing and offered only a blank gaze in return. Everything was moving so fast, like they could slip back into each other's lives tomorrow and not skip a beat. But that wouldn't solve anything. They still had their core intimacy issue to address, and bigger than that, Janie had to confess her neglect. Hannah might not be so quick to want her back in their lives once she'd heard the truth of it. "Is everything all right?" She flicked her gaze to Hannah's glass.

Hannah blinked and sighed deeply. "I guess I still can't fool you." She gave a half smile. "I'm worried I'm going too fast. I'm so grateful that you're here, and I got carried away. Will you stay if I dial it back?"

Janie swallowed against more guilt pressing on her throat. Her behavior was making her wife paranoid. She picked up her fork and speared a chunk of chicken. "I'm staying," she said. *At least until I confess, and you kick me out.*

"This is really incredible," Hannah said after her first bite of the carbonara. "We should cook together more often."

"We should do a lot of things more often," Janie said, without thinking.

Hannah set down her fork, her dark eyes searching Janie's

face. "Like what?"

Like be honest. Like trust each other with the hard stuff. Janie could almost see Maria sitting opposite her, giving her an encouraging smile. *Like not carry secrets that are eating us alive.* "Like this," Janie said instead, gesturing around the dining room. "Having dinner. Talking. Being together without it being about logistics or the girls."

"I'd like that." Hannah reached across the table, palm up.

Janie looked at Hannah's hand, took comfort in the sight of all those familiar calluses from years of physical labor, and in the strength of those fingers that had held her through so much, including the birth of their three children. This might be the last time Hannah extended this grace. Janie took it and entwined their fingers briefly before returning to her plate.

They ate in silence for a few moments, the clink of silverware against china the only sound. Janie's mind consumed itself with the fear of voicing the truth. Hannah talked more about her upcoming paint projects, though Janie couldn't tell whether she was filling the space out of nervousness or because talking about her work instead of their relationship was safe. Whatever it was, Janie was grateful for it. She watched Hannah's hands move as she talked and that familiar pull of attraction, love, and longing tugged for her attention. This was the Hannah she'd fallen in love with. Passionate, creative, and fully present when talking about something she cared about, this was the wife she'd missed over the past months as Hannah's sole passion had become their children.

The conversation returned to an easier flow, moving from work to lighter topics. Hannah told Janie a funny story about yet another of Woody's latest flings and how it had ended, and then she talked about Lori's dad wanting RB to join him in New York for a few months to consult on his veterans' project.

They finished dinner and cleared the plates together, moving in that familiar rhythm once more. Hannah brought out coffee and the pastries her dad had picked up from the bakery.

"Living room?" Hannah asked, and Janie nodded.

They settled on the couch, closer than they'd sat in months. They weren't quite touching but were near enough that Janie could feel the heat of Hannah's body, could smell her cologne and the faint scent of paint that she could never quite wash away. "Thank you," Janie said. "For tonight. For the dinner, for the conversation, for...seeing me. I know I said it earlier, but I mean it. I've felt invisible for so long, and tonight, you made me feel seen again."

Hannah set down her coffee cup and turned to face Janie fully. "I'm sorry I made you feel that way. I got so consumed by the girls and trying to be a perfect mother that I forgot how to be a wife."

"We both got lost," Janie said quietly. "I don't think either of us meant for it to happen. It just...did."

"But we can find our way back," Hannah said. "Can't we?"

Janie's chest tightened at the uncertainty in Hannah's voice. This was the moment. This was when she needed to tell the truth, when she needed to trust that Hannah meant what she'd been saying all evening about seeing her, about working together, about finding their way back.

"Hannah," Janie said, then faltered. Her hands shook, and coffee sloshed to the edges of her cup.

Hannah took it from her and set it on the side table, then captured both of Janie's hands in hers. "Hey. What is it? What's wrong?"

"There's something I need to tell you," Janie whispered.

Hannah's expression shifted. Her concern gave way to a flickering of fear, but there was also something solid and steady in her gaze.

"Okay," Hannah said. "I'm listening."

Janie tried to speak, but the words wouldn't come. She'd rehearsed this most of the previous night in her depressing apartment. But now, faced with actually saying it out loud, her throat closed up.

"Whatever it is," Hannah said gently, "we can handle it. Together. I promise to be here for you."

Janie closed her eyes and tried to force back her tears. "You might want to rescind that promise," she whispered, "when you hear what I did."

"Janie." Hannah placed her finger under Janie's chin and tipped her face gently. "Look at me."

Janie forced herself to open her eyes.

"Whatever you're carrying," Hannah said, "whatever you haven't told me, I need you to trust me with it. Trust that I can handle it."

Janie took a shaky breath. Then another. Hannah waited, patient and present and solid in a way that made Janie want to both run away and stay forever. "It was the Saturday of the memorial for Rosie's mom," she finally said, her voice barely audible.

Hannah nodded and didn't say anything. No doubt she'd remember the two-day argument they'd had about Hannah attending it alone.

"I was so tired," Janie said, the words starting to come faster now. "We'd been up until the early hours of the morning, arguing. And I'd had a month of late nights dealing with that nightmare IP case. You left early for the memorial, and the girls were fussy, and I just..." Her voice broke.

Hannah squeezed her hands but still didn't speak.

"I got them breakfast and then tried to play with them, but I was barely functioning. I put one of their favorite movies on, and I sat down on the couch. Just for a minute. Just to rest my eyes." She gave up trying to fight the tears, and the hot burn of her guilt tracked down her face. "But I fell asleep. I completely fell asleep, Han. With three eighteen-month-olds running around."

"Okay." Hannah traced slow, small circles on Janie's hand. "What happened?"

"I don't know how long I was out. Maybe twenty minutes. Maybe longer. When I woke up, it was because Tia was pulling on my arm, and she looked scared. And I realized…" Janie clutched her chest, sinking deeper into her panic as she relived the day. "I realized Chloe wasn't in the room."

Hannah's grip on Janie's hands tightened, but her expression remained steady and focused.

"I checked everywhere. The kitchen, the playroom, their bedroom. And then I heard something in the girls' bathroom, the one we'd been meaning to finish childproofing but hadn't gotten to yet." Janie's chest constricted, pressing against her lungs and making it almost impossible to get the next words out. "The cabinet under the sink was open. And Chloe was sitting on the floor with a bottle of children's Tylenol. The purple kind. And there was…" She swiped at the mucus running from her nose as she began to sob. "There was purple around her mouth and on her hands. The bottle was mostly empty."

Hannah's face had gone very pale, but she didn't let go of Janie's hand.

"I tried to see how much she'd taken. Had the bottle been new or not? I couldn't remember. I tried to get her to spit it out, but whatever she'd put in her mouth was gone. And I just…I lost it. I was screaming and crying, Luna and Tia were crying because I was scaring them, and Chloe started crying because everyone else was crying."

"What did you do?" Hannah asked.

Janie blinked through her tears and tried to focus on Hannah. Her expression was still calm, but her tension pressed against Janie's soul. "I called 911, and they told me to bring her to the ER immediately. So I loaded all three girls in the car, and I drove to Northwestern. I was shaking so hard I could barely hold the steering wheel." The force of the sob that followed as she placed herself in that memory could've broken her ribs. "They took Chloe back right away, checked her blood levels, and made her drink activated charcoal. They said she hadn't ingested enough to cause liver damage, and that she'd be fine. But that I needed to be more careful about childproofing. That I was lucky this time." She wrapped her arms around herself, though she didn't deserve the comfort. She should suffer like she'd made Chloe suffer when she'd vomited from the treatment. "They reported it to CPS, obviously, and they called me that evening to say it'd been screened out, and they wouldn't be pursuing the case. They said accidents happen."

Hannah was very still, her face unreadable.

"And then you came home," Janie whispered. "Gabe had texted me to say you'd left the memorial, but you didn't get back for another five or six hours. I heard the door slam, heard you stumble upstairs and trip on the landing. I cracked my door open to make sure you were okay, and you tried to get in the room." She shook her head. "You were so drunk. You reeked of alcohol like someone'd smashed a bottle of bourbon over your head."

Hannah rubbed the top of her head and glanced away. "Someone did," she said. "I was looking for a fight, and I got one."

Janie bit her lip and held back her judgment. That was the kind of behavior her mother had said was an issue. "I closed the door on you. I wouldn't have told you anyway, even if you'd been sober. I was too caught up in my own shame. I failed them. I fell asleep and Chloe could've died."

Hannah looked at her as if all the puzzle pieces had fallen into place. "That's why you left."

"I woke up that morning and couldn't look at myself in the mirror. I went into the children's room, but I couldn't look at Chloe without seeing that purple around her mouth. And I definitely couldn't have faced you. The girls are your life." Janie dropped her arms and stared at the floor. "I *had* to leave. You don't come back from something like that. You don't even let it happen if you're a good mother. I'm unfit, Han. My mother's right: I'm not capable of taking care of my own children."

"Stop." Hannah's voice was sharp enough that Janie's head snapped up. "Stop right there. You're not *unfit*. You made a mistake. A human, understandable, could-happen-to-anyone mistake."

Janie narrowed her eyes. It looked like Hannah and sounded like Hannah, but there was no way she could just forgive Janie for what she'd done. Where was the anger and rage? "But it didn't happen to anyone," she said. "It happened to me, so it happened to *your* children. *I'm* the one who fell asleep. I'm the one who abdicated my parental duties. I'm the one—"

"You're the one who was fucking exhausted," Hannah said. "You're the one who was trying to do everything for three months: work full time, handle most of the childcare because I've been getting the garage up and running, manage our household, be a perfect mother and wife and professional. You're the one who was drowning, and I didn't see it. *I'm* the one who didn't throw out the life preserver."

Hannah pulled Janie into her arms, and she didn't resist. She collapsed against Hannah's chest, sobbing. But safe.

"I'm so sorry," Hannah murmured into Janie's hair. "I'm so sorry I didn't see how much you were struggling. I failed you so completely."

"You didn't—"

"I did." Hannah pulled back just enough to look into Janie's eyes. "You needed me that night, and I wasn't there for you. I should've asked more questions, made space for you to talk to me. But I was too obsessed with the triplets and the garage."

Janie stared into Hannah's eyes, searching for the judgment and the rebuke, but all she saw was acceptance and love. She couldn't put her feelings into words. She could only cry while Hannah held her and rocked her gently.

"Every parent has these moments," Hannah said after a while. "You know what happened this week? I was at the store with the girls. I turned my back for literally two seconds to grab pasta from the shelf, and when I turned around, Tia had somehow climbed halfway out of the cart. She was dangling, about to fall headfirst onto the floor. I caught her, but if I'd been one second slower, she could've slipped out and cracked her skull open."

Janie hiccupped and buried herself deeper into Hannah's

embrace. Was Hannah making that up just to make Janie feel better? Or was it true and all parents had near-misses with their children? Was her guilt universal?

"And last week," Hannah said, "I was so exhausted after a long day that I almost ran a red light with our girls in the car. All parents have those moments, where we're exhausted, and overwhelmed, and something could go wrong. That doesn't make you unfit. It makes you human."

"But I fell asleep—"

"You were *exhausted*. You'd been running on empty for months. And yeah, Chloe got into something she shouldn't have. But you woke up, realized what happened, and got her help immediately. That's what a good parent does. A bad parent wouldn't have called 911 or have worried about it at all. They wouldn't have carried the guilt and separated themselves from their children for fear of hurting them."

Janie wanted to believe Hannah's words, but the shame was so deeply embedded it had infiltrated her DNA.

"Why are you telling me this tonight?" Hannah asked gently. "Is it because of your mom? And what David said?"

Janie had almost forgotten the second part of the nightmare. "Partly. I know that the investigators will get the hospital record somehow, no matter how confidential it's supposed to be. And she'll use it." She blinked away the unwanted image of their girls being dragged away by her mother. They probably wouldn't even allow visitation. "But I've been talking to Maria, a new friend," she said and gave a hesitant smile. Her relationship with Maria was the only good thing to have come from this whole tribulation. "She made me see that keeping this secret wasn't good for any of us."

"Maria?" Hannah asked.

Janie recognized that tone and sat up from Hannah's embrace slightly. "Don't be like that. She's..." She pondered an analogy that would resonate with Hannah. "She's like my Yoda, all wise and knowing. And about a hundred years old," she added for a little levity and to ease Hannah's jealousy.

"That's the kind of friend I can get on board with," Hannah said and laughed lightly. "But I'll fight your fucking mother with every breath in my body."

"She can't take them," Janie said, fresh panic rising in her chest. "If she does, it'll be my fault. If I hadn't fallen asleep, if I had been more careful, if I was just a better—"

"Stop." Hannah cupped Janie's face in her hands, forcing Janie to look at her. "Your mother is not taking our children. We're not going to let that happen. Do you understand me? We're going to fight this, and we're going to win."

"But the ER records—"

"Show that you responded appropriately to an *accident*. That's what a judge will see, right? An exhausted parent, a moment of inattention, a child who got into something she shouldn't have, and a mother who immediately got her medical care. There's no neglect there. Or abuse. Making mistakes is just part of being a parent."

"You don't know that. What if the judge—"

"Then we'll have documentation showing everything we've done since. Carmen. My dad helping. Therapy. Better childproofing. All our friends vouching for us. We'll show that we took this seriously and made changes. That's what responsible parents do." Hannah thumbed the tears from Janie's cheeks. "But more importantly, we're going to do this together. Not you alone, carrying all this guilt and fear. Us. As partners. As a team."

Janie wanted to believe it. God, she wanted to believe it so much. "I'm so sorry I didn't tell you right away," she whispered. "But I was so ashamed, and I was so scared you'd look at me differently. That you'd see me the way I see myself, as someone who failed our children."

"I don't see you that way," Hannah said and inclined her head slightly. "I see someone who was drowning and didn't know how to ask for help. I see someone who made a very human mistake and has been punishing herself for it. I see my wife, who I love, who I've failed, and who I want to support through this."

The word "wife" buzzed through Janie like an electric shock. It was too presumptuous, too much like claiming something that was broken. "I thought you'd hate me."

"I could never hate you." Hannah pulled Janie back against her chest and stroked her hair. "I love you. I've always loved you. Even when we were apart, even when I was hurt and confused, I loved you. And nothing you tell me could change that."

They sat like that for a long time, Janie crying while Hannah held her, murmuring reassurances and being present in a way she hadn't been for so many months. Eventually, Janie's tears slowed, then stopped, leaving her exhausted and wrung out but somehow lighter.

"We need to tell David," Hannah said. "First thing tomorrow before your mother's lawyers blindside him with it."

"I know. Maria said the same thing."

"Smart woman, that Maria. When do I get to meet her?" Hannah pressed a kiss to the top of Janie's head. "Are you okay? I know that was...a lot."

Janie pulled back to look at Hannah. Really look at her. There was no judgment there, no disappointment, no hidden anger. Just love, concern, and determination. But she still couldn't quite believe it. "I thought you'd think I was unfit. I thought you'd agree with my mother."

"Never." Hannah wrinkled her nose. "You're an incredible mother, Janie. You're patient, and creative, and loving. Our girls adore you. And yeah, you made a mistake, but that one moment doesn't define you. It doesn't erase everything else you are."

"I don't know how to stop feeling like I don't deserve them," Janie said.

"Then let me help you remember that you do, and that you're the one who had the strength to build this family from the start." Hannah kissed Janie's forehead softly. "Let me show you. Every day. Until you believe it."

Something cracked in her chest, not breaking, but opening,

as if her heart wanted the light to get into the dark place Janie had created and sealed shut for too long.

"Do you want to stay tonight? Not with me. I've moved into the guest bedroom. But you could stay in the master, just to be close."

Janie's heart raced. Part of her wanted more than that. She wanted Hannah to invite her into her arms, into her bed. But she didn't want to move too fast either, and right now, she was caught up in the intense vulnerability of her relief. Anything they did tonight would be ill-conceived. They'd been building toward this for days, but it still felt momentous. "Are you sure?"

"I'm sure."

"Okay. But for now, can you just hold me like this, right here?"

Hannah squeezed her a little tighter. "Of course. I want you to know you're not alone in this anymore. I'm going to be better for you, I promise."

"Thank you," Janie whispered.

"For what?"

"For not hating me. For...still wanting me."

"Always." Hannah's breath was warm against Janie's neck. "I'll always want you. Even when things are hard. Maybe especially when things are hard. Thank you for letting me be here for you now when I haven't been for so long."

Janie laced her fingers through Hannah's, and for the first time in months, it was like she could breathe. The secret was out. The worst had been said. And Hannah was still here, still holding her, still choosing her.

"We're going to be okay," Hannah murmured. "All of us. We're going to fight this and win, and we're going to be stronger than we were before. I promise I'll never stop seeing you again."

Janie closed her eyes and let herself believe it.

They were going to be okay.

Together.

Chapter Seventeen

Solo had yet to become comfortable with visiting Rae's office. She'd much preferred the couple of Zoom sessions they'd had. But sitting in the waiting room with Janie beside her grounded her. They were actually on the same team for the first time in forever.

Janie's legs bounced, and she clasped her hands tight in her lap as she sat upright in the chair like she was waiting for a judge to pass sentence. Solo covered Janie's hands with her own, stilling the anxious movement. "It's going to be okay," she said quietly, not wanting the far-too-cool receptionist to overhear.

"I know. I just…" Janie took a shaky breath. "I haven't been here with you since I left. What if we can't—"

"We can." Solo squeezed her hands. "We're already doing it. Last night proved that."

Last night. Janie's confession, the tears, the relief of finally having everything out in the open: God, she was glad she'd asked Janie to come over. If she hadn't, how much longer would Janie have kept her secret? And at what cost? Most likely the custody of their children.

Solo had held Janie until she fell asleep on the couch, then gently woken her when it had gotten late. Janie had taken the master, and despite her desperation to join her, Solo had gone to the guest bedroom. She'd been sleeping there for a while now, breathing in the fading scent of Fenty mixed with Janie's on the pillowcases she hadn't washed. The last thing she wanted to do was push and have Janie think Solo wasn't respecting her vulnerability.

Solo didn't miss the relief on Janie's face when she stopped at the guest room. Clearly, she needed space to process everything, to believe that Solo really had meant it when she said Janie's confession didn't change how she felt. She had lain awake for hours, staring at the ceiling, thinking about everything Janie had told her. The accident. The guilt. The crushing weight of shame that had driven Janie from their home. Why *hadn't* she just told Solo about it? She wasn't just saying that all parents made mistakes just to make Janie feel better. And Chloe hadn't even been a little bit sick.

Underneath it all, a small, complicated knot of anger resided in her gut, and Solo wasn't quite sure what to do with it. But that was why they were here. Analyzing her feelings had never been her top priority, but she was smart enough to realize her marriage depended on her doing exactly that now. Like it or not.

The door to Rae's office opened, and Rae appeared with her usual calm smile. "Hannah. Janie. Come on in."

They got up and headed into the space that was decorated to promote comfort and safety, but sometimes it felt anything but.

"It's good to see you together," Rae said.

Solo closed the door behind them and hovered, waiting for Janie to choose her seat without pressuring her. Solo could've whooped and jumped in the air when Janie sat on the three-seater sofa they'd shared in their other joint sessions. "Is it okay to join you?" She didn't drop down beside her, wanting to respect her boundaries. Solo was tentatively hopeful about their reconciliation, but she remembered Rae saying that she should no longer expect to be welcome in Janie's personal space.

Janie gave her a small smile. "Of course."

She could tell from Janie's expression that she was both amused and impressed, and Solo chalked up the wife point.

"How have things been for you both?"

Solo glanced at Janie with a silent question: *Do you want to start, or should I?*

"We had a breakthrough last night." Janie touched Solo's

thigh all too briefly. "I told Hannah about...about what happened. The real reason I left."

Rae inclined her head. "Which was?"

Janie briefly explained the ER incident, all the while twisting her hands in her lap. "I finally told her everything."

"And how did that feel?" Rae asked.

"Terrifying. But necessary. It lifted the weight of shame enough so that I could finally breathe." Janie looked at Solo then back to Rae. "She didn't react the way I thought she would."

Solo screwed up her toes in her boots and tried not to react visibly. When had she become so unapproachable?

Rae nodded slowly. "How did you think she would react?"

"I expected her to blow up." Janie sighed deeply. "The girls are everything to her, and I thought she'd kick me out of the house. I expected her to take my mother's side and realize that I was right: I'm unfit to be a parent, and I'm a danger to our children." Her voice cracked slightly, and she placed her hand over Solo's. "But she didn't. She said I was human, and that all parents make mistakes."

Solo closed her eyes against the vivid memory of her near-miss at the grocery store just days ago. "Because it's true. Last Tuesday, I was at Jewel-Osco with all three girls. I turned around for literally two seconds to grab something off the shelf, and when I turned back, Tia was climbing over the side of the cart and was halfway out of it. She was going to fall headfirst onto the concrete floor."

Rae leaned forward slightly. "And what happened?"

"I caught her. My heart was pounding so hard I thought I was going to have a heart attack right there in the pasta aisle. And I thought—" Solo's throat tightened. "If I'd been one second slower, if I'd been looking at my phone or distracted by something else, my daughter would've cracked her skull open. Because I wasn't paying attention for *two seconds*."

"Did you tell anyone about it?" Rae asked.

"Not until last night, no. I just put Tia back in the cart, finished shopping, and went home. My dad asked if everything went okay, and I said I was fine." Solo looked at Rae. "Because that's what we do, right? We have near-misses and moments of terror, and then we just...move on and pretend they didn't happen. Act like we've got everything under control."

"Why do you think that is?"

Solo had been thinking about that since last night, lying awake in her bed while Janie slept down the hall. "Because dealing with emotions is harder than dealing with logistics. If I opened that door and told my dad how terrified I was, then I might have to face how overwhelmed I was. How much I've been struggling without Janie, and how badly I've failed as a partner."

"You haven't failed," Janie said quietly.

"I have though." Solo turned to look at Janie. "I made you invisible. I was so consumed by trying to be a perfect mother that I forgot to be your wife. And when you needed me most, when you'd just had the most terrifying experience of your parenting life, you couldn't talk to me."

Janie squeezed Solo's hand. "But it sounds like you were scared too."

"Being scared isn't an excuse," Solo said and took Janie's hand in hers when Janie pulled back slightly. "You were the one who found Chloe. You had to rush her to the ER and then sit there terrified, worried that our daughter might have been poisoned. And instead of calling me to come support you through that, you had to go through it alone, because I'd made you think you couldn't come to me. I'd made you think that I'd get angry and judge you...instead of sharing your fear and reassuring you that it'd be okay."

Rae let the silence sit for a moment. "Hannah, I'm hearing a lot of self-criticism. Is there anything else underneath that? Any other feelings about what happened?"

Solo hesitated. This was the part she'd been avoiding thinking about directly. This was where the small, complicated knot of anger that she wasn't sure she had a right to feel came into it.

"This is a safe space, Hannah." Rae looked at both of them in turn. "You both have to feel safe enough to share your deepest feelings with each other so that your mutual understanding can grow."

Janie touched Solo's thigh again, for longer this time. "Rae's right, Han. I can't go back to how it was before, so we have to be honest with each other, even if it's hard, and even if it hurts."

Solo tugged on her ear and rolled her neck. "Are you sure?" She didn't want to fuck this whole thing up when it seemed like they might be making progress.

Janie rubbed Solo's thigh and nodded. "I'm sure. Let's do this right."

"Okay," Solo said. "I'm a little angry. But not about the incident itself. I meant what I said about being human and making mistakes. But..." Damn her inability to find the right words. Why was she so bad at this? "I guess I'm angry about being left in the dark." She swallowed hard and met Janie's questioning gaze. "You left and let me believe it was all my fault. I thought that I was such a terrible wife you couldn't stand to be around me anymore. We'd been fighting so much, and I figured I pushed you too far, in so many ways."

Janie's face crumpled. "Han—"

Solo held up her hand. "Wait, let me finish. I'm not saying this to hurt you. I'm just doing what Rae asked us to do, and I'm trying to be open and honest. This whole time, I thought I'd driven you away. I beat myself up about it every single day. I tried to figure out what was so broken in me that my wife would rather live in a depressing apartment than come home."

Tears streamed down Janie's face, and Solo wanted to shut the hell up and just hold her. She wanted to pick her up and carry her out of the office, forget everything that had happened and start all over again. Clean slate. But that'd just be burying their heads in the sand, and eventually, they'd have to come up for air. And that air would be even more toxic. Solo owed it to herself, to Janie, and to their girls to lay everything out now. If they were going to start again, they had to do it right.

"Don't censor your feelings, Hannah," Rae said. "Janie needs to hear this, and you need to voice it."

Solo clenched her jaw and forced herself to look at Janie instead of Rae, or out the window, or at the boring books on the many wooden shelves. "And it turns out, the whole time, you were carrying this huge secret. This thing had less to do with me being a bad wife and everything to do with your own guilt and shame. And I'm angry that you didn't trust me with it sooner. That you let me believe I was the problem instead of being honest about what you were going through."

"I'm sorry," Janie whispered. "I'm so sorry."

"I know you are. And I'm not holding onto this anger," Solo said, surprising herself. "I'm just acknowledging it exists." She motioned to Rae. "Because Rae keeps telling me I need to be honest about my feelings instead of pushing them down and pretending everything's fine."

"That's exactly right," Rae said. "Thank you for sharing all that. It takes courage to acknowledge complicated feelings, especially when they might hurt someone we love." She looked at Janie. "How does it feel to hear Hannah express her anger this way?"

Janie wiped at her face with shaking hands. "It destroys me that she thought everything was her fault, and that she blamed herself for me leaving when the truth was..."

Janie's body heaved with the power of her sobs, and Solo drew her into her arms. She held her there until Janie's tears soaked her tee, and she'd calmed enough to straighten herself up. She took a tissue and wiped her makeup-streaked cheeks.

"The truth was I left because I couldn't face what I'd done. Because I was drowning in guilt and shame, and I didn't know how to ask for help. I was so...so lost. So unable to connect to the world around me. And then Chloe..." Janie rubbed at her forehead. "Hannah suffered because of my cowardice."

"Is that what you think it was?" Rae asked gently. "Cowardice?"

"What else would you call it? I ran away instead of facing my problems. I hid the truth instead of being honest. I let my wife take on all the blame when—"

"When you were struggling with untreated postpartum depression," Rae said.

The words hung in the air like a small explosion.

Janie went very still and deep frown lines creased her forehead. "What?"

"Janie, I was concerned about this in the first couple of sessions, but I wasn't certain of it. After what you've said today though, I think we need to name it explicitly. What you've been experiencing—the overwhelming guilt, the inability to forgive yourself for a minor mistake, the intrusive thoughts about being an unfit mother, the isolation, the feeling of being disconnected, the belief that your family would be better off without you—these are all classic symptoms of postpartum depression."

"Doesn't that happen right after birth?" Janie asked. "The girls are eighteen months old."

"It can actually manifest anytime within the first year, and in some cases even later, especially under conditions of chronic stress and sleep deprivation. You may have been dealing with it for longer than you're even aware," Rae said, her tone gentle and quiet. "And your symptoms were exacerbated by the traumatic incident with Chloe. All of that created a perfect storm of guilt and shame that your depression latched onto."

The floor dropped out from under Solo as the realization hit. "How did I not see it?"

"Because you were struggling with your own adjustment to parenthood," Rae said. "Postpartum depression often looks like exhaustion and normal parenting stress from the outside. And Janie obviously got very good at hiding it."

Janie shook her head. "I'm not depressed. I'm just... I'm a bad mother, and I failed my children."

"No," Rae said firmly. "You're a mother with postpartum depression who experienced a traumatic incident, and you didn't have the support structure to process it healthily because you were already in distress by the time it happened. There's a significant difference."

Solo took Janie's hand, and Janie gripped it like it was a lifeline. She almost cracked a joke about not breaking her bones, but it wasn't the time. A heavy ball settled in her gut as she realized she couldn't really remember the last time they'd joked together.

"I thought you might benefit from medication and some more intensive therapy," Rae said, "but I had to be certain, and I needed you to be ready to hear it. The guilt and shame you're experiencing, Janie, isn't proportional to what actually happened. Yes, Chloe got into a cabinet she shouldn't have. Yes, it was scary. But your reaction to it: the crushing guilt, the belief that you're unfit, the inability to forgive yourself is the depression talking, not reality."

"But my mother—"

"Your mother is obviously a manipulative narcissist who found your vulnerable spot and is trying to exploit it," Rae said.

The abrupt way Rae clasped her hands together hinted at a degree of anger toward Janie's mother, and Solo wanted to hug her for that.

Rae separated her hands and stretched out her fingers, as if conscious of showing her own feelings. "She's using your depression-fueled guilt against you. That's what abusers do."

The surge of protective anger toward Janie's mother was so fierce it took Solo's breath away. "So what do we do? How do we help Janie?"

"First, Janie needs to see a psychiatrist about medication options." Rae looked at Janie. "Depression isn't weakness, and it isn't something you can just power through with positive thinking. It's a medical condition that responds to treatment. Are you willing to try that?"

"Yes," Janie said, in between small, gasping sobs.

Rae waited until Janie finished wiping away her tears. "Second, we need to address the trauma of the incident itself.

What happened with Chloe was terrifying, and you never properly processed it. EMDR or trauma-focused therapy might be helpful there."

"Okay." Janie nodded slowly then glanced at Solo.

The fear in her eyes wrenched Solo's heart from her chest, and she inched closer. "Is it okay to hold you?"

Janie's sigh seemed to take all the breath from her lungs. "Please."

Solo wrapped her arm around Janie's shoulders and held her tight. "I've got you," she said and hoped to God that Janie would accept that she really meant it.

"And third," Rae looked between them, "you two need to rebuild your relationship. Not pick up where you were before Janie left but actually start fresh. You have to get to know each other again and remember why you fell in love in the first place."

"That's mostly on me," Solo said. "I'm the one who stopped seeing my wife." She kissed the top of Janie's head. "But last night was amazing. With the nanny interviews, and making dinner together, and talking honestly."

"That's a good start," Rae said. "But I want to give you some structured homework to do."

Solo couldn't stop the disgruntled sigh from escaping. The active listening they'd done a few weeks ago hadn't seemed to help, but then maybe she wasn't invested enough at that point.

Rae raised her eyebrows, tilted her head, and focused her eyes on Solo. "I'm going to give you some intentional exercises that will help you reconnect, but you *both* have to be engaged."

"I'm sorry." Solo held up her hands. "I'm here for it all. I'll do whatever I need to do," she whispered into Janie's hair.

Rae pulled out a notepad and started writing. "First, I want you both to make a list of ten things you love about the other person. Not 'she's a good mother' or 'she works hard,' but the specific things, like the small stuff that made you fall in love. I'm talking about quirks or habits, or moments you remember really vividly."

Solo nodded, already thinking about her list. The way Janie bit her lip when she was concentrating. The sound of her laugh when something genuinely surprised her.

"Second, I want you to go on actual dates," Rae said. "And I don't mean dinner at home after the kids are asleep. I want you to get dressed up and go out. Hold hands and pretend you're courting each other for the first time." She looked at Solo. "I know your initial reaction might be that it's logistically too complicated to achieve with three toddlers—"

"We have Carmen now," Solo said quickly. "And my dad. We can make it work." When Janie looked up into her eyes, Solo pressed her lips to Janie's forehead. "I'll make it work, I promise."

"Good," Rae said.

Her wide smile was genuine and encouraging, and there was something about it and the way she seemed to really be in their corner that reinforced Solo's belief that they could do this. That *she* could do this and be a great wife again without sacrificing her love for their girls.

"I'd like you to go on one date per week, minimum, to somewhere you've never been together before. A new restaurant, a museum you've never visited, or a gig to see a band you've never heard of. The point is to create new memories, not just reminisce about how good the old ones are."

"Okay. We can do that, right?" Janie eased out of Solo's embrace and touched her cheek gently.

"We can." Solo took Janie's hand and kissed her fingers. "And I can't wait."

"Third, I want you to have a weekly check-in with each other. Spend fifteen minutes where you each share something you're grateful for about the other person, something that's been hard that week, and something you need from each other going forward. This isn't about problem-solving or fixing something you think is broken." Rae looked hard at them both. "This is just about listening and acknowledging what's going on in each other's lives."

"Got it," Solo said.

"And finally," Rae set down her pen and looked at them seriously, "I want you both to practice radical honesty. You can't hide your feelings to protect each other. No more suffering in silence. If something's hard, you say it's hard. If you're angry, or scared, or overwhelmed, you name it. You can't rebuild trust without honesty, and you can't have intimacy without vulnerability."

Solo thought about her admission that she was a little angry about Janie keeping her secret. It'd been hard to say, but Janie hadn't crumbled. She hadn't run. Instead, she'd listened, and apologized, and owned her part in it. Solo became increasingly sure they could do this.

"There's one more thing," Rae said, looking at Janie. "You're going to need to tell the court about your postpartum depression and show that you're getting treatment."

Janie's face went as pale as Rae's office walls. "Won't that work against us?"

Rae shook her head. "No, it will make you look like a responsible parent who recognized she was struggling and sought help. The alternative is your mother's lawyer finding out you've been dealing with untreated mental health issues and using that to paint you as unstable. Getting help is a strength, not a weakness. And any good judge will see it that way."

Solo rubbed hard at her forehead and tugged her ear. "How would they find out? Isn't everything we talk about here confidential?"

"Of course it is," Rae said. "But Janie's mother has money. And that can buy unscrupulous people who are happy to do even more unscrupulous things, like searching through your trash for the box your new medication comes in, for example."

Solo huffed and squeezed Janie's hand. Maybe they should install cameras around the house's exterior. "We'll tell David tomorrow and get ahead of it."

Janie nodded, looking shell-shocked.

Rae went over to her desk. "I'm calling Dr. Vale, a psychiatrist colleague. She often keeps a little time each day for emergency appointments. Can you clear some time to do this today?"

"Yes."

Solo smiled at the firm intention clear in Janie's voice. "I'll call Gabe and—"

"No," Janie said. "I need to do this part on my own."

"But I want to support you with all of this." Solo frowned and looked over to Rae for backup." Surely this is something we should do together?"

Rae lowered the phone from her ear. "That's Janie's call, Hannah."

Solo snapped her gaze back to Janie. One of the reasons they were here now was her inattention to Janie's needs. She couldn't tread the same path, or this was all for nothing. "Okay. If that's what you want."

Janie squeezed Solo's thigh and gave her a small smile. "It's what I want *and* need."

After Rae had made the appointment for Janie, they scheduled more frequent therapy sessions and coordinated their weekly check-ins and dates. By the time they left Rae's office, Solo's head was spinning with information, plans, and feelings.

They walked to their cars in silence, parked side by side in the lot. When they reached Janie's car, Solo stopped her before she could get in. "Hey," she said. "Thank you for being willing to hear that I was angry. I know that couldn't have been easy."

"You had every right to feel that way." Janie rubbed at some dirt on the paintwork and didn't look at Solo. "You still do."

"I'm serious that I'm not holding onto it. I'm just trying to do this therapy thing right and do what Rae's telling me to do." Solo tucked a strand of Janie's hair behind her ear. "You're really okay about doing all of this? All of the homework, the dating, the honesty."

"It's about our future and what we want from it. I want this,

Han. I want us. And I'm willing to do the work to get there."

"Me too." Solo kissed Janie's forehead. "Come over tonight? We can work on the ten things we love about each other."

Janie's answering smile lit a fire under Solo's butt. God damn, she'd missed her beautiful, unguarded smile. *That* was definitely one thing for the list.

"I'd like that," Janie said.

Solo stuffed her hands in her pockets, not wanting to leave. "And call if you need me after you've been to the doc, okay?"

"I will."

"And Janie?" Solo waited until Janie met her eyes. "Everything you've been going through... I'm glad Rae named it. I'm glad we can treat it."

"I'm scared." Janie grasped Solo's shirt. "What if medication doesn't help? What if I stay like this?"

"We'll figure it out together. But Rae seems convinced it's going to help more than you think, and she's the expert." Solo looked down at Janie's hand scrunching her tee. She pulled her hands from her pockets and caressed Janie's soft skin, another thing for her list. "You're not a bad mom. You're a great mom with a medical condition. There's a huge difference."

Janie's eyes filled with tears again, but this time they looked more like relief than despair.

"How does seven o'clock sound?" Solo asked. "Come for dinner. We'll eat with the girls and Dad, and then after their bedtime, we can work on our lists."

"Okay." Janie let go of Solo's shirt. "I'll bring wine."

"Perfect." They stood there for another moment, Solo not quite ready to separate, and it seemed Janie shared the feeling.

Finally, Janie reached up and cupped Solo's cheek. "Thank you," she whispered. "For not giving up on me and fighting for us even when I was too broken to fight for myself."

"Always," Solo said. "I'll always fight for us." She hadn't realized the battle they were in before, but now that she did, she'd fight with every breath in her body, and then some. "Can I kiss you?"

She waited, and time seemed to slow around them until Janie nodded. Solo cupped Janie's face and pressed her lips to Janie's briefly with a soft kiss she hoped was full of the promises Solo had made.

She watched Janie drive away, then sat in her own car for a long moment, trying to make sense of everything that had happened in the session and everything that had to happen for their little family to be safe again.

Postpartum depression. It made so much sense now. Sure, Solo had exacerbated the problem with her own work schedule and issues. But their fights had been about more than that, even before the accident that had been the final straw.

Solo started her car and headed toward the garage, already looking forward to seeing Janie later. They were starting fresh and building something new from the pieces of what they'd broken.

They were going to make it. She could feel it.

And goddamn, did it feel fucking good.

Chapter Eighteen

DR. VALE'S OFFICE WAS nothing like Janie had imagined. Instead of the sterile clinical space she'd braced herself for, it was warm, with soft lighting, comfortable chairs, and a small fountain burbling peacefully in the corner. Still, Janie had clenched her hands so tight in her lap as they talked about her situation that her knuckles had gone white.

But hearing an actual doctor lay out aspects of postpartum depression so logically made it all seem so much more acceptable, and Janie clutched at her chest as the reality of what Dr. Vale was saying began to kick in. The relief crashed over her with such power that she couldn't control her reaction, and her resulting tears poured out.

Dr. Vale passed her the tissue box without comment, letting Janie cry it out. She tried to compose herself quickly. Sobbing in front of strangers had never been something she'd allowed herself to do. Her mother had drilled into her what weakness that was.

"The good news," Dr. Vale said, "is that PPD is highly treatable. A combination of therapy, which you're already doing with Rae, and medication can make a substantial difference. I'm going to prescribe you an SSRI, a selective serotonin reuptake inhibitor. It'll take a while to reach full effectiveness, but many patients start noticing improvements within the first fourteen days."

"What if it doesn't work?" Janie twisted the wet tissue in her hands. "What if I'm still like this?"

"Then we try a different medication, or adjust the dosage, or add additional support. This isn't a one-size-fits-all situation, and we'll work together to find what helps you." Dr. Vale clasped her hands together. "But Janie, I want you to understand something important: seeking treatment doesn't make you weak or unfit. It makes you a responsible parent who recognized she was struggling and took steps to get help. That's *exactly* what good mothers do."

Janie wanted to believe her. God, she wanted to believe her so badly.

They spent the final few minutes of the appointment talking about potential side effects, what to watch for, and how to take the meds. Janie had noticed Hannah had emptied their liquor cabinet, but now it looked like the wine would have to go too. Dr. Vale gave Janie her direct number and told her to call if she had any concerns.

Janie left the office, daring to believe she'd taken the first step toward accepting the diagnosis. She had a medical condition not a character flaw, and it was a condition that could be treated *if* she took the pills. She sat in her car in the parking lot for several minutes, staring at the prescription. The pharmacy was right across the street. She could fill it now and start taking it tonight, but first, she wanted to talk to someone who'd helped get her this far.

She drove to the café that had become her refuge and parked in her usual spot.

When she entered, Maria took one look at her and nodded toward the corner. "Your table is waiting," she said. "I'll bring coffee."

Janie sank into the familiar chair and waited. Maria returned a few minutes later with two coffees and a plate of conchas. She took a quick nibble, and the sweet bread was comfort in edible form.

"So," Maria said, settling across from her. "Tell me."

Janie took a long sip of the coffee that tasted a hundred times better than the java at any other café, and then she told Maria about everything that had happened since they'd last talked. Saying her diagnosis out loud made it feel a little more real. "It's good that it makes sense of everything I've been feeling, but it's terrifying too."

"How so?"

"I'm scared that the meds won't work, and that I'm too broken to come back from this."

Maria covered Janie's hand with her own. "You are not broken, mija."

"Did you suspect it could be PPD?"

"I've lived long enough to recognize when someone's guilt is bigger than what actually happened, but that can have many names. *Your* shame has teeth that don't want to let go." Maria squeezed Janie's hand and then returned to her coffee. "A friend of mine went through something similar years ago. She had twins, and about a year after they were born, she started having these intrusive and terrible thoughts about something happening to her babies, about being a terrible mother. She hid it for months because she was ashamed, and because, like you, she thought it meant she was broken."

Janie bit her bottom lip. Of course she wasn't the first mom to feel this way. Hearing about someone else's awful experience shouldn't make her feel better, and yet, it kind of did. "What happened?"

"Finally, her husband saw there was something wrong, and he made her see a doctor. She was diagnosed with PPD, just like you." Maria smiled. "The medication changed her life. She told me that it was like someone had turned down the volume on all the terrible voices in her head. She could finally hear herself think again, and she could be present with her children without the constant intrusion of guilt and fear."

Janie had so many questions, and Maria always seemed to have the answers or an anecdote, at least. But this time, Janie wasn't sure she was ready to hear those answers. She took a deep breath and thought about her family, recalled the hope in Hannah's eyes when they planned to have dinner together that night. She had to be strong. She owed Hannah and the girls that.

"Did it change her? The medication?"

"It made her more herself, not less. That's what good treatment does. It doesn't change who you are. It just removes the illness that's been dragging you down."

Janie picked at the concha on her plate. "I'm scared. What if I take it and I'm still like this? What if it proves that this is just who I am now?"

"And what if it works?" Maria asked gently. "What if, in a few weeks, you look at your daughters and feel joy instead of guilt? What if you can be present with Hannah without the constant voice telling you that you don't deserve her? What if you get yourself back?"

The possibilities sounded too enormous to hope for. "When I told Hannah everything, she didn't judge me, just like you said she wouldn't. She shared her own close calls with the girls. She said every parent makes mistakes."

Maria's eyes shone with unshed tears. "And how did that feel? Having your shame met with compassion?"

"Like I could breathe for the first time in months." Janie's heart ached at the empathy in Maria's gaze. Their connection had been so instant. Where would she have ended up if Maria hadn't jumped into her car that fateful Sunday? Her own tears were warm behind her eyes.

"That's what love does. It says you're human. You're worthy. You're not alone." Maria squeezed Janie's hand. "This is the start of your healing, mija. It is not the end of who you are, but the beginning of finding yourself again."

Janie blinked and released her hot tears. "I want to bring Hannah here to meet you. You've been such a huge part of my life this past couple of weeks, and I want her to know you and to understand what you've done for me."

Maria smiled widely. "I would love that. Bring her anytime."

"We have our first official date on Saturday," Janie said. "I'm going to suggest that we explore this neighborhood. We could end up here, if that's okay?"

"Of course it is. I'll keep your favorite table ready." Maria's expression turned more serious. "And Janie? I'm proud of you for being brave enough to get help and for trusting Hannah with your truth. Facing your demons and embarking on a healing journey takes real courage."

Janie wanted to argue that it was desperation, not courage, that had gotten her this far. But maybe that was the depression talking. Maybe Maria was right, since she usually was, and choosing to get help was the bravest thing of all.

After they'd talked some more about everyday things instead of their usual serious stuff, Janie caught sight of the time. "I'm sorry, I have to go." She grinned, feeling a little lighter than she had when she'd first sat down with Maria. "I'm going home to do our therapy homework." *Home.* Where her heart and her family were. It sounded good to her ears.

After she'd gotten up, Maria pulled her into a hug. "Remember, you're not alone in this anymore. You have Hannah, and Rae, and your medication." She gently cupped Janie's cheek. "And you have me. We're all here, ready to help you carry what is too heavy to carry alone."

Janie sank into Maria's embrace and let herself be held, let herself believe that maybe, just maybe, she was going to be okay.

***

After a few hours at the office, where she'd been slightly more focused, Janie went to the apartment to change and then drove to the house. The box of pills she'd picked up on the way to work sat in the center console, both foreboding and tempting. But she'd decided to take the first one tonight with Hannah, thinking of it as a symbol of her commitment to their family, and she wanted to share the moment.

She drew up alongside their house and cut the engine. Everything looked so normal from the outside. It was impossible to tell that she'd almost torn the foundations of their family down.

Had any of their neighbors even noticed her absence? Were they judging them? Janie pressed her palms together, closed her eyes, and took a few long, deep breaths. This wasn't the energy she wanted to take inside. She wanted normality, to help with the girls, eat together, soak in some of the comfortable domesticity she'd been missing out on while she'd...

Janie stopped herself again and exhaled loudly, focusing hard on releasing the negative energy. This evening was about moving forward.

She locked the car and headed up the path to the front door. When she took hold of the handle, a flashback of the day she'd left assailed her, when she hadn't quite been able to let go, simultaneously wanting to hold it closed so Hannah didn't emerge and convince her to stay while also struggling not to push it back open and return to the safety of her wife's arms.

The pulse in her head pounded hard, pressing against the back of her eyes, making her vision spotty and soft. She had to lean against the door to stop from sliding to the ground. *Deep breaths*. Janie glanced back at her car. No one knew she was here yet. She could turn around and leave, text and say she couldn't make it... She sucked in another burst of cool air. Rae would say this was the depression talking. Maria's friend had said the medication quieted the vociferous little bastard. Right now, all Janie could do was remember that her beautiful family was waiting for her on the other side of her fear.

She threw open the door, and the chaos was immediate and perfect. Tia and Luna ran to the door shrieking "Mommy! Mommy!" while Chloe hung back for the briefest of moments before joining in. Janie dropped to her knees and gathered all three of them into her arms, breathing in their shampoo and toddler-sweet smell, and her joy pushed her dread back a little, at least for now. "Hi, babies," she murmured. "I missed you so much."

Hannah came from the kitchen, dish towel over her shoulder, looking domestic and handsome in her jeans and shirt combo, mostly covered by an apron. Janie's heart expanded when Hannah gave her that soft, private smile that somehow conveyed *all* her love and desire. It was a smile Janie hadn't seen for a while, and seeing it now took her breath away.

"Dinner's almost ready," Hannah said. "Are you hungry?"

"Yes," she said automatically then shook her head and bit her lip. Their fresh start had to be rooted in honesty. Janie extricated herself from the girls as she stood, pressing her hand against her stomach. "I've got a cannonball in here, and it feels like it could explode into a thousand cramps and spasms. I'm a little afraid to feed it."

Hannah frowned and rushed over to Janie. "Are you okay? Do we need to get you to the hospital?"

"Who's going to the hospital?" Hannah's dad came into the hall from the living room and scooped up Tia and Luna into his arms, while Chloe clung onto Janie's leg like a limpet.

"No one," Janie said. "I'm just...nervous, I suppose."

"Come and get the girls settled at the table while I finish up dinner." Hannah took Janie's hand. "Everything's going to be great."

Janie could've wept at the comfort and safety Hannah's simple physical touch gave her, and she nodded, trusting her wife. "Okay." She unpeeled Chloe from her leg and lifted her up to follow Tom into the dining room.

By the time they'd managed to get their three wriggling worms into their seats at the table, Hannah had brought in a giant cauldron of her special homemade beef chili and all the fixings.

Janie gestured to the side dish of ground beef. "Still not converted to Hannah's idea of chili, Tom?"

He rolled his eyes. "I spent too long in Texas to think of this as chili but," he grabbed the side of meat and dumped it into his dish, "the extra beef lowers the ratio of beans to meat, so I'll grin and bear it."

Hannah picked up a cornbread muffin and waved it at him.

"You could always cook your own meals."

Tom spooned a huge helping of chili into his bowl and laughed. "Nah, not having to think about that is the second-best thing about living with you."

"What's the first?" Janie asked.

Tom nodded toward the triplets. "Those three tiny terrors." He smiled softly, and his eyes went glassy.

Janie glanced at Hannah and saw her expression was identical. Envy tugged at her heart. Their father-daughter relationship was a far cry from the one Janie had experienced. Tom had dropped his whole life instantly to come to Hannah's rescue, and he seemed more than happy in their house. She nibbled the inside of her cheek as it occurred to Janie that she didn't know what his longer-term plans were. Or was this it?

"Is that enough?"

Janie only heard Hannah's question distantly. "Sorry, what?"

Hannah held a half-full bowl aloft. "Chili. Is this enough?"

"It's perfect, thank you." Janie took it from her and pushed away the issue of Tom's living arrangements for future consideration.

They fell into easy conversation as they ate, and the girls told as elaborate stories as they could with their limited vocabulary about the park, the ducks, and the dogs they'd seen that day.

It was all so normal. So beautifully, preciously normal.

After dinner, they bathed the girls together, and then read bedtime stories side by side, their shoulders touching, taking turns with the characters. Janie loved the way Hannah immersed herself in the acting, creating wild and ridiculous voices that made the girls giggle adorably. When the triplets were finally asleep, they went back down to the living room. Tom left a note on the table saying he'd gone to the bar to watch the game with his friends. Janie had no idea *which* game, or even which sport, but it was nice that he'd already met some new people. Maybe he really was here to stay. Again, she shook that potential issue away. She and Hannah had far more pressing problems to deal with, starting with their therapy homework.

"I picked up some special notebooks from Four-Sided." Hannah retrieved a paper bag from the sideboard and brought it over to the couch. She sat beside Janie and held the package to her chest. "I spent ages trying to find the right ones," she said, then offered them to Janie.

"I didn't think about *where* we'd write our lists." Janie rubbed at her brow. "I'm failing at this already."

"No, you're not." Hannah ran her thumb over the back of Janie's hand. "We could've written on any of the fifty pads in the house, but I've been a crappy wife, and I wanted to do something special." She pushed the paper bag at Janie again. "C'mon, I'm excited about this. I want to see which one you'll choose."

Janie smiled. She hadn't seen Hannah so exuberant about anything other than their children in a while. She made a mental note that Hannah's child-like enjoyment of things should go on her list.

She reached into the bag and pulled out two journals, one covered in cute baby elephants on a safari-type background, and the other featured a flock of white doves on a stylized blue sky. Matching pens sat in loops on the paper's edge. Janie flicked through them to check the paper type, and her smile grew wider.

"That's your favorite, right?" Hannah bounced on the sofa. "You like the grid paper for neatness, right?"

Janie ran her fingers over the smooth paper and nodded. "I do." She turned the books over and flexed them in her hands. "I love soft cover more than hardback too."

Hannah wiggled her whole body, and her eyes lit up. "I remembered. That's why I went to Four-Squared. It—"

"Was the first stationery store we went into together when I needed a new pen for work." The memory jolted through her, and she chuckled. "You were so patient while I tried all the different options."

Hannah shrugged. "It had to be right."

Janie had gotten used to that particular mantra and had even come to expect it after Hannah continued to sweep Janie off her feet in the first couple of years of their relationship. When the triplets came along though, she took it to the extreme, making Janie feel like she *couldn't* get it right. The realization slammed into her, and she clutched her chest.

Hannah's eyes widened, and she scooched closer. "What's wrong?"

She was about to dismiss it, but Rae's voice in her head reminded her they had to be honest. Janie paused a second longer before she shared her thoughts.

Hannah dropped back into the couch and put her hands behind her head. "I added to the pressure, didn't I? I made your depression worse."

Janie turned sideways and tucked her legs underneath her. She traced lines on Hannah's forearm, along the muscle Janie liked to watch move and dance while they made love. The hit of desire struck her almost as hard as the recent realization. God, her emotions and hormones were going haywire. "That doesn't matter now," she said. "What matters is this, right here. I told you because I don't want to keep secrets, not because I want to make you feel bad."

Hannah tugged at her ear. "Honesty's kind of painful, isn't it?"

Janie nodded. "It can be. But it can be wonderful too. I can *honestly* say that you're my gibbon."

Hannah laughed loudly. "I remember watching that program with you in Vegas when we first met."

Janie nodded. "In between all the sex," she whispered.

"You're a bad influence." Hannah's eyes twinkled mischievously. "You're making me want to ditch this homework and spend the rest of the night making out." She looked down at the journals on the edge of the sofa. "But this is important stuff... right?"

Janie arched her eyebrow at Hannah's wavering resolve. "Right," she said and picked up the notebooks again. "And I get to choose."

Hannah's eyes sparkled for a different reason. "Yeah, and

then I can explain why I chose them."

Just for fun, Janie held one in each hand and looked between the two for way longer than was necessary, because she'd known which one she wanted from the moment she pulled them from the wrapping. When Hannah looked like she might explode if Janie didn't pick one soon, she clutched the dove book to her chest and thrust the elephants toward Hannah.

"Yes!" Hannah took it from her and held it in the air like a trophy, then she beamed a megawatt smile at Janie. "Okay, so you want to know why I bought the ones I did?" She barely waited until Janie had nodded. "I got the doves for you because they're a symbol of a new beginning, which is what we're doing. And I got this one for me because I never want to forget who you are to me ever again. I always want to remember our love and who we are together."

Janie's heart swelled against her chest, and she ran her fingers along Hannah's jawline. "That's so thoughtful. I love it." She kissed Hannah's cheek and stayed that way, so close, breathing in her scent for a moment longer before she drew away and waved her journal between them. "Homework."

Hannah swallowed hard enough for Janie to hear, and she had to blink a few times before her eyes lost their drowsy desire. "Homework," she said and sighed deeply.

Janie shifted to the other end of the couch and began to scribble. With each thing she thought of, she found herself grinning like Lewis Carroll's Cheshire Cat, and in no time at all, had to stop herself at ten when she could easily have written one hundred things. She looked up at Hannah, who either had already finished or hadn't begun because she couldn't think of anything. "Could you go first?" Janie edged forward, hoping Hannah's list was finished, and she was just allowing her fear to catastrophize. "I'm feeling pretty unlovable," she said after Hannah frowned.

"Sure." Hannah took a sip of wine and put her pen back in its loop on the book. "Okay. Ten things I love about you," she said.

Janie sneaked a peak and saw that Hannah had underlined the task three or four times. She braced herself, not sure what to expect.

"One," Hannah said, her voice soft. "The way you bite your lip when you're concentrating on something. You scrunch up your face a little bit, and it's the cutest thing I've ever seen."

Heat rushed up Janie's neck and into her cheeks. She hadn't realized Hannah had noticed that.

"Two: how you always save the last bite of dessert for me, even when I tell you to just eat it. You cut it in half and insist we share, like you don't want me to miss out on anything *ever*."

"I do do that," Janie said. "Remember that red velvet cake?"

Hannah nodded. "At Freddie's. Before we went to the theater to watch *Princess, Priestess, Witch*."

Janie remembered that night. Gabe had practically puppeteered Hannah into complimenting Janie. "It was our last date night before I moved into the guest room."

"And the first one we'd had in months." Hannah huffed out a long breath. "I'm sorry I stopped making time for you."

Janie put her finger to Hannah's lips. "Don't. That's the past." She flicked her gaze to Hannah's page. "Keep going. I'm enjoying this."

Hannah kissed Janie's finger. "Three: the fierce, protective look you get in your eyes when someone you love is threatened. I saw it when we were talking to David about your mother, and I've seen it a thousand times with the girls. It's like watching a lioness protecting her pride."

A steady warmth, warning of imminent tears, began to rise behind her eyes. But Janie didn't try to stop it. She didn't want to hide her emotions from Hannah; she didn't want to hide anything from her again.

"Four: your laugh when something genuinely surprises you," Hannah said, switching her focus between her journal and Janie. "I'm not talking about the polite laugh you use for clients or strangers, but your full, unguarded laugh that sounds like pure joy. I haven't heard it enough lately, and I miss it."

"I miss it too," Janie whispered.

"Five: the way you talk to the girls like they're mini adults, always explaining like they're capable of understanding. Six: how you sing so beautifully when you're cooking, or in the shower, or just moving around the house even though you swear you sound like a strangled cat." As Hannah continued through the list, her handwriting became less legible not because of her scrawling but because of Janie's tears falling on the paper as she read along. "Seven: the little crease that appears between your eyebrows when you're worried about something. Eight: how you text me random thoughts and pictures through the day just to share them and make me smile. Nine: how you always remember tiny details about people's lives and ask about them later. That makes people feel so special." She stopped and looked into Janie's eyes. "*You're* so special. And finally, though I could fill this whole book tonight, a new favorite is the way you look at me, like you're doing right now, like you can't quite believe I still love you, when the truth is I've never stopped and never will." Hannah passed Janie a tissue and swiped at her own tears with another one. "Your turn?" she asked gently.

"Okay." Janie wiped her face and re-opened her own notebook. "One: your creative passion when you talk about your work. Your whole face lights up when you're describing a paint technique or showing me a color you mixed. You become this other version of yourself, completely absorbed and present."

"Does that count as just one?" Hannah gulped.

"Yes, it does. Now shush and just listen, or I won't get through this." Janie tapped Hannah's leg. "Two: the gentle way you handle the girls even when you're exhausted. I've watched you be patient through tantrums and messes when I know you're running on empty, and it's one of the most beautiful things I've ever seen."

As Janie read through her list, she could recall a hundred examples of each little thing, and the recollections filled her heart and nourished her soul. "And ten," she said, "is the way you fought for us. Even when I'd given up on myself, even when it would have been easier to let me go, you fought. You kept showing up. You didn't let me disappear into my shame. And I'll spend the rest of my life being grateful for that. For being given a second chance, and for keeping our family together."

They sat in silence for a moment, both crying, and Hannah wrapped her arms around Janie and held her tight. The weight of being truly seen by Hannah overwhelmed her, making it impossible for her to speak.

"We're going to make it," Hannah finally said, "aren't we? We're actually going to make it through this."

"Yeah," Janie said, and for the first time, she really believed it. "I think we are. I was thinking about our first date. What if we spend Saturday afternoon walking around Pilsen? Maria's told me so much about the neighborhood, and I'd love to explore it together. See the murals, check out the shops, maybe grab some street tacos. And we could end up at Maria's café." She glanced away briefly. "I told her I wanted to bring you to meet her. She's been such a huge part of my healing, Han. I want you to know her, to understand what she's done for me."

"I'd love that." Hannah tucked a strand of hair behind Janie's ear. "What time should I pick you up?"

Janie shook her head. "I'll pick *you* up," she said and wiggled her eyebrows. "Just like I did in Vegas. Two o'clock? That'll give us a few hours before the café gets too busy."

"It's a date."

Janie smiled. How crazy to be planning a first date after several years of marriage. But still, something fluttered in her chest, though it wasn't something she thought she could say out loud just yet. Maybe anticipation or even hope... Whatever concoction it was, something dangerously close to joy was swimming around in there.

She remembered the medication she'd shoved in her purse and pulled it out. "I thought I'd take this now."

"Is that why you didn't want wine with dinner?" Hannah asked. "I didn't want to say anything in front of Dad. That's not my story to tell."

Janie nodded, popped the medication into her mouth, and washed it down with a swallow of water. *This is the beginning. Not the end of who I am, but the beginning of finding myself again.* With Hannah watching her intently, it was every bit as symbolic as she'd anticipated. "Thank you," she said. "For today. For the list. For seeing me."

"Thank you for trusting me with your truth," Hannah said. "And for taking that first pill." She leaned in and kissed Janie, soft and sweet, and full of promise. "Can you stay tonight?"

Janie could. Of course she could. And God, she wanted to, even if she stayed in a separate room again. Nothing was waiting at the apartment... Except work. The therapy sessions had meant she'd missed hours at the office, and she had to play catch up tonight. "I have to work to make up some time. I'm sorry." She glanced at her phone and saw it was nearly ten. "I have to go."

"There's no need to apologize." Hannah caressed Janie's cheek. "But please don't exhaust yourself, okay?"

"I won't."

Hannah walked Janie out to her car and held the door open for her. Janie got in, and Hannah seemed hesitant to let her go.

"You'll be back Saturday?" Hannah asked, leaning in the open window.

"I promise." Janie reluctantly drove away, more hopeful than she'd been in months. Tomorrow, she'd take the second dose of medication. The day after that, the third. Day by day and week by week, she was going to get better. She was going to enjoy her gorgeous wife and their beautiful children.

Now all she had to do was hold onto that thin strand of optimism when the black dog of her depression tried to tug it from her like a chew toy.

Chapter Nineteen

Solo checked her reflection in the hallway mirror for the third time in ten minutes, adjusting the collar of her button-down shirt, then smoothing it down again. She'd changed twice already. Her first outfit had been too casual, and the second too formal. She'd finally settled on dark jeans and a slim-fit burgundy shirt that Janie had always said brought out the warmth in her eyes.

"You look great, slugger," her dad said from the living room, where he was building an elaborate block tower with Chloe. "Stop fussing."

"I'm not fussing." Solo moved away from the mirror, then immediately turned back to check her hair.

"You're definitely fussing," her dad said, sounding amused. "It's just Janie. Your wife, remember? The woman you've been married to for two years."

"It's our first real date since..." She wasn't quite sure how to finish that sentence. Since they'd started trying to put the pieces back together? The theater date last month was forced and unnatural, and she'd been too preoccupied, desperate to get back for the triplets. God, she'd been an ass.

"Since you decided to fight for each other," her dad said gently and grinned. "Maybe you *should* be nervous about it."

Solo abandoned the mirror and collapsed onto the couch beside him. Luna immediately crawled into her lap, and Solo automatically adjusted to accommodate her, before pressing a kiss to her daughter's curly hair. "We Zoomed with David yesterday," she said. "Janie from her office and me from the garage. She told him everything about the ER incident."

Her dad grumbled. "How did that go?"

"Better than Janie expected. He was frustrated we didn't tell him sooner, but he understood why. He still thinks we're in good shape even after he'd reviewed the medical records. They show it was an accident, and we've taken steps since then by childproofing and employing Carmen." She nudged him. "And we've got you hanging around too. David's confident Janie's mother doesn't have a case."

He raised both eyebrows and stared at her, clearly waiting for more. He could always hear the "but" before she said it.

"But it's still terrifying. The hearing is in three weeks, and until then, we're just... waiting and hoping Janie's mother doesn't find something else to use against us."

"You're doing everything right," her dad said. "Both of you. And you're doing it together. *That's* what matters."

Tia wandered over and thrust a picture book at Solo. "Mama read."

"Mommy is coming soon, baby girl. How about Grandpa reads you this one?"

"When Mommy coming?" Tia's face scrunched up with the kind of concentration only a toddler trying to understand time could achieve.

"Very soon. Maybe ten more minutes?"

"Ten minutes," Tia said seriously, like she had any concept of what that meant.

Solo's phone buzzed.

I'm outside. Should I come in?

Her stomach did a complicated flip. "She's here," she said, unnecessarily loud. She stood and popped Luna on the playmat, but she protested with a squawk. Solo went back to her phone and texted Janie. *Do you want to come in to see the girls?*

"Go." Her dad shooed her toward the door. "Have fun. Don't worry about your little terrors. Carmen will be here in an hour, and everything is under control."

"I know, but shouldn't the girls see their mommy?" She grabbed her keys from the tray by the door.

"Han." Her dad put his hands on her shoulders, looking at her seriously. "Your mother and I had rough patches. There were times when we couldn't see past our own hurt to see each other. You know what saved us? We kept showing up. We kept choosing each other. That's what you and Janie are doing. So go. Show up for your wife. Choose her."

Her phone buzzed again.

Would it be okay if I didn't? I really want this time to be about us. I can come in after our date night. Does that work?

Solo hugged her dad quickly, then kissed each of the triplets. "Be good for Grandpa and Carmen. I'll be home later."

"Much later," her dad said and gave a knowing smile. "Don't rush. You two need this."

Solo grabbed her denim jacket, more for something to keep her hands busy than because she needed it in the warm September afternoon, then headed outside.

Janie was leaning against her car, wearing a dress Solo had never seen before. It was deep green with small white flowers, fitted at the waist and flowing to just above her knees. Her hair was down and caught the afternoon light. Solo's mouth fell open like she was a cartoon character. Janie looked fresh and achingly familiar all at once.

Solo jogged down their path and closed the gate behind her. She wanted to pull Janie into her arms and kiss her, then maybe scoop her up and take her upstairs to show her how much she'd missed her. But first dates were about taking it slow. Weren't they?

"Hi," Janie said then bit her bottom lip.

"Hi." Solo couldn't stop staring. "You look... Wow."

"Yeah?" Janie looked down at herself like she'd forgotten what she was wearing. "I bought it yesterday. I thought...fresh start, new dress," she said and shrugged.

"It's perfect. You're perfect." Solo moved close enough to touch Janie but held back, and for a moment, she just stood there, taking her in as if she was seeing her for the very first time.

"So. First date."

"First date." Janie nodded. "Are you ready to be swept off your feet?"

"You're going to do the sweeping?" Solo chuckled.

Janie arched her eyebrow the way she did when she was practically daring Solo to push. "Yes. *I'm* going to do the sweeping."

"Then I'm ready," Solo said, enjoying Janie's familiar queen-like confidence. "Sweep away."

Janie's eyebrow dropped, and she inclined her head toward the Lexus. "Hop in."

Solo happily did as instructed. Their time together was already feeling new and exciting, and she couldn't wait to enjoy every second of it. She didn't really take notice of the route and was happy enough to simply stare at her wife's profile, something she wasn't sure she'd get to see with any kind of regularity ever again. Janie was clearly following some internal map, and she seemed lighter today as she sang along to the radio, one hand on the wheel and the other occasionally reaching over to touch Solo's knee. Each touch darted warmth through Solo's chest.

She thought about asking how Janie was feeling about their Zoom with David yesterday, but she didn't want to bring the vibe down. And today was supposed to be just about them, reconnecting and rediscovering each other. For now, Solo wanted to ignore the ball of dread sitting in her guts and just *be* with her wife.

They drove through neighborhoods that shifted and changed, past the Loop with its towering buildings and through pockets of residential streets until Janie pulled into a parking spot on 18th Street.

"It's crazy that we haven't been here together," Solo said before she got out of the car. She got a hit of incense and noticed they were parked outside some kind of spiritual shop.

The woman inside came to the door and seemed to study them both for a long moment. "If you're looking to make sure this sticks, I've got a great spell for second chances."

Solo did a double take and backed away. "Uh, no. We're good on our own, thanks."

The woman looked at them both again for longer than was comfortable, and then she winked. "Yeah, you will be," she said and turned back into her shop.

"That was strange," Solo said when Janie came alongside her.

Janie laughed lightly. "That kind of thing is normal around here. Wait until you meet Maria."

"I'm looking forward to that," Solo said and held out her hand, not wanting to assume Janie would be good with the physical contact. She almost did a little celebration jump when Janie intertwined their fingers. "I want to meet the woman who's been taking care of my wife when I couldn't."

Janie kissed Solo's cheek. "Don't go there. We're focusing on being there for each other from here, okay?"

Solo nodded, and when they started walking, she immediately understood why Janie had fallen for this neighborhood over the past couple of weeks. Murals covered nearly every available surface, massive, colorful pieces that transformed ordinary buildings into art galleries. A skeletal Día de los Muertos figure smiled down from one wall. A woman's face, rendered in stunning detail, gazed out from another, her expression both fierce and tender.

"This one's my favorite," Janie said, stopping in front of a mural that depicted a phoenix rising from flames, its wings spread wide and brilliant with gold and crimson. "I came across it a few weeks ago, and I stood here for twenty minutes, staring at it."

Solo took in the mural, understanding why it would speak to Janie. "Rising from the ashes," she said quietly.

"Yeah." Janie squeezed Solo's hand and lifted it to her chest. "That's what it feels like. Like everything burned down, and now we're building something new from what's left."

The art and Janie's sentiment took away Solo's ability to say anything remotely clever, so she said nothing at all and simply let the beautiful weight of it all settle in her heart.

They walked hand in hand through the neighborhood, stopping to admire murals, peeking into shop windows, just existing together in a way they hadn't in so long. Solo relaxed more with each step, and the constant tension she'd been carrying for weeks slowly began to unwind.

They paused in front of a mural of intertwined hands that were different shades of brown, tan, and cream, all holding each other up. It reminded her of Gabe, and Shay, and RB, and Woody. That's exactly what they'd done for her and for each other for years. She took a photo to show them and scanned the QR code in case the artist did commissions. She'd love something like that in her area of the garage. "Can I ask you something?"

"Anything."

"When you left, where did your mind go?" Solo had wanted the answer to this question since Rae had put a name to Janie's suffering, but she didn't know if it'd be okay to ask. Now though, as everything seemed to be slipping back into place, albeit a new place, she figured Janie could decide whether or not to share her experience. "I know your body went to some apartment, but where did *you* go?"

Janie was quiet for a long time. "I went to a place where I didn't have to see disappointment in anyone's eyes. Where I could just be small without having to pretend I was okay." She squeezed Solo's hand. "In the moment, it seemed like the only option."

Solo swallowed against her constricting throat, like one of the giant hands from the wall had reached out and wrapped itself around her neck. "I'm sorry that I made you feel like you had to hide from me."

"It wasn't your doing. Maria kept saying that I was building my own prison." Janie tugged Solo forward. "Come on. The café is just around the corner. I want you to meet her."

The café was small and welcoming, with mismatched furniture and walls covered in local art. The smell of coffee and fresh bread wrapped around Solo like a hug. A few people sat scattered at tables, working on laptops or reading, but the place had a quiet, comfortable energy despite the sizeable line waiting to be served.

Behind the counter stood two older women. Solo guessed they were in their sixties, and both had silver-streaked, almost black hair pulled back in loose buns. Their faces were lined with countless experiences.

"Janie!"

"Mirta, Maria, this is Hannah, my wife."

Janie said the last word with a kind of quiet pride that filled Solo's chest with joy. One of them nodded and said hello before she continued to serve their long line of customers. The other, maybe slightly older and definitely more attractive, came around the counter to greet them. She moved with a grace that seemed almost theatrical and carried herself with a confidence that clearly came from experience, not arrogance.

"I am Maria," she said and took Solo's hands in hers, studying her face with an intensity that should have made her uncomfortable but somehow didn't. "Finally we meet. I was beginning to think Janie would never bring you to our little corner of the world."

Solo smiled, a little envious at the way Maria's eyes seemed to take in everything and *know* everything at once. "Janie's told me how you've helped her. Thank you for being there for her when she needed someone."

"Ah, but she's making it sound more noble than it was." Maria released Solo's hands and gestured toward a corner table. "I just made coffee and let her talk. Sometimes all people need is the space to be themselves without judgment."

They settled at the table, and Mirta brought over coffee and pan dulce without being asked and was gone again before Solo had finished withdrawing her wallet.

Maria grasped Solo's wrist and shook her head. "No payment required. I'm sure Janie will explain later." She narrowed her eyes. "So you are the woman who holds Janie's heart in her hands? The artist who paints cars."

"Guilty," Solo said, trying to ignore the interrogation vibe Maria was emanating. "I prefer 'automotive artist' if we're being fancy."

"And you're good?" Maria asked. "Janie says you're brilliant, but Janie is biased."

"I'm decent," Solo said, the odd feeling that she was being evaluated for something important growing. "I love the work. I love the challenge of taking something rusty or forgotten and making it beautiful again."

"Mmm." Maria sipped her coffee. "And that's what you're doing now, yes? With your marriage?"

Solo blinked, taken aback by the directness.

"Maria," Janie said, but Maria waved her off.

"What? I'm old. I get to be blunt." She turned back to Solo. "Your wife came to me broken, convinced she was unfit to be a mother, too ashamed to be honest with the person who should have been her partner. So yes, I'm asking if you are taking this seriously? Are you really committed to rebuilding your marriage? Or are you just going through the motions because of your children?"

"Maria!" Janie's face flushed a brighter red than one of the feature walls.

Having her love for Janie challenged by a complete stranger wasn't exactly how she thought their first date would go, but Solo found herself smiling anyway. She liked Maria's fierce protectiveness on Janie's behalf. She'd clearly become attached to Janie and genuinely cared for her, and she definitely wasn't afraid to attack on Janie's behalf. Solo had that with Gabe and the rest of the gang, but Janie had no one in her corner, not even her stupid family.

"I'm committed," Solo said after she tugged off a piece of the sweet bread and rolled it between her fingers. "And not just because of our daughters, though they're part of it, but because I love Janie." There was a warmth in Maria's expression that somehow made it easy to open up. She'd had to learn to explain herself to Gabe when Solo served under her, but she hadn't quite extended that learning to her wife. So this should have been alien, but after a few therapy sessions with Rae, Solo was beginning to see that she needed to be more open if she didn't want to end up alone. She reached deep inside her heart and rooted around. "I failed her. I made her invisible when she needed to be seen, and I shut down when she needed support. I'll never make those mistakes again."

Maria studied her for another long moment, then nodded, apparently satisfied. "Good. Because your wife," she gestured at Janie, "she is special. She is worth fighting for. And if you hurt her again, you will answer to me."

"Deal." Solo held out her hand, and Maria shook it solemnly.

"Okay, can we please stop acting like I'm not sitting right here?" Janie asked quietly.

Mirta laughed from behind the counter. "Maria does this with everyone she loves. Last week she interrogated the mailman because he seemed too friendly."

"He was flirting with you," Maria said. "I was protecting your honor."

Mirta threw up her hands. "He was doing his job, viejita."

Solo smiled at the easy banter between them, trying to figure out their relationship. Sisters? Partners? Something else entirely?

"Mirta is supposed to be my silent partner," Maria said, as if reading Solo's mind. "Though she too often ignores the 'silent' aspect of her title and believes she's in charge."

"Because I *am* in charge," Mirta said and laughed loudly. "You just haven't accepted it yet."

The exchange didn't clarify their relationship, but it didn't really matter, and Solo didn't want to push, especially when they'd only just met. They spent the next hour at the café, and by the end of it, she'd been completely charmed. The older woman had a way of storytelling that was captivating. She'd traveled all over the world, mentioned at least six countries that she'd lived in, and she spoke four languages fluently. She talked about art, music, and literature with the kind of casual knowledge that came from genuine passion and deep knowledge, and the kind of emotional intellect Solo coveted just a little.

"Wait," Solo said, something clicking in her brain. "Did you say you lived in Buenos Aires in the eighties? And you were involved in theater?"

"For a time, yes." Maria glanced at Mirta, who shrugged.

"Maria Flores?" Solo leaned forward. "You're Maria Flores, the *actress* from Guatemala who conquered Hollywood? I knew you looked familiar! My mom loved your movies. She made me watch *La Frontera Invisible* a dozen times."

For the first time since they'd met, Maria looked slightly uncomfortable. "That was a long time ago."

"You won an Academy Award," Solo said, memories of time with her mom flooding back. Her mom, on the couch with six-year-old Solo curled up beside her, watching this beautiful, talented actress command the screen. "Best Supporting Actress for *Where the River Ends.* I remember my mom crying during your final scene."

"People forget," Maria said quietly. "Time passes. That was another life."

"But what an amazing life," Solo said. "To create art like that, to move people to tears. That's an incredible gift."

Maria's expression softened. "I had a good run. But everyone's time in the spotlight ends eventually. And when mine did, I found I didn't miss it as much as I thought I would." She glanced around the café with obvious affection. "This is better. Quieter. More real."

"You gave it up?" Solo asked. "But you were so successful."

"Success isn't always what we think it will be." Maria gazed out the window and seemed to see beyond the buildings across the street. "The industry changed. Or maybe I changed. I got tired of pretending, of being someone I wasn't. And then I fell in love with someone who couldn't be with me publicly, and I had to make a choice: my career or my truth."

Solo understood that look, that weight. "You chose yourself."

"I chose love. And honesty. And a life where I could breathe." Maria's smile was bittersweet. "I don't regret it. Though there are days when I miss the work, the craft of it, the challenge of becoming someone else."

"You move people here," Janie said, "in a very different way, through your wisdom and compassion for all the broken people who stumble into your café."

Maria laughed, a genuine, delighted sound. "Perhaps. Though I prefer to think of it as simply being present. Anyway," she placed her hands over Janie's and Solo's, "you have much better things to be doing than keeping two old women company. It is time for you to go."

Janie nodded and smiled at Solo. "I just need the restroom, then we'll head home."

Maria watched Janie disappear around the corner of the counter then she turned to Solo. "Take care of her," she said and squeezed Solo's hand. "She's stronger than she thinks, but she's still fragile. The shame hasn't fully released its grip yet."

"I know," Solo said. "I'm trying."

"Don't just try. Do." Maria's gaze was intense.

This was all so surreal. Janie had stumbled across a real-life Yoda. Solo had to push a giggle down, so all she could manage was a nod.

"And don't let her mother anywhere near those children. That woman is poison."

"We won't." All humor evacuated her body, and Solo clenched her jaw.

Maria squeezed her hand a little harder. "You're good for her. I can see it in how she looks at you. Like you're home."

Solo's throat tightened. "She's home for me too."

When Janie returned, Maria and Mirta said their goodbyes

with hugs. Solo offered her hand but was pulled into a bone-crushing embrace that didn't match their gentle, elderly appearance, and they made her promise to come back soon. As she and Janie walked back toward the car, the late afternoon sun was turning everything golden, and Solo couldn't help but think the weather was siding with their attempt to rebuild their lives.

"She's amazing," Solo said. "I can't believe you've been hanging out with a former movie star and didn't tell me."

"I didn't know," Janie said. "She doesn't exactly advertise it. With all the stories she tells and the café running on goodwill, I had a suspicion there was more to her background than she'd shared with me, but she obviously wants to keep that part of her life private. I think she likes being just Maria now, not Maria Flores the actress."

"Is that why she wouldn't accept payment?" Solo slipped her arm around Janie's waist, and Janie leaned into her.

"Yeah. I think maybe some people pay, like tourists, but mostly, the café's used by her community, and she wants them to feel safe and looked after."

Solo smiled and nodded. "That's a wonderful thing. It's kind of what Gabe's doing at the garage, except queer people still have to pay."

Janie laughed and leaned into Solo a little harder. "So not the same?"

Solo shrugged and laughed too. "I guess not... Thank you for sharing your friends with me. I can see why you like it so much here."

"I wanted to. I wanted you to see where I've been while I've been away from you and to meet the people who have been helping me. Maria's been..." Janie paused and bit her bottom lip, clearly searching for the right words. "She became a competing voice in my head, one that told me I deserve good things and that I'm not as broken as the *other* voice tells me I am."

"You're not broken at all." Solo pulled Janie in tighter. "You're healing. There's a difference."

They reached the car, but instead of getting in, Janie turned to face Solo, her back against the passenger's side door. The setting sun caught in her hair, turning it bronze and gold, and Solo's breath caught. How could she have stopped seeing how beautiful Janie was?

"I don't want to go home yet," Janie said quietly.

"No?" Solo was enjoying this time together too much for it to end so quickly, for their reality to push back in. "What do you want to do?"

Janie put her hands on Solo's shoulders, and Solo pulled her in closer on auto pilot, their bodies fitting together in that familiar way they always had.

"I want..." Janie ran her fingernail over Solo's bottom lip. "I want to keep being just us for a little while longer. No responsibilities, no triplets needing us, no legal cases hanging over our heads. Just us."

"Okay." Solo's heart pounded against her chest, and other things pulsed in hope. She gently slipped a lock of Janie's hair behind her ear, not wanting to push anything. "What did you have in mind?"

"I made a reservation at a hotel downtown." Janie's cheeks flushed pink. "We don't have to use it if you're not ready, but I thought maybe—"

Solo kissed her. Not tentatively or carefully like she thought she'd have to do while they slowly found their way back to each other, but deeply, desperate with all the want and love and longing she'd been holding back. Janie made a small sound of surprise, then melted into it, her fingers digging into Solo's shoulders.

Solo pulled back, breathing hard. "Take me to the hotel," she said. "Please."

Janie's smile was wide and confident. It was the same smile Solo had come to know as a sure-fire indication of her sexual arousal.

Janie wrapped her hand around the back of Solo's neck. "Yeah?"

"Yeah." Solo kissed her again, softer this time. "I want you. I want this. I want us to remember what it feels like to just be together without the weight of everything else."

"Get in the car," Janie said, already moving around to the driver's side. "Before I can't wait for the hotel and just drag you into that alley over there."

Solo laughed, giddy and reckless in the best possible way. She climbed into the passenger seat, and as Janie started the car and pulled into traffic, Solo reached over and held her hand. "I love you," she said. "I've missed telling you that."

"I've missed hearing it." Janie brought Solo's hand to her lips and pressed a kiss to her knuckles. "You've got some making up to do."

"I love you. I love you. I love you." Solo punctuated each repetition with a squeeze of Janie's hand. "There. That's a start."

Janie laughed her full, uninhibited, and joyful laugh. "You're ridiculous," she said.

"You love it."

Janie glanced over at Solo and nodded, the love in her eyes clear. "I really do."

They drove through the city as the sun painted the sky in shades of pink, orange, and purple, and Solo smiled widely. She couldn't help but hope they were finally driving toward their future instead of running from it.

Chapter Twenty

THE HOTEL LOBBY WAS elegant in an understated way, with its marble floors, soft lighting, and foliage everywhere. Janie couldn't have cared less about any of it; she wanted to be safely ensconced in any of its many rooms as soon as possible, and this fancy décor didn't figure into that desire one bit. The front desk was staffed by a young man who barely glanced up as Janie gave her name, then he handed over a key card with a professional smile that suggested he'd seen countless couples check in without luggage and thought nothing of it.

"Thank you," Janie said, her hand shaking as she took the card. Almost instantly, the warmth of Hannah's hand was against the small of her back, steadying and grounding her with ease.

"Are you okay?" Hannah whispered into her neck.

"Nervous," Janie said as they walked toward the elevators. "Is that crazy? Being nervous about this?"

"No." Hannah traced small circles against Janie's spine through the thin fabric of her dress. "I'm nervous too."

The elevator arrived empty, and they stepped inside. The doors slid shut, cocooning them in mirrored silence. Hannah stood slightly behind her, close enough that Janie could feel her warmth, and she caught Janie's gaze in the mirror.

"We don't have to do anything," Hannah said softly. "We can just talk. Order expensive room service. Watch bad action movies from the nineties. I'm here for whatever you need."

Janie turned to face Hannah and cupped her face gently. "I need *you*," she said, her voice hoarse. "I need to remember what it feels like to be yours. To be us in *this* way." She kissed Hannah hard, wanting her to feel that need like it was driving all the blood in her body.

Hannah brushed her thumb across Janie's cheekbone. "You've always been mine. Even when we were apart, I wished to God that you were still mine, that you *wanted* to be mine."

The elevator chimed their arrival at the eighth floor, and they walked down the carpeted hallway in charged silence. Janie fumbled with the key card until Hannah's hand covered hers gently, helping guide the card against the slot until the light turned green.

The room was pretty and more than Janie needed for tonight. All she was interested in was the king-size bed with its crisp white linens and fresh new possibilities. There was a sitting area by the window overlooking the city lights, and strategically placed soft lamps cast everything in warm amber. Under other circumstances, it would've been nice to order something to eat and watch a movie.

But Janie's thoughts were mostly on making use of that big bed to reclaim her wife. To reclaim herself.

She set her purse down on the small table in the center of the room, hyperaware of Hannah behind her, of the door clicking shut, of the fact that they were alone in a way they hadn't been in months. No children who might wake up and interrupt them. No father tactfully retreating to give them space. Just them.

"Janie." Hannah's voice was soft. "Look at me."

Janie turned, and the expression on Hannah's face nearly undid her. She could see Hannah's desire in the way her eyes had gone dark, in the tension in her shoulders. But there was also tenderness and the kind of reverence that made Janie feel simultaneously vulnerable and powerful.

Janie tried to identify the other emotions racing around her mind, vying for her attention. One of them...one of them she really didn't want to acknowledge or give voice to. But this fresh start was about honesty, wasn't it? And if she couldn't be honest on their first date, would that set the tone for this new journey and doom it from the very beginning? "I'm scared," she said after quieting her inner conflict.

"Of what?"

"I'm scared of not being enough for you anymore. That I've forgotten how to be with you like this. I'm frightened that you'll touch me and realize..." Janie's breath stuttered. "You'll realize I'm not the woman you married, or the woman you think I am. The one you want and need me to be."

Hannah was within touching distance in three strides. She cupped Janie's face and lifted her chin gently, forcing Janie to meet her gaze. "You're still the woman I married. And I love every part of you: the scared parts, the sad parts, the parts that are still figuring out how to be okay. All of it. I just need you to be you."

"I have stretch marks now," Janie said, the words tumbling out along with unbidden watery sorrow. This wasn't the way this was supposed to be going. The ragged desire that had dragged Hannah to the hotel had run for cover when the tar began to advance along the horizon of her conscious mind again. "My body is different. I'm softer, and there's this heaviness," she pressed her hand to her chest, "here, inside me. Like I'm carrying something dark that might never go away, something that's become part of me against my will."

"I know." Hannah traced the track of Janie's tears with her thumbs. "I know you're struggling. I know the postpartum depression isn't just going to magically disappear because we're working on our relationship. But Janie, you're here. You're fighting. You told me the truth even though you were terrified. That's the bravest thing I've ever seen."

Janie arched her eyebrow, quite certain she didn't believe that. Hannah had been a soldier and seen things Janie could only have nightmares about. "I don't feel brave."

"You don't have to feel it for it to be true." Hannah pressed a kiss to Janie's forehead, achingly tender. "And as for your body," she ran her hand down Janie's neck slowly, "you grew three whole beautiful and amazing humans inside you. You're a goddamn miracle."

Fresh tears spilled over, and Hannah kissed those away too, first from one cheek, and then the other, soft and patient and so full of love that Janie's chest hurt.

"I want this," Janie said, clutching at Hannah's shirt. "I want you. But I'm... I'm so scared of disappointing you."

"You could never disappoint me." Hannah slid her hands down to Janie's waist and pulled her closer. "Let's go real slow. We can stop anytime. This is about us reconnecting, not about performing or being perfect. Okay?"

Janie nodded, not trusting her voice.

"Can I kiss you?" Hannah asked.

Janie's lips twitched at the request. After they'd gotten together, Hannah hadn't needed to ask that question. But this was different. She was asking permission for so much more than a simple kiss. "Please," she whispered.

Hannah kissed her slowly, like they had all the time in the world. Her lips were soft but firm, and Janie melted into the familiar sensation and the solid safety, her body remembering even if her mind was slow to accept it. Hannah's hands stayed on Janie's waist, not pushing, only holding, and a sharp pang of realization coursed through her. Hannah was holding back, moving gently, like Janie was a fragile, brittle vase.

Janie pulled back slightly so their lips parted. "You don't have to be so careful with me. I'm not going to shatter."

"I know. But I like being careful with you. I like taking my time." Hannah traced the strap of Janie's dress with her fingers. "I've missed this so much. I've missed *you*. And I don't want to rush a single second."

She kissed Janie again, deeper this time. Janie released her death-grip on Hannah's shirt and started exploring, drifting her hands up over Solo's shoulders and into her short hair that tickled Janie's fingertips, relearning the shape and the feel of her. Hannah moaned softly against Janie's mouth, and the vibration of it traveled through her whole body.

Hannah moved to the tiny pearl buttons at the front of Janie's dress. She pulled away slightly and met Janie's gaze. Janie nodded, ignoring the voice in her mind that was telling her Hannah would soon realize this was a mistake.

Hannah undid the first button slowly and then continued downward, revealing a little more of Janie with each one, ramping up both her desire *and* her anxiety. Hannah pressed gentle kisses to Janie's collarbone, the hollow of her throat, and the swell of her breast above her bra.

"God, you're beautiful," Hannah murmured against her skin. "So fucking beautiful."

"I'm not—"

"Yes, you are." Hannah looked up at her, and the intensity in her eyes stole Janie's breath. "You are."

Hannah continued with the buttons, unhurried and methodical. By the time she reached the last one, Janie's whole body trembled, not from fear but from anticipation and need, and from the overwhelming notion of Hannah truly seeing her again.

"Do you remember our first night together?" she asked.

Hannah smiled and wiggled her eyebrows. "I'll *never* forget that." She tapped her forehead. "It's burned into my brain."

Janie took Hannah's hand and kissed each of her fingertips. "You were in more of a hurry to take off my dress that night."

"This is different," Hannah whispered. "Back then, I just wanted to get laid, and I had no idea I'd found someone so special." She shook her head, never taking her eyes from Janie's. "But I nearly lost you. And I had no idea that the last time we made love might be the *last* time we made love. This is a gift, and I want to take in every second."

Janie parted her lips, wanting to respond to the beauty of Hannah's sentiment. But words eluded her, and she feared that even if she found some, they wouldn't make it out of her mouth without the choke of tears.

Hannah pushed the dress off Janie's shoulders, and it pooled at her feet. Janie stood there in the black, lacy underwear she'd purchased at the same shop as the dress yesterday, fighting the urge to cover herself. She'd been ridiculous, buying a new outfit and sexy underwear, thinking it might solve their problems, thinking it might hide her ugliness, inside and out, somehow.

And now Hannah was stepping back.

Janie watched her face carefully for any hint of disappointment or hesitation. But there was only wonder and reverence. "You're staring." She tried for humor, but her vulnerability sang louder than anything else.

"I'm memorizing," Hannah said and traced her fingers along the textured skin of a stretch mark that ran from Janie's hip toward her navel.

"They're taking their sweet time to fade," Janie said, barely hearing her own voice. She looked down at the road map of lines marring her skin. They'd changed considerably from the raised red slashes immediately following the birth of the triplets, but for her, they pulsed like live train tracks across her body.

"They're part of you, so they're beautiful. *You're* beautiful." Hannah splayed her hand over Janie's stomach, the soft, rounded part that hadn't existed before the triplets, that Janie had tried so hard to hide under loose clothes. "This body made our daughters. This body is a fucking miracle, Janie."

The tears came again, and Janie didn't try to stop them. Hannah pulled her close and held her while she cried. They weren't sad tears as such. The tiny little drops were filled with something more complicated: self-loathing, loneliness, shame. Months and months of it. And standing almost naked in front of her wife, whose tender gaze couldn't have been more loving and supportive, the slow, painful shedding of those feelings truly began.

"I'm sorry." Janie hiccupped. "I'm crying all over your shirt." She brushed uselessly at the wet patch on Hannah's button-down, the one that made her eyes pop. "This is supposed to be sexy."

"This is sexy," Hannah said, her expression serious. "You being honest about what you're feeling and trusting me with your vulnerability. You've never been sexier."

Janie's heart sped up as Hannah guided them toward the bed. Hannah sat on the edge and pulled Janie to stand between her legs.

"Your turn," Hannah said, looking up at her. "If you want to."

Janie looked at her hands. They'd stopped shaking for now, at least. She ran her fingers along Hannah's collar then popped each button slowly, revealing the sports bra underneath, the flatness of her stomach, the familiar landscape of her body.

Hannah shrugged out of the shirt and tossed it aside, then pulled her bra over her head. She wasn't shy about her body and never had been. Janie supposed that came from her years in the Army, but she didn't know for sure. However Hannah's confidence had come about, Janie envied it. Hannah's willingness to be naked made Janie love her all the more, because she was letting herself be vulnerable in a different way and offering herself without reservations or caveats.

Janie traced the defined muscle of Hannah's shoulders, the evidence of hours spent working on cars, tanks, and armored vehicles. Her strength was one of the things Janie loved about her. She followed the line of Hannah's shoulders with her lips, kissing and nibbling, making her way down the center of her chest. "I missed you," she whispered against Hannah's skin. The power of what they were doing caught up with her and almost dropped her to her knees. "I missed us."

"I'm right here," Hannah said hoarsely. "I'm not going anywhere."

Janie looked up, recognizing the need in Hannah's voice, and their eyes locked. For a long moment, she simply stared into Hannah's eyes. She wasn't sure exactly what she was looking for, or what it would even look like if she knew. What she did find was a deep ocean of love, a yearning that went beyond physical desire but one which still needed that intimacy to fully reconnect, to become who they were together. Her heart knocked against her ribs, as if trying to reach out for Hannah and bring her back inside, where she belonged. This was Hannah, her wife. The woman who had seen Janie at her absolute worst and was still here, still choosing her, still looking at her like she hung the moon.

Hannah cupped Janie's face. "Do you want to keep going?"

Janie placed her hand over Hannah's. "I do." She swallowed, the rising heat determined to take control of her mind as well as her body. "God, I do."

Hannah winked and slipped her hands around Janie's back. "This is new too, right?" She gave a wicked grin, unhooked the bra easily, and slid it from Janie's shoulders.

Janie fumbled at Hannah's belt buckle. She tugged it hard, but the damn thing wouldn't come loose. "Get these off," she said, pulling at Hannah's jeans' pocket.

Hannah chuckled. "Are you in a hurry now?"

Janie shrugged. "I want to feel your skin against mine."

Hannah shed her jeans, boxers, and socks in seconds. Then she pulled Janie down onto the bed and rolled them over, so they were facing each other, bodies aligned, chests pressed so close they could Morse code their love in heartbeats.

"Hi," Hannah said softly as she pushed a few strands of Janie's hair behind her ear.

"Hi," Janie said, managing a watery smile as tears welled once again.

Hannah kissed her, slower now, less desperate and more intentional. She slid her hands down Janie's spine and over her hips, as if mapping out her body with loving curiosity. When she cupped Janie's breast and squeezed, Janie arched into the touch with a gasp.

"Sensitive," Hannah murmured and did it again. She circled her thumb over Janie's nipple until Janie was squirming against her.

"Please," Janie said, not entirely sure what she was asking for but knowing she needed more of Hannah's touch.

Hannah rolled Janie onto her back and settled above her, propped on one elbow so she could look down at Janie's face while she continued her exploration. "I can't believe I almost lost you," she whispered, her voice catching.

Janie swallowed hard and wrapped her hand around Hannah's neck. "I almost lost myself. You had no chance."

"But now I've got a second chance." Hannah grinned and kissed Janie's nose. "And I'm not going to waste it."

She traced patterns on Janie's stomach and beneath her breasts, and Janie's repressed passions began to unfurl under the attention. The part of her she'd locked away tight, probably since she'd given birth, was finally ready to resurface under Hannah's gentle and practiced touch.

Hannah rested her hand on Janie's hip. "Tell me what you need."

"I need you to touch me," Janie said, clasping her hand over Hannah's. "*Really* touch me. Like you mean it."

"Oh, I mean it." Hannah's eyes were dark and intense. "I thought I might never get to touch you again... I'll show you I mean it."

She slid her hand over Janie's panties, and even through the sheer fabric, the touch sent shockwaves through Janie's system. She hadn't been touched like this in so long... She hadn't let herself be touched, hadn't *wanted* to be touched, and her breathing quickened as the whole situation threatened to overwhelm her.

"Are you okay?" Hannah asked, her hand stilling.

"Don't stop." Janie grasped Hannah's shoulder. "Please don't stop."

Hannah hooked her fingers into the waistband of Janie's underwear and pulled them down, disposing of them swiftly so they were both naked, skin to skin, and the intimacy of it made Janie's throat tight.

Hannah returned to between Janie's legs, and with no barrier, her fingers slid through Janie's wetness with a sureness that spoke of years of knowing Janie's body, of understanding without words what she needed.

"God, Janie," Hannah whispered. "You're so—"

Whatever she was going to say was lost when Janie pulled her into a kiss that was more teeth than finesse. All the desperation and need and love she'd been holding back poured out at once, like hot lava from a once-dormant volcano. Hannah responded in kind, her fingers finding their rhythm, her mouth swallowing Janie's gasps and moans.

But then Hannah slowed down, gentled her touch, and pulled back just enough to look at Janie's face. "Not like this," she said. "I don't want to rush this. I want to see you. I want you to see me."

She shifted her position, settling more fully between Janie's legs, and this time when she touched her, she held Janie's gaze. The eye contact was almost unbearable. The intensity too much. The connection too raw. Janie fought against the tar trying to weigh down her eyelids to close her eyes, to make her hide from the brutal honesty of this moment, but Hannah shook her head.

"Stay with me," Hannah murmured. "I want to watch you come apart. I want you to see how much I love you while it's happening."

Janie's breath hitched as Hannah's fingers found that perfect rhythm, that perfect pressure, the combination that Hannah had learned years ago and clearly hadn't forgotten. But this wasn't just physical; the way Hannah looked at her, the way her free hand cupped Janie's face so tenderly, the way she murmured "I love you" over and over like a prayer made all of it incredibly spiritual.

Her pleasure built slowly, a wave gathering force ready to smash her against the shore, and her hot tears streamed down her temples as Hannah circled her thumb over Janie's clit. Hannah curled inside her just right, keeping her eyes locked on Janie's with the intensity of knowing her down to her bones.

"Let go," Hannah whispered. "I've got you. Just let go."

And Janie did. The orgasm crashed over her, releasing not

just the physical sensation but something deeper, like all the tension, fear, and shame of the past months was breaking apart and washing away with the receding tide. She cried out, arching her back, her fingernails digging into Hannah's shoulders, clutching her close, and through it all, Hannah watched her. Her anchor, her lover, her wife.

When Janie finally came back to herself, her body racked with deep, wrenching sobs that had nothing to do with the pleasure and everything to do with the emotional weight of what had just happened.

Hannah gathered her close and kissed her forehead. "I've got you," she murmured into her hair. "You're okay. I've got you."

"That was—" Janie shook her head, unable to finish the sentence. There weren't words for what that was.

"I know," Hannah said, her voice thick with emotion. "I know, baby."

They lay tangled together for a long time, with Hannah tracing soothing patterns up and down Janie's back. Her sobbing subsided, and her tears eventually slowed. Janie melted into Hannah's arms, wrung out and raw and more vulnerable than she'd ever been, but also so much lighter. Those dark things that she'd locked inside her chest had finally broken free.

Eventually, Janie found the energy to move, and she shifted so she could look at Hannah. Her eyes were shiny, and she was clearly on the edge of crying. Janie kissed each of her eyelids, acknowledging Hannah's vulnerability without bringing verbal attention to it. Hannah blinked, and a stray tear escaped. Janie thumbed it away gently. "Your turn," she said.

Hannah wrinkled her nose. "Since when do we take turns?"

"Since today." Janie tugged her closer and draped her leg over Hannah's hip. "Or maybe never again. But right now, I need to. I need to make you feel what you just made me feel." She pushed Hannah onto her back, and Hannah let out a moan. It was small, almost nothing, but in their intimate language, it was practically a shouted declaration of Hannah's desire. "Let me take care of you," Janie whispered, and Hannah nodded.

Janie took her time, re-learning Hannah's body: the dip of her waist, the sharp jut of her hip bones, the way her breath stuttered when Janie ghosted her hand over Hannah's ribs. Minutes later, when Janie finally slid her hand between Hannah's legs, Hannah pushed her hips upward to greet her, and the sound she made was desperate, so delightfully desperate and dripping with desire.

"I've missed this," Janie said, sliding her fingers through Hannah's wetness. "I love making you feel this way."

Hannah took Janie's free hand and laced their fingers together. "I love you making me feel this way."

Janie worked her slowly, carefully, watching for every reaction, every tell. She knew Hannah's body as well as she knew her own, knew exactly how to touch her, where to press, when to speed up or slow down. All of it rushed back to her. But this time was different, like Janie was rediscovering Hannah and claiming something precious that had almost been lost.

Hannah's eyes locked on Janie's face, the weight of her gaze like a physical presence. There was trust there, and love, and a kind of desperate hope that made Janie's chest ache.

"I love you," Janie said, her thumb finding Hannah's clit, circling with the pressure she needed.

Janie added another finger, and Hannah arched off the bed with a gasp. Janie kissed her with the same desperate hope still lingering in Hannah's half-lidded gaze. She infused it with everything they'd been through and everything they were rebuilding, tried hard to calm Hannah's fears and her own, though they'd quieted in the aftermath of her climax.

Hannah came with Janie's name on her lips, her whole body tensing and then releasing, and a fierce pride and gratitude washed over Janie. This strong, beautiful, imperfect woman was hers. They were each other's.

When Hannah's breathing finally evened out, Janie carefully withdrew her hand and cuddled into Hannah's side, pressing her glowing body to Hannah's equally sweaty one. Hannah wrapped her arm around her and held her close, and they lay there in silence, just breathing. Just being.

"That was..." Hannah whispered.

"Yeah. That was something." Janie didn't have the words either, and really, did they need them? It was the feelings, the residual connection that mattered so much more than labeling what they'd just done and how they'd come together again.

"Are you okay?"

Janie considered the question seriously. *Was* she okay? The depression was still there, of course. The weight in her chest hadn't magically disappeared, despite the mind-blowing orgasm. The fear about the custody hearing was still there, adding more pressure. The guilt about Chloe and the ER visit was hanging around too, though maybe slightly less crushing than before.

But underneath all of that, there was something new. Or maybe not new. Maybe it was just something she'd forgotten resided inside her. Hope, and connection, and the bone-deep certainty that she wasn't alone. And she hadn't been since she'd met Hannah. "I'm not perfect. And as amazing as you were just now," she said and wiggled her eyebrows, "I'm not healed. But I am okay." She snuggled in closer. "I'm better than okay."

"Good." Hannah kissed the top of Janie's head. "Because I need you to know that wasn't just physical for me. This wasn't just about reconnecting sexually."

Janie frowned. "I know."

"Do you?" Hannah shifted so she could look at Janie's face. "Because I need you to really understand that I see you, Janie. And not just as the mother of my children, though you're so wonderful at that job. But as *you*. As my wife and partner. As the woman I want to spend my life with."

Fresh tears spilled over, and Janie let them fall once more. "I thought I'd lost that. I missed you seeing me that way."

"You didn't lose it. *I* lost sight of it for a while. But I'm going to keep seeing you every day. Even on the hard days, and when the depression is bad, and when we're exhausted, and the girls are driving us crazy. I'm going to make sure you know that I see you, and I promise never to stop again."

"What if I can't always see myself?" Janie asked quietly, giving voice to the rising worry in her mind. "What if the depression doesn't get better with the meds? What if I have days where I can't remember why I'm worth fighting for?"

"Then I'll remember for both of us." Hannah cupped Janie's face and thumbed away her tears. "I'll remind you every single day if I have to. You're worth it, Janie. You're worth every fight, every hard conversation, every moment of doubt. You're worth everything to me. You always have been, and you always will be."

Janie kissed her, soft and slow, and full of hope for what they were rebuilding. When they pulled apart, Hannah grinned widely.

"You know what I just realized?" Hannah asked.

"What?"

"We have an entire hotel room to ourselves. No kids who might wake up. No responsibilities until tomorrow. We could order room service. Take a bath. Make love again. Or just sleep for a little while."

Janie ran her finger over Hannah's lips. "Just sleeping with you sounds perfect."

"Yeah?"

"Yeah." Janie nestled closer against Hannah's chest, her heartbeat steady and strong against Janie's ear. "Let's just be us for a little while longer." With Hannah's arms around her and Hannah's breath warm against her neck, she was truly at peace for the first time in months.

They had a long road ahead, with all the therapy, the custody hearing, and the daily work of rebuilding trust and connection. The medication would take a while to really kick in, and the depression might never be fully gone. There would be hard days, maybe even hard months.

But she had this. She had Hannah, and vice versa. Their love was big enough for their children and for each other, and their hearts had room for both kinds of devotion.

And that, Janie thought as sleep crept closer to claim her, was more than enough.

It was everything.

Chapter Twenty-One

SOLO WOKE TO THE bright city lights filtering through the hotel curtains, her body pleasantly exhausted. Every muscle ached in that good way, the kind that came from hours of reconnecting with the woman she loved most in the world.

Janie was sprawled across her chest, with one of her legs over Solo's hips pinning her down, and her face was pressed into Solo's shoulder. Her breathing was deep and even, peaceful, like she didn't have the weight of...*everything* on her mind. Solo's arm had gone slightly numb under Janie's weight, but she didn't want to move. The moment was too precious, too fragile, like any shift might shatter it and bring down the beauty of the previous hours.

She studied Janie's face in the artificial yellows, pinks, and blues of the cityscape's illuminations, smiled at the way her eyelashes cast shadows on her cheeks, the small crease between her brows that appeared even in sleep, the soft parting of her lips. *Beautiful.* She was so goddamn beautiful it made Solo's chest ache. She hoped she'd made Janie grasp how much Solo worshipped her when they'd made love. And Jesus, it was definitely that. There'd been such desperate intensity, followed by slow, exploratory tenderness, and maybe her favorite of all, the sleepy, almost dreamlike final bout that had left them both trembling and overwhelmed.

Solo thought about her therapy sessions and knew she wouldn't have been here now without Rae's patient intervention. She doubted she could've even begun to understand Janie's depression, but she was still plagued by the feeling that it was so unfair. Janie was such a wonderful human being, such a gentle soul. She didn't deserve what had happened—what was still happening—to her, and it made Solo want to hurt someone. If only she could find the source, the reason. But there was none. Although she could direct some of her rage toward Janie's mother, for sure.

Her stomach turned at the reminder that the custody threat still loomed large, and they still had hard work ahead of them. But last night had been a turning point, like they'd finally found their way back to the foundation of what they were, not just as parents but as lovers. It was as if they'd rediscovered the two people who had chosen each other once and would continue to do so every day. And Solo was willing to fight anyone and everyone to keep her little family safe now that it was back together again.

She bit her lip. They *were* back together again, weren't they? This had sealed it, surely... Doubt gnawed at her gut, adding to the tension Janie's mom had set in motion.

Janie stirred slightly, her hand flexing against Solo's ribs, and Solo pressed a kiss to the top of her head. They had to leave this bubble and return to reality, to the triplets, to the garage, and to the legal battle with Janie's mother. But for just a few moments longer, Solo wanted to hold onto this peace and the hope that they were going to be okay.

Janie made that cute little sound she always made when she wasn't quite awake but not fully asleep either, and she burrowed closer. Not wanting to think about getting up and going home just yet, Solo tightened her arm around her wife's waist.

My wife. She tested out the words in her head. They'd never stopped being married, of course, but it had been too long since Solo had really fulfilled the truth of that word. Janie was her wife, her partner, and the woman she wanted beside her through everything.

The sky outside continued to shimmer with the spotlights dotting Lake Shore Drive, shifting colors and fading high in the clouds that were keeping the stars at bay. Solo thought about their daughters and the morning routine that would start in just a few short hours. Tia would be the first to wake, climbing out of her crib and padding to Solo's bedroom to announce that it was morning even though the sun was barely up. Chloe would follow soon after, never wanting to be left out. And Luna would be the last, needing to be coaxed awake with promises of pancakes or cartoons.

Solo's chest tightened with longing. She missed them. Even after one night away, she missed the weight of their small bodies, the chaos of their demands, the way they smelled like baby shampoo and sweet popcorn. But she'd enjoyed every single second of her date with Janie, and she was sure they'd reclaimed the part of their relationship that had been buried under the weight of parenthood.

Janie shifted again, and her eyes fluttered open. For a moment, she looked disoriented, then she focused on Solo's face and smiled, her gaze soft, sleepy, and full of contentment.

"Hi," Janie murmured, her voice rough with sleep.

"Hi." Solo brushed a strand of hair away from Janie's face. "How are you feeling?"

"Sore in the best possible way." Janie smiled then wrinkled her nose and dipped her gaze slightly. "Hopeful."

"Yeah. Me too." Solo glanced at the clock on the nightstand. It was way past midnight, and its neon digits declared an end to their fairytale night. "I should probably head home before my clothes turn to rags," she said and sighed deeply. "The girls usually wake up around six thirty, and I don't want to confuse them about where I am."

Janie bit her lip and nodded slowly. "Of course. I'll drop you off."

Solo looked into Janie's eyes, trying to decipher the emotions that had flittered across them. "Come with me," she said, venturing into shaky territory.

"Really?"

"Yes. Come home with me." Solo's conviction increased with each syllable. "I don't mean to stay. I know we'll have to take things slow and build up to you moving back in. Unless you *do* want to stay. Then you can. Obviously." She waved her hand, trying to stop herself waffling. "But come for breakfast and be there when the girls wake up. Let's start our day together, and maybe we can create some new Sunday traditions." When Janie's eyes filled with tears, Solo hoped to God they were the good kind.

"You want me there?"

"Of course I do. And so do the girls." Solo cupped Janie's face. "But only if you're ready. I'm not pressuring you. If you need more—"

"No." Janie shook her head emphatically. "No, I want to. I want to be there. I want to start our day together."

"Yeah?" Relief flooded through Solo, so intense it made her dizzy.

"Yeah."

They got dressed quickly, both fumbling with clothes and buttons in their haste. Solo kept stealing glances at Janie, at the way her dress hung slightly askew, at the marks on her neck and collarbone Solo had made in the throes of passion, at the way her hair was gloriously messed up from their night together.

"What?" Janie asked, catching Solo staring.

"You look thoroughly…loved," she said and grinned. "It's a good look on you."

Janie flushed pink. "You're ridiculous."

"You love it."

"I really do."

They checked out of the hotel, receiving only a slightly raised eyebrow from the young person behind the desk, and Janie drove them home through the somewhat quiet streets of early morning Chicago. In between watching Janie's profile and the concentration in her expression, Solo looked out over the lake and toward the horizon that was so distant, it made the water seem like an ocean. The beautiful sight got her thinking how much she loved that they were raising their kids in a place where they got all the benefits of a city as well as this.

When they pulled up to the house, Janie grasped Solo's thigh and squeezed a little too hard.

She placed her hand over Janie's and eased it up slightly. "Are you okay?"

"I'm nervous. I don't know why. This is my house. And yet..."

"But this is different." Solo lifted Janie's hand to her lips and kissed her knuckles. "You're coming home for real."

Janie didn't respond. She just nodded repeatedly, as if she couldn't stop.

Solo stroked Janie's hand. "We don't have to make a big deal about it. We can just...let it be."

Janie let out a long breath. "Okay," she said and got out of the car.

Solo took her hand, and they crept up the path and into the house as quietly as possible, mindful of the rest of the sleeping household. The door of her dad's bedroom was closed, and the triplets' room was silent. They'd timed it perfectly, arriving about an hour before the girls would start waking up. Solo held onto Janie's hand, a little scared that if she let go, Janie might run down the stairs and out of the house again. She gestured to their bedroom. "You're sure?"

"I'm sure."

In their bedroom, they stripped off their clothes, changed into PJs and climbed into bed. When Solo pulled Janie close, she tucked herself against Solo's side with a sigh that seemed to come from a deep, hidden place.

"I missed this bed," Janie whispered.

"I missed you *in* this bed."

They lay there in the quiet dimness, and that unsteady, off-beat rhythm of her heart, the one she'd become aware of since Janie had first moved out of their marital bed, settled. This was how it was supposed to be: Janie in her arms, in their bed, their home. Together.

"Thank you," Janie said softly.

"For what?"

"For not pressuring me." Janie moved her hand from Solo's stomach to her chest.

Solo kissed the top of Janie's head. "From now on, I'm always going to do whatever you need."

They dozed lightly until the bedroom door was pushed open, and right on schedule, Tia stood in the opening, silhouetted and small in the half light of the hallway. Janie stiffened slightly in her arms, and Solo touched her back gently. "It's okay," she said and prayed it really would be. "Look who's here!" She uncoupled herself from Janie and switched on the bedside lamp.

"Mommy! Mommy!" Tia tumbled along the carpet in toddler-turbo running style and began to clamber onto Janie's side of the bed. "Mommy help!"

The oxygen came back into the room with a whoosh when Janie reached out from under the comforter without further hesitation and hoisted Tia onto the bed and between the two of them.

"Good morning, baby girl." Solo kissed the top of Tia's head, breathing in her unique toddler scent.

"Mommy home," Tia said, clumsily sticking her hand in Janie's face.

"Yep," Solo said, holding in the choking sob that reached up her throat. "Mommy came home." She sniffed the air when Tia kicked her legs up into the air. "Smells like someone needs changing."

Janie threw back the covers and lifted Tia into her arms. "I've got you. Let's go see if your sisters are up yet."

Solo followed Janie back to the triplets' room, practically gliding across the carpet thanks to the joy lifting her heart.

By the time Janie had changed Tia's diaper and gotten her into fresh clothes, Chloe was awake too, and Luna was beginning to stir gently. When they finally seemed to register Janie was in the room, they burst into giggles and cute little exclamations. Solo inclined her head slightly, waiting for the inevitable thundering of Griff's heavy paws up the stairs as he realized the girls were awake and ready to play. Seconds later, he was in the bedroom too, with that happy look on his face like it was Christmas and he'd just ripped open the hugest box of bones in the universe.

Her dad appeared in the doorway, took one look at the scene and smiled. "Good night?" he asked her quietly.

"The best," Solo said, her heart pressing against her chest like it might burst with the amount of love contained within its walls.

He drew her into a bone-crushing hug. "Good. It's about damn time."

Once they got the girls dressed and ready, they went downstairs and made breakfast together. Janie scrambled eggs while Solo handled pancakes, both of them dodging triplets who were determined to assist in their own special way. Her dad supervised from the table, drinking coffee and offering unhelpful commentary like it was a football game and the triplets were on the offence.

"I was thinking," he said as Janie plated the eggs. "You two seem to have things well in hand now. And Carmen's working out great. Maybe it's time I think about moving on."

Solo froze, spatula suspended over the griddle. She hadn't wanted to think about this part of being reunited with Janie. Having him there had been such a lifeline. She wouldn't have survived without his steady presence, his help with the girls, and his gentle wisdom whenever she'd faltered, which had been a lot. "You don't have to go," she said quickly. "We love having you here. Right, Janie?"

"Of course. You're always welcome," Janie said.

But her response was a beat too slow, and Solo caught the hesitation, filing it away to think about later. Her dad noticed too, of course he did, and he gave a sage nod.

"I'm not leaving tomorrow," he said. "But I don't want to overstay my welcome either. You two need to figure out your rhythm as a family again, and that's going to be a lot easier without an extra person in the house."

Solo flipped the pancake as it started to burn. "But—"

"We can talk about it later," her dad said, stopping Solo in her tracks. "For now, let's just enjoy breakfast."

They ate together, and the triplets made their usual mess. Solo tried to push away the sudden anxiety about her dad leaving. She'd gotten so used to having backup, but she'd also enjoyed spending so much time with him again. The thought of going back to just her and Janie, even though that's what she wanted, seemed like it might be too much for the two of them to handle and too soon to try.

As if she was able to read Solo's mind, Janie took her hand and held her gaze, her understanding clear. They'd figure it out together.

On Monday morning, Solo walked into the garage feeling mighty pleased with herself. Sunday with Janie and the girls had been a lazy dream of a day filled with cartoons, playtime, and naps. Janie had stayed until after dinner before heading back to her apartment. Solo hadn't wanted her to leave, but she had to work, and her files were there. Solo didn't press the issue, not wanting to pierce the bubble of happiness they'd created over the weekend. They'd kissed goodbye at the door like teenagers, and Solo had watched Janie drive away, a smile on her face instead of an ache in her chest.

"Well, well, well," Woody said, the moment Solo entered. "Look who's glowing like she got some."

"Shut up," Solo said, then grinned widely.

"Oh my god, you did!" Woody whistled. "You totally did!"

Gabe emerged from the office, followed by Shay. "Did what?"

"Solo had sex!" Woody announced to the entire garage.

"Jesus Christ, Woody." Solo punched RB's shoulder, but in truth, she'd been desperate to get to work to share the news with her chosen family. "Can I have coffee before we discuss my sex life?"

"Nope." Shay motioned to the couches. "Spill. Now."

They gathered in the break room, and Solo told them everything. Not the intimate details of Saturday night, but everything else about her perfect weekend. When the conversation inevitably turned to the custody battle she and Janie were gearing up for, the lightness she'd been feeling when she walked in began to fade, and fear invaded the vacuum.

"That fucking woman," Gabe said, her expression fierce. "What can we do? How can we help?"

"Testify as character witnesses," Solo said. "David, our lawyer, said we need to line up people who can speak to our fitness as parents."

"I'm in," Gabe said.

Shay nodded. "And me."

"Me too. I can lie as good as anyone," Woody said and clapped Solo on the shoulder.

"Obviously." RB shrugged. "Though I'm probably not the most credible witness given my general life choices."

"You run a successful business, and you're loyal to your people." Solo kicked RB's shin lightly. "That counts for something."

"When's the hearing?" Gabe asked.

"I'm not sure yet." Solo glanced at her phone, hoping that might prompt David to call with exactly that information. "Early October maybe."

"And how's Janie handling it?" Shay asked.

Solo thought about Saturday night, about Janie breaking down in her arms during the hours of talking and reconnecting between the sex. "She's scared. We both are."

Gabe's expression softened. "I'm proud of you for fighting for your family and being vulnerable enough to let Janie back in. You're doing the work, and that's amazing."

Gabe never said shit she didn't mean, and Solo's throat tightened. "Thanks. That means a lot."

"We've got your back," RB said. "Whatever you need. Testimony, someone to intimidate Janie's mother in a parking lot—"

"Not that last one," Shay said, shaking her head.

"Fine." RB threw up her hands and rolled her eyes. "But the

offer stands if things take a turn."

Woody leaned back in her chair. "So are we going to talk about the fact that you and Janie are back together? Like, for real?"

"We're working on it," Solo said, not wanting to jinx it. "We're taking it slow. She stayed over on Saturday night, but we haven't talked about her moving back in permanently yet."

Shay arched her eyebrow. "But you want her to."

"Of course I do. But I also want to do it right. We have to do the work Rae gives us and build a foundation that's going to last. We can't rush back in and end up falling into the same patterns that broke us the first time."

"Smart." Gabe gave Solo the thumbs up. "Hard, but smart."

Solo could've talked more, but the demands of the workday pulled them apart. She headed to her current project of a custom paint job on a restored Mustang and lost herself in the familiar rhythm of the work. But all day, her mind kept drifting back to Janie and the past two days, and to the tentative, fragile hope that they really were on a solid path to reconciliation.

Her phone buzzed with a text. *Thinking about you. Can't wait to see you tonight.*

Solo grinned and typed back: *Me too. I love you.*

I love you too. See you at seven?

Six would be better. But I'll take whatever I can get.

She pocketed her phone and returned to her work, but she couldn't stop smiling. They had the custody hearing looming, and now maybe her dad was leaving. They had the daily challenges of parenting triplets, running the business, and managing Janie's depression, and all the other complications of life. But they had hope, and while a little of that could be a dangerous thing, maybe a truckload of it would be enough to outweigh the suffocating fear.

Chapter Twenty-Two

THE SAME ABSTRACT ART on the walls, the same white-noise machine humming by the door, the same slightly-too-soft couch that made it hard to sit up straight. Of course none of it would have changed. But Janie could, and she had, or at least, she *was* changing. And other things had changed since their last session. Like her relationship with her wife.

It'd been five days since everything had shifted between them. Sunday had been a beautiful day with the triplets, giving Janie the chance to re-establish her connection with the girls too. Monday and Tuesday had been crazy at work as even more authors added their names and works to the class-action suit. She'd worked so late that she'd stayed at her apartment both nights, but she and Hannah had texted constantly through the days and talked on the phone for a couple of hours before bed. Work had been a convenient excuse to give Janie a little distance after the emotional maelstrom of the weekend. She wanted to be sure she really was ready to go home.

Janie glanced at Hannah sitting beside her, flicking through a gallery of car restoration photos, and touched her leg.

Hannah looked up at her immediately. "Sorry. Woody wanted me to send some of my pics for the garage website." She dropped her phone in her lap. "Are you okay?"

Janie nodded. "I was thinking about how things have changed in the last week."

Hannah took Janie's hand and traced circles on the back of it with her thumb. "Good changes?" she asked, not meeting Janie's eyes.

"Good changes." She tipped Hannah's chin up with her

fingertip. "Are you doubting us?"

"God, no." Hannah grasped Janie's hand. "I'm just hoping you're happy."

The door to Rae's office opened, and Rae came out with her usual warm smile and kind eyes, radiating that air of patient empathy that had made Janie feel safe enough to start opening up in the first place. She'd been reluctant to take Rosie's referral, but now she couldn't imagine seeing anyone else.

"Janie, Hannah. Come on in."

She and Hannah settled on their usual couch, and Janie held tight to Hannah's hand, not because she was anxious, but because she *could*. And because Hannah wanted her to.

Rae settled into her chair across from them, notepad in lap, and studied them both for a moment. "You two look different," she said. "What's changed since I saw you last week?"

Janie glanced at Hannah, who gave her an encouraging nod. "We did the ten things homework," she said. "And we went on our date."

"How did those things go?"

"The ten things was..." Tears prickled Janie's eyes. "It was really good, and it was a timely reminder of why we fell in love in the first place."

"And the date?" Rae asked.

"We went to Pilsen," Hannah said. "We walked around for a while and looked at the street art." She glanced at Janie and smiled. "Janie took me to meet Maria, the woman who's been helping her."

"That's significant." Rae nodded and made notes. "Janie, how did it feel introducing Hannah to someone who's been important to your support system?"

Janie nibbled on her lip for a moment, trying to figure out the best way to express that. "I was conflicted," she said, touching Hannah's thigh when she frowned slightly. "I met Maria moments after I left Hannah, the day after the ER incident. It was quite surreal, but looking back, it kind of feels like fate. Maria became the one person I could talk to when I'd shut out everyone else. I wanted Hannah to meet her. But I was worried that the new part of my life wouldn't be able to co-exist with my family life."

"Worried in what way?" Rae asked.

"That Hannah might not like Maria. Or vice versa." Janie fiddled with a stray piece of hair, unable to look at Hannah in case there was hurt in her eyes. "Hannah has her ex-Army buddies, and she's had them for a long time, but..." She swallowed, fearing the possible judgment. "I've never really had friends like that, not people I can count on to be there, whenever and however I need them. Maria's friendship feels magical, and nourishing, and supportive in a way I could never have imagined."

Rae stopped writing. "And you don't want to lose that now that you've had it?"

Janie shook her head. "Hence my concern."

"And was it warranted?" Rae asked.

"I don't think so," Janie said and met Hannah's gaze again. "Was it?"

"No." Hannah touched Janie's cheek gently. "I thought Maria was nice. And even if I hadn't, I would never want you to stop seeing someone who meant so much to you."

The tight band around Janie's heart eased a little. "I'm sorry I didn't tell you that earlier."

Hannah's answering smile was easy and full of love. "It's okay, but I don't want you to be scared of sharing anything with me. I want you to be happy, and if Maria helps with that, I'm all in."

"Thank you," Janie said.

Rae scribbled some more then looked up again. "And what happened after you met Maria?"

Heat zipped up Janie's spine and flushed her neck. "I booked a hotel room, in case we wanted somewhere private to talk or..." She shrugged slightly and studied the delicate painting above Rae's desk. "We reconnected."

Hannah gave a low chuckle. "*Really* reconnected."

Rae smiled. "And how was that?"

"Intense," Janie said. "Emotional. But also a little bit scary. Like we've opened the door that leads to us again, and now we have to figure out how to walk through it without falling back into old patterns."

"What old patterns are you worried about?" Rae asked.

"Me disappearing into the girls and making Janie invisible," Hannah said immediately. "And seeing Janie just as their mother and forgetting she's my wife, a person, with her own needs beyond those of the family."

"I don't want to stop being honest when I'm struggling." Janie gripped Hannah's hand again. "I want to stop trying to be perfect and just be real. That's a hang-up from my parents, but it's one I'm finding it tough to let go of."

"They're important patterns to be aware of," Rae said. "And the awareness itself is a huge step. What are you going to do differently this time?"

"We're going to check in more." Hannah half turned to Janie and took both her hands. "And try to talk about what we need instead of assuming the other person knows."

"I'm going to be more honest about when I'm having a bad day," Janie said. "I'm going to try not to hide it and pretend everything's fine. I went to the doctor you recommended last week and got a prescription for antidepressants."

"That's a significant step." Rae made a note. "How do you feel about that decision?"

Janie sighed deeply. "More conflict, honestly. It feels like I'm admitting defeat or something, and I'm worried it won't fix anything. But Maria told me about a friend who took them, and they worked really well, so I guess I'm also a little relieved that I might not have to white-knuckle through every day anymore."

"Taking medication for depression isn't defeat," Rae said gently. "It's recognizing that you have a *medical* condition that responds to *medical* treatment. You wouldn't refuse insulin if you were diabetic, would you?"

"No, of course not." The two examples seemed like opposite

ends of the scale, but that kind of thinking wasn't going to help.

"And we're going to make time for just us," Hannah said. "We'll keep having a date every week. We've got Carmen now, and she's working out great, so that makes it easier for us to be together on our own."

"All of that sounds excellent." Rae nodded encouragingly. "So where are you two at now? Logistically, I mean. Janie, are you still at the apartment?"

Janie nodded. "But we want to talk about me being home more."

"How often are we talking?" Rae asked.

Hannah bounced in her chair. "I was thinking maybe every other night. That gives Janie a few nights at her apartment if she needs space, but it also lets us build a routine together."

Rae focused on Janie. "How does that feel to you?"

"I think that'll work well. I want to be with Hannah and the girls, and I want to go home. But I also don't want to rush back into something and have it fall apart again."

"That's very self-aware too." Rae looked between them. "What about Hannah's father? Is he still living with you?"

"Yeah, but we've been talking about that." Hannah placed her hand on Janie's thigh. "We have a big backyard, and there's side access to the property. We're thinking about building him a tiny house back there. That'll give him his own space, but he'll still be close enough to see the girls regularly."

"And how do you feel about that, Janie?"

"I like it," Janie said. "I mean, Tom's been great. He's been really supportive at a time when Hannah needed him most. He didn't hesitate to upend his whole life to help. But having the house to ourselves feels better to me. Tom still gets to be close to his granddaughters, and they get to see him every day, but we get our house to ourselves again."

"That sounds like a creative solution that respects everyone's needs," Rae said. "When would you staying over more regularly start?"

"Tonight?" Hannah looked at Janie hopefully. "If you're ready?"

"I don't have a bag with me." Janie's heart raced, but Hannah's tender expression quieted her anxiety. "But I could swing by the apartment and pick some stuff up. I'll have to work for a while after the girls have gone to bed."

"That's okay. I understand," Hannah said, her voice gentle. "But tonight, just come home. Please."

Tears threatened to spill over again as Janie nodded. "I will."

Rae smiled. "I think this is excellent progress. But I want to make sure you're both being realistic about what this means. Being together again is a big adjustment. You're going to have moments of friction, times when you get on each other's nerves, and times when the old patterns try to reassert themselves." She held up her hands. "That's normal. The key is to keep communicating, keep being honest, and keep coming back here to help you process things when you need to."

Hannah nodded. "We will."

Rae smiled then checked in about the custody case. They filled her in on the timeline, with the hearing scheduled in three weeks.

"That's a lot of stress on top of rebuilding your relationship," Rae said. "Make sure you're truly supporting each other through that and not just focusing on presenting a united front for the court."

"We're trying," Janie said. "David is preparing us well. But I won't deny that it's scary."

"Of course it is. Your mother is threatening your family. But from what you've told me, you have a strong case. You're engaged parents, you're working on your relationship, and you have support systems in place. A judge is going to see that."

Janie nodded and tried to soak up Rae's positivity. The niggling doubt that her mother was going to ruin everything wouldn't fade or quiet though. They talked some more about Janie's depression and methods for Hannah to support her, and

Rae gently ended the session.

Out in the parking lot, Hannah took Janie's hand. "You're sure about tonight?"

"I'm sure," Janie said and got in the car. "I want to be with you and the girls."

"Then I'll see you at home." Hannah closed the car door, her smile so full of hope it made Janie's chest ache.

On Thursday morning, Janie woke to the sound of small feet padding down the hallway and Tia's voice calling "Mommy! Mommy!" She rolled over, reaching across the bed to find Hannah was already gone, likely heading off the triplets before they could invade their bedroom.

"Give Mommy five more minutes," Hannah said in the hallway. "She's still sleeping."

Janie threw back the comforter and swung her legs out of bed, powered by the desire to see the beautiful faces that belonged to those voices. She pulled on a pair of sweatpants and headed to the triplets' room, where she found Hannah changing Chloe's diaper while Tia and Luna bounced impatiently on Tia's bed. She stood in the doorway and watched for a little while, thinking that she'd almost lost all of it. "Morning."

Three little faces lit up. "Mommy!"

Tia and Luna scrambled over the cot's lowered side and wrapped their small arms around her legs, their voices competing to tell her things about their dreams, and their stuffed animals, and the birds they could hear outside.

Hannah looked up from the changing table and smiled softly, her gaze warm and full of love. "Good morning."

"Morning." Janie scooped up Luna and Tia, breathing in their sweet scent. "Did everyone sleep okay?"

"Like three little logs, right?" Hannah finished with the diaper and lifted Chloe down. "Want to help with breakfast?"

"Yes. Absolutely."

They moved downstairs together, the triplets trailing between them, and fell into a rhythm that seemed like a distant memory, one Janie's depression had tried to force her to forget. Hannah started coffee while Janie filled sippy cups with milk. Hannah pulled out eggs and bread, and Janie settled the girls at their little table with coloring books to keep them occupied. She and Hannah moved around each other in the kitchen with ease, and something tight in Janie's chest unfurled, as if ready to embrace their renewed future.

This was what she'd been missing out on with her self-imposed isolation. Not just being with the girls but the two of them as a team.

Tom appeared in the doorway, already dressed for the day. "Well, this is a nice sight," he said, smiling at them. "Both my girls making breakfast."

"Morning, Tom," Janie said and sank into his strong embrace.

"Good to have you here, Janie." He hugged her tighter. "The house feels complete when you're in it."

"Thank you," was all she could manage in response, and even that came out croaky and weak. She caught Hannah's gaze, and the combination brought tears to her eyes. Janie looked away quickly and concentrated on the chaos of their breakfast routine instead of the overwhelming beauty of *belonging*.

They ate breakfast together, with the triplets being overly demanding: more juice, more toast, help with cutting their eggs into even smaller pieces. Janie happily indulged them, recognizing their behavior for what it was.

"They'll get used to that," Hannah said.

"They're just acting out a little." Janie ruffled Tia's hair and was rewarded with a huge smile. "They'll calm down when they realize I'm here to stay." Even as she said it, the cogs began to whir. What was she doing, going back to the apartment tonight? Why separate herself from them again when everything felt so good? And if it got too much, she could always leave once the kids were in bed.

Carmen arrived at eight to take over, and Hannah and Janie got ready for work with the efficiency of having done this dance a thousand times before.

At the door, Hannah kissed Janie goodbye with a passionate intensity that made Carmen tactfully turn her attention to the triplets.

"See you tomorrow," Hannah murmured.

Janie grasped a handful of Hannah's tee and pulled her close. "Or I could come back tonight," she said without overthinking the implications.

Hannah's eyes brightened, and she grinned widely. "Tonight? Are you sure?"

Janie nodded then kissed her hard. "And maybe there could be less sleeping," she whispered and nibbled Hannah's ear. Hannah practically melted against her.

"Aw, that's not fair."

"It's plenty fair when it's a promise of more to come." Janie gave Hannah's chest a light shove. "Go, paint some magic."

Hannah winked. "Yes, ma'am."

After Hannah left for the garage, Janie drove to her office. The day passed in a blur of meetings, phone calls, and paperwork, all of which she breezed through, feeling more focused and present than she'd been in weeks. She went for lunch with Austin and filled him in on how things were going.

"That's great news," he said. "Does that mean you won't be dropping any more C-bombs on Katherine?"

Janie flushed, embarrassed at the reminder of her behavior that night. "That wasn't my proudest moment, but it depends on whether she keeps her distance or not. A couple of weeks ago, she made it clear that she's interested in me. And for some reason, she seems to think it's reciprocated."

Austin waved his hand. "Then she's seriously deluded. It's always been Hannah for you. Any idiot with eyes can see that."

Janie laughed lightly. She'd been the idiot who couldn't see it for herself for a little while, but Austin was right. Her short-lived attraction to him had just been a confusing aspect of her depression, and Hannah was her north star. She had been since the moment they connected.

That evening, she pulled up curbside behind Hannah's car and cut the engine. *Home.* She could still do this, couldn't she? They weren't moving too fast, were they? She drew in a deep, cleansing breath and headed inside, anxious but eager for whatever the night held. After being mobbed by the triplets, she and Hannah made dinner while Carmen kept the girls busy. Just as Carmen left, Tom returned from his new racquetball club, and they ate together.

Bathtime was a challenge Janie had missed. Tia splashed water everywhere, Luna refused to get her hair washed, and Chloe kept trying to drink the bathwater no matter how many times they told her no. By the time all three were clean and in pajamas, Janie and Hannah were soaked, and Janie's heart could barely contain the joy the evening had created.

"Bedtime stories, Momma." Tia thrust her favorite book about a boy sparrow toward Janie.

Chloe tugged on Janie's slouch pants. "Yeah, story!"

After a quick change into dry clothes, they read stories, all five of them curled up on the giant sofa at the far side of the triplets' bedroom, and one book became three until finally, the girls were settled in their cribs with their various loveys and the nightlights switched on.

Janie and Hannah retreated to their bedroom and collapsed on the bed. "Oh my god," she said. "I forgot how exhausting they are."

"Right? And that's with Carmen *and* Dad helping out. It's no wonder we were drowning before." Hannah rolled onto her side to look at her. "You did great today. Did it feel okay?"

Janie sighed deeply, the ability to think returning slowly after a whirlwind few hours. "I was terrified I wouldn't be able to slip back into the mom routine and that I'd lost my connection with them."

"You didn't lose anything. It's all still there." Hannah tucked a strand of damp hair behind Janie's ear. "How are you feeling?

For real?"

Janie didn't respond immediately, something she was working hard on. The instant answer was usually a broad stroke paint brush that covered up the truth of it, and they'd promised each other honesty. She was exhausted, yes. Overwhelmed, a little. But underneath all that... "Happy," she said. "Tired and happy. Is that weird?"

"Not even a little bit." Hannah's smile was soft. "Are you still glad that you came over again?"

"More than," Janie said. "I won't lie and say that I wasn't anxious. I don't want to rush things, but I so wanted to be home again tonight." She caressed Hannah's cheek. "Back in your arms and in our bed."

Hannah kissed the top of her head. "You're exactly where you belong."

Janie closed her eyes for a moment and listened to the steady beating of Hannah's heart, its rhythmic certainty quieting the rest of the noise in her head. Conscious she could easily drift into the welcome embrace of sleep, she tapped Hannah's chest. "Your dad's developing quite the social life."

Hannah chuckled. "Right? It's starting to feel like we've reversed roles, and he's just coming home for dinner and to get his laundry done. And, I don't know, are we supposed to wait up for him tonight? Make sure he gets home okay after a night out with his new buddies?"

"I almost want you to wait on the stairs for him, tapping your watch when he stumbles in, all buzzed."

Hannah laughed again, the rumbling sound echoing in Janie's ear. "I talked to him earlier about the tiny house idea."

Janie scooched around and rested her head on Hannah's stomach so she could look at her. "What did he say?"

"He loves it." Hannah traced light circles on Janie's shoulder. "He's already researching designs and costs. Apparently, he's been thinking that he'll be in the way when you come home for good and wasn't sure what he was going to do, but he likes the idea of having his own space while still being close to the girls."

Janie pushed Hannah's tank top up slightly to touch her skin. "He doesn't want to head back to Florida then?"

Hannah entwined their fingers. "He said that place was killing him, and he's made some fast friends here." She frowned. "Do you *want* him to go back to Florida?"

"I want him to go wherever makes him happy." Janie uncoupled their hands and gently followed the lines on Hannah's palm. "The girls certainly seem to love having him around, and an extra babysitter so we can have our date nights is *definitely* a good thing." She kissed Hannah's stomach, ignoring the twinge of jealousy at Hannah's relationship with her dad. Tom had always been kind to Janie and like a father to her, but that hadn't negated her wish for things to be different with her real father. "When would you build it?"

"Spring, probably. Now wouldn't be a great time to start a big project like this. But that gives us time to plan it, figure out exactly what we want, and get permits." Hannah shrugged. "He's also going to look at property in the area in case we can't get the right permissions."

"You sound excited." Janie smiled when Hannah moaned as she dragged her fingernails along Hannah's forearm. "It seems like you've enjoyed having him around."

"I really have." Hannah bit her bottom lip and glanced away briefly. "I guess I didn't realize how much I missed him."

"So at least one good thing came out of my meltdown," Janie said and raised her eyebrows.

"More than one thing." Hannah twirled a strand of Janie's hair between her fingers. "Can you remember the last time we lay in bed, just talking and being with each other?"

Janie shook her head and continued her slow exploration of Hannah's lines and contours. "It's nice."

"He really likes you, you know? He's been worried about you, and he's so glad you're coming home."

Happy tears edged her eyes. Her depression had convinced

her she was worthless and unlovable, but her family *wanted* her home. "I like him too. And I'm glad he'll still be close. The girls love him."

"They really do." Hannah caressed Janie's cheek. "But I also really like the idea of it being just us in the house again. Our family. Our space. Does that make sense or does it make me a bad daughter?"

Janie laughed lightly. "I think it makes perfect sense, and I like it just being us too." She slipped her hand under Hannah's tee and ran her finger over Hannah's nipple, thinking of her early morning enthusiasm to do something other than sleep in their bed tonight. But she seriously lacked the energy to put her desires into action, and her hand stilled.

Outside, ordinary life continued. The faint sound of the occasional car passing, a dog barking somewhere down the street, the normal sounds of their neighborhood. The normal sounds of *home*. She snuggled in, trying to get even closer to Hannah's body.

"We should probably shower," Hannah said but made no move to get up.

"We should probably do a lot of things," Janie murmured, equally immobile.

"Tomorrow?"

"Tomorrow," Janie said and shifted to the little spoon position.

"Thank you for coming home again tonight." Hannah kissed Janie's neck. "I know it might be a little scary, but I'm really glad you're here."

"Me too." Janie pushed her butt further into Hannah's crotch. "Even though I'm exhausted and smell like toddler bathwater."

"You smell perfect," Hannah said. "You smell like home."

Janie heard the smile in Hannah's voice and began to drift on the seas of sleep.

"You still awake?" Hannah murmured into Janie's hair.

Janie startled, then let out a long sigh as she pulled Hannah's arm around her. "Barely."

"I love you."

"I love you too," Janie whispered and began to drift again, the exhaustion of the day pulling her under. But just as she was about to slip into sleep, her phone buzzed on the nightstand. She tried to ignore it, but it buzzed again. And then a third time.

"You should check that." Hannah nudged her gently. "It might be important."

All the important people in her life were tucked up safely in bed, but she reached for her phone anyway and squinted at the bright screen in the dark room. Three texts from David.

Janie's entire body went cold. Behind her, Hannah propped herself up on one elbow.

"What is it?"

"David. He says my mother filed a motion." Janie's voice sounded thin and scared, even to her own ears. "He says it changes things."

"Christ," Hannah said, "why did he wait until this late to send a nuclear missile into our house?"

Janie dropped her phone onto the table and turned into Hannah's arms. "He was in San Francisco for another case this week. It's probably just the time difference."

"What kind of motion?" Hannah asked.

"He doesn't say." Janie's earlier contentment evaporated like morning mist in the early sun. "He wants us to call him first thing tomorrow."

They lay there in the darkness, no longer relaxed, both of them wide awake. Janie's mind raced through possibilities, each one worse than the last. Emergency custody. Expedited hearing. New evidence. Had her mother discovered the ER incident? Why didn't David just say that? Could there be something else? Something she'd fabricated?

"Whatever it is, we'll handle it," Hannah said.

She said the words calmly, but Janie could still hear the tension in her voice. "What if we can't?" The words slipped out before Janie could stop them. "What if she's made something up? What if—"

"Janie." Hannah wrapped Janie's hands in her own and gripped tight in the darkness. "We'll handle it together. Let's try to get some sleep."

Janie turned again and snuggled back in, but as she lay there, staring at the phone, that little box of doom, and listening to Hannah's breathing gradually slow back toward sleep, she couldn't shake the feeling that the other shoe had finally dropped. They'd had six perfect days. Six days of reconnecting, of hope, of believing they might actually make it through this.

And now her mother had made her next move.

Her phone didn't buzz again to furnish her with more information, with something that would tell her exactly how bad this was going to be. The recalcitrant block of plastic and circuits lay useless now.

She couldn't sleep. All she could think of was courtrooms, and judges, and her daughters crying for her as her mother dragged them away.

Chapter Twenty-Three

SOLO STARED AT HER dad's rudimentary plans for the tiny house spread across the dining room table, but the numbers and measurements kept blurring together. She'd been looking at the same page for ten minutes, unable to focus on square footage or electrical requirements because her mind kept circling back to yesterday's phone call with David.

Janie's mother wasn't waiting for the scheduled court date three weeks away; she'd filed an emergency hearing and was pushing for temporary custody immediately, claiming "new evidence of parental neglect."

What new evidence? The ER incident, probably. David had been maddeningly vague, saying only that he'd know more after reviewing the filing in detail and that they shouldn't panic. But how were they supposed to not panic when "temporary custody" meant Janie's mother could have the girls within days?

"You're going to burn a hole in that paper if you keep staring at it like that," her dad said from the doorway, two mugs of coffee in his hands.

Solo looked up. "Sorry. I can't concentrate. I keep thinking about—"

"The court thing. I know." He set the coffee down in front of her. "Is Janie still at work?"

"Yeah. She had depositions all afternoon." Solo rubbed her eyes. "She'll be home around seven."

The word "home" had an almost miraculous taste on her tongue, even after Janie had stayed over this whole week instead of alternating with nights at her apartment. They fell asleep together and woke up together and navigated the ongoing chaos of triplet parenthood together. It'd been all but perfect, with a few moments of friction, and times when Janie's depression tried to derail them, but they were working through it.

Or they had been, until Janie's mother threw another grenade into their lives.

"You know," her dad said, pulling out a chair and sitting down across from her, "I've been thinking about the timeline for the tiny house."

She pushed away the papers and grabbed her coffee. "I'm not sure I want to talk about this right now. I have other things pressing for my attention."

"Actually, I think the distraction might do you good." He drew the plans closer to him. "I was thinking we could break ground when the weather starts to warm up in March. We'd get the foundation poured and the framing up before it gets too hot. I reckon we could be move-in ready by June."

"That fast?"

"Tiny houses are quick to build," he said. "That's part of the appeal. And I've got a buddy from the hardware store who's a retired contractor. He's bored out of his mind and looking for a project." Her dad smiled. "But in the meantime, I think you and Janie need your space back, so I'm going to look for a short-term rental. Me making myself tactfully scarce isn't going to work for the next six months."

"You're not in the way—"

"Hannah," he said, "I love being here. I love seeing you and my granddaughters every day. But you two are rebuilding your marriage, and that's hard to do with your old man underfoot. Six months is nothing in the scheme of things. And when we build the tiny house, I get to stay close, but you get your privacy. Win-win."

Solo's throat tightened. This hadn't been the plan, and she wasn't sure she was ready to lose an integral part of her new support system just yet. "I don't know what I would have done without you."

"You would've figured it out. You're stronger than you give yourself credit for." He reached across the table and squeezed her hand. "You always have been. But I'm glad I could help. And I'm proud of you for turning to me and not alcohol."

Solo pulled her hand away, unable to meet his gaze. He'd rescued her too many times from that rathole when she was younger. "Woody and RB appreciated it too," she said, recalling the day she took a crate of liquor to their place after Janie had just left. "I had to be strong for the girls. I couldn't lose myself in a bottle like I have before."

He nodded. "Still. That takes guts, slugger, and I'm proud of you."

"Thanks, Dad," she said quietly.

He cleared his throat. "Anyway, I'm not going anywhere. By June, I'll be fifty feet away in a much cooler living situation, and I won't have to face the shame of telling my new buddies that I'm living in my daughter's fancy house."

Solo grinned. "When you put it like that." Her phone buzzed with a text from Shay: *Game night tonight. Our place. 7pm. Bring snacks. You in?* Right. She hadn't seen the gang outside of work since volleyball night, and they'd want to be updated on how things were going with Janie.

Can't. Janie's coming home around 6 and we need to talk about the court stuff.

Bring Janie. You both need this. Plus we need to talk strategy. Everyone's going to be there. Partners too. No bugging out or you have to tell Gabe when you get to work.

Solo hesitated, then paraphrased the texts for her dad. "What do you think?"

"I think you should go. I'll handle things here. You and Janie could use some time with your people."

She swiveled her phone around and around on the table. She wanted a taste of normality, but everything was so far from normal right now. "Are you sure?"

"Positive. Carmen left that pasta bake in the fridge, so I'll heat it up for the girls. We'll do bathtime and stories, and everyone will be asleep by eight. It's Friday night: you should go. Blow off some steam and get your heads right for whatever's coming."

Solo nodded. "Okay, we will." She texted Shay to say they'd be there and then Janie to see if she wanted to come. It would be the first group thing Janie had done since the Brewster auction, and Solo hoped she'd say yes. She didn't wait for a response, knowing Janie would already be busy with work, and headed out to the garage after kissing the triplets goodbye.

Work gave her some respite from the scenarios racing around her head, and at lunch, Gabe and Shay made her promise she'd be there later. She managed to get away around five after finishing a custom job earlier than expected. Solo opened the front door, anticipating a full front assault from the girls, but the place was eerily quiet. The thought that this could be her new status quo if Janie's mother won custody slammed into her chest like an engine block, and she had to grasp the stair rail for support.

The opening lines of "Let It Go" floated into her consciousness, and the reason for the unusual silence became apparent. Solo walked to the living room and stood, unnoticed in the doorway, watching the girls draped all over her dad and Carmen. She raised her eyebrow when she saw Carmen's arm over the back of the sofa, her fingers tenderly stroking her dad's neck. Did this complicate things or make them better? She sighed loudly, not wanting to deal with that particular question right now.

The triplets screamed, leapt off the sofa, and launched themselves at Solo's legs, and all was right in the world again. She threw her dad a questioning look, and he shrugged, clearly not aware she'd seen the affectionate display. She tumbled to the floor with the girls, deciding to tackle that later. *Much* later.

When Janie got home just after seven, her hair was escaping from its bun, her makeup was slightly smudged, and her shoulders were tight with tension. Solo met her at the door and pulled her into a hug before she could even set down her bag.

"Rough day?" Solo murmured into Janie's hair, hoping she hadn't changed her mind about going out.

"The depositions ran long. And I kept checking my phone every five minutes to see if David had called with more information about my mother's motion." Janie pulled back to look at Solo's face. "Did you hear anything?"

"Nothing yet. He said he'd call tomorrow after he reviews everything in detail."

Janie's face fell, and Solo hated her hopeless expression. "Hey," she said, cupping Janie's cheeks. "We're going to get through this. Whatever she's claiming, we'll fight it."

"But what if—"

"No what ifs. Not tonight." Solo kissed her softly. "Tonight, we're going to Gabe's for game night. Dad's handling bedtime. We're going to spend a few hours with people who love us."

Janie looked like she might argue, but then she sagged against Solo. "Okay, yeah. That actually sounds good."

"Go say hi to the girls then change into something comfortable."

Thirty minutes later, they were in Janie's car heading to the gang's apartment in South Wabash, with an assortment of beer, wine, and snacks in the back seat. Janie hadn't spoken since they'd stopped at the store, and now she was just staring out the window.

Solo reached over to take her hand. "You okay?"

"Just tired." Janie blew out a long breath. "I haven't seen the gang properly for weeks. What if they hate me? I feel like I'm going to be terrible company."

Solo ran her fingers over Janie's palm. "You don't have to be *on* for them. They're our people. They've seen us at our worst."

"Have they though?" Janie whispered. "They've seen you struggling. But me? I just...disappeared. I left you alone with three babies while I hid in a depressing apartment feeling sorry for myself."

Solo pulled into a parking spot near Gabe's building and turned to face Janie properly. "First of all, you weren't feeling sorry for yourself: you were drowning in postpartum depression. Second, they don't judge you. Rosie's been in your corner from the beginning. She understands mental health struggles better than anyone. RB will probably make some inappropriate joke to break the tension, Woody will be quietly supportive, Shay will probably mother-hen you, and Gabe will go into military strategist mode about the court case."

Janie gave her a small, tight smile. "You're probably right."

"I'm definitely right. Now come on. Let's go spend some downtime with the army we have on our side."

The sound of laughter hit them as soon as Solo opened the door. Inside, the living room was already full. Woody was sprawled on one end of the couch, RB was perched on its arm, and Shay and Rosie were curled up together on the other end. Solo figured Gabe and Lori were in the kitchen.

The apartment was neat, with leather furniture, framed vintage truck posters, and a bookshelf full of military history and mechanics manuals. Lori and Rosie's influence was starting to show in small ways: a couple of throw blankets in soft gray and baby blue, a potted plant on the windowsill, and actual curtains in the living room instead of the blinds RB had put up a couple of months ago.

"There they are!" Woody jumped up and pulled Solo and Janie into a hug.

"Be cool, Woody," Shay said, unfolding herself from the couch.

She was wearing a fitted sweater and skinny jeans that looked high chic in a way that Shay managed effortlessly. The femme energy she exuded in a room full of butches always made her stand out.

Shay pulled Solo into a hug, then turned to Janie with a warm smile. "Hey, Janie. Glad you could make it."

Rosie was right behind her, immediately wrapping Janie in a

gentle hug. "How are you holding up?"

"I'm..." Janie's voice wobbled. "I'm okay."

"You don't have to be okay," Rosie said softly. "Not with everything going on."

Solo recognized the tone Rae used and was reminded again why Rosie had been such a good therapist before switching to marketing, though Shay had mentioned she was considering returning to therapy.

Gabe emerged from the kitchen with a stack of pizzas, and Lori trailed behind her with a tray of vegetables and dip.

Gabe pulled Solo into a bro hug, then embraced Janie in a more traditional way. "Glad you could make it. Beer? Wine?"

"Beer," Solo said and looked at Janie. "And non-alcoholic wine for you?"

"Yes, please." Janie tugged hard on Solo's hand.

Janie's fear and tension practically radiated from her, and Solo draped her arm over Janie's shoulder. "It's okay," she whispered. "Everyone here loves you. Not like I do, obviously, but they love you." She squeezed Janie's shoulder lightly and winked.

They settled in the living room after everyone refreshed their drinks. Gabe sat in her armchair with Lori snuggled between her legs, Shay and Rosie settled back on their end of the couch with Woody on the other end, and RB dropped onto the floor. Solo and Janie squeezed together on the loveseat, and the easy nature of the gathering began to seep into her bones. She exhaled and melted into the soft upholstery. She hadn't realized how much she'd needed to be surrounded by her people until right now.

"So," Shay said, "let's talk about the elephant in the room. Janie's mom is being a nightmare, and we're going to be testifying. Tell us what we need to know."

"David's going to prep you individually," Solo said. "But basically, you'll be asked about our fitness as parents. What you've seen when we're with the girls, whether we seem stable and capable, that kind of thing."

"Easy," Woody said. "You're both great parents. The girls are happy and healthy and clearly loved. What kind of monster tries to take kids away from parents like you?"

"The kind who wants control of a trust fund," Janie said quietly.

"Can you walk us through what's going to happen?" RB asked, leaning forward. "At the hearing?"

Janie took a breath, and Solo smiled as she shifted into lawyer mode, straightening her spine and raising her head high.

"Both sides will present their case. My mother's lawyer will try to paint us as unfit. They'll talk about me leaving the house, our demanding jobs..." Janie scanned the room and sighed. "And they'll probably make veiled comments about our lifestyle. Our lawyer will counter with evidence of stability: our new nanny, Carmen, the couples' therapy, the strong family support system, and our character witnesses. The judge will ask questions, review all the evidence, and make a ruling."

"And this emergency motion?" Gabe asked.

Solo practically jumped from her seat and stood to attention at the sound of Gabe's command voice, the one that had led them through combat zones *and* some other sticky situations. "We don't know yet what new evidence she's claiming," she said, though she had a damn good idea. "David's reviewing the filing, but he's got other clients too. So we don't know the details yet, but she's asking for temporary custody while the case is pending, which would mean the girls would go to her immediately."

"Absolutely not," Shay said. "That's not happening."

"We're doing everything we can to prevent it," Janie said. "But my mother has resources. And she knows how to present herself as the concerned grandmother."

"What about character witnesses for Janie specifically?" Lori asked. "Not just as a parent, but as a person?"

"That's where Rae comes in," Shay said. "And that guy Austin from Janie's law firm, as well as your assistant, right? They can all speak to who you are."

Janie gave a quick nod, but her entire body tensed against

Solo's. She hadn't really gotten close to anyone, and she didn't have the chosen family and friends like Solo did. Only Maria had penetrated that fortress, and David had said it would seem desperate to bring in a character witness who'd only known Janie for a couple of weeks.

"Rae will talk about the postpartum depression." Rosie looked toward Lori. "As Janie's therapist, she's seen Janie actively working to get better."

Lori nodded at Rosie. "And you can talk about how Janie has been helping you with your loan fraud. I know we're both new to the group, but we've seen how tight you all are, how you have each other's backs, no matter what."

Tears burned Solo's eyes, and she stared up at the ceiling, trying to fight them off. "You guys don't have to—"

"Stop," Shay said, but her tone was affectionate. "We're family. This is what family does."

They talked through the timeline, the strategy, and what each person should emphasize in their testimony. Gabe, as Solo's former commanding officer, would speak to Solo's character and reliability. Shay would talk about the garage, about Solo's work ethic and dedication to both her business and her family. Woody would discuss Solo's commitment to her responsibilities. RB would...well, RB would probably say something inappropriate, but she'd also fiercely defend Solo's fitness as a parent.

After about an hour of legal talk, Shay stood up and stretched. "Okay, enough of that. We're supposed to be having game night, not a war council. Who wants to play Mario Kart?"

"Oh, you're going down," Woody said, already reaching for a controller.

Solo laughed. "You say that every time and then RB destroys you."

"That's because RB is secretly a gaming prodigy." Woody stuck out her bottom lip. "It's unfair."

"I just have good hand-eye coordination," RB said and grinned widely.

They played for an hour with trash talk flying, Woody getting increasingly competitive, and RB quietly dominating. Shay's running commentary had everyone laughing, her natural charisma filling the room. Solo noticed how Rosie watched Shay with obvious adoration, how they kept finding excuses to touch, fingers brushing, their hands always seeking each other out in small intimate gestures that spoke of a relationship still in that giddy early phase. It was the same way Gabe and Lori moved around each other, careful but magnetic, still learning each other's rhythms but clearly falling hard.

A pang of something that wasn't quite envy registered in Solo's gut. Wistfulness maybe. She and Janie had been like that once, in the beginning. And they were finding their way back to it, but it looked different now. Scarred and harder won, but maybe stronger for it.

During a break between rounds, Shay cornered Solo in the kitchen while she was grabbing more beer.

"How are you really doing?" Shay asked. "And I don't want more of the brave face bull that you're putting on for everyone. I want the truth."

Solo leaned against the counter. When Shay took the time to talk, Solo always listened. "Terrified." She took a long pull on her bottle, hoping she might swallow some of her emotions along with the beer. "But fucking angry too. Who does Angela think she is? She failed as Janie's mom so now she wants a second chance with *our* kids? It's fucked up."

"It is." Shay grasped Solo's shoulder, her penetrating gaze looked right into Solo's soul. "What else?"

"I'm trying not to fall apart because Janie needs me to be strong."

"You know it's okay to not be strong sometimes, right?" Shay raised her eyebrows and stared at her. "You can still be the baby of the group who doesn't have it all figured out."

"I'm not the baby anymore," Solo said, a little taken aback when she realized she meant it. "I'm a mother of three. I'm fighting for my marriage and my family. I'm...I'm an adult now."

Shay smiled. "Yeah, you are. And you're handling it really well. We were worried that you'd spiral when Janie left and maybe fall into old patterns and start drinking too much. Or even shut down completely."

Solo's chest tightened. "I won't lie, I thought about it. I was on my knees literally and figuratively the morning Janie left. But then I heard my girls calling for me, and I knew I couldn't. My whole family needed me, and I wasn't going to let them down."

"Your *whole* family," Shay said, giving Solo that same intense gaze. "Not *my girls* need me."

Solo frowned. "What?"

"You said 'my whole family needs me,' not 'my girls need me.'" Shay leaned against the counter beside her. "That's growth, Solo. A few months ago, everything was about the kids. Gabe and I talked about how worried we were that you'd lost yourself in motherhood, and lost sight of your marriage."

Solo was about to protest but stood down quickly enough. She couldn't argue that Shay was wrong. "My girls mean so much to me," she said slowly. "But they're not everything. Janie's my world. I learned my lesson. Being without her nearly killed me, and I'll always see her as more than just the mother of my kids."

"That's what's going to get you through this," Shay said and slapped her hand against Solo's chest. "That right there. The fact that you've learned to balance being a mother and a wife and yourself, all at once."

Gabe walked into the kitchen and stopped in the doorway. "You two having a moment without me? I'm hurt."

"Just giving Solo the Shay Washington wisdom treatment," Shay said and ran her knuckles over Solo's buzz cut.

"Then all will be well in your world," Gabe said and grabbed another bucket of beer. "Now can we get back in there before everyone dies of thirst?"

They returned to the living room, where Janie was deep in

conversation with Rosie and Lori. Solo caught the end of Rosie saying something about therapy approaches and Janie nodded, looking more relaxed than she had when they'd gotten there.

"Your turn, Gabe," RB said. "I'm tired of destroying Woody's ego."

"My ego is indestructible," Woody shouted, thrusting her controller in the air.

"Your ego is definitely something," Shay said, and everyone laughed.

They played for another hour, the energy lighter. Shay kept the mood upbeat, cracking jokes and trash-talking with Woody in a way that had everyone in stitches. At one point, she turned to Janie and said, "You know, if your mom tries anything in court, I'm happy to testify about what a badass lawyer you are. What you're doing for Rosie is scary good."

Janie's cheeks flushed. "You think?"

Shay nodded. "Your mom's lawyers have no idea who they're up against."

Solo watched Janie's face transform: she sat up a little straighter, and some of that lawyer confidence crept back in. Solo smiled at Shay and raised her bottle. She always knew exactly what someone needed to hear and how to say it.

Around ten, Janie's phone rang. She looked at the screen and went pale. "It's David." The room went silent as Janie put it on speaker. "David. What is it?"

"I've reviewed the motion," David said after half apologizing for the late call. "Your mother's uncovered the ER incident. She's requesting temporary custody until the hearing."

His words hit Solo like a sucker punch. "How? Aren't those records supposed to be confidential?"

"They are," David said. "But no doubt she has investigators who'll do anything to get the information they need."

"What do we do?" Janie asked, her voice shaky.

"We fight it. I've already drafted our response. But you need to be prepared. There's going to be an emergency hearing on

Monday morning. The judge will hear both sides and make a ruling on temporary custody."

"Monday," Janie whispered. "Two days."

"I'll email you both the details tonight. In the meantime, document everything. Your routines with the girls, Carmen's schedule, therapy appointments. Show stability and consistency."

After David hung up, the room stayed deathly still. Solo looked at Janie's stricken face, then at her crew.

"So," Woody finally said, her usual levity replaced by something harder. "Monday. That means we have a couple of days to make sure you're ready to show that judge you're the best fucking parents those girls could ask for."

"We'll all be there," RB added quietly. "Whatever you need."

Shay stood up, and Solo saw that look on her face, the same one Gabe got when she was planning a mission. They'd been friends long enough to think alike in almost all situations, but especially ones like this.

"Okay," Shay said. "Here's what we're going to do. Tonight, Solo and Janie go home and get some sleep. Tomorrow, we help them document everything. We'll come over, take photos, help organize records, whatever they need. Sunday, we do a practice run, where you," she pointed at Solo, "are going to practice staying calm and confident under pressure. Monday morning, we show up to that courthouse, and we don't let them take those babies."

Rosie got up to stand beside Shay. "You'll walk into that courtroom with an army behind you."

"Damn right," Lori said softly, and Gabe squeezed her hand.

Janie was crying now, and Solo pulled her close. They were surrounded by their people, their army, and even though everything was kind of falling apart, there was something steady beneath the fear.

They weren't alone. They were never alone.

In the car driving home, Solo reached over and took Janie's hand. "We're going to win this," she said, trying to convince herself as much as Janie. "We have to."

But Janie just stared out the window at the passing lights, her hand limp. "What if we don't?" she finally whispered. "What if Monday morning, a judge decides I'm unfit? That we're unstable? What if I have to watch my daughters get taken away by my mother?"

Solo didn't have an answer. She just gripped Janie's hand tighter and drove them home, toward their sleeping children, toward whatever the next few days would bring.

Two days. They had two days to save their family.

And Solo had never been more terrified in her life.

Chapter Twenty-Four

JANIE HAD THROWN UP twice before they even left the house Monday morning. The first time was right after she got out of the shower, the anxiety hitting her so hard she barely made it to the toilet. The second was after she'd gotten dressed in her most conservative navy suit, the go-to one she wore to court when she needed to project competence and stability, and realized her hands were shaking too badly to fasten the buttons. She got there in plenty of time, but splash-back on her suit forced a change of outfit.

She was sitting on the edge of their bed, half-dressed and crying, when Hannah came in. She wordlessly finished buttoning Janie's shirt, then pulled her into a hug that Janie wanted to stay in forever.

"We're going to get through this," Hannah murmured into her hair. "Whatever happens, we're going to get through it together."

God, how Janie wished that were true. But if everything went against them today, would Hannah really not blame her for losing their children? And she couldn't shake the image of a judge, a total stranger who knew nothing about them and nothing about how much they loved their daughters, getting to decide their family's fate in a matter of hours. It seemed ironic that she'd been more than happy with the ability of a hundred judges in her cases deciding the fate of her client. Maybe this was payback for her cavalier attitude.

She finally disentangled herself from Hannah's embrace, and they went downstairs to wait for the Uber she'd ordered. David had insisted they didn't drive, probably sensing that neither of them were fit to navigate the mayhem of Monday's morning traffic, and though Tom had offered to take them, Janie politely declined. The last trip in his back seat had left her with palpitations and deep nail marks in her palms.

Maria had already arrived, and she pulled Janie into a warm and deep embrace. "Everything will be fine, mija."

"Thank you for coming to look after the girls," Janie said, choosing not to acknowledge Maria's statement. She wanted to believe her, more than anything, but doubt burrowed deep in her mind, warning her of impending doom.

Hannah showed Maria to the playroom and returned with Tom, who then stood at the door like a sentry ready for battle. Janie hadn't seen him in a suit since their wedding. They had people in their corner and on their side, but all of it might mean nothing in the face of Angela Evans and her legal entourage.

Janie froze at the base of the stairs, staring at her phone screen and the little black car moving toward their house. Hannah touched the small of her back, and she almost collapsed against her.

"It'll be over soon," Hannah said.

Her words didn't provide the comfort they were supposed to. Over didn't necessarily mean the right result. Over could mean her life as a mother was done, and she'd never get to hold her beautiful little girls ever again. Because if a judge was going to take her children away, why would they allow her visitation rights? Lawyer logic tried to creep in but didn't make it past the barking black dog of her catastrophizing.

"The car's here," Tom said, opening the door.

The cool air rushed in, wrapping her in even more doubt. The October morning was crisp and clear, the kind of day that should have imbued hope but instead loomed like a mockery. How dare the weather be beautiful when Janie's entire world could be about to collapse? Hannah's hand was once again at her back, gently ushering her out of the house and toward the Uber. She got in and shuffled across to the center, then stared out the windshield, not particularly fixing on a point of interest. If the driver braked hard and she shot through the windshield, at least this nightmare would be over.

She was vaguely aware of Hannah putting her seatbelt on for her, as if she'd sensed Janie's nonchalance about her own mortality, and then she fell away from the surroundings of the interior and the chatter of their driver into a kind of echoey trance. She didn't want to engage in small talk with a stranger when the custody of her beloved children hung in the balance. How was she supposed to entertain inane drivel about the latest sports game or the state of the country's politics when she could be two hours away from becoming childless, no longer able to claim the title of mom?

She partially emerged from the vaguely meditative state when she became aware of Hannah squeezing her hand.

"We're here."

Hannah's voice was distant, as if Janie were hearing her through a seashell. A vivid and beautiful memory of her grandma with her at the beach, each with a seashell pressed to their ears, presented itself in her mind, and she smiled. All of her special childhood memories were with Grandma Susan, but she didn't want her own children to have that same experience. *She* would be different. And that meant not letting her vindictive, greedy mother anywhere near the girls. A thread of steel wound its way from the base of her spine and up into her mind, fortifying her for the battle ahead. Suddenly, sound returned and everything became crystal-sharp.

She grasped Hannah's hand tightly. "She's not taking them away from us."

Hannah tugged Janie closer. "Damn right she isn't."

David hurried across the sidewalk to open the door and helped Janie out of the car. "You reminded Maria not to answer the door for anyone and to call me immediately if anyone shows up claiming to have a court order, yes?"

"Yes." Janie arched her eyebrow, briefly offended at the implication she might've forgotten something that important.

But she hadn't been her usual, logical self throughout this ordeal, so his question was vaguely justified. She glanced over to the main entrance and saw Gabe, Lori, Shay, Rosie, Woody, and RB were already there, looking like they were about to launch some kind of queer military operation.

"Ready?" David asked, more gently this time.

Janie looked at Hannah, who took her hand. "No," she said. "But let's do it anyway."

As they approached the steps, their people surrounded them. Gabe fell into step on Hannah's left, her presence solid and commanding. Shay took up position on Janie's right, her usual bright energy replaced by something fierce and protective.

"You've got this," Shay said quietly.

Janie leaned her head on Shay's shoulder for a moment and sighed deeply. "Thank you for coming."

Inside, the courthouse was all marble and echoes and too many people moving with purpose. That was usually a familiar comfort, but today it felt foreboding. But Janie shook it off, determined to maintain the fortitude that had coursed through her in the car.

David led them to a courtroom on the third floor, and Janie's stomach dropped when she saw her mother already seated with her lawyer, a severe-looking woman in a predictably expensive suit. She was currently reviewing documents with a focus that made Janie's legal instincts scream danger.

Her mother looked up as they entered, and something flickered across her face very briefly. Surprise, maybe, at the size of the group accompanying Janie. Or perhaps calculation, already figuring out how to spin the presence of such a motley crew of individuals. But it was milliseconds before her mother's expression smoothed into the perfect mask of concerned grandmother, and nausea rushed up Janie's throat once again.

"Don't look at her," Rosie said softly, placing her hand on Janie's shoulder. "Look at us. Look at Hannah. Look at everyone who's here for you."

Janie nodded and forced herself to focus on Hannah instead and on the set of her strong jaw, the way she stood straighter when she was nervous, as if she was on parade again. Then there was the tiny muscle twitching in her cheek that meant she was holding back her surging emotions.

Hannah turned and gave her a small, tight smile. "We're going to get through this."

The court officer called them to order, and everyone else settled into the gallery seats.

"Remember," David said, looking at Hannah, "this isn't a full hearing. It's just an emergency motion to determine temporary custody while the main case is pending."

Janie arched her eyebrow and meant it this time. "Just" felt like a joke when a negative outcome would mean her daughters being ripped away from them.

Judge Morrison entered, her sharp eyes and expression giving away nothing. A small sprig of hope fluttered in Janie's stomach; surely a Black female judge would be more sympathetic to the challenges they faced, more understanding of—

Don't be stupid. That was her mother's kind of thinking, making assumptions based on demographics. Judge Morrison would rule based on the law and the evidence. Nothing more, and nothing less.

"This is an emergency motion for temporary custody filed by Angela Evans, maternal grandmother of," Judge Morrison glanced at her notes, "Tia, Luna, and Chloe Rogers-Evans, currently in the custody of their parents, Hannah Rogers and Janie Evans."

Hearing the girls' full names, so formal and legal, made Janie's chest hurt. They were her babies, not cold names on a legal document.

"Ms. Bradford," Judge Morrison said, looking at Angela's lawyer. "You have the floor."

Bradford stood with a confidence that came from years of winning, and Janie fought to control the bile rising from her roiling guts. She would be confident too, confident that her girls belonged with her and Hannah.

"Your Honor, my client filed this emergency motion due to credible concerns about the safety and wellbeing of her granddaughters. The parents have been separated for over a month, during which time, one parent, Janie Evans, abandoned the family home and the children. While Mrs. Evans has recently begun staying at the home on what appears to be an ad-hoc basis, there is no consistent, stable living arrangement."

Hannah gripped Janie's hand hard under the table, making her hiss. David shot them a worried side glance.

"Furthermore," Bradford said, "there is evidence of serious neglect. Last month, one of the children ingested medication while under Mrs. Evans' supervision, requiring emergency medical treatment. While the child recovered, this incident was never reported to my client, suggesting a pattern of hiding dangerous situations." Bradford pulled out documents and handed copies to the bailiff, who passed them to the judge and to David.

"We don't have to report anything to *her*," Hannah muttered, and David shot her a warning look.

"Finally, Your Honor, both parents are engaged in demanding careers that make adequate childcare challenging. While they have hired help, the instability of their relationship, combined with Mrs. Evans' recent abandonment of the home and history of neglectful supervision, creates an unsafe environment for three toddlers. My client is simply seeking temporary custody to ensure the children's safety while the court determines long-term arrangements."

Bradford sat down, looking pleased with herself, and Janie wanted to scream. While almost everything Bradford had said was technically true, it was completely devoid of context. She'd weaponized facts, twisting them into a narrative that painted Janie as neglectful and Hannah as overwhelmed.

"Mr. Adams," Judge Morrison said, looking at David.

David stood and adjusted his tie. Sharp, precise, and ready for battle. She'd seen him do it a hundred times.

"Your Honor, Ms. Bradford's characterization is not only misleading but borders on malicious. Let's address each claim in turn." David pulled out his own stack of documents. "First, the separation. Yes, Mrs. Evans moved out of the family home in early September while dealing with postpartum depression. But she remained in constant contact with her children, continued to provide financial support, and has been actively working on her marriage through couples therapy. She hasn't 'abandoned' anyone, least of all her children. She's a mother dealing with a medical condition who took temporary space to get help." He handed some documents to the court officer. "Here are records from their therapist confirming regular appointments, and a letter from Mrs. Rogers-Evans' physician documenting her diagnosis and treatment plan for postpartum depression."

Janie ignored the spark of shame at her diagnosis being spoken out loud and in public so freely. She had to accept it was nothing to be ashamed of, or she'd never emerge from under its vast, dark influence.

"Second, the ER incident," David said softly and glanced at Janie with a sympathetic smile. "Yes, there was an incident where one child ingested a small amount of children's Tylenol. Mrs. Evans responded immediately and appropriately by taking the child to the emergency room. The ER report shows no finding of neglect. The physician noted that the mother was 'appropriate and concerned throughout' and that this was an accidental ingestion requiring no treatment beyond an activated charcoal administration." He paused to let that sink in. "The parents subsequently improved all childproofing measures and hired professional help. Clearly, this isn't evidence of neglect. It's evidence of responsible parenting. They learned from a close call and took action to prevent future incidents."

Janie caught Hannah's gaze and gave her a tight smile. God, how she wished they hadn't run out of childproof locks just as they'd gotten to the bathroom they'd reassigned for the girls.

"Finally, the claim of demanding careers and inadequate childcare. Your Honor, Mrs. Hannah Rogers is an equal partner in a successful automotive customization and repair business, and Mrs. Janie Evans is an attorney in private practice. Both have structured their work schedules to prioritize their children. They've hired a full-time nanny, Carmen Reyes, who I'll be calling as a witness, and they have a strong support system," he gestured to their chosen family in the gallery, "which is evident from the number of people who've shown up today to testify on their behalf."

Janie and Hannah checked over their shoulders, and both of them smiled at their assembled army.

"This emergency motion is not about protecting children," David said, his voice hardening. "It's about my client's mother attempting to gain control of a substantial trust fund established by her own mother for these children. Mrs. Angela Evans was passed over for that inheritance in favor of her daughter—my client—and is now using the legal system to try to access those funds through her granddaughters."

Bradford shot to her feet. "Objection! That's a baseless accusation—"

"I have documentation," David said. "Mrs. Angela Evans attempted to contest her mother's will a number of years ago and lost. The trust is ironclad and managed by Mrs. Janie Evans for the benefit of the children until they turn eighteen. However, if Mrs. Angela Evans were to gain custody, she would control those assets as the children's guardian."

Judge Morrison held up a hand. "I'll review the documentation. Ms. Bradford, unless you have evidence to contradict Mr. Adams' claims, I suggest you sit down."

Bradford sat, but her expression was thunderous, and her previous confidence seemed to have slipped away.

"I'd like to call my first witness," David said. "Carmen Reyes."

Carmen came forward from the gallery, and a rush of

affection overcame Janie. Carmen had dressed in her nicest clothes, and now she took the stand with a dignity that made Janie's throat tight.

After Carmen was sworn in, David said, "Ms. Reyes, how long have you been working for the Rogers-Evans family?"

"About two weeks now. Full-time, Monday through Friday and some weekends."

David nodded. "And in that time, what have you observed about the parents' fitness and the children's wellbeing?"

Carmen sat up a little straighter and looked toward Judge Morrison. "They're excellent parents. Both of them. Hannah is very hands-on, very loving with the girls. She knows each of their personalities, what they like and don't like, and how to calm them when they're upset. And when Ms. Janie is home, it's the same thing. Those girls light up when they see their mommies."

"Have you observed anything that concerns you about the children's safety or care?" David asked.

"No, never. The house is fully childproofed. I've worked in a lot of homes over the years, and theirs is one of the safest I've seen for toddlers. The girls are healthy, happy, well-fed, and well-loved. They have routines and structure. And most importantly, they have two parents who clearly adore them."

Bradford cross-examined, trying to get Carmen to admit that Janie wasn't there every day, that Hannah sometimes worked long hours, and that the house had been chaotic when Carmen first started. But Carmen held firm, her responses calm and unshakeable.

When Carmen stepped down, David called Hannah's dad.

Tom Rogers took the stand with quiet authority. He testified about moving from Florida to help Hannah, about the love and dedication he'd witnessed, and about the three little girls who were thriving in their home.

"Have you ever had concerns about your granddaughters' safety in your daughter's care?" David asked.

"Not once." Tom frowned and shook his head. "Hannah

is an incredible mother. Her mom would be so proud..." He paused and cleared his throat before continuing. "Yes, she's been struggling, but any parent of triplets would find it hard. But she's never put those girls at risk. She's asked for help when she needed it, which is what good parents do."

"And her wife, your daughter-in-law?" David pointed to Janie. "What's your impression of her as a mother?"

"Janie loves those girls fiercely." Tom smiled widely at Janie. "You can see it in every interaction. She's been dealing with postpartum depression, and she's been getting help for it. That takes courage."

Bradford tried to shake him on cross, implying that he was biased because Hannah was his daughter.

Tom laughed. "Of course I love my daughter. But I love my granddaughters too. If I thought they were in danger, I'd be the first one saying so. And they're not."

Next up was Gabe, and Hannah's shoulders visibly dropped as Gabe took the stand.

"I served with Solo—Hannah—in the Army," Gabe said. "She was part of my unit, and I trusted her with my life on multiple occasions. I trust her with her daughters' lives now. She's one of the most responsible, capable people I know."

Shay followed, her natural warmth making her testimony feel personal and genuine. "I've known Hannah for years, and I work with her every day at the garage. I've seen how she talks about her girls. She lights up. And since Janie's been coming back home, Hannah has become more balanced. She's happier, more herself. These are two people who love each other and love their kids. That's what I see."

RB testified about Hannah's work ethic and reliability. Woody, despite Solo's concerns, managed to be both sincere and appropriate in her testimony about Hannah's dedication to her family.

David called Rosie, and Janie's breath caught. As a former medical professional, Rosie's words held even more weight.

"Janie is one of the strongest, most compassionate people I've ever met. When I was going through a hard time with a family crisis, Janie was there. She cared, and she's helping me resolve everything."

"Ms. Morgan, you have a background in psychology, correct?" David asked.

"Yes. I was a therapist for over a decade before recently transitioning to marketing."

"And in your professional opinion, does postpartum depression make someone an unfit parent?"

"Absolutely not," Rosie said, her eyes flaring angrily. "Postpartum depression is a medical condition affecting up to twenty percent of new mothers. What makes someone unfit is refusing to acknowledge it or get help. Janie recognized she was struggling and took action. She sought therapy, took medication, and continued to communicate honestly with her wife. That's exactly what a responsible parent does."

Bradford's cross-examination was aggressive, trying to get Rosie to admit that Janie's departure from the home was abandonment, and that the depression made her unreliable. But Rosie held her ground, her therapist training evident in how she calmly redirected every attack.

Lori's testimony about observing Hannah with her children and seeing nothing but love and competence was brief but impactful, and Bradford's cross of Rae Trent was almost desperate, as if she'd realized she might be on the losing side for once.

"I'd like to hear from the parents directly," Judge Morrison said. "Mrs. Evans and Mrs. Rogers, please stand."

Janie's legs were like water as she stood. As if sensing it, Hannah grasped her hand.

"Mrs. Evans," Judge Morrison said, her voice neutral, "tell me about the ER incident."

Janie swallowed hard. "I was exhausted. I'd been up most of the previous night with Luna, who had an ear infection. The next day, I fell asleep on the couch while the girls were playing. I woke up when I heard Tia crying. Chloe had gotten into the bathroom cabinet and had a bottle of children's Tylenol. I immediately called 911, took her to the ER, and stayed with her until the doctor confirmed she was fine."

Judge Morrison tilted her head. "And why didn't you tell any of this to your mother?"

"Because my mother and I have a difficult relationship, and it never occurred to me to tell her anything. It isn't as though she's been involved in the girls' lives since they've been born, though she's been critical of my parenting choices. I didn't want to give her more ammunition to use against me." Janie sighed deeply and shook her head. "I realize that sounds like I was hiding something, but at the time, I was just trying to protect myself from her judgment."

The judge pressed her lips together tightly and nodded, but there was still no clear emotion in her expression. "And the separation from your home and wife?"

"I was drowning. The postpartum depression had gotten so bad that I couldn't see straight anymore. I was so confused... about *everything*." Janie thought about how she'd mistaken her need for friendship as attraction with Austin and rubbed hard at her forehead. "I was failing my daughters and my wife. I thought leaving would somehow protect them from me." Tears edged out of her eyes, and she wiped them away with the back of her hand. "It was the wrong choice. I should've stayed and gotten help. But I'm getting help now. I'm on medication, I'm in therapy, and I'm working on my marriage. I love my daughters more than anything in this world, Your Honor. The thought of losing them—" Her voice cracked, and she couldn't finish. Hannah tightened her grip on Janie's hand.

Judge Morrison turned to Hannah. "Mrs. Rogers, your mother-in-law's lawyer has painted a picture of an overwhelmed single parent barely holding things together, including having a problem with alcohol. How do you respond to that?"

"I *was* overwhelmed." Hannah shrugged. "But I *don't* have an issue with alcohol. Triplets are hard. Triplets when your wife is struggling with postpartum depression and you're trying to run a business and be everything to everyone is really hard. But I wasn't alone for long. My dad came through for me, and I have my crew from the garage, who helped in so many ways. And most importantly, I have my wife again." She lifted Janie's hand to her lips and kissed her knuckles. "She's not just the mother of my children. She's my partner, my wife, my person. We're stronger together than apart, and we're figuring out how to be better for each other and for our girls."

Judge Morrison glanced across at Janie's mother before returning her gaze to Janie and Hannah. "What would temporary custody with the grandmother mean for your family?"

Hannah's jaw tightened. "It would destroy us. My daughters don't have a relationship with their grandmother; she's seen them maybe three times since they were born. They don't *know* her. Being taken from their home, from us, from everything familiar would traumatize them. And it would devastate Janie and me. We're not perfect parents, but we love those girls with everything we have." She tugged on her ear and cleared her throat. "Please don't take them away from us."

Judge Morrison nodded. "You may sit," she said. "I need some time to review these documents. Court is adjourned, and we'll reconvene in an hour."

Everyone stood for her to leave, and the courtroom fell silent except for the rustle of papers from her mother's lawyer. In her peripheral vision, Janie saw her mother and Bradford gather their things to leave, but Janie kept her gaze fixed forward. She could practically feel the burn of her mother's glare, but she didn't succumb to the temptation of meeting her eyes. She didn't trust herself not to say something that her mother would use against her.

"Do you want to get some air?" Hannah asked.

Janie shook her head. "I'm not going anywhere. Maybe the

judge won't be that long."

David swiveled his chair to look at her. "I can wait here and call you back. Perhaps you should get a drink?"

"No," Janie said, more firmly this time. She shouldn't have to justify her desire to stay to her own lawyer. She gestured to the jug of water and glasses on their table. "That'll be fine if I need it."

"Okay." David held up his hands. "Okay. Then we all wait."

Janie sat back in her chair and closed her eyes. She imagined a circle of three colors, orange, purple, and green to represent their girls, and outlined in red to represent Hannah's protection, and then she concentrated on her breathing. Little splotches of black crept in at the edges of her vision as her thoughts wandered to her mother. She acknowledged them before quickly pushing them out of the picture to refocus on the bright globe. She felt Hannah's steady presence beside her, not demanding attention or conversation, but just *there*. This was her family unit, and she couldn't—she *wouldn't*—lose it.

The time slipped past in a haze of steadily counted breaths and deliberate dismissals of the dark presence of her mother. The court officer announcing the judge's return drew Janie back into the room, and she opened her eyes slowly. Her mother and her lawyer were also back.

Janie yawned and quickly covered her mouth. She hadn't slept much last night, not because of the babies for once, but because every time she closed her eyes, she saw the word unfit printed somewhere official, somewhere permanent. She kept her hands folded tightly in her lap, fingers pressed together as though they might drift apart if she didn't keep them contained.

Hannah's knee was warm against hers, solid and present. Janie leaned into it without meaning to.

Judge Morrison adjusted her glasses and looked down at the file, then up again. "This matter was brought to the court as an emergency."

The final word landed in Janie's chest, familiar and wrong. Everything had been an emergency once. Every feeding, every cry, every spiraling thought at three in the morning. Now she was learning that panic didn't make something true.

"Emergency relief is reserved for situations involving immediate danger to children," the judge said. "I have heard no such evidence today."

Janie swallowed hard and pressed her nails deeper into her palms.

"Your Honor," Bradford said quickly, "we also raised concerns regarding the mother's postpartum depression—"

Janie's heart lurched. Hannah's hand closed around hers, tight enough to hurt, as though anchoring her to the moment where she was still allowed to be a mother.

"A condition which is being treated and managed," Judge Morrison said. "One which has been verified by a licensed psychiatrist."

Janie blinked.

"Postpartum depression is not parental unfitness. It is not neglect. And it is not an emergency." Judge Morrison punctuated her sentences with finger stabs to her desk. "What concerns this court is that mental health was raised here not as a matter of care or safety, but as a litigation strategy, exploited in an extremely callous manner."

Janie stared at the wood grain of the table blankly, vindicated but exposed at the same time, like the judge was protecting her but only because she couldn't do it for herself.

David stood. "Your Honor, at this time we move to dismiss the petition in its entirety for lack of standing and failure to state a claim."

Janie's breath snagged, and Hannah pressed her leg harder against Janie's.

"Granted," Judge Morrison said.

Just like that. The word echoed in Janie's head, searching for understanding. Could it actually be over?

"Under Illinois law," Judge Morrison continued, "a non-parent seeking custody must establish standing by clear and convincing evidence of parental unfitness or extraordinary circumstances. The petitioner has done neither. Both parents are present and are fit. And I believe the children are safe."

The judge's statement wrapped around Janie like a blanket, and she warmed in its comfort. In a court of law, she was being pronounced fit and safe.

"Furthermore, there is no evidence of abuse, neglect, abandonment, or incapacity."

"Your Honor," Bradford said, "we would request that the full custody hearing—"

"There will be no full custody hearing," Judge Morrison said, sounding more and more irritated with the lawyer. "The petition is dismissed with prejudice."

The room tilted. Janie exhaled, the sound torn from somewhere deep and fragile. She pressed her forehead to Hannah's shoulder, just long enough to remind herself that this was real, and it wasn't a beautiful dream where she and Hannah won, and her mother failed.

"Let me be clear for the record."

Janie looked up, her heart jumping into her mouth. Was there a but?

"This action was brought under the guise of concern." Judge Morrison adjusted her glasses. "But the evidence establishes an improper purpose. Filing an emergency petition without factual basis is a serious abuse of this court's process. Mental health stigma has no place in custody litigation."

Tears gathered behind Janie's eyes, uninvited once more, but she didn't fight them.

"The court further orders that the petitioner is barred from filing any future custody or visitation actions regarding these children without prior leave of court."

A soft sound rippled through the gallery. It wasn't applause, not quite, but Janie could almost feel the desire of her gathered friends to shout out in celebration.

The judge looked directly at Janie's mother. "These children are not leverage. They are not assets. And they are not a trust instrument." She brought down her gavel. "Court is adjourned," she said and swept out of the courtroom.

For a moment, Janie stayed where she was, her fingers laced with Hannah's, breathing in and out like she'd been taught. Behind them, their family buzzed quietly. They were the people who'd believed in them when they could barely believe in themselves, and Janie would never forget that.

She was still shaking when Hannah leaned close. "See? We're good parents. The judge said it."

Janie's breath hitched. She wanted to believe it. God, she wanted to believe it. She looked down at their intertwined fingers, then up at Hannah, who'd stood by her through all of this. "I was so scared," she whispered.

"I know." Hannah's thumb traced circles against her palm. "But you're still here. Our babies are still ours. We're going to be okay."

The weight began to lift from Janie's chest. Not all of it, and maybe it never would, but enough to breathe. Enough to hope. "I love you," she said.

Hannah's eyes shimmered. "I love you too."

Around them, the courtroom was emptying. David and their friends were standing, probably waiting to embrace them. But for just this moment, it was only the two of them. They'd built their perfect little family, and they'd survived the darkness of the past few months. They'd fought her mother, and they'd won. Janie was battling with herself and maybe she could say she was winning sometimes too.

She rose, her legs unsteady, and Hannah pulled her close. Over Hannah's shoulder, she caught a glimpse of her mother's rigid back as she left, with Bradford trailing behind her. There was no satisfaction or triumph in that, only a quiet, exhausted relief.

"Come on," Hannah murmured against her hair. "Let's go home to our babies."

Home. To the chaos, and the sleepless nights, and the tiny hands that reached for her. The life they'd made together, messy and imperfect, was hers again.

Chapter Twenty-Five

JANIE WAS BARELY VISIBLE over the stacks of discovery documents for the AI copyright case. She had a share of thousands of pages of training data logs, licensing agreements, and technical specifications to comb through, and her eyes had started to blur around page three hundred of the first pile.

When her assistant, Amanda, tapped lightly on her open door, Janie could've wept with relief for the distraction. "Come in," she said, beckoning her in. She saw the apprehension in Amanda's eyes, and Janie's relief switched to high alert. "What's wrong?"

Amanda glanced behind her as if she were afraid the boogeyman might be lurking close by. She met Janie's eyes again and briefly bit her bottom lip. "Your mother's here. I told the front desk to convey you were too busy to be disturbed, but she's insisting on seeing you."

Janie sighed deeply, and an instant pressure developed in the hollow just below her ribs. It wasn't quite fear, not anymore, but something adjacent to it, like the muscle memory of that emotion, a phantom limb reaction of a childhood spent trying to anticipate her mother's moods, criticisms, judgments. She should've expected her mother would pull something like this. The fact that she hadn't managed to bypass the reception desk and storm straight to Janie's office was likely only because Phillip was on vacation, and the receptionist was new and probably had no idea who Angela Evans was.

The last time her mother had appeared unannounced at Janie's office, it had been to threaten her. She'd weaponized Janie's worst fears and deepest shames, and she'd taken what little confidence Janie was clinging to and pulverized it into dust.

But that was before the emergency hearing. Before Judge Morrison had looked at Bradford, her mother's lawyer, and essentially called bullshit on the entire case.

That had been three days ago. Three days of Janie breathing a little easier, sleeping a little better, and allowing herself to believe it might actually be over.

But apparently not.

"What would you like me to do?" Amanda asked.

Janie could tell the front desk to send her mother away. She could have security escort her out if necessary. She could refuse to engage. Any of those options were well within her rights. She didn't owe her mother much before all of this had begun, and now that she'd tried to take the triplets away, Janie owed her nothing at all. She'd be justified in stepping over her body in the street if her mother had collapsed.

But even as she thought it, Janie knew she wouldn't. Because some part of her, the part that was still eight years old and desperate for her mother's approval, needed to know why her mother was here. Again. Especially after such a humiliating loss. What could she want? Was there any possibility, however remote, that her mother had come to apologize?

Janie took a deep, steadying breath. "Send her in."

Amanda's expression indicated she might be impressed. Her assistant knew very little about Janie's complicated relationship with her mother, but she knew Angela Evans' reputation. Taking her on was no small thing.

Janie didn't bother straightening her desk or checking her appearance in the compact mirror she kept in her drawer. Instead, she simply sat in her chair, hands folded on her lap and waited.

Her mother walked through the door looking exactly as she always did: Chanel suit in dove gray, pearls at her throat, hair styled with the kind of perfection that required a standing weekly appointment. Everything about her screamed old money, good breeding, and the kind of wealth that didn't need to announce itself because everyone already knew. It was a façade that hid something ugly and twisted beneath.

Janie had spent most of her life trying to live up to that standard. Trying to be polished enough, successful enough, respectable enough to earn her mother's pride. Looking at her mother now, why had she ever wanted to?

"Janie," her mother said.

"Mother."

Her mother closed the door behind her and settled into one of the comfortable armchairs on the far side of Janie's office. She crossed her legs at the ankle in that way she'd drilled into Janie as a teenager. Knees together, ankles crossed, hands folded in lap: the posture of a lady.

"Thank you for seeing me."

Janie didn't respond. She had nothing to say to the woman who'd birthed her and was mother in name only. Her mother's mouth tightened slightly, the only outward sign of her displeasure, and it was so tiny, the average person would've missed it. Janie didn't. She never had, but then her mother hadn't tried that hard to hide it before.

"I wanted to speak with you about the court's decision." Her mother tapped her long nails rhythmically on the wooden arm of the chair. "To clear the air, as it were."

"There's nothing to clear." Janie looked pointedly at her mother's hand, and remarkably, she ceased her drumming. "The judge dismissed your case, with prejudice. It's over." God, how good that sounded out loud.

"Yes, well." Her mother's tone suggested the judge had made some kind of clerical error rather than a well-reasoned legal ruling. "The judge made her position quite clear. Though I still maintain that my concerns were valid, I recognize that the court doesn't share my perspective."

The pressure beneath Janie's ribs subsided, and a fiery flicker in her chest began to rise. Not anger yet. More awareness of her mother's careful phrasing, and the way she was framing the judge's decision as a difference of opinion rather than calling out her malicious attempt to take Janie's children merely for financial gain. "Your concerns were never valid," Janie said, keeping her voice level despite the desire to scream the words. "They were fabrications designed to support a financially motivated custody claim."

"That's not fair—"

"The judge literally said you were using the legal system to try to access a trust fund you have no legal right to." Janie leaned forward in her chair and narrowed her eyes. "Those exact words are in the official record," she said, tapping her desk for emphasis on each word. She relaxed against the back of her chair and tried to maintain a neutral expression when really, she wanted to revel in the newfound steel she was displaying in the face of her mother's usually overwhelming presence.

Then Janie saw it. A slight crack in her mother's composure. The skin tightened around her eyes. A quick clench of her jawbone visible in her gaunt cheeks. Even the hint of a flush creeping up her neck. Her mother wasn't quite the behemoth she wanted everyone to believe she was.

"Your grandmother's will was a betrayal. After everything I did for her, all the years I spent caring—"

"You didn't care for her," Janie said and clenched her own jaw at the memory of her mother's desertion. "You visited her twice a year and complained the entire time about how inconvenient it was."

Her mother's head twitched. "That's not true."

But it was. Janie remembered her grandmother in that big house in Lake Forest, alone except for her housekeeper and her cats. Remembered her mother's sighs and eye rolls whenever Grandma Susan called. *Your grandmother wants us to visit again. As if I don't have better things to do than listen to her complain about her rare form of arthritis.*

But Janie had loved those visits. And she'd looked forward to all the school vacations she'd spent with her too. She loved her grandmother's sharp wit and sharper mind, and she adored the way she'd looked at Janie like she actually saw her. Like Janie was interesting and worthwhile, and not just a reflection of her mother's expectations. "Grandma Susan left you out of the will because she knew you'd waste it," Janie said quietly. "She told me that, right before she died. She said she was leaving everything to me because I was the only one in the family who understood the value of money and who wouldn't treat it like it was infinite."

Her mother's face went white, then red. "She had no right—"

"She had every right." Janie clenched her toes in her shoes, praying that the channeling of her grandma's gumption would continue. "It was her money and her choice."

"I'm her daughter—"

"And I'm her granddaughter. I'm the one she actually spent time with. I'm the one she trusted." Janie leaned forward. "Why are you really here, Mother? Because if you came to apologize for trying to take my children, you're doing a terrible job of it." She noted the way her mother's hands clenched in her lap, another tiny crack in her perfect composure.

"I came because despite everything, you're still my daughter. And I don't want this..." her mother waved her hand in the air as if the issue were tangible and touchable, "unpleasantness to permanently damage our relationship."

There it was. Not an apology. Not even close. Just a desire to smooth things over, to maintain the appearance of family harmony so her mother could continue to have access to Janie. And through Janie, possible access to the money.

Because if something happened to Janie, the trust would go to the girls. And if Angela was the loving grandmother, the involved family member, she'd have a much stronger case for guardianship than if she was estranged.

Her mother's visit wasn't about reconciliation: it was about positioning.

"You tried to take my children," Janie said, her voice steady as a sense of calm rippled gently through her. It was as if Grandma Susan was right beside her, holding Janie's hand, giving her strength. "You stood in front of a judge and claimed I was an unfit mother. You weaponized my postpartum depression to try to prove I was a danger to my own daughters. You hired investigators to dig into my life looking for dirt." She took a breath. Listing all her mother's foul tactics out loud in quick succession rammed home the depths her mother had plumbed, just for money, and rage whispered louder beneath the surface of her calm. "You made it clear that the only thing that matters to you is that trust fund, and you were willing to destroy my family to get access to it."

"That's not... I never said..." Her mother's careful mask slipped further, revealing the inner ugliness in her eyes that she worked so hard to hide. "I had legitimate concerns about the children's safety."

"No, you didn't." In the face of her mother's continued protests, Janie's bubbling anger subsided. Something colder and clearer rose in its place, as she recognized her mother's desperation and her lack of control, both so completely out of character. "You've met the girls three times in their entire lives. You don't know their names without checking your phone. You know nothing about them because you've never cared enough to know anything about them."

"I *care* about my granddaughters."

Janie scoffed. "You care about their *trust fund*."

Her mother stood abruptly. "How dare you speak to me this way? After everything I've done for you."

"What *have* you done for me?" Janie stood too, and she was taller than her mother. She had been since she was thirteen but had spent so much of her life trying to make herself smaller, more palatable, less threatening. Now, she actually looked down at her. "You paid for college, yes, but you held it over my head every time I made a choice you didn't agree with. You criticized my career, my marriage, and my decision to have children. You made it clear that nothing I did would ever be good enough."

Her mother grasped the back of her chair, her nails digging into the soft leather. "I had high standards because I wanted you to succeed—"

"You had high standards because you wanted me to reflect well on you. You wanted me to be an extension of your image, not my own person." Years of suppressed words and emotions rose in Janie's throat, fighting to finally get out and be heard. "When I told you I wanted to go to law school, you said I would struggle. When I told you I was gay, you said I was confused and that it was a phase I'd grow out of. When I told you I was marrying Hannah, you said I was making a mistake because she wasn't from the right kind of family."

Her mother sneered. "She isn't—"

"The right kind of family?" Janie clenched her jaw and shook her head. "What does that even mean? Hannah is kind and loyal and hardworking. She's an incredible mother. She fought for our marriage even when I'd given up on it. She's everything you're not."

Her mother's expression turned to stone. "You're overwrought. The postpartum depression is obviously still affecting your judgment—"

"Don't." Janie's voice was sharp enough that her mother actually took a step back. "Don't you dare use my mental health as a weapon again. It's a medical condition that affects thousands of women." She grasped the edge of her desk, needing something to keep her in place lest she give in to the years of hurt and express it physically. "I'm treating it with therapy and medication, and I'm doing better every day. Having depression doesn't make me a bad mother any more than having diabetes or asthma would."

"But staying with that woman—"

"*That* woman is my wife." Janie tightened her grip on the warm wood in her hands. Attacking her was one thing, but her rage rose in decibels when her mother attacked Hannah. "She's the love of my life. And she's more family to me than you've ever been."

The words hung in the air between them, sharp and final. Janie watched her mother's face cycle quickly through the emotions of shock, hurt, fury before she settled back into that careful mask.

But it didn't quite fit anymore. Janie could see the cracks, and the desperation underneath. The fear that she'd miscalculated was now visible, as was the knowledge that she'd pushed too hard and lost any chance of getting what she wanted.

"Your grandmother wouldn't have wanted this," her mother said, her voice sounding smaller and almost pleading. "She wouldn't have wanted you to cut yourself off from your family."

"You're not my family," Janie said, and the truth of her blunt statement settled into her bones. "Not in any way that matters. Family shows up. Family supports you. Family doesn't try to take your children away because they want access to money."

"I was trying to protect them—"

"You were trying to control me like you've been trying to control me my entire life." Janie moved around her desk and walked toward the door; her grandma's gumption was fading as the consequences of the conversation were beginning to take root. She needed her mother out of her space. "I'm done, Mother. I'm done trying to earn your approval and trying to be who you want me to be. I'm done allowing you to make me feel small and insufficient. I have a family who actually loves me. I don't need you."

"You can't just—Janie, please..." Her mother's voice actually broke. "You're all I have."

And there it was. Not *I love you*. Not *I'm sorry*. Just *You're all I have*.

Because Janie's father had left her fifteen years ago, tired of the criticism, the impossible standards, and the way nothing was ever good enough. Because her mother had alienated any *real* friends with her competitiveness and her need to constantly one-up everyone. Because she'd built her entire life around appearances and status and money, and now she was sixty-one years old and completely alone but for the sycophants and shallow sidekicks.

A heaviness sank down into the pit of Janie's stomach. Was it pity? Perhaps a little, but mostly, it was exhaustion. "You could have had me," she said quietly. "If you'd actually been interested in knowing me instead of controlling me. If you'd supported my choices instead of criticizing them. If you'd shown up for my wedding, met my wife with an open mind, been excited about your granddaughters instead of seeing them as obstacles to money you think you deserved."

"I never meant—"

"But you did. And you do." Janie opened the door, a clear dismissal. "I hope you figure out how to be happy, Mother. I really do. But I can't help you with that. I have my own life to live, and my own family to love. And you're no longer part of it."

Her mother stood beside the chair, still clinging to it for a long moment, her perfectly made-up face flitting through emotions Janie wasn't interested in reading. Then she smoothed her skirt with hands that trembled slightly and walked toward the door.

She paused in the doorway, not quite looking at Janie. "When you were little, you used to tell me you loved me every night before bed. Do you remember that?"

Of course Janie remembered. She remembered being five years old, then six, then seven and all the subsequent years after that, desperate for her mother's affection, saying I love you like a talisman that might ward off criticism or earn a smile instead of a correction. "I do," Janie said.

"You haven't said it in years."

That was because she'd learned that saying I love you just gave her mother another tool to manipulate her. Another pressure point to exploit. Love, to her mother, had always been conditional. Transactional. Something earned through compliance rather than freely given. Janie swallowed against her dry mouth, the rawness of this exchange worsening with every word. "No," she said. "I haven't."

Her mother blinked rapidly, something Janie had never seen before. Whatever was going on behind her mother's crumbling façade, Janie didn't want to know. It was too late. Whether her mother was hurt, or angry, or even if regret was swimming around in her dark soul somewhere, Janie no longer cared. "Goodbye, Mother."

"Goodbye, Janie."

And then her mother was gone, her Louboutin heels clicking down the marble hallway toward the elevators, and Janie was alone in her office with the door still open and her heart pounding hard against her chest like it was trying to escape.

She closed the door softly. And then she just stood there, breathing, feeling like she'd run a marathon, or climbed Mount McKinley, or done something equally exhausting and monumental.

She'd just cut ties with her mother. Completely and finally.

She dropped into the chair her mother had just vacated and sat with her feelings, as Rae had impressed upon her to do. Beyond the galloping panic and the disappearing gumption, what was it straining for recognition?

Freedom.

The word settled into her consciousness with surprising clarity. She was free. She'd been carrying that weight for far too long, and she'd just hefted it from her shoulders.

Janie stared at the discovery documents from the AI copyright case that had seemed so important an hour ago. Now she was somewhat disconnected from it, like that was someone else's work, someone else's life.

Her phone buzzed. *How's your day going?*

Janie stared at Hannah's perfectly timed message for a long moment before responding. *My mother just came to my office. I told her I'm done, and I cut ties completely. I think I'm okay. I don't know. I feel weird.*

I'm coming to get you.

Janie smiled. Her handsome, strong rescuer wife clearly wasn't about to let her deal with the aftermath of this alone. *You don't have to. I'll be fine.*

I'm already in the car. Be there in fifteen minutes x

Janie set down her phone, and tears burned the back of her eyes. They didn't *feel* like sad tears. Not really. They were a simple, emotional release after she'd finally opened the pressure valve after years of keeping it screwed down tight.

She thought about the way Grandma Susan had looked at her when Janie told her she was gay. She'd been freshly out, terrified to tell her family but needing to tell someone. Her grandma had listened, nodded, and said, "Your mother's never going to understand you, sweetheart. She doesn't have the capacity. But that's her loss, not yours. You build your own family. You build your own life. And you don't let anyone tell you how to live it."

Janie moved to her desk and pulled up the trust documents on her computer. It was something she did occasionally when the imposter syndrome got bad, when she needed to remember that someone had believed in her and thought she was capable and trustworthy, someone worth investing in.

Thank you, Grandma. Thank you for seeing me. For believing in me and protecting me even after you were gone.

Her office phone rang, and she let it go to voicemail. Right now, all she wanted to do was sit in the quiet, processing and feeling.

And remembering.

She remembered being eight years old, sitting at the dining room table doing homework while her mother corrected her penmanship. "Your Gs are too round, Janie. You need to make them more angular. People judge you by your handwriting."

She remembered being sixteen, coming home from school excited about making the hockey team, only for her mother to say, "Sports are for people who don't have the brains needed to do something important with their lives. Why didn't you try for the debate team?"

She remembered being twenty-two, calling to say she'd been accepted to law school, and hearing, "Well, I suppose it's something that you got a place. It'll be interesting to see if you keep it."

Every memory was like that. Every moment of pride, achievement, or joy undercut by criticism, by the suggestion that Janie should have done better or been more, tried harder. And underneath all of it, the constant message was *You are not enough. You will never be enough. No matter what you do, it will never be good enough for me.*

Janie had internalized that message so thoroughly that it had become part of her operating system and the background hum of her life. It was the voice in her head that said she was failing, insufficient, and fundamentally flawed.

That voice sounded a lot like her mother's.

But it had become Janie's voice and had been for so long that she couldn't remember a time before it. The same voice told her she was a bad mother for falling asleep when Chloe got into the medicine cabinet. It told her she didn't deserve Hannah's love. And it told her she should be able to handle everything—work, kids, marriage, and her mental health—with ease and without help, and definitely without ever admitting that she was drowning.

That voice was her mother's true legacy. The inheritance her mother had already given her was more impactful than any trust fund could ever be. And far more negative and damaging.

Now though, Janie was done listening to it. She picked up her phone and called Rae, who answered on the second ring.

"Janie? Is everything okay? We're not scheduled until Thursday."

"I just cut ties with my mother." Janie almost laughed as she said it. "Completely. She came to my office, and I told her I was done, that I didn't need her, and I have my own family to protect.

And I feel...I think I feel good. But also weird. Like I'm waiting for something bad to happen."

"That's normal," Rae said gently. "You've spent your entire life in a painful relationship with your mother. Ending it is huge. It's grief and relief, plus guilt and freedom all mixed together."

"I don't feel guilty," Janie said, smiling as she realized she really meant it. "I thought I would. But I just don't."

"That's growth," Rae said. "That's you recognizing that you deserve to protect yourself from people who hurt you, even if those people are family."

"She said I used to tell her I loved her every night when I was little, but I hadn't said it in years." Janie rested her head against her chair and sighed. "I couldn't even remember the last time I'd said it. Because I don't think I do. Love her, I mean. I don't think I have for a long time."

"That's okay. You're allowed to not love someone who's consistently hurt you. Blood relation doesn't obligate you to maintain a relationship, especially one that's toxic."

"My grandmother gave me complete independence from my mother and allowed me to find my way out from under the darkness of her shadow."

"And now you're doing the same thing your grandmother did," Rae said gently. "You're protecting yourself and your children from someone who sees you as a means to an end rather than someone worthy of unconditional love."

Something clicked into place in Janie's mind, and the hollow ache under her ribs receded. "Yeah, I am."

"How does that feel?"

The warmth in Rae's voice seeped out of the phone and encased Janie in a blanket of comfort and acceptance. "Powerful. Scary. Right."

"All of those are appropriate responses," Rae said. "Listen, I know we're not scheduled until Thursday, but if you need to come in earlier—"

"No, I'm okay." Janie smiled again, realizing she really meant that too. "Hannah's coming to pick me up. I just wanted to hear someone tell me I wasn't crazy for slicing my mother from my life."

"You're *not* crazy. You're healthy. You're setting boundaries. You've chosen yourself and your family over someone who's consistently demonstrated that she doesn't have your best interests at heart. You've done exactly what you should be doing."

After they hung up, Janie sat in the quiet of her office and thought about the family she'd been fighting for. About what it meant, what it should mean, and what she wanted it to mean for her daughters. She thought about Hannah, who'd fought for their marriage even when Janie had given up on it. She'd been patient with Janie's depression, her fears, and her inability to believe she deserved good things. Hannah saw Janie, really *saw* her, and loved her anyway.

She thought about Tom, who'd never once made Janie feel like an intruder or a failure. He made her coffee exactly how she liked it and told her stories about Hannah's childhood that made Hannah groan with embarrassment.

Her mind flitted to Hannah's crew, who'd shown up to that courthouse like an army and testified on their behalf. They'd made it clear that Janie was part of their family too, not because she'd married into it but because she'd earned it by being real, by letting them see her struggles instead of pretending to be perfect.

Her bouncing brain settled on Maria, who'd given her a safe place to fall apart and put herself back together. Without her, Janie didn't want to even contemplate where she might've ended up. The totally bizarre nature of their initial meeting, when Maria had tapped on Janie's car window and then settled in the passenger seat without invitation, had been like a scene from the kind of weird movies that killed at the Sundance Film Festival.

All of that was family. It wasn't DNA, or obligation, or financial entanglement. It was choice: choosing to show up. It was seeing and being seen. Family was love that was freely given instead of conditionally withheld.

Janie's phone buzzed again.

I'm downstairs. Come when you're ready x

I'll be down in a few minutes x

Janie gathered her things and turned off her desk lamp. She glanced around her office, at the law degree on the wall, at the photos of Hannah and of the triplets on her desk, and then at the stack of case files that represented her career, which was still her passion and her choice, and something she was damn good at despite her mother's doubts.

This was her life, one she had built for herself. And it was great. It was enough. *She* was enough.

Janie walked out of her office, locked the door behind her, and headed for the elevators. For Hannah. For home. For the family she'd chosen and who'd chosen her back. And she smiled widely. *Now* the nightmare was truly over, and she could concentrate on becoming the person she'd always wanted to be.

Chapter Twenty-Six

SOLO SAT IN HER truck outside Janie's office building, engine idling, watching the glass doors for her wife to emerge so she could get her home, hold her tight, and make sure she was actually okay.

The text about Janie's mother had hit Solo like a physical blow, not because it was bad news, but because she knew what it would've cost Janie to do that. To finally stand up to the woman who'd spent Janie's entire life making her feel small and never nearly good enough.

She wanted to hunt down Janie's mother and tell her exactly what she thought of her exploitation of her daughter's vulnerabilities. She'd wanted to do something, anything, to fix this for Janie. But Janie had spent her whole life with people trying to tell her what to do and what choices to make. What she needed now was someone to just be there and "hold space," as Rae called it, for whatever she was feeling. Solo had to let Janie process in her own time and in her own way.

So she sat in the gentle heat of the sun shining through her windshield, gripping the steering wheel hard, heart in her throat, hoping this wouldn't push her back into the oblivion of a deep depression.

When the doors finally opened and Janie walked out, Solo's breath caught. Janie looked *different*. She didn't appear to be the broken, dejected daughter like Solo had feared. There was no hint of devastation, or fragility, or any of the things Solo had braced herself for.

Janie looked tired, sure. That was a constant state of being when you were raising triplets and working full time. But she also looked lighter somehow. Like the impossible weight of her mother's expectations were no longer bearing down on her.

Solo leaned across to push open the passenger door, and Janie climbed in. For a moment, they just looked at each other, with Solo taking in Janie's red-rimmed eyes and careful composure, scanning for cracks in case Janie was hanging onto an outward professional appearance while she disintegrated inside.

"Hi," Janie said finally.

"Hi." Solo tucked a strand of hair behind Janie's ear. "You okay?"

"I don't know. Maybe." Janie's laugh was shaky. "I told my mother I was done with her, and I didn't need her anymore. When she left, I called Rae, and now you're here, and I'm wondering if I actually disowned my own mother or if I hallucinated the whole thing."

"You did it." Solo cupped Janie's face, sure it was true. "You stood up for yourself. That's amazing."

Janie's eyes filled with tears. "Why do I feel so strange about it? I should feel good, right? Relieved at least. But I just feel...like I'm in some sort of limbo, and I have no idea what's supposed to happen next."

Solo didn't respond for a second while she tried to pull up another kernel of knowledge she'd learned from Rae. "You've spent your entire life in survival mode around your mother. Maybe your body doesn't know what to do with the feeling of being safe from her yet. It'll take time." She stroked Janie's cheekbone with her thumb. "And that's okay. We've got plenty of that together."

Janie nodded and put on her seatbelt. "Can we go home? I just want to be with you."

"Yeah. Of course." Solo put the car in gear and pulled out into traffic. They drove in silence for a while, Janie staring out the window at the city passing by, and Solo stealing glances at her whenever she could take her eyes off the road.

"Carmen has the girls until eight," Janie said eventually. "She and Tom took them to the park, and then they're going to get pizza. He texted while I was waiting for you."

Solo smiled. "So we have the house to ourselves for a few hours."

"Yeah." Janie glanced at her briefly. "Would it be okay if you stayed with me for a little while? I know you probably need to get back to the garage—"

"The garage will be fine without me. Gabe and Shay have everything under control; they always do." Solo took Janie's hand and pressed it to her lips. "I'm exactly where I need to be."

They pulled in to their parking spot twenty minutes later, and some of Solo's own tension eased as soon as she saw their house. Home. It was their safe place, the space they'd built together and nearly lost but were building again, with stronger foundations this time.

Inside, Solo helped Janie out of her suit jacket and watched her set down her bag with the kind of careful precision that indicated she was holding herself together through sheer force of will. Solo recognized that look. She'd seen it on Janie's face a hundred times over the past few weeks. One wrong word, and she'd completely fall apart. "Come here," she said, opening her arms.

Janie walked into them like she'd been waiting for permission, and then she was pressed against Solo's chest, shaking and making small, wounded sounds that shattered Solo's heart into pieces. "I've got you," she murmured into Janie's hair. "You're safe, I promise."

They stood there in the entryway for a long time. Her back started to ache from holding Janie's weight, and the afternoon light shifted and changed through the windows. But Solo didn't move, or suggest they go sit down or get comfortable, or do anything other than this, because this was what Janie needed right now. To be held, and to fall apart.

Eventually, Janie's shaking subsided, and her breathing evened out. She pulled back just enough to look at Solo's face.

Her eyes were red and swollen but clearer than they'd been in weeks.

"Sorry," Janie said. "I'm a mess."

"You're not a mess. You're working through something huge." Solo brushed tears off Janie's cheeks with her thumbs. "You don't have to apologize for having feelings."

"I think I'm expecting her to call or show up again and find some new way to make me feel guilty for choosing myself over her."

"And if she does, we'll handle it." Solo squeezed Janie's waist a little tighter. "But I don't think she's going to. It sounds like you made it clear that you're done, and she knows she can't manipulate you anymore. She lost her power over you."

"Has she?" Janie whispered. "Because eight-year-old me is still hanging around, not quite knowing what she's supposed to do with what just happened."

Solo took Janie's hand and led her to the couch. She tugged her down so they were sitting close, and then she pulled Janie's legs over hers. Her mind whirred with Rae's words about the *inner child* and how important it was. "That eight-year-old kid deserved better," she said. "She deserved a mother who saw how incredible she was. How smart, and kind, and brave. That kid deserved unconditional love, and she didn't get it, and that's not her fault. That's your mother's failure, not yours."

"When she left the office, I felt an elated kind of freedom, but I think that was just adrenaline-fueled. Reality's setting in now." Fresh tears spilled down Janie's cheeks. "I don't know how to stop hearing her voice in my head, telling me I'm not enough and I'm a failure. All I hear is that I'm a bad mother, a bad wife, and a bad daughter. A bad everything."

"I know, baby. But that voice is a liar." Solo squeezed Janie's hand. "You want to know what I see when I look at you?"

"What?"

Janie glanced up, and the wounded, hopeful look in her eyes tore at Solo's heart. "I see you fighting. You keep showing up even though it's hard, even though your brain is telling you that you don't deserve good things. I see you love our daughters so fiercely it takes my breath away. You're being brave enough to admit that you're struggling and asking for help. You're working your ass off every single day to be better, do better, and feel better." Her voice cracked, and she cleared her throat. "I see my wife, my partner, and the woman I want beside me through everything for the rest of my life. And I am *so* fucking proud of you for standing up to your mother."

That prompted more tears, and Solo pulled Janie close again.

"I'm so tired," Janie whispered. "I'm so tired of fighting and trying to prove I'm worthy. I'm sick of waiting for the other shoe to drop."

"I know, baby, I know." Solo relaxed back into the sofa, taking Janie with her, while she cried out weeks of accumulated fear, stress, and trauma. All of it poured out in harsh, painful sobs that made Solo's chest ache with the desire to take it all away.

But she couldn't. It wasn't hers to take, Rae would say. Solo could only hold Janie through it, only be present, patient, and steady while Janie fell apart and put herself back together.

Eventually, the crying subsided into hiccups, then quiet breathing. Janie pulled back and looked at Solo with swollen eyes and the kind of raw vulnerability that made Solo want to build walls around her, protecting her from everything and everyone who'd ever hurt her.

"I love you," Janie said. "I don't think I say it enough. But I love you so much it scares me sometimes."

Solo kissed the top of Janie's head. "Why does it scare you?" she asked, though she often had the same thought.

"Because I'm afraid I'll mess it up and disappoint you. One day, you might realize you and the girls would be better off without me."

"Funny. I think the same thing all the time." Solo's heart fought against the crushing pressure of Janie's devastating lack of self-worth. She had to keep talking, keep telling her the same things in the hope that sometimes Janie would really hear them. "Janie, look at me."

Janie shifted and met her eyes.

"I would never be better off without you." Solo shook her head and chuckled lightly. "I'm barely functional when you're not here. The past few weeks we've been apart, I was surviving, not living. I was going through the motions, taking care of the girls, going to work, but it was like half of me was missing. You're not a burden, or a disappointment, or someone I'm settling for. You're my person. And you make me want to be better, do better, try harder." She caressed Janie's cheek. "I need you to believe that."

Janie nodded slowly. "I'm trying."

"I know. And I'm going to keep telling you. Some days you'll hear me, and some days you won't; I know what Rae said about that." Solo leaned in and pressed her forehead against Janie's. "But we're in this together. All of it. The good days and the bad ones, and the days where you can't get out of bed because the depression is too heavy. I'm here for all of it."

Janie sighed deeply. "What did I do to deserve you?"

"You didn't have to do anything. You just had to be you." Solo kissed her softly. "That's always been enough for me."

Janie kissed her back, tentative at first, then deeper, her hands coming up to run over Solo's buzz cut. The kiss shifted from comforting to something charged with need, and want, and the kind of desperate hunger that came from nearly losing something precious.

"I need you," Janie whispered against Solo's lips. "I need to feel something other than scared and exhausted. I need you to show me how much you want me."

"God, I do." Solo moved her hands to Janie's waist and pulled her closer. "Do you have any idea what you do to me? How much I crave you?"

"Show me." Janie's eyes were dark now, pupils blown wide. "Please show me."

Solo stood and tugged Janie up with her. They moved through

the quiet house toward their bedroom, and she was hyperaware of every sound. The creak of floorboards, their breathing, the rustle of clothes.

After she'd closed the door to their bedroom, Solo turned to face Janie, and the vision stole her breath. Janie was backlit by the late afternoon sun coming through the curtains, and she looked ethereal. Beautiful and heartbreakingly vulnerable.

"I don't want to be gentle," Janie said quietly. "I don't want careful and tender. I need to feel alive. I need to feel something other than this weight in my chest."

Solo understood the need to escape her own head through physical sensation; she'd been doing that for years before she met Janie, before she found a love that filled the hole in her heart. She understood the desire to be consumed by something other than doubt and an endless loop of negative thoughts. She kissed Janie hard, backing her toward the bed. "Tell me what you need."

"You. All of you. And hard."

They undressed each other quickly and with none of the slow reverence from the hotel nearly two weeks ago. This was urgent, almost frantic. Janie's hands shook as she unbuttoned Solo's jeans, and Solo nearly ripped Janie's blouse in her haste to get it off.

When they were both naked, Solo pushed Janie onto the bed and crawled over her, pinning her wrists above her head as she moved. Janie arched up against her with a gasp, and a surge of power, desire, and overwhelming love coursed through Solo's body like an electric shock. "You're mine," she rasped. "Mine to love and mine to protect. Say it."

"I'm yours," Janie gasped, her breath already ragged. "I'll always be yours."

Solo released Janie's wrists and made her way down Janie's body with her lips, teeth, and tongue, marking a path from Janie's throat to her breasts. Janie's small, desperate sounds went straight to Solo's core, and she ground her hips restlessly against Janie's.

"Please," Janie whispered. "Han, please..."

Solo moved lower and spread Janie's legs wide. She looked up to meet Janie's eyes. She was flushed and panting, her pupils so dilated her eyes looked black.

"I love you," Solo said. "Please don't forget that, not even for a second."

Janie closed her eyes briefly and nodded. "Sometimes I just don't know why."

"Then let me show you." Solo put her mouth on Janie, and Janie cried out loud enough that Solo was grateful the house was empty. She worked Janie's core, listening to the sounds she made, feeling the way her body responded, and chased her pleasure, desperate for her actions to demonstrate the depth of her love.

Janie came hard and fast, her hands fisted in Solo's hair as she arched off the bed. But Solo didn't let up and kept going until Janie begged her to stop, oversensitive and trembling.

"I can't," Janie whispered.

"You can." Solo looked up at her. "One more. Give me one more." She slid her fingers inside and returned her mouth to Janie's clit. It wasn't long before Janie's whole body went rigid then shattered apart again. Her orgasm was quieter and deeper, and Solo felt it in the way Janie's entire body relaxed, like every bit of tension from the past few weeks ebbed away with the final soft shudders.

Solo crawled back up Janie's body and gathered her close. She pressed kisses to her damp forehead, her flushed cheeks, and her trembling lips. "Okay?" she murmured.

"More than okay," Janie said. "That was... God, that was exactly what I needed."

Solo smiled, overly pleased with herself as she always was after making Janie come. It was one of those feelings that just never got old. "Good."

They lay there for a while as Solo traced lazy patterns on Janie's stomach. Janie's breathing gradually evened out. The afternoon light continued to shift and change, casting long shadows across their bed.

"Your turn," Janie said eventually, shifting so she was fully facing Solo.

She inclined her head. "We don't take—"

"I want to." Janie slipped her hand down, over Solo's stomach and between her legs. "I want to make you feel as good as you just made me feel."

Solo's breath hitched at Janie's touch. She was less urgent, more exploratory, like she was relearning Solo's body, mapping out what made her gasp. She let herself get lost in it, in the pleasure, the intimacy, and the simple perfection of being with her wife like this.

She came with Janie's name on her lips and Janie's eyes locked on hers, and her orgasm rippled through not just her body but also her soul. This connection, their love, this partnership...it was everything. It was Solo's whole world.

She flipped Janie onto her front and took her from behind, hard and quick, and Janie moaned into the pillow, muttering expletives and threatening bodily harm if Solo dared to stop. As if she would. One. Two. Solo stopped counting as Janie came over and over for her, pulling her in, demanding more, soaking up Solo's stamina as if each orgasm energized Janie instead of draining her.

Afterward, they lay tangled together, sweaty, sated, and utterly spent.

"I don't want to move," Janie murmured against Solo's shoulder. "I want to stay here forever."

"We can stay like this a little longer." Solo kissed the top of her head. "We've got time."

"*Time*," Janie said, enunciating the word like it was foreign. "When did we last have time? Just the two of us, with no rushing and no obligations?"

"Too long," Solo murmured, pulling Janie on top of her. "Way too long."

They drifted in that half-asleep state that came after great sex. Janie's body cooled against Solo's skin, her heartbeat slowed, and the comfortable weight of Janie on her body grounded her in the moment.

"I'm scared I'm going to wake up tomorrow and that voice will be back," Janie said into the darkness of the room. "It'll tell me I made a mistake, and that I'm selfish for choosing my own happiness over maintaining a relationship with her."

"And what if it does?" Solo asked gently.

Janie lay her head on Solo's chest and sighed deeply. "Then what do I do?"

"Then you tell me." She traced her finger along Janie's nose and gently tapped it. "And we deal with it together. We talk about it, we call Rae, and we remind you that the voice is lying. You don't have to fight it alone anymore. That's what I'm here for."

Janie was quiet for a long moment, and Solo thought she might have fallen asleep. She continued to tangle her fingers through Janie's long, silky hair, almost tickling herself, and waited.

"I'm not good at asking for help," Janie said finally. "Admitting when I'm struggling is...so alien."

"I know." Solo wrapped her arms around Janie and squeezed. "But you're getting better at it. Lately, you've been telling me when you're having bad days. You've been honest about the depression and your fears. That's huge progress."

Janie huffed quietly. "It still feels like weakness."

"It's not weakness. Talking about something this hard takes strength." Solo pulled another pillow beneath her head so she could look at Janie's face properly. "You know what weakness looks like? It looks like my mom refusing to admit she had breast cancer until it was too late to treat effectively. It looks like me trying to handle triplets, a business, and a failing marriage all by myself instead of asking for help. Weakness is pretending you're fine when you're not. Strength is saying 'I'm struggling and I need support.'"

Janie's eyes filled with tears again. "How do you always know the right thing to say?"

Solo laughed, remembering her desire to have Gabe in her ear not so long ago when Janie was packing to leave. "I really don't. I fuck up all the time, but the therapy is helping me so much. I'm trying, same as you." She brushed away a tear that had escaped down Janie's cheek. "We're both trying. That's what matters."

"Promise me something," Janie said.

"Anything."

"Promise me we'll never stop talking to each other. Even when it's hard and we're scared of each other's reaction." Janie trailed her finger along Solo's collarbone. "Promise me we'll keep showing up and keep fighting for this." She tapped Solo's heart.

"I promise." Solo kissed her softly. "I promise to always talk to you and be honest about what I'm feeling and what I need. I'm never going to let work, or the kids, or anything else make you invisible again." She clasped Janie's hand to her chest. "I promise with all my heart to see you, *really* see you, every single day."

"I promise too," Janie said. "I promise to tell you when I'm struggling instead of hiding it. I'll ask for help instead of trying to be perfect. And I'll keep trying to trust that you love me even on the days when I really don't know why you would."

They sealed the promises with a kiss, slow and deep, full of everything they'd survived and everything they were building.

Outside, the sun was setting, painting their room in shades of gold and amber. Soon, her dad and Carmen would bring the girls home, and the house would fill with toddler noise, dinner preparations, and bedtime routines. But for now, it was just the two of them, the core of their family, in this beautiful moment, choosing each other again.

"I don't regret what I did today," Janie whispered, her lips caressing Solo's skin. "Is that terrible?"

"No. You did what was healthy for you. And for us and the triplets."

"I think…I think I've been wishing for a different mother all these years instead of accepting the mother I actually had. Today, I finally stopped wishing for something that was never going to happen."

Solo nodded. "That took courage, babe."

"Or maybe just exhaustion." Janie laughed softly. "I got too tired trying to earn love from someone who's incapable of giving it freely."

"Now you can use that energy for the people who *do* love you like that. For our daughters and me." She kissed Janie again. "But especially for yourself."

"For myself." Janie nodded. "That's the hardest one."

"I know, but you'll get there. We'll get there together." Solo's phone buzzed on the nightstand, but she ignored it. Right now, nothing was more important than holding her wife and reaffirming their promises to build the foundation they needed for whatever came next.

They'd survived a level of hell. The separation. The custody case. The secrets, and shame, and fear of losing everything they'd created together. And they'd come out the other side stronger.

"We should probably get up," Janie said without making any move to actually do so. "Everyone will be home soon."

"Five more minutes and then we're done," Solo repeated the line from one of the girls' favorite animated movies and pulled her closer.

Janie chuckled. "Okay. Five more minutes."

They lay there in the fading light, arms wrapped tightly around each other, and contentment settled in Solo's chest. She had her perfect little family back together again, and that was all she'd ever needed.

Chapter Twenty-Seven

On Wednesday evening, Janie pulled into the garage parking lot at six thirty and frowned. Why were all the second-floor lights on when Hannah had texted saying she'd be waiting outside? And if she was still working late, she would've left the bay doors open. She always said she liked the flow of air even in the cooler months.

Something didn't feel right. Janie tried not to catastrophize and grabbed her phone to text Hannah, then noticed she'd missed a message twenty minutes ago.

Can you come inside? I'm in the office doing paperwork.

Paperwork on any night would've been an early Christmas miracle. Hannah hated the administrative tasks of being part-owner in the garage, and Janie was certain Shay and RB handled most of it. But paperwork on a Friday night when they were supposed to be heading home for family dinner and a movie with the triplets was nearly impossible to believe.

The side door was unlocked, which was also weird. Gabe was serious about security almost to the point of paranoia, especially now that they had so many expensive tools and rare cars with custom paint jobs inside.

Janie stepped into the dark hallway leading to the main garage floor and heard multiple voices, low and conspiratorial, coming from the main bay. Her heart thudded louder against her ribs. Had something happened? Was Hannah okay?

The lights blazed on and a chorus of voices shouted, "SURPRISE!"

Janie screamed and clutched her chest, her heart lurching to her throat. It took her a few seconds before she settled and began to take in the scene. The garage bay had been transformed from a steel and grease pit to a celebratory space with string lights, decorations, and a banner reading "CONGRATULATIONS, SOLO & JANIE." In the back, near the tire station, was a table loaded with food and a beautiful floral arrangement, and the space was filled with what looked like every person she cared about in the world grinning at her like maniacs.

Hannah was front and center, looking absurdly pleased with herself, and tears sprang to Janie's eyes as she started laughing. "You butthead." She clicked her way across the concrete floor toward Hannah and shoved her shoulder. "I thought something was wrong. I thought—"

"Sorry for the mild heart attack." Hannah grinned and pulled Janie into a hug. "But we wanted to celebrate."

"Celebrate what?"

"You." Hannah pulled back and held her at arm's length. "Us. We fought, and we won."

Janie looked around at the gathered faces: Gabe and Lori, Shay and Rosie, Woody, RB. Tom was holding a squirming Chloe while Luna hung onto his other hand, and Tia kept Carmen's arms full. There were some people she didn't recognize, including a couple of women in Sanctuary polos, an awkward-looking woman in a bow tie, and a redhead with a Flower Loft apron on. But they all faded into the background when she locked eyes with her precious friend. "Maria?" Janie's voice cracked. "Mirta?"

"We wouldn't miss this for anything, mija," Maria said, crossing to pull Janie into a warm hug.

Janie relaxed into the embrace and inhaled the scent of coffee and cinnamon coming from Maria's hair. "I can't believe you all did this." She stayed in Maria's arms, sniffling a little, overwhelmed by the love in the room, by the fact that all these people—her *family*—had shown up for her. "This is... I don't even know what to say."

"Say you'll eat," Woody called out. "Because Gabe and I cooked, and if you don't appreciate it, we'll be devastated."

Janie hoped that wasn't true. They were both wonderful people, but neither of them was known for their culinary skills. "You cooked?" She looked at Gabe, praying for her to say she was joking.

Gabe shrugged. "We ordered it from Bonnie's and arranged it nicely on serving platters. That counts, right?"

Everyone laughed, and Hannah took Janie's hand, leading her further into the space. Up close, and now that she was a little less on edge, Janie could see the thought that had gone into this. She spotted plenty of her favorite foods amongst the inevitable pizza and beer. Even the wine they always shared on their anniversaries was chilling in an ice bucket.

Janie tugged on Hannah's shirt. "When did you plan all this?"

"This week. I wanted to do something to mark what you've done. I wanted to celebrate you choosing yourself and choosing us. And to remind you that you have a chosen family who loves the hell out of you."

Janie couldn't speak for a moment, like her throat couldn't possibly be wide enough to allow her gratitude out. Rosie came up beside her with a glass of wine, Shay hugged her, and Janie found herself surrounded by people wanting to congratulate her and to tell her how proud they were.

"Mommy!" Chloe pulled away from Tom and rushed up to her.

Janie swept her daughter up in her arms and breathed in a big hit of her perfect toddler scent.

Tom put his hand on her shoulder. "I'm proud of you," he said quietly. "After everything you've been through and survived, you're still smiling. You're a fighter, Janie. My daughter and my granddaughters are lucky to have you."

"I'm lucky to have you too," Janie said. "You've been more of a parent to me than my own mother ever was."

His eyes got shiny, and he cleared his throat loudly. "Well, you're family. This is how it is."

There was that word again. Family. Not of blood, or of

obligation, but a family through choice. And here was hers, showing up and loving her unconditionally.

Chloe squirmed to get down, then toddled toward where Luna and Tia were "helping" RB look through a box of car parts. Janie watched them for a while, her heart so full it ached.

"Hey." Gabe offered a glass of wine. "You doing okay? Not too overwhelmed?"

"Overwhelmed in the best way." Janie grasped the drink gratefully and took a big swallow. "Thank you for everything you've done for us. I'm so glad you're here."

Gabe smiled. "Solo would've killed us if we hadn't shown up. She's driven us all insane this week, texting in the group chat at all hours to make sure everything was perfect. "

Janie stared across at Hannah, and her stomach flipped at the sight of her wife in a crisp polo shirt and dark jeans, snug in all the right places. "She's pretty perfect herself."

"Don't tell her that. Her ego's already big enough." Gabe grinned then shook her head. "Seriously though, you two have come through something that would have destroyed most couples. You should be proud."

"I am," Janie said. "I'm scared, but proud."

"Good. Fear means you're paying attention." Gabe clinked her beer against Janie's glass. "To new beginnings."

"To new beginnings." She didn't miss the way Gabe quirked her eyebrow, like she was warning Janie not to screw it up again. Janie didn't blame her. Hannah had been the baby of their group for a long time, and they were all hyper-protective of her.

"Be careful with Solo," Gabe said. "She's not the superwoman she pretends to be."

"I will, I promise." Janie kissed Gabe's cheek then made her way around the room, talking to everyone, accepting hugs and congratulations, and feeling *seen*.

Lori pulled her aside near the makeshift bar RB had set up. "I know we don't know each other that well yet," Lori said, "but I wanted to say that watching you and Solo fight for your family has been inspiring. My parents have always had this incredible marriage, and I used to think that kind of love just happened naturally, that you either had it or you didn't. But seeing you two actually work at it and choose each other every day, even when it's been so hard, has made me realize that the best relationships are the ones people fight for."

"Thank you." Tears edged Janie's eyes again, and she blinked them away. "That means a lot." She gestured toward Gabe. "You both seem really happy."

"We are." Lori's smile was soft. "Though I have to admit, being around all of Gabe's crew with the history they share can be a little intimidating sometimes."

Janie took Lori's hand and squeezed gently. "You fit though. I can see the way Gabe looks at you, and the way everyone's welcomed you. You belong here."

Before Lori could respond, Shay swept in with Rosie in tow.

"Enough serious talk," Shay said. "We're here to celebrate. Janie, c'mere, we need to show you something."

Shay and Rosie led her to a corner where a collage of photos had been stuck to the wall, of Janie's memories going back years. Janie and Hannah on their wedding day. The garage crew in their Army days. The triplets as newborns. Janie's grandmother at her law school graduation. Christ, Hannah was set on ruining her eye makeup tonight.

"Solo put this together," Shay said. "She wanted you to see your history, your family, and all the people who've loved you and shaped you."

"And my old college friend, Alyssa, brought in the gorgeous flowers," Rosie said.

She gestured to the redhead in the leather apron, who was in animated conversation with the tall masc in the bow tie Janie had spotted earlier. The woman looked even more awkward now, if that were possible.

"It's all so..." Janie touched the soft petals of a yellow rose. "Please thank her for me." She stared at the photo of her grandmother. Even in a two-dimensional snapshot, the unconditional love in her grandmother's eyes was obvious as she smiled at the camera, her arm around Janie. She closed her eyes, feeling the strength and warmth of Grandma Susan's love around her, and she could almost hear her voice: *Build your own family, sweetheart. Build your own life.* Janie opened her eyes and smiled. "It's beautiful." She pointed to the picture of the garage crew with some desert in the background. "Hannah looks so young. You all do."

"She still does." Shay chuckled. "She'll always be the baby of the group, even if she has grown up some."

Janie nodded, knowing how much Hannah treasured her place in their little group.

"Your grandmother would be proud of you," Rosie said softly. "You really fought for yourself and your family."

"I hope so." Janie touched the photo gently. "Grandma Susan is the one who made all of this possible. The trust fund allowed Hannah to invest in the garage, it bought our house, and it gave us the resources to fight my mother's custody case. She protected me even after she was gone."

"Sounds like she really saw you," Shay said. "That's a rare gift to receive."

"I was so grateful for it." Janie wrapped her arms around herself. "Especially as I got older and realized my mother wasn't really looking at me, let alone seeing me."

Rosie placed her hand on Janie's shoulder and rubbed gently. "I know that feeling."

Janie sighed and put her hand over Rosie's. "I'm sorry. I'm being insensitive, given..."

"Given that my mother just died?" Rosie shook her head. "No, you're not. You made the decision I couldn't, and I'd probably still be in a toxic relationship with her if she hadn't OD'd. You're really strong, Janie, and I really admire you for that."

Janie swallowed, not sure how to respond without ending up in tears again, and she'd cried more in the past month than she had in her entire life. It was time to start smiling, so she simply accepted the compliment and smiled.

An easy silence followed, and Janie settled in the moment, juggling her joy at the time she and her grandmother had shared with her grief that she wasn't there to share the joy now.

"So," Rosie said and nudged her, "I have news that I'm desperate to share even though this is your party."

Janie laughed. "I'd be grateful for the spotlight to shift, honestly."

"I'm going back to being a therapist. There's an opening at the LGBTQ center. They want someone who can work with their young people. It isn't going to be anything like my private practice, but it feels right."

"Rosie, that's amazing!" Janie hugged her. "You're going to be incredible."

"Do you think?" Rosie bit her lip and frowned. "I'm terrified I won't be any good at it anymore."

"You'll be great," Shay said firmly, draping her arm over Rosie's shoulders. "And you're going to help so many people from our community."

"Exactly." Janie clasped her hands together. "All those kids who are struggling and think they're broken, who've been disowned or their parents have tried to stop them being who they are..." She shook her head. "You're going to make such a difference. God knows you'll be needed now more than ever."

Rosie's eyes got shiny, and Shay pulled her close and kissed her forehead. Happiness surged through Janie as she watched. They'd found each other and were building something beautiful, just like she and Hannah had. Her gaze drifted back to the collage, and she took the time to study each photo. She found herself fixating on one from their wedding day, both of them laughing at something off-camera, joy radiating from every inch of the image.

Hannah came to her side and placed her hand on the small of Janie's back. "That's the one I kept staring at too," she said softly.

"We look so young." Janie leaned into Hannah's solid body. "So sure of ourselves."

"We had no idea what we were getting into." Hannah laughed lightly. "No clue about the sleepless nights, or how we'd lose ourselves in being parents. This family life has really tested us." She sighed deeply and wrapped her arm around Janie's waist to pull her in closer. "But I'd do it all again. Every single hard moment. Every fight, every struggle, every night I lay awake terrified we weren't going to make it."

Janie turned in Hannah's arms to look at her, eyebrows raised. "Even the part where I left?"

"Even that. Because you came back, and we're stronger for it." Hannah caressed Janie's cheek, a wistful look in her eyes. "This version of us has survived the worst, and we're still here. We're better than the naive version in that photo. We know what we have now *and* what it's worth."

Janie pressed her face into Hannah's chest. "I'm so glad you never gave up on me."

"I couldn't. You're my person, and you always have been." Hannah took her hand. "Come on, there's something else I want to show you."

Hannah led her through the garage and upstairs to her little office in the back, the space where she did her design work. Sketches of custom paint jobs covered the walls alongside photos of completed projects. On her drawing desk lay a rich red leather-bound portfolio Janie hadn't seen before. "What's that?" she asked.

"Open it."

Janie flipped open the cover, and her breath caught. Inside were dozens of sketches, all of the same subject: *her*. Janie reading on the couch. Her laughing with the triplets. Janie asleep in their bed, hair spread across the pillow. Her profile backlit by morning light. Some were detailed and precise, others just quick drawings, but all of them were rendered with such care, such attention and love that Janie's throat tightened. "When did you do these?" she whispered.

"Over the past month. I started right after you left, actually." Hannah moved to stand beside her, looking down at the drawings as she put her hand on Janie's hip. "I couldn't sleep most nights, so I'd sit up and draw. At first, I was just trying to remember what you looked like when you smiled. I was desperate to hold onto the good parts of us. But then it became something else. I started to see you again, not just as the mother of my kids, but as you. The whole, complex, beautiful person I'd somehow stopped really looking at."

Janie came to the final sketch of her in the courtroom, sitting at the defendant's table. Hannah had captured something in her expression that Janie hadn't known was there: not just fear but determination. Strength. "The custody hearing." Obviously, they both knew the location, but she vocalized it anyway, wanting to make the connection between that and the emotions Hannah had captured tangible.

Hannah nodded. "I watched you sit there and face down your mother's lawyer, face down all that fear, and it made me even more proud of you. And I wanted to immortalize that version of you." She pointed to her own scribble below the drawing. "The fighter."

Janie's hands shook as she flipped back through the pages. There was one of her with Maria at the café, leaning forward in conversation. One of her in her work clothes, briefcase in hand, looking fierce and professional. Another of her sitting on the couch, holding all three triplets at once, face scrunched up with effort but smiling. "I had no idea you drew like this."

"I guess I stopped when I went in the Army, and I don't get much time now either." Hannah shrugged. "I had no idea I was going to show you, to be honest. But when I decided to throw this party, I knew I had to." She took Janie's hand. "These taught me to see you again. And what I saw was someone incredible, someone worth fighting for." She cupped Janie's face and kissed her softly. "Someone I never want to stop looking at."

Janie stared into the seemingly bottomless love in Hannah's gaze. "I don't know what to say."

"You don't have to say anything," Hannah said and kissed her again. "I just wanted you to know that even in the worst moments, even when we were apart and everything felt impossible, I saw you. And I'm never going to stop seeing you."

Janie pulled Hannah into a kiss that was equal parts gratitude, love, and promise. When they broke apart, Hannah held her tight, and they stood there in the quiet of her office, foreheads pressed together, breathing each other in.

"Thank you for that," Janie whispered and flicked a glance at the sketchbook.

"I'm glad you like it."

A knock on the door made them both jump, and RB stuck her head in. "Sorry to interrupt whatever disgustingly romantic moment you're having, but I need everyone in the main bay. I have an announcement."

"We'll be right there," Hannah said.

After RB disappeared, Janie looked back at the portfolio. "Were you just showing me this, or do I get to keep it?"

"It's yours," Hannah said and cast her eyes downward as her face flushed. "I'm just happy you want to keep it."

"Of course I do." Janie wrapped her hand around the back of Hannah's neck and pulled her in for one last kiss. "You're so talented."

They returned to the main garage hand in hand, with Janie steps lighter yet more solid, as if Hannah's gift had reminded her of something fundamental: she was loved and, most importantly of all, she was enough.

Across the room, RB's voice rose above the general chatter. "Okay, okay, everyone shut up for a second. I have an announcement."

The room quieted, and everyone turned to RB, who looked uncharacteristically nervous. "So," she said, shifting her weight from foot to foot. "I've been offered a temporary position." She ran her hand through her hair, adjusting her quiff slightly. "In New York."

There was a collective intake of breath, and Hannah's grip on Janie's hand tightened.

"What kind of position?" Gabe asked.

RB looked across at Lori. "Working with Hank on his veterans' housing project. He needs someone to help launch the first shelter, someone who understands the population, who can do intake and assessment, and someone who's not going to take shit from bureaucrats. Apparently, I fit the bill."

Janie nodded, remembering Lori and her dad telling everyone about the project at Lori's birthday meal a couple of months ago. It'd been clear then that RB was excited by the proposal.

"Are you going to take it?" Woody asked quietly.

RB glanced around the room. "I think so. It's only for a few months, like a sabbatical, basically. Long enough to get the shelter up and running, train the permanent staff. But it's good work. Important work."

Hannah shifted beside Janie. "But the garage—"

"Will be fine without me for a few months," RB said. "You guys can handle things. And it's not forever. I'll be back by spring, probably earlier. But this feels like something I need to do."

Gabe stepped up to RB and grasped her shoulder. "You should do it. I knew Hank had lit a fire under your ass when he talked about it."

"Really?" RB's shoulders visibly dropped an inch. "You're not pissed I'm bailing?"

"You're not bailing, you're growing." Shay moved to the other side of RB and punched her arm. "After Hank told us about his plans, we've all been talking about how we could do more, how we wanted to help vets who're struggling. You're actually going to do it." She raised her wine glass. "That's something else to celebrate."

RB's eyes shone. "I'm going to miss you assholes."

"We'll miss you too," Hannah said. "But we'll see you over the holidays, right?"

Her grip on Janie's hand tightened to the point where Janie had to tap Hannah's forearm, but Hannah relaxed when RB nodded.

"You can count on that," RB said. "That's one of the things we promised we'd always do once we were all civvies again."

"Plus," Woody said, "maybe you'll actually learn to fold your clothes properly while you're living in New York. The rest of us are tired of your slob habits."

The room erupted in laughter, the tension breaking. RB flipped Woody off and grinned. "My slob habits are part of my charm."

"That's definitely one word for it," Gabe said. "It's not the *right* word, but..." She grabbed RB around the neck and scrubbed the top of her head.

The party continued, people breaking into smaller conversations, the energy warm and celebratory.

Janie slipped her arm around Hannah's waist. "Are you good?"

Hannah cleared her throat and looked everywhere but at Janie. "Uh-huh."

Janie put her finger under Hannah's chin and made her meet her eyes. "It's short-term, Han. She'll be back before you know it."

Hannah tilted her head slightly. "I hope you're right. Hank's project is the kind of work RB was born to do, and it's national. What about when Hank wants to open the next one in Boston, and the next one in DC?" She threw her arms out and clenched her jaw. "New York could just be the start."

Janie grasped Hannah's hands and stilled them. "Whatever happens, you won't lose her. She'll always be there for you."

Hannah looked into Janie's eyes. "Like you will be?"

Her vulnerability almost undid Janie, and she pulled Hannah into her arms. "Yes, like I will be. Always."

"Okay," Gabe shouted, startling Janie. "Let's get back to the party!"

A while later, Maria approached Janie as she placed some spring rolls and satay sticks on her plate. They moved to a quieter corner of the garage where they could actually hear each other over the loud music Woody was DJing badly.

"You look happy, mija," Maria said. "As if, perhaps, you might one day be at peace."

"I'm working on it." Janie gave a small smile, recognizing that Maria was one of the few people to understand that she'd be a work in progress for a long time, possibly until she died. But that was okay. That was life. "I'm starting to feel like myself again. And I'm not constantly waiting for something bad to happen." She wrinkled her nose. "Just maybe every other day."

Maria chuckled. "You're healing," she said then sipped her wine before looking over the edge of her glass at Janie. "Have you heard from your mother since the confrontation?"

"No. And I'm hoping I never will." Janie went silent for a moment. Saying that aloud made it even more real, and the truth of it comforted her soul like a home-crocheted blanket wrapped around it. "I think she got the message."

"Good. You deserve to live free of her judgment and manipulation. It's time for you to live the life you want, not the one she thought you should have."

"You helped me see that. You, and Rae, and Hannah all helped me see that I was worth fighting for." She held out her hand, and Maria took it. "Thank you."

Maria's smile was warm. "You've always been worth fighting for. You just needed to believe it yourself."

They talked for a while longer about inconsequential things, until Janie plucked up the courage to quiz Maria on her past. They'd spent so much of their time unpicking Janie's issues, but Janie wanted to explore a deeper friendship with Maria now that she was on the right track. "Do you ever regret walking away from Hollywood?"

"Never. Because what I gave up was performing, pretending, living for other people's applause. What I gained was authenticity. Truth. A life that's mine, lived on my terms." Maria looked around the garage and gestured to the gathering of Janie's friends and family. "This is what matters. Community. Love. Being there for each other, no matter what. Fame, and money, and other people's opinions are all worthless in comparison."

"My grandmother used to say something similar. She said the only thing that mattered at the end of your life was whether you loved well and were loved in return." Janie swallowed hard. "I miss her."

"Your grandmother was a wise woman."

"She was." Janie glanced over at Hannah talking animatedly to RB, probably getting her to promise to come home. "I wish she could see the life I'm living."

"I think she knows." Maria tapped her nose and looked upward. "And I think she's very proud."

Hannah caught her eye and wandered over to them. "Sorry to interrupt, but the girls are getting cranky. We should probably head home soon and get them to bed."

"Of course." Maria hugged Janie warmly. "Thank you for letting me be part of this celebration. It's been an honor watching you find your strength."

After Maria and Mirta left, Janie helped wrangle the triplets into their coats while Hannah wound the party down and thanked everyone for coming.

Gabe and RB pulled Hannah aside near the door, and Janie watched them talk in low voices, heads close together. Instead of being envious, as she once had been, joy rose in Janie's heart. Their friendship had been forged in the fires of war and would last forever, regardless of distance or time. Janie's friendship with Maria had risen from the ashes of a different war, one Janie fought with herself, but she knew in her heart, it too would last for years to come. And she'd treasure it like the precious find that it was.

Shay refused their help to clear up, and Carmen and Tom volunteered to take the girls so Hannah and Janie could have a little alone time on the drive home.

"Thank you," Janie said after they slipped into her car, "for loving me enough to do something this thoughtful."

Hannah clicked her seatbelt into place then covered Janie's hand with her own. "You deserve to be celebrated. I wanted you to know how many people love you and are in your corner."

"I know it...at least for today." Janie rested her head on Hannah's shoulder, and Hannah pulled her closer into her arms.

They sat there for a moment in the quiet of the car, and Janie sighed quietly as that love settled deep in her bones. This was home. It wasn't the house with the triplets' toys scattered everywhere and the crayon masterpieces on the walls. It wasn't the garage with its smell of motor oil and paint. It wasn't, and would never be, any physical place.

Home was right here with Hannah's arms around her, facing the future with the certainty that no matter what came next, she didn't have to handle it alone. Whatever hard days and challenges were thrust before her, no matter how difficult the ongoing work was to manage her depression while being a mother, and a wife, and herself, they'd face it, and overcome it, together.

"You're the strongest person I know," Hannah said, her voice thick with emotion. "I want you to know that too."

Tears slid down Janie's cheeks, but she no longer cared about her makeup. These were good tears, filled with gratitude and overwhelming love. "I couldn't have done any of it without you," she said. "You saved me, Han. You saved us."

"We saved each other."

Hannah's kiss levitated Janie from her leather seat, filling her with the same excitement and thrill as the touch of Hannah's lips had when they'd kissed for the first time. She moaned into Hannah's mouth and deepened the kiss, the rest of her responding, eager to go further. When Hannah pulled back,

Janie stuck out her bottom lip. "Tease."

Hannah grinned. "It's not teasing if I follow through when we get home," she said.

Janie threw the car into reverse. "That's as good as a promise, and you—"

"*Always* keep my promises," Hannah said and wiggled her eyebrows.

Janie pulled out of the parking lot and headed toward their house, their daughters, and the promise of love in so many forms. She looked over at Hannah and the small smile playing on her lips, and Janie's heart expanded with so much love she thought it might burst from her chest.

She thought about her grandmother, about Maria, about all the women surrounding her and showing her what strength looked like. She thought about her mother and the decades of shame, criticism, and impossible standards that Janie had finally relinquished her death grip on.

She thought about her daughters, about the family she'd chosen and who'd chosen her back, about the garage crew who'd become her tribe, and about their messy, imperfect, and absolutely beautiful life.

And she thought about Hannah and the promises they'd made to each other: to keep talking and showing up. To keep fighting for their love and their family, and the life they were building together.

The depression guaranteed she'd have bad days. The triplets would be challenging, especially as they headed toward puberty and their teen years. Work would be stressful, and life would throw them curveballs.

But she wasn't alone to face any of it.

And that made all the difference.

Janie pulled into the curb and turned off the Lexus, but neither of them moved to get out. They just sat there for a moment, hands clasped between them, looking at their house lit up from within.

"Ready?" Hannah asked.

Janie squeezed her hand. "Ready."

They walked up the path together, toward the warmth, the light, and the unconditional love waiting inside; toward their daughters and their bright, beautiful future; and toward everything they'd fought for and everything they'd won.

Toward *home*.

Janie stepped inside, and the bedlam of bedtime routines, toddler giggles, and Tom's laughter from the kitchen cascaded over her. She smiled widely, knowing, deep in her core, that this was everything she'd ever wanted and needed. She'd finally found her way back to herself, not to the person her mother had wanted her to be, or the perfect version she'd tried so hard to become, but the real Janie. Flawed and struggling. Brave and loved.

Exactly as she was meant to be. And with the woman she was meant to be with.

Something profound struck her so hard and definitively that it almost took her breath away. She didn't need every fear named, or every wound explained, or every doubt unraveled. What mattered was that the unspoken no longer stood between them, and they were safe inside the love they chose, again and again.

AUTHOR'S NOTE

Thank you for reading *Unspoken*. If you enjoyed Solo and Janie's second-chance romance, I'd really appreciate you popping a review on Amazon for me! And if you haven't read any of my other books, maybe you'd like to try my number one US bestseller, *Stunted Heart*?

Unspoken is the third in the Windy City Romance series. If you're eager to find out who might get their own happily ever after in book four, *Unseen*, copy this link into your browser (BookFunnel will take you to a mini eBook of chapter one of *Unseen*):

https://wifeyromance.news/WCR4

www.helenaharte.com
Follow me on Instagram, TikTok,
and Facebook at AuthorHelenaHarte

Ship of Dreams by Brey Willows
Two rival captains, one deadly mission, and secrets that could set the skies ablaze.

Women in War Historical Romance series by E.V. Bancroft
On the Edge of Uncertainty
First love, second chance, last hope.
Encrypted Hearts
Can they survive the chaos of war, or will secrets tear them apart?
Virgin Flight
In the battle between duty and desire, can love win?
Warm Pearls and Paper Cranes
A family torn apart by secrets. The only way forward is love.

The Promise by Addison M Conley
When the world keeps pulling you under, who do you reach for?

Back to Back by Jo Fletcher
When Fred and Ruby's worlds collide, can love rise from the rubble?

Heart of the Storm by Ally McGuire
Sometimes a storm is just what you need to clear the skies ahead.

Brave Enough to Love by Valden Bush
In a dance between truth and sacrifice, can they rewrite the rules of love?

The Dak Farrell series (FBI Thrillers) by Robyn Nyx
Dead Pretty (Book One)
An FBI agent, a TV star, and a serial killer. Love hurts.
Dead Ringer (Book Two)
Three bodies. One killer. No motive?

Medea by JJ Taylor
Who will Medea become in her battle for freedom?

Stunted Heart by Helena Harte
Two women who don't do forever. One night that says otherwise.

Fragments of the Heart by Ally McGuire
Love can be the greatest expedition of all.

The Here Together series by Jo Fletcher
Here You Are (Book One)
.Can they unlock their hearts to find the true happiness they both deserve?
Here in My Heart (Book Two)
In the golden glow of a South of France autumn, two very different lives collide.

Dark Haven by Brey Willows
Even vampires get tired of playing with their food...

The Chase Stinsen Adventures by Robyn Nyx
The Golden Trinity (Book One)
Two experts. One legend. Zero trust. Old flames. New enemies. Ancient secrets.
The Copper Scroll (Book Two)
The hunt for the Ark could give her the world. Or it could cost her the one thing that matters most.

Green for Love by E.V. Bancroft
All's fair in love and eco-war.

Call of Love by Lee Haven
Separated by fear. Reunited by fate. Will they get a second chance at life and love?

Where the Heart Leads by Ally McGuire
A writer. A celebrity. And a secret that could break their hearts.

Stolen Ambition by Robyn Nyx
Daughters of two worlds collide in a dangerous game of ambition and love.

Cabin Fever by Addison M Conley
She goes for the money, but will she stay for something deeper?

The Helion Band by AJ Mason
Rose's only crime was to show kindness to her royal mistress....

An Art to Love by Helena Harte
Second chances are an art form.

Let Love Be Enough by Robyn Nyx
When a killer sets her sights on her target, is there any stopping her?

Nero by Valden Bush
Banished and abandoned. Will destiny reunite her with the love of her life?

Judge Me, Judge Me Not by James Merrick
One man's battle against the world and himself to find it's never too late to find, and use, your voice.

Music City Dreamers by Robyn Nyx
Music brings lovers together. In Music City, it can tear them apart.

Scripted Love by Helena Harte
What good is a romance writer who doesn't believe in happy ever after?

Call to Me by Helena Harte
Sometimes the call you least expect is the one you need the most.

What's Your Story?

Global Wordsmiths, CIC, provides an all-encompassing service for all writers, ranging from basic proofreading and cover design to development editing, typesetting, and eBook services. We specialise in helping self-published authors get their books into the world but also help authors find a traditional publisher or agent.
Another part of our work is charity and community focused, delivering writing projects to under-served and under-represented groups across the UK, giving voice to the voiceless and visibility to the unseen.

To learn more about what we offer, visit: www.globalwords.co.uk

A selection of books by Global Words Press:
Desire, Love, Identity: with the National Justice Museum
Aventuras en México: with Farmilo Primary School
Times Past: with The Workhouse, National Trust
Young at Heart with AGE UK
In Different Shoes: Stories of Trans Lives with Trans4Me
Our Pride: with Nottinghamshire Healthcare Trust